Hex Appeal

Hex Appeal

LINDA WISDOM

SOURCEBOOKS CASABLANCA™
AN IMPRINT OF SOURCEBOOKS, INC.®
NAPERVILLE, ILLINOIS

Published by Sourcebooks Casablanca, an imprint of Sourcebooks, Inc.
P.O. Box 4410, Naperville, Illinois 60567-4410
(630) 961-3900
FAX: (630) 961-2168
www.sourcebooks.com

Library of Congress Cataloging-in-Publication Data

Wisdom, Linda Randall.
  Hex appeal / Linda Wisdom.
    p. cm.
  ISBN-13: 978-1-4022-1400-4
  ISBN-10: 1-4022-1400-6
  1. Vampires—Fiction. I. Title.
  PS3573.I774H49 2008
  813'.54—dc22

2008018162

Printed and bound in the United States of America
QW 10 9 8 7 6 5 4 3 2 1

*For Laurie McLean. Agent, good bud, and
the one who keeps me in line. Well, as best as she can.
I owe ya big time!*

Chapter 1

"YOU SHALL PAY, NICK GREGORY. THIS I VOW. YOU SHALL suffer and scream for a mercy I shall deny you." Jazz's parted lips trailed across Nick's collarbone. She ran the tip of her tongue up the taut lines of his throat while her fingers danced their way down his abs following the line of crisp hair lower still.

"Mercy," Nick whispered as her fingers wrapped around his erection. He lay naked on his bed, legs slightly spread to accommodate Jazz's bare thigh draped over his.

"But we've just begun, darling," she purred, nipping his earlobe just hard enough to cause him to jump in response, then soothed the bite with her tongue. "You must lie there very still while I have my way with you."

"Feel free to do what you will—soon enough it will be my turn." He lowered his voice to a husky growl that made promises she knew he would keep. Her body quivered in anticipation.

But for now, it was her turn and she intended to make the most of it.

Leaning back, she admired the view. Sheer male beauty stretched out beside her. Nick had kept himself in excellent physical condition in life and, as a member of the undead, his well-honed body would never deteriorate. She tangled her fingers in the light dusting of dark brown hair on his chest. She knew many women admired a hair-free chest, but she liked to see a bit there, as long as the man didn't look as if he needed a good chest waxing. No, Nick's was just right. Surrendering to temptation, she lowered her head to nibble on a dark brown nipple that peeked out among the hair. It peaked to a hard nub and brought another groan to his lips.

"Wuss," she teased, dividing her attention between both nipples, alternating with tiny nips of her teeth and soothing licks of her tongue. She glanced up under the cover of her lashes. "Why no nipple rings? So many vamps love them as bling."

Nick made a face. "Not my style. Makes me think it would be too easy to loop a chain through it. Make me a slave."

"Hmmmm," she giggled and hummed as she mouthed her way down to his navel. "The picture that conjures up. . ."

"Seems like you've already conjured something very much up." His eyes followed as she cupped her hand around his straining cock, slowly stroking from root to tip in a rhythm that had him clenching his teeth when her other hand gently cradled the sac beneath.

"I ask that thee render me that which I deserve. Because I say so, damn it!" She finished with her own version of "so mote it be" on a wave of throaty laughter right before she raised her body up over him and settled on him with perfect ease. She straddled his hips, bending her long legs alongside his.

"What? No foreplay?" He grasped her hips, although she needed no help in finding a rhythm. It had been written in their blood ages ago.

She leaned forward and brushed her mouth across his, tickling the seam of his lips and teasing the tips of his fangs, darting out before they could prick the tender skin. "We had foreplay at the movies," she breathed against his mouth. "And during the drive home when I unzipped your jeans and. . ." she deliberately paused for effect, "it's time for the main event, fang boy." She moved in a circular motion, tightening her core to massage him with her inner muscles.

Nick suddenly jackknifed his legs, flipping her onto her back with ease.

"You are so right, mi'lady. But I'll be the ringmaster for this show." He dipped his head, kissing her deeply. The scent of arousal grew thick in the room. He reared back until his cock left her folds. As she whimpered the sorrow of her loss, he thrust forward, filling her once again. With each deepening stroke, she arched up, meeting him as his equal.

Jazz looked up, smiling at the dark intensity of his features.

Her smile faltered a bit when she saw the arousal turn to something else, as his expression sharpened and his eyes turned a burning red. The growl that traveled up his throat turned into a feral hiss. Before she could react, his fangs lengthened and he dipped his head. Pain shot through her as his fangs pierced the sensitive skin of her throat.

Why isn't my blood making him sick? Everyone knows a witch's blood will sicken, and can even kill, a vampire! She wanted to shriek, to fight back, but her heavy limbs refused to obey her commands. Lights danced before her eyes and she feared instead of her blood killing Nick, he would kill her.

Jazz's eyes popped open as she shot up in bed, her hand pressed against the side of her neck where pain still radiated. Nick lay slumbering beside her.

Fear, memory of searing pain, and just plain fury warred inside her. She looked down at the source and let her temper—and fist—loose.

"You son of a whore!" She threw a punch to his bare abs that could easily have broken her hand. Not that she would have noticed. "*You bit me!*"

"What? What?" Nick scrambled away from her flying fists and fell out of bed. He grasped the covers and stared at her as if he was positive she'd somehow lost her mind. "What in Hades is wrong with you?"

"You bit me!" She slid off the other side of the bed and hurried around the room, keeping her hand pressed against her neck. Pain and anger translated to red and purple sparks flying around her.

"Bit you?" Confusion mingled with being just plain pissed off at being awakened with a punch to the stomach. "I was *asleep,* damn it!" He hauled himself to his feet and stood there in all his naked glory. For once, Jazz's cold stare warned him that she wasn't admiring the view. He stared at her hand covering her throat but saw no signs of blood or trauma to the skin. He refused to believe he would take her blood without permission, asleep or not. In all their times as lovers he hadn't even given her a hickey. He also kept a close eye on her free hand. The last thing he wanted was witchflame thrown at his favorite part of the body. "Damn it, I didn't bite you!"

With one hand applying firm pressure to her neck, she struggled to pull her jeans on one-handed. "You practically tore out my bloody throat," she snarled, still feeling the ache of her flesh.

Nick crouched slightly, his hands thrust outward. "Will you stop using the word 'bloody'?"

She blinked back the tears that threatened to leak out. "Get out."

"What?" Even with his super hearing, he knew he couldn't have just heard what she said.

She breathed hard as if pushing back tears. Or absolute terror. "I said *get out!*" She stalked around the room, still keeping him out of reach, snatched up his jeans and T-shirt, and threw them at him. The clothing bounced off his chest and fell back to the floor. "Get out and do not ever come near me again." She refused to look at him as she gathered up her own clothing. "Because if you do I *will* stake you. I cannot believe you bit me!" Tears and anger made a nasty combination.

Nick's jaw worked furiously. A witch with Celtic origins might have a legendary temper, but so did a vampire with the blood of a Cossack. "This is *my* room. *My* apartment."

Jazz froze in the act of pulling her cotton top over her head. She stared at the navy and cream swirled print comforter that had been tossed to the floor, navy sheets that were likewise thrown every which way, and furniture that suited a centuries-old vampire. None of the stark colors that dominated her own suite of rooms. She finished pulling on her top, then picked up her leather tote bag. "Fluff! Puff! Where are you two? You better not have left the apartment!" she shouted when she discovered it was empty of two items. The errant slippers popped into the room and scampered over to her feet. Sensing the turmoil in the air, and guessing the cause, the fluffy predators snarled and gnashed their razor-sharp teeth at Nick, clearly showing they considered him the enemy in this battle. Jazz quickly stuffed her underwear, the top she'd worn the night before, and a hairbrush into her leather tote bag and slung it over her shoulder. "If Rex sees those man eaters, you'll be permanently banned from the boardwalk along with them," Nick warned, jumping into his jeans as he followed her to the door.

She sniffed at the mention of the boardwalk manager who ruled his kingdom with an iron fist. "He's not the boss of me." She glared at him. "And neither are you."

"Jazz, what in Hades' name is going on? How can you say I took your blood when there's no sign I did! Damn it, show me where I bit you!" Nick was fast on her heels as she raced up the stairs to the building's main floor. Ground-eating strides took her down the hallway to the double glass doors. Nick wasn't worried about the early morning light. His advanced age as a vampire along with heavily tinted glass of the doors helped protect him against the sun. He was confused, and more than a little ticked off, by her accusation. But it was clear Jazz wasn't going to stick around to talk about it.

He gingerly rubbed his palm over his bare abs. If he'd been a mortal man he would probably have had his share of cracked ribs. The heavy glass door almost hit him in the face as she slapped her palm against the surface and pushed it open, sailing through and not looking back. He kept the door open long enough to holler after her, "And why can't you hit like a girl?"

He stared at her retreating figure and realized that wasn't one of his finer moments.

Jazz was relieved it was still early enough that it seemed no one was stirring on the boardwalk. With the slipper bunnies *non gratae* in the carnival area, she had to make sure not to be seen by the boardwalk manager, who made ogres look like sweet pussycats.

"What the hell do you think you're doing bringing them here?"

Jazz froze. "Five steps," she muttered, staring at the parking lot that was so near yet so far. "Just five lousy steps." She turned around. "Well, aren't we up early!" She used her perkiest witch voice. "How are you, Rex?"

Rex (no one ever learned his last name) was a horror filmmaker's dream—if he wanted someone who looked like a nightmarish thug. Six-foot-four with a square-shaped body built like a Sherman tank, the man looked as if he'd been a former professional boxer. The misshapen nose, cauliflower ears, and slight droop to the left side of his mouth, along with arms the size of tree trunks and the stance of a long-time fighter, showed he wasn't your everyday human. He looked as if one deep breath would split his plaid cotton shirt à la the Incredible Hulk. Standing stoically in front of her, he glared at her feet. Fluff and Puff took one look at him and squeaked in alarm.

"Cowards," she muttered.

"I told you if I ever caught you bringing those damn garbage disposals on the boardwalk again you'd be banned for life," he snarled. "*Your* life."

"They're not doing anything," she argued. She'd had a bad night and no coffee yet, so by now she was feeling pretty snarky. "They have rights too."

"Not here they don't." He stabbed a sausage-shaped finger in the direction of a sign posted off the walkway. "No pets allowed on the boardwalk and they were banned from here last year."

Jazz hid her grin at the sound of the slippers' shrieks of outrage at being considered pets. "Now that's just insulting them."

He leaned in, exhaling air that reeked of a serious lack of Listerine. "Insulting them is the least of their problems. Those fuzzy chompers were out on the boardwalk doing the only thing they know how to do. I oughta feed them to a wood chipper."

She thought better of getting back in his face. Her olfactory senses could only take so much. The gross breath was bad enough, but his body odor was beyond nasty. She'd need to inhale bleach to get the stench out of her nostrils. "They're magickal. You can't touch them and you know it." Smug sounds from Fluff and Puff backed up her haughty claim.

He scowled. "Don't be so sure about that. I've got a carnie missing and those damn slippers were seen in the vicinity."

Jazz felt the cold stealing through her bones. "No way. You tried that accusation before and it didn't work. Besides, contrary to legend, they haven't eaten a human in centuries."

Rex shoved his face into hers, forcing her to rear back. "There's no accusation this time. Only fact. Those *things* have fallen off the wagon, because Willie is missing."

"You're accusing them of eating Willie? Give me a break, Rex! There's no way they'd touch him even if he was smothered with Grey Poupon. They don't like anything with Were-blood and I don't care what you say, Wereweasel blood is the worst." She privately thought the Ferris wheel operator was the perfect picture of his ancestry. Willie's sharp features mirrored the animal he turned into once a month. "So you'll have to look elsewhere for a patsy, because no way am I letting you accuse them of something we both know they didn't do."

At that precise moment, Fluff began coughing and stretching his neck until he hacked loudly. A large black button popped from his mouth. As they say, timing is everything.

Jazz and Rex stared at the boardwalk's logo stamped on the button. She felt a hitch in her stomach that had nothing to do with indigestion. While it didn't look good, she wasn't about to back down.

"He's always picking up things," she said swiftly.

Rex crouched and gently touched the button with his beefy forefinger. "It's Willie's."

Jazz couldn't argue with his statement, since Rex could easily sense any essence belonging to the creatures that worked for him, whether they were members of his pack or not.

He straightened up and jabbed his finger at her. "It ate Willie!"

"And I say he didn't," she argued. "I told you. They don't like Weres."

His heavily scarred face transformed into something even viler. "They're coming with me."

"You can't touch them," she stated, ignoring her slippers' squeaks of dismay. "They're mine by right. I rescued them from Dyfynnog's castle."

"And they ate a living being," Rex reiterated. "That gives me the right to take them into custody. You're not the only one with witchy connections, missy, so don't give me any shit that just because you rescued their furry asses you can protect them."

Missy? What was it with men reverting to their chauvinistic ways? "They were with me all night." She ignored her gargoyle's voice reminding her that the slippers had come into the room when she called them.

"They need to be taken before the Witches' Council and destroyed for their actions."

Jazz felt her balance teeter as Fluff and Puff practically hopped off her feet in their agitation at Rex's words.

"They're not going anywhere until there's rock-hard proof that they ate Willie," she said with a bravado she didn't feel inside. The Witches' Council wasn't her favorite place and she wasn't their favorite witch. She was on 100-year probation as it was.

"I have one of Willie's shoes with his blood on it and tufts of fur. Plus, I have this." He held up the button.

"That's not saying it's his blood or their fur. I have the right to investigate the matter." She felt the hole she was rapidly digging for herself. If the slippers ate Willie, she was going to throw them in a wood chipper herself! She had enough trouble with the Witches' Council without the slippers adding to the mix.

Rex paused.

"You know I have the right to invoke protection for them until the truth is discovered," Jazz pushed.

"All right," he said grudgingly. "You have two weeks."

"The usual time is thirty days."

"Two weeks and be grateful for it. All you're going to find out is that your *things* ate Willie. And make sure they don't go anywhere." He turned and walked away.

Jazz's hand started to rise up, her fingers outstretched. "May you. . ." She abruptly snapped her mouth shut. "Oh no, you are so not going to be the cause of more banishment time for me." She glared at Fluff and Puff, who'd been giggling and blowing raspberries at the retreating Rex. "You've really done it now," she scolded. "Just wait until we get home." She ignored their continued grumbles as she made her way to the parking lot. At the moment, all that mattered to her was that she'd had a few hours of good sleep and that her destination would offer her coffee and, with luck, a muffin.

It took Jazz all of ten minutes of scanning the empty parking lot to realize she had walked over to the boardwalk instead of driving.

Fear and anger still mingled inside her and her neck hurt like hell, even if she couldn't feel any wounds or find any sign of blood. Considering the sensation of feeling Nick literally rip her throat open, she should be able to see *something*. And her neck wouldn't be hurting if he hadn't done something there.

And Nick. Why hadn't he gotten sick when he took her blood? At the very least, he should have suffered from one hell of a case of heartburn, since a witch's blood is poisonous to a vampire.

"It doesn't make sense." Her whisper hung in the air, creating questions she had no answers for.

Needing to think things out, Jazz took a circuitous route home, stopping at a twenty-four-hour Starbucks for a Venti white chocolate mocha for herself and ignoring Fluff and Puff's pleas for a cinnamon roll. With the charges Rex wanted to level against the slippers, she knew he had the right to demand they be taken into custody. But that didn't mean she didn't have more than her share of doubts about Willie's sudden disappearance. Were-carnies tended to wander more than mortal carnies did. If she wanted success she knew she'd have to start looking for the Wereweasel before he ended up states away.

She sipped the hot liquid, savoring the rich chocolate taste mingling with the caffeine as she walked past storefronts that wouldn't open for another couple of hours. That was fine with her, since she wasn't in the mood to stop and chat, or even shop.

"Why does Nick have to ruin things when everything was going so well?" she muttered, taking another swig of her drink instead of sitting down and giving in to tears.

Since they had vanquished Clive Reeves a few months ago, Jazz and Nick had taken up where they had left off over thirty years ago, but with one major difference. This time around they made love more than they fought. They'd even had actual conversations. Some of them ended up with verbal outbursts, but she didn't consider those times fighting. More a difference of opinion.

Jazz was still convinced The Protectorate wanted Nick to rejoin their ranks. Especially after Flavius's death. Nick had taken the loss of his sire, and close friend, hard. Jazz gave him time to mourn the vampire's passing but refused to allow him too much time. Not when there was a chance The Protectorate might try to use Nick's guilt to persuade him to carry on Flavius's work. She had always felt the group, set up centuries ago to govern the vampire race, used Nick's strong sense of good and evil to further their own cause. That they would use him until there was nothing left but an empty husk.

As a former noble Roman officer, Flavius had thrived in the environment. Nick's human role as a Slavic soldier meant he was well suited to his role as an investigator in The Protectorate, but Jazz hated his working for them. Hated how they used him. She wanted to believe him when he told her he'd left The Protectorate, but then he let slip they'd hired him to find out who was destroying vampires. She saw it as their chance to lure him back into the fold. She found it difficult to believe his claim that he only took the assignment for the hefty retainer they offered and once he received payment after Clive Reeves was killed by his victims and his mansion imploded, he was out of it.

Jazz found no compunction in checking his answering machine messages on the sly. As suspected, The Protectorate still called with offers. She wondered what would happen when, like the Mafia, they made him an offer he couldn't refuse. To ensure that couldn't happen, she deleted the messages before he could hear them. She just hoped he never found out what she did. Nick was big on privacy issues.

As she headed home, one thing stuck in her head. Her cell phone hadn't rung once since she left the building.

"Stubborn vampire." She lobbed her empty cup into a nearby trashcan and scuffed her way down the sidewalk.

"Stubborn witch," Nick muttered, tossing a bag of O neg in the microwave and setting it to warm. "What makes her think I'd risk my stomach, not to mention my existence, in taking her damn poisonous blood?" The minute the microwave dinged, he opened the door and withdrew the plastic bag.

He knew some of his kind who drank directly out of the bag, but he preferred to be more civilized than that. He kept a variety of beer bottles as his beverage holder of choice, his own little way of keeping his life somewhat normal. . .as far as human standards of "normal" go.

As he lifted the blood-filled Schlitz bottle to his lips, a memory jogged his brain. Flavius laughing at the Heineken bottle Nick used one night while his sire chose a Baccarat crystal wine glass.

The heart that no longer beat twisted a bit in his chest. Before, it could be years between times he and Flavius saw each other, but Nick always knew that the elder vampire was somewhere in the world. Available by phone or e-mail. If Nick needed him, he was there. Then a madman used evil magick to turn the powerful vampire into a shade and it took the combined efforts of Nick, Jazz, and even Irma to send Flavius to the land of shadows where vampires went when their lives were extinguished.

Nick knew many vampires, but Flavius was more than that. He was his sire. His brother.

And now Nick was alone.

As he lowered the bottle, his eyes settled on a photograph tacked to the refrigerator by a magnet shaped like a fortune cookie—Jazz sitting on the wooden railing on the boardwalk pier, the setting sun a brilliant blaze of orange and gold behind her and just as dazzling as her smile. Denim shorts displayed legs that seemed to go on forever while her turquoise and white checked crop top trimmed in lace was feminine and flirty. Her hair was piled high in a messy knot with ends drifting in the ocean breeze.

Anyone looking at the picture wouldn't believe that she was 700-plus years old and had more magickal power in her fingertips than many had in their entire bodies.

No one, not even Flavius, made Nick feel well and truly alive the way Jazz did.

But, other than great sex, what did he give her? Make her feel? Even after all these years, did they truly have what was required between a couple? Especially when that couple was made up of a witch and a vampire?

He swallowed the rest of the rapidly cooling blood. His appetite was gone, but after last night, he needed the nourishment.

And he needed rest.

He returned to his bed, to sheets that smelled of Jazz's perfume. He quickly stripped off his jeans and climbed into bed, burrowing against the pillow she'd used.

The pull of daybreak wasn't strong, but he hadn't rested much lately, so his eyelids drooped quickly.

"Perchance to dream," he murmured, as his body shut down for the daylight hours.

"You are in so much trouble," Jazz told Fluff and Puff, setting them on her chaise then heading for her closet. She stomped all the way to the rear and placed her hand against the back wall. "My secrets are here. My secrets are dear. I ask that you open for me." The wall trembled under her touch and silently slid to one side. A faint light shimmered inside, illuminating the interior that held magickal items Jazz rarely used, and one item she never thought she would have to use. She paused at the entrance, taking several deep breaths to calm her racing pulse. She walked over to one dark corner that was faintly illuminated by the glow coming off a fair-sized cage. Magick covering the bars prickled her skin as she picked it up and carried it out of the room. The wall silently slid closed.

Fluff and Puff's chatter ceased as they watched her carry the cage into the room and set it on the bed. Jazz ignored their squeaks and cries of alarm as she murmured the words to release the cage door.

"I have no choice. Do you realize what will happen to you if I can't prove your innocence? Rex can go to the Witches' Council and demand you be destroyed. And I would have no option but to give you over to them." When she picked up the wildly struggling slippers, angry sparks flew around the room as they fought her every step of the way. Jazz gritted her teeth against the painful magick skimming up her arms. She hadn't been leading Rex on when she said they were protected. Magick did shield Fluff and Puff, and the slippers were drawing on that power now. She knew she'd have a major headache by evening. "So sad. Bunnies been bad. Don't let me fail. Bunnies must go to jail. Because I say so, damn it!" She pushed them into the cage and quickly secured the seal on the door before they could escape. Sparks from bunny tantrums bumped up the atmosphere in the room to the point of suffocation. "Stop it! Do you think I want to use this?" She swallowed the anguish she felt. "I know Dyfynnog used this cage to keep you two prisoner, but I have to keep you secured. Or would you rather I hand you over to the Witches' Council like Rex wants?"

She took their sudden silence as their assent. Their black eyes shot accusations at her as she moved around the room. In the end, Jazz escaped to the bathroom so that she didn't have to listen to their angry muttering. She had a feeling their incarceration wouldn't be pleasant for them or for her.

"Why isn't there a mark?" Jazz leaned across the graceful, deep, rose-colored bowl that doubled as her bathroom sink to peer into the oval mirror. All she saw was an unblemished neck. She knew a vampire could lick a bite and it would heal instantly, but she had jerked away from Nick, so a mark, if not a lot of bruising, should still be visible. She touched her fingertips to her neck, felt tenderness along the skin's surface, but that was all. Her moss-green eyes widened at the memory of the pain she felt at the time, but even there she couldn't find the answers she was seeking.

She straightened up and ran over to the tub, turning off the water before it overflowed. She had decided a long hot bath was in order. The silence from the bedroom was deafening. She was positive Fluff and Puff were pouting big-time, since no one pouted better than her bunny slippers. Well, unless it was her. She had a pretty good idea once they were freed they'd be taking vengeance on anything of hers they could reach. It was up to her to vindicate them of a crime she was certain they didn't commit, but she feared in the end she'd be the one punished. The slippers knew how to hold a grudge and even more how to make someone suffer. She made a mental note to put heavy-duty wards on her closet.

"Choices, choices." She ran through her large selection of body washes and body creams, most of which smelled like a bakery. Since she wanted comfort, she chose a body wash inspired by the scent of creamy hot cocoa and set aside a like-scented body cream and a shimmering body powder that reminded her of marshmallows. When she was in total witch mode, she wore a heavier, spicy scent. Otherwise, she stuck to what she called the "fun stuff." The many bottles and jars in the bathroom cabinet were proof of her addiction to good smells.

The rubber duckies lining the edge of the tub perked up as they watched her ready her bath. When Blair gave

Jazz a collection of rubber duckies last summer, Jazz didn't expect the duckies to pretty much take over the tub anytime they could. Many an evening she walked in to find it filled with water and the duckies playing their own version of *Battleship*.

"All right, guys, behave," she gently scolded them, as one rubber ducky wearing Joe Cool dark sunglasses emitted a squeaky wolf whistle before hopping off the ledge and into the warm water. The others followed him into the bubbles, quacking their pleasure as they bobbed up and down in the mild waves.

Jazz switched on her CD player, stepped into the steaming water, and activated the whirlpool jets, settling back against the curve at the end that cradled her neck with just the right touch. She closed her eyes and tried to ignore the outside world as the soft sounds of Celtic Woman floated through the room and the rubber duckies started scrambling back up onto the ledge, taking turns diving into the water.

She sunk further down in the water and allowed the many jets to massage her body from toes to shoulders. Soon she was lulled into a light doze.

She suddenly felt the faintest of touches brush over her toes. She smiled and shifted her feet from her dream tormentor, not really trying to escape. She couldn't remember the duckies trying this game, but they did love to play, so she'd go along with their fun. Then she sensed the hint of fingertips trail along her ankles and up her calves. This time she couldn't escape, nor did she want to. Instead, she parted her legs a bit in a less than subtle invitation. Her smile dimmed to a slight frown as the phantom fingers stroked her inner thighs and upward. The closer they reached her core, the colder the touch became, even in the heated water, until she felt as if needles of ice pricked her skin and pain radiated through her body. A sense of something not quite right invading her dream state brought her back to awareness and she jerked away. Water splashed over the side of the tub as she sat upright looking around the room, but nothing appeared out of place. She was alone in the room.

Even in the heated water she felt chilled. The music still played and sounds of Fluff and Puff growling complaints added further background noise. She turned her head and found the duckies now perched on the ledge. They all had a faint look of alarm on their yellow-orange faces and their beaks moved in silent distress. She leaned over the side of the tub and peered through the open bathroom door where she could see that her suite's double doors were closed.

But that didn't stop the sensation that the atmosphere in the rooms had drastically changed, and not for the better. Jazz quickly climbed out of the tub and opened the drain. She wrapped a bath sheet around her body, swiftly drying her skin. Normally, she would take her time and smooth on body cream and dust herself with the shimmering powder, but this time she wanted to be out of there as soon as possible.

Once wrapped warmly in her robe, she went to her trunk for sage and began burning it in pots scattered around the bathroom and bedroom. She needed to cleanse the air and purify the rooms.

She had no idea what brought her so rudely awake, but she knew one thing: whatever the fingertips that had caressed her intimately belonged to, they weren't even remotely human.

Even after smudging the rooms, Jazz still felt a bit out of sorts as she dressed in aqua terry drawstring pants with an embroidered strawberry doubling as decoration and back pocket, and a matching hoody. Tiny strawberries decorated her flip flops. She kept her makeup minimal. She tried a hint of plum eye shadow and black mascara to highlight her green eyes and a dusty rose blush with shimmer in it that echoed her lipstick. Today she wanted the color to boost her unsettled spirits.

She left a pair of angry slippers behind as she exited the room.

"Wow, look at you," Krebs, aka Jonathon Shaw, III, greeted her when she sauntered into the kitchen and pulled a bottle of citrus-flavored sparkling water out of the refrigerator. "No bad scary witch today?"

She thought of the black leather pants and black silk shirt she'd almost put on in an attempt to feel like the big bad scary witch after a bath that had turned less than relaxing.

"Maybe I'll go more suburban witch." She tried to picture herself driving an SUV or minivan with kiddies headed to Little League or soccer practice. She shuddered at the idea. She twisted the bottle cap off and drank half the bottle in one gulp. "Do you want to take a drive up the coast? Stop and get dinner somewhere?" *Pretend all was normal with the world even if it wasn't.*

Krebs looked at her bright, almost perky, self and then down to his T-shirt, faded to the color of ancient bones, and tan and navy plaid pajama pants. His dark-brown hair stuck up in unruly spikes. Not as a fashion statement, but only because he hadn't cleaned up yet.

"Um, we're not even at lunchtime yet."

"We could do it for lunch instead of dinner. I'm free," she suggested with a brightness she didn't truly feel. "Or even drive up to Santa Barbara, do some sightseeing, then have dinner. Come on. It's a gorgeous day. Let's enjoy it." *Let me escape my haunted bathroom and pissed off slippers for awhile.*

"I—ah—I don't think so. Thanks anyway." He developed a sudden interest in his coffee mug. "Besides, I think that ghost of yours gropes me when I ride with you."

Jazz snorted as she drank her water, then coughed. "Irma's too much of a lady to do that." No way in Hades she'd admit that she'd seen the irascible ghost do some braille on Krebs's very nice male bod the last time he rode with them. She guessed while he couldn't see Irma, he could sense when she was taking liberties with him.

Bad ghost! Bad!

"And that's not all," he lowered his voice. "And this has only been in the past few months, but sometimes when I've been in the carriage house, I swore something was humping my leg."

She swallowed the hysterical laughter that threatened to erupt. She hadn't mentioned the dog to him yet and wasn't looking forward to the day she did. She knew Krebs was allergic to dogs. Luckily he wasn't allergic to a spirit dog.

"Come on, Krebs," she whined. "We haven't had a fun evening out in a while."

He continued stirring his coffee even though she knew he drank it black and wouldn't need to stir it.

"I've got work," he mumbled.

"All work and no play make Krebsie a dateless boy." She took her keys off the board near the back door. "Okay, but you're going to miss out on some awesome seafood, terrific conversation, and a scintillating evening with *moi*." She blew him a kiss and sailed out the door.

The crusty tones of Humphrey Bogart along with loud weeping greeted her as she activated the carriage house door, watching it swing outward.

Casablanca. She heaved a sigh as she entered the carriage house. Irma sat back in the cushy recliner Jazz had gotten her with a lace hanky dangling from one hand as she dabbed at her eyes. She stared at the TV, mouthing the final words.

"Okay, Rick and Louis will be the best of friends. How about a drive?" She tossed her keys from one hand to the other.

Irma covered her nose with her hanky and honked. No delicate sniffs for her.

"He just let her leave," Irma sobbed.

Jazz ignored the fact that she cried buckets when she first saw the movie at the Rialto Theater in 1942.

"That's the war for you. Tell you what, let's cruise the coast. That will cheer you up." She climbed in the car and started up the engine. A moment later, Irma was in the passenger seat. "Grab some dinner."

"*You'll* grab some dinner," Irma grumbled, tucking her hanky in her dress pocket. Her navy print dress looked as freshly pressed as the day she was laid to rest in it. She never forgave her lying, adulterous husband for choosing an unflattering style for her eternity wear. "I'll just sit in the car like one of those bobbling hula girls people set on the dashboard."

"You in a bra top and grass skirt is something I so do not want to picture. Besides, you can leave the car now. Go sit on the beach or something. Find a stick and throw it for the dog to fetch." She eyed the furry behemoth that lay next to Irma's chair. "He needs some serious exercise."

"What good is my ability to leave the car if I can't come in with you?" Irma argued.

"Oh no, not after that day in Taco Bell." Jazz shuddered at the memory.

"It wasn't my fault that ghost-hunting crew was in there having lunch," Irma huffed. "Or that one of their people sensed me."

Jazz knew it wasn't Irma's fault, but it didn't make the insanity of that time or the panicked customers running out of the restaurant when the psychic ghost hunter jumped up with his camera any easier to remember. "Look, I'll park where you have a great view of the beach," she promised, activating the remote for the doors then backing down the driveway. "That way if you change your mind you can walk down to the sand and enjoy the sunset."

When Jazz reached the street she heard the faint tinny sounds of the carousel's calliope coming from the boardwalk. She resolutely ignored the lure of the Midway and turned in the opposite direction.

As she drove toward the Pacific Coast Highway she swore she felt a whisper of a touch along the inside of her leg. The contact was unsettling, since she knew it had nothing to do with the dog.

"Assure me this will work," a low voice echoed against the chamber's stone walls.

"My work never fails."

"Good, because if it does, you will never leave this room." The speaker opened the large iron door and left the room.

The one left behind returned to his task.

Flickering candlelight highlighted the ancient text etched in parchment lying on the antique oak table. The words written in an arcane language long forgotten by many in the magick world were etched in the blood of its creator's enemies just as the parchment was crafted from its enemies' skin. Long fingers ending in similarly long nails polished so brightly that they glowed black in the candlelight traced the lines of text. A low guttural voice repeated the spell over and over, but what made the words even more powerful was the drawing placed next to the text.

A drawing of Jazz Tremaine that was so lifelike, so exquisitely real, she could have stepped off the paper. Every bare inch of flesh detailed in the drawing was absolutely perfect.

Chapter 2

JAZZ DROVE UP TO SANTA BARBARA, WHERE SHE INDULGED in some shopping, then returned home at a leisurely pace, finally stopping in a small funky coastal town that looked like a movie set straight out of the 1940s. The seafood restaurant she chose sat on stilts overlooking the beach with a bar displaying fishing nets, colorful glass floats, and starfish for decoration. She ignored the looks of frank male interest directed her way as she was seated on the deck with a glass of wine and a perfect view of the sunset.

The morning's events had left her feeling uneasy. If Nick hadn't bitten her, why did it feel so real at the time? And just what in Fates' sake happened in the tub? Two unsettling dreams in less than twenty-four hours could not be a coincidence.

She mentally vowed not to use the tub again until she thoroughly cleansed it. And not with Scrubbing Bubbles either.

She may have been half-asleep at the time, but what touched her in the tub didn't feel like a dream.

Meaning. . .if that was the case, then the same could be said for what happened at Nick's apartment.

Meaning. . .magick.

She preferred to dismiss that thought because she honestly didn't want to think someone was casting spells against her. It was bad enough that she now had to find out what happened to Wereweasel Willie before Rex lost his patience and reported the slippers to the Ruling Council. He may have agreed to give her time to find out what happened, but Rex also believed in his own time-table, one that didn't always agree with anyone else's.

Plus for now, she just wanted to relax and enjoy the evening. Her eyes focused on the horizon, admiring the play of gold, orange, and red on the ocean heralding the sunset. The faint silhouette of a porpoise jumping into the air and diving back into the water as the sun finished its descent caused her to smile. The votive candle set on the small round table flickered wildly in the ocean breeze, casting shadows across her face.

"You know, it's never a good thing to see a pretty lady sitting alone."

Pretty lady? Jazz mentally summed up her unwanted visitor before she turned from the view to see who was interrupting her peace and quiet. One look told her she had it right on the mark.

The man standing by her chair was about six feet tall with sun-bleached blond hair arranged in a tousled way that said he spent more time on his grooming than she did. His perfectly maintained tan was meant to show off his baby blues, and gym-toned pecs and six-pack abs were visible under a—natch—blue polo shirt tucked into designer jeans. A quick downward glance showed tanned bare feet shoved into Top-Siders that she'd bet her favorite cauldron had never stepped onto a boat deck.

She smiled. "Sometimes the lady prefers to sit alone." *Go away before I turn you into a gingerbread boy and have you for dessert.*

Not accepting her mental hint, he flashed his bleached pearly whites and took the seat across from her. He set his whiskey glass down on the table.

"I'm Thad."

"Of course you are." She enjoyed his faint annoyance that his charm wasn't getting through to her. It would have been so tempting to see what he'd look like as a frog. Or maybe a hermit crab. They were at the beach, after all. But she didn't think the Witches' Council would see it as improving his lot and she had that hundred-year's probation to think about.

"You're not local. I would have remembered you." Thad's eyes were centered on her breasts. "Where are you from? L.A.?"

"Yes." She was always grateful her breasts weren't centerfold material, but obviously Thad only cared she was female. She didn't need to be psychic to know that.

His smile almost glowed bright in the candlelight. "Maybe you'd like some company and after dinner we could have a drink at my place. I've got a cozy place just up the beach." He reached across to touch her hand.

Okay, she was *this* close to turning him into a sea urchin, no matter what the Witches' Council would do to her.

"Sweetheart, our table is ready." There was no warning someone stood behind her chair or even a hint of warmth at her back, but she didn't need either to know who stood there. For a second, she even enjoyed the deer-in-the-headlights look on ole Thad's face. She lifted her hand, feeling the slide of fingers through hers as Nick rested their clasped hands on her shoulder. "This is Thad, darling," she purred.

"Thad," Nick growled with just enough emphasis to make his point known.

"I didn't know." Thad rose so hastily his drink glass tipped over, spilling whiskey on his jeans. He didn't appear to care as he walked to the end of the deck and rushed down the stairs leading to the beach.

"Well, that was rude." Jazz looked up. "And don't you look tall, dark, and dangerous?" Nick did look dark and utterly dangerous in a black silk shirt left open at the throat tucked into black slacks and black loafers she hazarded a guess were Italian made. Probably left over from his wardrobe when working for the Protectorate and their unlimited coffers. The evening breeze ruffled his dark hair and the candlelight etched shadows across his jaw.

He cocked an eyebrow. "Rude? Me or him?"

"You for running off my impromptu date. Him for, well, running." She allowed him to effortlessly pull her to her feet. "I gather you weren't lying about our table being ready."

"Not at all." He rested a hand against the sweet hollow in the base of her spine as they followed the hostess through the restaurant to a window table.

Jazz didn't bother asking Nick how he managed to find her. How he tracked her down had been a gift he'd never shared and she doubted he ever would.

In record time they gave their orders and were left alone.

"You do realize I'm sticking you with the check?" She sipped her wine, watching the light from the candle flame play over his face. Judging by the hint of color in his skin, she guessed he'd recently fed, and if she wasn't mistaken, he'd also made use of the spray tan booth membership she set up for him at a nearby tanning salon. At least he looked more outdoorsy than the tanning bed color Thad sported. Come to think of it, a tanning bed would turn Nick into a crispy critter, which, in her opinion, would be a waste of a perfectly good vampire.

"So that's why you ordered the Surf and Turf for yourself and the lobster for me?" He glanced up as the waitress deposited a glass of merlot in front of him. He would drink enough to appear polite while he knew Jazz would also nibble on his food.

"And I plan to have their Kahlua cheesecake for dessert." Jazz toyed with the idea of telling him what had happened in the tub, but what would she say? *By the way, sweetheart, some specter played touchy-feely with me under the bubbles today.* She hadn't detected any hint of magick in the room, but she refused to believe she'd dreamed it happening or that magick wasn't involved. No, whatever she felt was as strong as what she'd felt in the early morning hours when she was positive Nick had taken her blood. She refused to believe either was her imagination.

"Did you do some heavy-duty running to get up here right after sunset, or use another method?" she asked. She'd always been curious about a vampire's method of transportation other than the usual mortal means, but Nick was close-mouthed about the vampire ways. She pretended only mild curiosity, but damn him, he knew different. The faint grin on his lips told her he saw through her ploy.

"Do you mean something like 'Beam me up, Scotty'?"

"If the bat fits." She narrowed her eyes, trying to imagine him as a winged creature of the night.

"Be nice. I saved you from Thad." He lifted his glass in a silent toast. "He saw you arrive, admired your sexy convertible, and obviously saw you as some bored Hollywood wife who was looking for action he would be only too happy to provide."

"Little did he know I'd just use him and abuse him," she drawled, well used to Nick's gift of reading minds. She wasn't surprised that Thad's mind wasn't all that difficult to navigate.

"And he would have loved every minute of it."

Jazz stared at the platter set before her. Considering she'd eaten little all day, it was no wonder she was starving. After she eyed Nick's lobster she knew she would be making short work of the luscious crustacean along with her own meal.

The things she did for the man.

"Just roll me out of here," Jazz said with a contented sigh as they later exited the restaurant.

"I could have done something with my lobster," Nick muttered.

"My idea was better." She patted her over-full tummy. "But the cheesecake may have been over the top. You were smart to stick with just coffee."

He chuckled. "As if I had a choice." He grabbed her hand and pulled her around the side of the restaurant. "A walk seems to be in order."

"Augh! Carrying me would be more like it." She bumped her shoulder against his, but tugged off her flip-flops as they trudged through the sand. Nick took her sandals from her and draped an arm around her shoulders.

"I honestly don't recall taking your blood." The salt-tinged evening breeze caught up his quiet words and seemed to blow them out to sea.

Jazz winced at the memory of how her morning had begun. While she now questioned what she felt or if it was a dream, the faint throbbing in her neck was a vivid memory.

"It was all so real," she said softly. "A hot sexy time and then you biting down." She paused. "I honestly felt as if it happened." Her fingers absently fluttered toward her neck. "Still feel. . ." Images flashed before her eyes like a horror movie. Suddenly, her dinner wasn't settling so well.

Nick rubbed his hand down her arm in a comforting manner.

"I need to know what you dreamed. Perhaps I can figure out what happened."

"I don't do well with blood, you know that. I'd need an Alka-Seltzer before even talking about it."

"Pretend you're watching a movie." He steered her toward an outcropping of rocks and settled her against one that was shaped like a seat.

"Great, Freddy Krueger time." She breathed in through her nose. "We were, ah, making love." That was a memory she could deal with. "And as it got more intense, you took charge the way you like to." She shot him a look when he opened his mouth. "My story. My way. Simple. You were on top. Your eyes turned red, then you leaned down and tore into my throat. I screamed and wondered why my blood didn't make you sick. Next thing I knew I was yelling at you and exiting your apartment as fast as I could go." She flinched when his fingertips moved over the affected area.

"A dream with pain is nothing unusual," he murmured, continuing to caress her skin in soothing strokes. "There are those who would pay a fortune to have such a dream. They would welcome such pain."

"Well, they can have mine for free." She stopped, recalling what had happened before the definitive moment. "The last part, that is."

"Why do you think you had the dream?"

"Bad Thai food. Who knows? Maybe a holdover from what happened before." There was no need to explain her choice of words. They both knew what "before" meant.

"Magick?"

She shook her head. "I thought of that, but it doesn't make sense and it didn't feel like a magick I'm familiar with. I haven't pissed off anyone enough to do something like this. Well, I haven't!" she protested, easily reading his skepticism.

When the wind picked up Nick stood in front of Jazz, protecting her from the chill. His fingers moved from her throat to her hair, tangling themselves among the heavy strands. The idea of snuggling into his arms and kissing him grew stronger by the moment.

Jazz gave in to temptation, since Nick was the best kind of temptation. Their tongues tangled as she slid her fingers between the buttons of his shirt, stroking his skin while he palmed her breast through silk and lace.

"Mmm, even better than chocolate," she murmured, once she had a chance to take a breath.

"What's better than chocolate?" His amusement washed over her.

"You. Although, I have to say some days I'd go for the chocolate." She feathered kisses over his face.

"I'd rather go for you." He kissed the top of her head and wrapped her tightly in his arms.

It didn't take much effort for Nick's slacks to hang open and Jazz's to end up around her ankles. He picked her up and she wrapped her legs around his waist as he lowered her onto his erection. She kept her arms around his neck, pressing her cheek against his as he moved his hips in cadence with hers. There was no urgency in their movements, none of the heat of before, but a soft gentle loving that brought a big smile to Jazz's lips and the same with Nick. As her body tightened around his, she breathed his name against his skin. He didn't lower her back to her seat on the rock for a moment, instead preferring to hold onto her.

"You sure know how to show a girl a good time, Nick Gregory," she said, looking as dreamy as she felt.

"I do my best." He helped her dress.

At the sound of laughter and barking, they turned to see Irma standing at the water's edge while the dog raced up and down, chasing the incoming waves.

"Come back before you drown!" Irma shouted to the dog, who ignored her entreaties to return to her.

"Did she ever name him?" Nick asked.

Jazz shook her head. "Irma's tried out names, but so far he doesn't seem to like what she's come up with. But then, I wouldn't want to be called Fluffy or Pooh Bear."

Nick winced. "They don't work for me either."

"Oh, I don't know, I can see you as my l'il Pooh Bear," she cooed. "Do you want a ride back to the city? Easier than flying back, even if I would like to see you in bat form."

He smiled. "Only if I can drive." He grasped her hands and pulled her to her feet as she called out to Irma to join them at the car.

"No way I'll share the passenger seat with Irma, and the bench seat isn't wide enough for all four of us."

"Except if I sit there, she'll distract you while she's groping me." They walked up the sand toward the restaurant parking lot. "I like my idea better."

"Better than her complaining that I'm hogging the seat. I'll have to find a way to get the dog to ride in the trunk. That should be fun since he appears to be afraid of small spaces." Her laughter floated across the air. "I'm not used to seeing you look so dapper. It's a nice change from the jeans and T-shirts you seem to live in nowadays."

He inclined his head to her compliment. "Thank you."

She dug her toes into the sand as she walked. "Yes, very sexy in that dark dangerous way."

Nick chuckled and shook his head. "I'm not going to get lucky tonight, am I?"

She turned around and danced backwards. A broad smile lit up her face. "We'll see."

❖❖❖

Coffee. She needed lots of coffee. Turn the Pacific Ocean into dark rich French roast or chocolate mint that she could swim in. She wasn't fussy.

Jazz's eyelids felt glued together the next morning as she made her way down to the kitchen. Krebs sat at the table with a plate of bacon and eggs in front of him. Jazz went straight for the mug sitting by the plate and held it reverently in both hands as if the contents held the gift of life.

"That's my coffee."

"I don't care." She didn't bother to inhale the caffeine fumes. She slugged it back.

"What did you do last night?" He stared at her more rumpled than usual pajamas and hair sticking every which way. "Your eyes are carrying a whole set of luggage there. Maybe even a few steamer trunks."

She plopped in a chair and rested her cheek on the table. "I don't think I slept very well last night."

"Ya think?" He picked up the mug and refilled it along with filling a second mug for himself, which he placed well out of her reach. "Maybe you and the vampire should consider tapering off on the hot and heavy sex. Does he look as bad as you do?"

"There was no sex, no hot and heavy, no nothing," she mumbled against her hands. "Nick got a call during our drive back and he had to see a client. All I remember is coming home and falling asleep, but it wasn't a nice sleep." She frowned as she tried to recall what exactly disturbed her rest. She mentally backtracked through her evening. Drive up the coast. Ick factor with the dog slobbering all over her during the drive. Tanning-bed bronzed

Thad hitting on her. Nick. Romantic dinner by candlelight. Walk on the beach and some serious making out. Nick driving them home and ignoring Irma's complaints that Nick wouldn't take up as much room next to her as Jazz did. Jazz threatening to banish the ghost to the trunk with the dog. Then there was that one last attempt on Nick's part to persuade her to stay at his place, which was incredibly tempting, but after what happened the previous night, Jazz had no difficulty in saying no. Then by the time she got home all she wanted to do was collapse on her bed. Even washing her face seemed like too much work.

And now she was sucking down coffee as if it was the only thing between her and sanity.

Right about now, it just might be.

Krebs sighed and pushed his plate over to her, then got up and started fixing a second batch.

"You didn't look much better yesterday. What's going on?" In no time he had eggs scrambled and bacon straight out of the microwave for himself.

"Just having trouble with sleep." She picked at her food. "Maybe I shouldn't have asked for a loaded baked potato to go with my Surf and Turf. Or have eaten Nick's lobster. But then it could have been the Kahlua cheesecake," she thoughtfully concluded.

"Gee, ya think?" Krebs looked a little green. "Oh, you got a call on the house phone." While they each had private phone lines, a central line was installed for any calls considered not personal. "Seems she couldn't get you on your cell or any other way and wanted to make sure you'd call her back."

"Who?"

"Thea. She's the romance novelist, right?"

Jazz groaned. She guessed there was also an urgent "contact me" message on the wallmail, but she hadn't bothered looking at it when she got home. Of course, Thea's idea of urgent was 180 degrees different from hers. To Thea, a broken nail or learning her hairdresser was out of town was fodder for a breakdown. And if one of her books fell off the NYT list, well, get the designer straitjacket ready, because Thea would be curled up in a corner in a fetal position convinced her life was over. Jazz was convinced that Thea created the word diva. As a world-famous historical novelist, she had found her niche. Of course, it helped she had her own true experiences and stories from her witch sisters as material for her books. Seven hundred years of romantic adventure gave her plenty of inspiration without having to do any serious research. It also provided her with a penthouse apartment in Manhattan, flats in London, Paris, and Milan, along with a couture wardrobe and an incredible collection of bling that rivaled JLo's.

"If someone cursed her, she's on her own." She drank more coffee and picked up a slice of bacon, waving it like a banner. "She's a twit. I love her, but she's still a twit."

Krebs grinned. "She said something about coming out to L.A. and wanting to get together for dinner. She also said I'm more than welcome to join the two of you."

"The woman is a witch piranha."

"I'll have you to protect me." He refilled their coffee mugs. "So, are you going to tell me why you couldn't sleep last night? Because, I'm serious, Jazz, you look like hell."

"Thank you so much," she snarled, but without the heat she normally could conjure up. She was too tired even to send the plates to the sink so that they could wash themselves. She rinsed them off and placed them in the dishwasher.

"Then go back to bed." He stretched his arms over his head.

She shook her head. "Can't even if I want to. I've got a job up in the Hollywood Hills. Remember when I eliminated Martin the Sleazebag's cursed cookie jar? Seems word got around."

"Aren't you afraid someone in the film industry will decide to make a movie about you? Or write a book?"

"I take care of that in my own little way. The idea might strike them, but it leaves as quickly as it arrives." She dug her fingers into her scalp and rubbed vigorously. The copper-red waves floated upward as if hit by an electric shock.

"Does Nick like football or soccer?" Krebs asked, sipping his coffee.

Her still sleep-deprived brain tried to assimilate the question. "Huh?" Not articulate, but at the moment she couldn't do any better.

"Football. Soccer. Usually accompanied by beer and chips, but I guess he'd want to skip that part. I know the games are during the day, but you said he can go out on cloudy days and the weatherman said this Sunday will be overcast. I thought maybe he'd like to come over and watch the game with me."

Jazz tried to picture Nick sprawled on the leather couch in the family room, knocking back a brewski and munching on nachos. Well, munching on the nachos wouldn't happen, but he could show up wearing a football jersey in honor of his favorite team with his face painted in team colors. She added a blooming beer belly to the picture. The illusion shattered inside her mind like glass.

"I—uh—I don't know."

"Can I have his phone number? Invite him over?"

Jazz's first thought was to give him a reason why he couldn't call Nick, but Krebs knew what Nick was, had even heard a very edited story of what happened out at the Reeves' estate, so could she really lie to him and say no, he and Nick couldn't have a play date? She grabbed a piece of paper off the notepad by the phone and scribbled across it.

"Most of the time his answering machine picks up, so just leave him a message. Maybe some guy bonding is what he needs now."

"Sheesh, Jazz, show some enthusiasm here," he groused. "You'd think we were going to have some hookers in."

"For all I know you will." She rolled her eyes as she carried her coffee mug out of the kitchen. Considering the way things had been going lately, she wouldn't be at all surprised this weekend to see Nick parked on the couch, beer can in one hand and that plate of nachos in the other. And wouldn't that make a fun Kodak moment?

As she crossed her bedroom, she determinedly kept her gaze from the blank wall that seemed to glow and throb with the graceful script scrawled across it.

Where in Hades are you? Wallmail me now!

"Later, Thea," she muttered, almost running to the bathroom as if her witch sister could see her from 3500 miles away. Still, with Thea anything was possible.

Jazz ignored her reflection in the bathroom mirror as she went through the motions of showering and washing her hair. As she stood under the spray, she thought back to her restless night. She knew she'd had odd dreams but couldn't recall any of them, which was uncommon for her since she usually remembered her dreams in detail. She practically drowned herself in peppermint-scented body wash, hoping the sharp fragrance would wake her up.

By the time she dressed and amped her makeup with a glamour illusion to cover the bags under her eyes, she felt ready to kick some magick ass.

The feeling lasted until she stepped outside and stared at a disaster. Ear-splitting yowls warred with deep-throated barks.

"No, no, no, no, no," she muttered, running into the yard and almost twisting her ankle in a freshly-dug hole. She ran toward the southern magnolia tree that dominated a corner of the yard where the ghostly dog pushed against the trunk with his front paws while barking at a ball of furious fur hunched on a high branch.

"Pepper! My Pepper!"

"Damn!" Jazz muttered, racing to the tree and avoiding the many holes in the grass at the same time. "It's all right, Mrs. Sanderson," she called out to the silver-haired woman peering over the fence.

"Why is my Pepper acting as if something's after her?" the woman asked looking bewildered. "My baby's afraid of heights!"

"I'll get Pepper down and bring her over to you," Jazz promised, forcing herself not to look at the dog who'd finally stopped barking and now watched her with his head cocked.

"Maybe I should stay here and assure her everything will be all right. She's so frightened," Mrs. Sanderson's voice quavered.

"You're upset and it could be making her more upset. Go in and fix yourself a cup of tea. I'll get her right now." Jazz gave the elderly woman a tiny magickal nudge to encourage her to no longer be a witness to what Jazz needed to do.

"Perhaps you're right." She turned away and made her way to the house.

Jazz waited until she heard the patio door slide shut then looked up at the white Persian cat who stared at her with the fury only a cat could display.

"Down you go. Ignore your foe. Because I say so, damn it!" She held out her hands and the cat landed in her arms. "Ow!" She eyed the scratches on her arms. "A thank you wouldn't have hurt," she muttered, before she glared at the dog. "You get in the carriage house right now. Bad dog!"

As Jazz crossed the yard to head next door, she muttered the words to restore the grass to its usual pristine lush greenery.

"This is why I don't have pets," she growled.

"My land, these aren't houses around here. We're looking at mansions from the Travel Channel." Irma's mouth dropped open in shock as they drove up the winding road. Heavy wrought-iron gates and call boxes set at the end of driveways barred unwanted visitors.

"Most of them are multi-million dollar estates," Jazz said, wishing the house numbers were easier to read. But then, up here residents tended to pay the big bucks for privacy. She glanced at the sheet of paper scrawled with the directions Patrice Sanibel had given her. "We need to find a 1920s Spanish-style house with the name Hacienda Nights. It will be on a bronze plaque by the gates."

Irma fumbled in her handbag and pulled out a pair of blue catseye glasses complete with blue rhinestones along the flared edges.

Jazz groaned. "Irma, you're dead! You don't need glasses anymore!"

"That's what you think. I keep putting off using them and I'm not going to do that anymore." She practically hung over the open window to peer at the houses. "Do you think they all have swimming pools?"

"It's a law out here," she quipped.

Irma's head whipped from side to side. "Will we see Marilyn Monroe's house?"

"One, this isn't a celebrity sightseeing tour. Two, she lived in Brentwood."

Jazz finally pulled over to the side of the road and held out her hand, palm curved upward. "Who needs a GPS?" she gloated. "Bouncing ball of light. Find house of Spanish night. Do it fast and do it right. Because I said so, damn it!" The moment the words left her lips, a glowing purple ball the size of a baseball appeared in her palm. It rose slowly into the air and zipped over the T-Bird's hood. "I shouldn't have used the word fast," she muttered, quickly pulling out onto the road.

"Up there, on the left." Irma pointed toward a road sign.

Jazz made a quick turn, staying on the fiery heels of the glowing ball that now slowed down and hung in the air in front of gates guarding a driveway that curved upward. "Thank you," she called out. The ball winked *you're welcome* and disappeared.

Jazz pushed the call button, identified herself, and waited for the gates to swing open.

"Can I go in with you?" Irma asked.

"No."

"Can I wander in the gardens?" She peered at the colorful flora surrounding the house.

"No." Jazz parked the car in front of a curve of concrete steps leading to the front door. A smaller ornate gate stood at the bottom. "I don't need my client freaking out if she happens to sense you."

"Then do you mind if I smoke while you go in there and do your ritual?" Irma was getting downright snarky by now. "You wouldn't let me bring my baby along and you know he gets lonely. I guess I should have stayed home and watched *Judge Judy*."

"Your 'baby' turned the backyard into holes a gopher would envy and terrorized the neighbor's cat. Mrs. Sanderson swears the cat is so traumatized she probably won't leave the house for weeks."

"It's a known fact dogs and cats don't get along," Irma pointed out. "It wasn't his fault. It was his nature."

"He needs to change his nature. And he needs a name. Since he doesn't seem to want to move on, you'd better come up with one. And please don't play the radio while I'm gone. Or smoke."

"How can I play the radio when you have the keys?" Irma's smirk didn't fool Jazz one bit and she noticed there was no promise given on keeping the car a No Smoking zone.

"Maybe because you found a way to do it, as I discovered that morning I left Nick's and you'd played the radio all night."

"I was listening to a very good all night station."

"It still killed the battery!"

"Which you brought back to life."

Jazz shook her head as she got out of the car and closed the door behind her. A burst of chilly wind coming down the hills wrapped around her, making her grateful she had zipped the warm liner into the waist-length black leather jacket that topped her dark purple silk blouse and black jeans. She had her hair pulled back in a tight French braid revealing silver hoops with four moonstones embedded in the metal along with her favorite moonstone pendant and ring. Since she wasn't sure what kind of curse she was going to be dealing with, she wanted to look her witchy best.

Considering the expensive real estate, she was surprised when the lady of the house answered the door instead of a maid.

"Ms. Tremaine. I've been expecting you." Patrice Sanibel smiled and offered her hand. She was the picture of the ideal trophy wife wearing a peachy-pink silk T-shirt and matching fitted slacks. Her high-heeled slides matched the outfit perfectly. Her golden brown hair was streaked with highlights and tucked behind her ears. Jazz had no doubt the diamonds winking from her ears were real and flawless. "Thank you for coming. Would you care for some coffee or something cold to drink?" Her smile turned a bit uncertain. It was then that Jazz upped her age a good ten years. She guessed Patrice had seen an excellent plastic surgeon.

Jazz was surprised by the warm welcome, since most of her clients were either so freaked out they were ready to offer their firstborn to get rid of the curse or acted superior as if it was a major inconvenience for her to be there. Instead, Patrice was acting as if Jazz was a friend who just happened to stop by for a visit.

"Uh, iced tea would be nice," she replied, figuring the woman needed this chat time first. And it might even help her relax.

Patrice led her outside to an umbrella-shaded table on a patio overlooking a swimming pool that could have easily handled the entire U.S. Olympic team with room left over. A fountain in the center of the pool sprayed a watery rainbow into the air. The spa looked as if it was part of a fairy tale grotto. Since the day was a bit chilly, patio heaters were on, adding necessary warmth. For once, it was a minimum smog day, so Jazz kicked back and enjoyed the view of the city. She loved the funky three-story Victorian house near the beach that she and Krebs shared, but she wouldn't mind being up here at night when the lights burst forth in their colorful glory. Maybe they'd let her come up and hang out. She'd even bring a nice bottle of wine. Provide some munchies. Maybe even bring Nick up. She wondered how they'd feel about a vampire in their house.

She slipped on her sunglasses and allowed herself to slide into the zone.

Oh yeah, she so could do this.

"Here we are." Patrice walked out carrying a tray bearing two glasses filled with iced tea, a small glass bowl bearing wedges of lemons and limes, and a china plate filled with treats that had Jazz's mouth watering.

"I rarely indulge since it means extra time with my trainer," Patrice explained, transferring a small raspberry tart to her plate.

"Mrs. Sanibel," Jazz began, after squeezing a lime wedge in her tea and taking a sip.

"Patrice, please."

Jazz nodded. "Patrice. You have a lovely home."

Her face lit up. "Thank you. It was built in 1926 for a popular silent film star. We moved in about fifteen years ago. I had discovered a box of old photographs showing how the house looked back then and I wanted to re-create that ambiance. I was lucky enough to track down and find many of the original furnishings." She looked over the area with the air of a woman who enjoyed her surroundings for what they gave her and not for its value. Jazz silently bet that Patrice's husband only saw the dollar value in every blade of grass.

"Patrice, I realize this may be difficult for you." Jazz knew she would have to force the issue or sit here and make nice for longer than necessary.

The other woman's coral-glossed smile slipped just enough to let her know she held on to her control by a thread.

"My husband can never know you were here," she said softly, as if fearing she would be overheard.

Which explained why no household help hovered around.

Jazz took her time debating between a fudgy pecan tart and something that looked rich and decadent. In the end, she chose both. She didn't have a trainer ruling her weight.

"Patrice, why do you feel you have been cursed?"

Patrice's smile remained fixed on her lips, but tears now glistened in her eyes. She kept just enough control to keep them from falling and smudging her makeup. She pushed back her chair and stood up. "Please, bring your tea and plate." She gestured toward a set of sliding glass doors that led into a master suite. The suite was larger than Jazz's entire floor at home.

Jazz couldn't help herself. She envied the tiny spotlights set above the bed, equally small twinkling lights embedded in the walls, and a bed large enough to house a Third World nation. Shades of amber, taupe, and turquoise gave the room the feel of a restful oasis. Jazz could easily have curled up on the bed and taken a nap. But as she walked further into the room she felt a shift in the air. It was subtle, but there, teasing the edge of her perception.

She circled the room, seeking the spot where she sensed the magick was the strongest. She found it the moment she reached the doors shielding the walk-in closet. She glanced at Patrice who stood with her arms wrapped around her body as if she was cold. She looked downright miserable as she nodded.

Taking that as an invitation, Jazz opened the double-doors and stared at racks of clothing that rivaled most department stores. The minute she crossed the threshold she felt the sensation of something wrong smack her in the face.

Oh yeah, someone had done a magickal number on the lady.

For a moment she studied the small monitor set in the wall that appeared to hold an inventory of every item in the closet. Shelves held shoes of every color, heel height, and for every occasion. Another held handbags. Dresses, evening gowns, and casual clothing were categorized according to need and color. She even found the "hidden" safe that she was sure held some of Patrice's less expensive jewelry—meaning anything that cost under a million. Everything a Hollywood trophy wife would need for her lifestyle.

Except something tainted the interior. It grew stronger as she moved deeper into the closet until it was strong enough she fancied she could smell it.

"Some kind of illusion spell," she murmured after a moment of allowing it to sink in.

"There's something in here, isn't there?" Patrice stood in the doorway, her arms still wrapped around her body.

Jazz nodded. Her fingers itched to pluck a teal fine wool dress from the rack that looked as if it would feel like silk against her skin and see how it would look on her. "What made you suspect your closet had been cursed?"

"It was nothing in particular. I came back from a week at a spa getaway with a couple of friends. When I walked in here I felt a sense of something wrong. I thought our daughter had raided my closet again and put it down to that."

"But there was more," Jazz prompted, having a pretty good idea where this was going.

"It wasn't long after my return that I noticed that people started treating me differently. They acted as if I wasn't there. Not even a subtle snub, but I didn't feel as if it was the usual snub I've seen among the people I know. Yet, all of a sudden I didn't receive as many lunch invitations as I used to and friends didn't call as often to suggest a shopping trip. Even my hairdresser wasn't readily available as before." Patrice sat down in a chair near the closet. "I—ah—I thought that my husband's position was in jeopardy. If you are on the way out, you suddenly don't exist among your circle. Then I thought he might be having an affair." She looked away, uncomfortable with divulging private fears to a stranger. Her discomfort turned to embarrassment. "At first, I thought of hiring a private investigator to find out the truth. I felt foolish doing so, so instead I saw. . .a psychic." She grimaced.

Jazz continued prowling the area, looking for the hot spot, so to speak. Clothing and shoes—she noticed they were in her size—made it a bit difficult.

"Who did you see?"

"Marlena. She's in Venice."

Jazz nodded. "I know of her. She's very good. What did she say?"

Patrice took a deep breath. "The minute I walked in, she said that my clothes had been hexed by my husband and if I wanted to have my life back again, I would need to have the hex removed. I remembered my husband mentioning how you had eliminated a

curse from something in Martin Reynolds' house."
Amusement lit up her eyes. "And what you did to him
when he tried to cheat you. I never liked Martin, so I
knew you were the right person to contact."

Jazz grinned. "I hope it took him all night to bury
every tiny piece from that smashed cookie jar." She
paused by a rack of handbags. She pushed a button that
caused the rack to roll back and another rack to roll forward. She rose up on her tiptoes and peered into the top
rack that was empty.

Yep, right there. Small, unnoticeable, and powerful
enough to render a woman socially invisible to any who
knew her.

Jazz was excellent at curse elimination and she knew
she could take care of the charm with little effort. At the
same time, she had a few revenge spells up her sleeve
and it sounded like Patrice's bastard of a husband would
need a few, or ten, to bring him in line for doing something like this to an obviously nice woman who didn't
deserve this treatment.

Chapter 3

JAZZ SHOOK OUT HER ARMS AND HANDS AS SHE THOUGHT about the best way to handle the charm. "Patrice, could you bring me a piece of your husband's clothing? Say, a handkerchief or T-shirt?"

When Patrice returned holding a snowy white T-shirt, Jazz stopped her at the threshold. "Until I get this taken care of, I don't think you should come in," she suggested, taking the shirt out of her hands. She returned to the racks and reached up, using the shirt to pick up the small charm. Even through the silky cotton Jazz could feel the magick humming through her body. She didn't like what she held one bit. She would have liked nothing better than to place it on the floor and smash it to smithereens, but she knew some charms had a failsafe built in that would allow the charm to back-fire on the destroyer. The last time she faced one of them her car was blown up. The T-Bird, and Irma, sur-vived, but the few minutes Jazz thought they were gone were the longest of her life. It wasn't something she cared to repeat.

"What is it?" Patrice remained just outside the thresh-old and craned her neck for a closer look.

"A charm holding an illusion spell," Jazz explained.

"Illusion? Do you mean he put some kind of *spell* on me?" Horror coated her words like ice.

"Not on you. The spell was created to basically infil-trate your clothing. It was hidden up high where it could-n't be seen, but had the power to cover your closet. The illusion was that you didn't exist." She carefully wrapped the fabric around the charm and set it on a small table in the middle of the closet.

"Invisible? But you see me? Others have." Patrice shook her head, having difficulty in understanding.

"It's not that kind of invisible. Essentially, you be-come someone beneath their notice." She searched for an easy example. "The way many people view clean-ing staff and waiters in a restaurant. They don't exist in their world."

Patrice covered her mouth with her hands. "Who would make such a disgusting thing?"

"Not all leave a signature. This is one of those. I don't think this was crafted in the States." Jazz sifted through her brain, looking for the right counter-spell. She knew she had to be careful to ensure it didn't backfire on her. While there were times she didn't mind flying under the radar, she didn't want to be invisible to her friends. Al-though that kind of invisibility could come in handy around any enemies she encountered.

"Cole was in Brazil the month before my spa vaca-tion," Patrice said. Realization hit her hard. "And here I thought he changed toward me because so many others had also. But it wasn't the same. His was deliberate. Why would he do this to me? I can't believe he hates me that much! I've done so much for him. Sat on committees, planned social functions, attended every premiere he thought was important, made friends with women who don't have a thought within their heads other than their next Botox treatment." Patrice paced back and forth, her face taut with fury. "Perhaps he's not having an affair now, but if he did something this horrible that means he's planning something. He's planning to get rid of me, and what better way than for me to be snubbed by everyone. He knew I'd end up feeling so rejected by everyone important in the business that I'd leave him instead of him leaving me because I wouldn't want his career to suffer. That *bastard!* It was my family's money that gave him his start! My father gave him the needed financing for his production company! By the time I finish with him I'll own that company!"

Jazz smiled. She always believed that determination and sometimes anger were definitely better than self-pity. And there was nothing better than a Hollywood wife on the warpath. She was positive Patrice could come out of this situation much better than if the charm hadn't been found and she'd martyred herself on her husband's behalf. She also guessed the woman knew where a lot of figurative bodies were buried. As her eyes fell on the cloth bundle, an idea started to form.

"Patrice, where is your husband's closet?"

"Why. . .?" The woman's gaze followed Jazz's. Comprehension hit fast. She nodded, a hard decisive jerk of the head. She led Jazz to the other side of the room on the other side of a bathroom Jazz knew she could also easily move into. She gestured for Patrice to stay out of the room as she walked inside and searched for just the right place. After ten minutes, she found what she was looking for. She turned and looked at Patrice.

"It's your choice."

Patrice's chin quivered, but she took a deep breath and looked stronger than she had since Jazz first arrived. "Do it."

Jazz set the bundle down and carefully unwrapped the charm.

"Charm that hides. Charm that bides. Hold the one who wished this spell. Set her free. Leave her be. She will rise and he will fell." She winced at the bad grammar even if it did rhyme. "Let him who wished it have the darkness that covered her. Because I say so, damn it!" When she touched the charm, she felt the immediate shift in the magick move from feminine to masculine. Once it was placed in the corner of a high empty shelf, she felt the power fan out and engulf the room. In no time, it had literally become a part of the closet and every piece of clothing.

"Is it done?" Patrice asked when Jazz stepped out of the room.

She nodded. "From now on anything he wears will in the same sense render him invisible to anyone in his surroundings. Just as what happened to you, it won't be in the literal sense, but he'll find himself without lunch invitations, golf dates, movie premieres." She grinned.

Patrice squared her shoulders and walked over to her closet, stepping inside. Clothing, shoes, and handbags started flying out. Within minutes, the floor was filled with designer wear and accessories. When she reappeared she was breathing hard but looked happier than when Jazz first arrived.

"It seems only right I do a little shopping this afternoon," she announced. "In fact, if there's anything here you'd like, you're more than welcome to it. I'd say we wear the same size."

"I thought you went in there to banish a curse. How did you manage to go shopping too?" Irma stared at Jazz exiting the house loaded down with clothing on hangers and shopping bags dangling from each arm. In no time, Jazz had the trunk filled so she dumped several bags piled high with shoe boxes in Irma's lap. They promptly fell to the seat.

"The woman owned never-worn Jimmy Choos and Manolos to die for and now they're all mine," Jazz announced starting up the car. "Along with some choice Prada and Kate Spade bags," she said with a reverential sigh, glancing at the bags in the passenger seat. "And the clothes," she sighed, "she's my size."

"Why would she give you all of these?" Irma peered inside the bags that rested through her ample bosom.

"She's redoing her closet. Among other things." Jazz thought of the woman who wasted no time taking charge of her life. She guessed that ole "King" Cole would be in for quite a few surprises when he got home to his castle that night. Especially since when she left the house Patrice was already on the phone with the home security agency requesting someone change all the security codes and locks. She also had put a call in to her attorney. Jazz doubted Cole would be staying at any five-star hotels anytime soon.

"She gave you all this used clothing instead of paying you?" Irma wrinkled her nose.

Jazz thought of the very nice check tucked in her jacket pocket that she'd be depositing in the bank before she headed home with her loot. "Oh, I got that too. The woman is a saint." She started up the engine and took off with the radio blaring Wayne Newton. "Not the station I had it set to," she said with a scowl.

"I had to have something to do while you were in there being given new clothes and. . ." she leaned over and sniffed, "eating chocolate when you know very well I sat out here with nothing to do."

"Then don't come with me next time." She briefly toyed with the idea of coaxing Irma to ride along with Krebs in his hot Porsche. Since she could finally leave the T-Bird there was no reason why Irma couldn't go to any car she chose.

"Even if I can leave, I'm so used to this seat that it's not easy to always exit the car. There's times I feel as if I'm still cursed to stay in the car," Irma argued.

"Don't say that! It makes it sound like I'm still cursed with you and I thought we'd taken care of that." Jazz zipped down the road, eager to sort through her new wardrobe. She wondered what Nick would think of a little black strapless number that was perfect for the dance floor.

Then there were all those La Perla scraps of silk and lace. She had never owned lingerie that exquisite and she knew Nick would appreciate them even more than she did.

She would just have to make sure he didn't try to rip them off her. Lusty vampires were so hard on clothing.

Wearing cocoa brown yoga pants and a gold-colored crop-top that revealed more than it covered, Jazz sat barefoot and cross-legged on the carpet, gazing at everything she had laid out on a purple silk cloth. She had arisen that morning with the intention of doing anything it took to stop whatever troubled her sleep.

"No more bad dreams," she murmured, picking up a purple bag and adding a mixture of mugwort, lemonbalm, lavender, chamomile, and valerian. Before she pulled the drawstring tight she added a milky blue moonstone. "Sweet dreams each night. Sleep well and tight." She thought of the unsettling nights she'd been having. "Because I say so, damn it!"

Not about to stop there, she flattened her body to the floor and carefully nudged a broom under the bed, the bristles pointing to the foot. It was her own method of a dreamcatcher. "No more bad dreams."

She moved around the bedroom and sitting room lighting cleansing incense. She knew it would take more than enchanting the bed. She needed to treat all the rooms in the house. Once she finished, she felt a calming air float around her, infusing her with serenity. Surroundings guaranteed to give her a good night's sleep.

"It's all magick," she whispered with a smile.

It was a simple task. Run in, get her money from Dweezil, and run out. She figured it wouldn't take more than thirty seconds, tops.

Except she was dealing with Dweezil.

The minute Jazz stepped inside the customer area of All Creatures Limo Service she knew Dweezil had finally done it.

He had lost his ever-lovin' mind.

After Dweezil fired Mindy and she left to start up a car service fully backed by her family's money, he had gone through office staff like a cold sufferer went through tissues. Every time Jazz came in, someone new manned the counter. A few were pretty decent. Most of them weren't. But this new one. . .

"May I help you?" This receptionist's voice was low and deliberate as if she had to carefully think through each word.

Hmm, this one could last longer than most. Jazz stared at the tall, rail-thin woman with unhealthy grayish skin. Her hair could only be described as dusty white and was pulled back in a severe bun. Without even a smidge of makeup for color, the woman looked like a living, so to speak, black-and-white photograph. As she spoke, tiny flakes of skin drifted down to the counter. She was falling apart. Literally.

"I'm Jazz. I'm one of the drivers."

"Oh yes." She tapped a pencil against the counter causing the little fingernail on her left hand to fall off and bounce on the surface. She ignored the nail lying by her hand as she picked up the phone. "I'll announce you to Master Dweezil."

"No need." Jazz breezed past, wrinkling her nose at the faintly musty smell of long dead flesh.

"But he insists all visitors be announced!" As she spun around, a few patches of loose skin drifted through the air.

"He insists on a lot. That doesn't mean he gets it." Jazz opened the inner office door and slipped inside, closing it behind her. "Honestly, D, with so many creatures looking for work, you have to hire a zombie?" She dropped into the chair in front of his desk. "And insisting she call you Master Dweezil? A bit much, isn't it?"

Dweezil looked up from the paperwork he had been reading and groaned. For a moment it looked as if the incredibly hairy bits above his eyebrows were wriggling on their own. She always swore those things were real caterpillars. "Whaddya want?"

"It's payday." She smiled brightly. "So don't worry, I won't be here long."

He opened his desk drawer, pulled out an envelope, and tossed it across the desk. "As if my fuckin' life isn't bad enough."

"Proof of that is standing out front behind your counter. Someone whose nails and skin fall off isn't exactly good for customer relations. I won't even go into office hygiene requirements."

"Grevia's a good worker," he mumbled, his skin turning a darker olive shade while a burnt almond smell emanated from his skin. Proof he was feeling pretty agitated. But then Dweezil usually was disconcerted. "So don't give her any shit."

"Yeah, like my complaints trump your tantrums." Jazz narrowed her gaze in thought when Dweezil didn't snap back at her. Snitty moods were his natural state. A downcast Dweezil was unusual. "Okay, what's wrong now?"

For a moment she thought he was going to cry and she didn't think she could handle that. Not that Dweezil had anything to recommend him in the looks department, but a morose Dweezil was downright scary.

"What has me going?" he repeated. "Just the worst thing in the world. I've lost some of my best clients. It was bad enough that you lodged a complaint against Tyge Foulshadow and he was banished to the Realm of the Undesirables." His voice ended up on a high note. For a moment the windows shimmered as if they'd shatter from the sound. His normal raspy ground glass voice could cause a person's head to pound. When he was upset, well, ears had been known to bleed.

"Gee, D. I'm so sorry I lost you your favorite client just because the oozy grotesque arranged to have me captured by an insane creature who wanted to keep me for a sex pet while he drained my boyfriend of all his blood. I guess if I was a better person I would have let bygones be bygones. *Not!* Foulshadow deserved everything he got and more."

"But he paid in gold bars!"

She winced at the assault on her eardrums. "D? Can you lower it a few million decibels? I swear that voice could cause a stroke." Jazz pulled her earlobes. "Listen. You'll just have to get over it. I don't think he'll be leaving that realm anytime soon."

Dweezil fumed. "And it gets worse. You can't imagine what's been going on here." His voice grew shriller by the moment.

"No, but I'm sure you're going to tell me."

"It's that elf bitch! She's stealing all my business!" Dweezil snarled and began pacing the length of his office with short jerky steps. This wasn't easy considering he was seven feet tall with an olive-colored body that resembled a dead asparagus with a messy mud brown thatch of hair on top that looked as if it had been stuck on by a preschooler in arts and crafts class. He paused by one of the shelves and plucked off an ancient Greek dildo. He made strange crooning sounds, stroking the worn leather surface lovingly, seeming to use the erotic tool as a pacifier. A small ripple showed under the fine wool of his specially tailored Armani jacket, slithering its way downward.

If Dweezil's third hand ended up anywhere near his second dick, she was so out of there!

"Uh, D, what did we agree on about using the B word?" She kept her gaze focused on a point just past his left ear which was turning a deeper shade of olive-green the more agitated he became.

The burnt-almond scent again flared throughout the room and he bared his yellowish-green jagged teeth at her. She bared her pearly whites back at him, and he started to swear. Whenever he got this upset, the odor not only became more foul, but so did his language, which was usually limited to the F word.

"*Dweezil!*" Jazz shouted.

He jumped, dropping the dildo at the same time his hidden third arm whipped out of his pants and returned to its hidden sleeve inside his jacket. He glared at her then picked the sex toy up, tenderly transferring the object to the shelf. Jazz tried to generate some anger, but felt pity for the great lout instead.

"Okay, can we get back to your so-called problem." She held up her hand to stave off his protest. "Fine, traumatic event. How do you know Mindy is cutting into your business?"

Dweezil returned to his desk, dropping down onto his black leather chair. "Ficus told me he saw Kreen at The Crypt and he left in a brand new black Hummer limo." His black eyes glowed with a strange yellow light where the irises would have been.

Jazz knew Kreen to be a vampire with a penchant for sweet young things. He rated second on her list of *Who I Want To See Torn Into Tiny Pieces*. "And you don't have a Hummer limo, new or otherwise." She glanced at his collection of vintage erotica and sex toys. "Don't be so cheap, Dweezil, and get one."

"Maybe I could afford the fuckin' Hummer if I wasn't overpaying some of my drivers," he snarled. "Or if someone hadn't blown up an almost new specially fitted limo."

"Give me a break, D! That vehicle was almost eight years old. Besides, the crew had to replace the air filter after every trip with Foulshadow. So don't blame me. Maybe you could afford the feckin' Hummer if you didn't spend all your profits on vintage erotica and sex toys," she pointed out, unaware her own temper was bringing out her Gaelic roots. She wrinkled her nose and sneezed as an extra burst of burnt almond attacked her nostrils. "Damn it, D! If you don't calm down, I'm outta here." She started to rise to her feet.

"All right, all right." He waved her back down. "There's more."

Jazz swallowed her sigh, hating to think what else could be going on to send Dweezil into a tizzy. "Such as?"

"Such as I've lost six workers in the last week." He fiddled with his sleeve. His extra-long fingers stroked the fine cotton. "Little fuckers went to work for that elf bi. . ."

he caught the warning glint in Jazz's eye, "*her*. They say she's paying better. She only hired them so she can ruin me." He continued stroking the sleeve the way he'd stroked the dildo and glanced up. "You have to go talk to Mindy. Tell her to give me my workers back. And if she won't, do some witchy thing to make her give them back."

"No, I don't have to talk to her. And no way I'm casting any hexes just because you think you've been wronged." She idly examined her nails and realized it was past time for a manicure. Maybe she'd opt for a pedicure and even a massage while she was at the day spa. *Thank you, Patrice, for the great idea.* "When you think about it, it's surprising they hadn't left sooner." She'd been present when Dweezil went on one of his rampages and fired everyone. She figured this time the dwarves got fed up and went elsewhere. "Maybe they went where they'd feel appreciated. They work hard, D, and you know you don't pay them a fraction of what they really deserve. I've seen how some of those cars come back and it's downright disgusting."

"I'm a wonderful guy to work for." He held his arms open in an expansive gesture. "They got every fuckin' thing they need here! I even give them time off when they're sick! Maybe I don't pay them for it, but I don't make 'em come in and get everybody else sick. Most of 'em haven't had such a good paying job since they played those Munchkins in *The Wizard of Oz*."

"Yeah, you're a saint, D. You keep on thinking that." She pushed herself out of her chair. "Why all this concern about Mindy? How many limo services have you forced out of business over the years? She'll be gone in a year and all your clients will return claiming you're the only one who treats them right." She noticed the way he fidgeted in his chair and ignored it. She was tired of cleaning up Dweezil's messes. The last time she got involved her car had been blown up. If it hadn't been cursed, her beloved T-Bird, and Irma, would have been no more. And she really would have missed that car.

"You owe me. I lost money when the insurance company wouldn't pay up on the limo that got destroyed when you drove up to that mansion."

"Maybe if you used a legitimate insurance company instead of the fly-by-night firm you went with to save money, you'd have a replacement vehicle," she pointed out. "And thank you for all your concern on my behalf. I could have been killed up there from all the vamps running out." She almost *was* killed up there, but that was something she'd keep to herself. Even if Dweezil knew, he still wouldn't offer sympathy.

"It was that damn clause that said they wouldn't pay on damage caused by magick. Print was so small you couldn't read it with a microscope." He pulled in a deep breath. "Fine, I'll pay you to go talk to her."

Jazz was sorely tempted to find out just how much he would pay. For Dweezil to be willing to part with coin he kept as close to his icky breast as Scrooge kept his fortune in his coffers meant that he was really worried.

"I'll think about it. Don't think that means anything," she warned him when she saw that he perked up. "I only said I'd think about it."

Dweezil hopped out of his chair and remained on her heels as she left his office and strode into the reception area.

Grevia was occupied talking to a tiny creature that couldn't be more than two feet tall and was wrapped in a dark cloak. Its squeaky chatter reminded Jazz of the Jawas in *Star Wars,* except this one's lineage didn't involve trading or scavenging. She knew for a fact the Skiznogs' gifts lay in the stock market.

"I still can't understand why you hired her," she said, pulling Dweezil toward the door. He hissed and reared back as the afternoon sun touched his face.

"She keeps things running smoothly and doesn't give me any shit like some people I could name," he muttered, retreating further.

Jazz rolled her eyes. "Honestly, D, the sun won't hurt you."

"My kind gets skin cancer very easily." He patted his face, checking to see if lesions had blossomed just from that minute exposure.

She was tempted to ask him about his kind since she had never seen another creature like Dweezil, but past experience taught her he preferred to keep his heritage a secret. For all she knew he came from the same galaxy far far away as the Jawa-like Skiznogs.

"Look at her, D. She's flaking all over the place. Do her a favor and fire her. Find someone who will remain in one piece," she whispered, giving the receptionist a quick glance. Luckily Grevia was still occupied with the two-foot-high client. Flakes of skin littered the counter like gray dust. When Dweezil refused to look at her, the truth popped on like a lightbulb. "Oh for Fates' sake! You bought her!" She silently counted to ten then counted again. "You bought a zombie to work for you."

"Zombies don't bleed and they're efficient." He didn't admit his guilt, but then he didn't have to. It was written on his olive-skinned face.

"And it's considered slave labor."

He held up his forefinger to make a point. "Well, yes, but it's not illegal as long as I provide housing for her."

Jazz threw up her hands. "But it should be. It's wrong, D, and you know it. Fine, but once her body parts start falling off, and they will, you'll be losing customers." She pushed the glass door open.

"You'll still go see Mindy, right?" he called after her.

She ignored his plea and headed for her car. Irma took one look at her face and for once didn't say a word.

"Idiots. All men are idiots no matter what species they are," Jazz muttered once they were on the road.

"It took you this long to figure that one out?" It seems Irma was determined to have the last word after all.

When Jazz stepped inside the house, she stared at the stack of boxes near the front door.

"Wow, Krebsie, you gave the UPS man a workout today. How many more computers can you put up there?" she teased.

"They're not all mine." Krebs carefully pulled computer parts out of a large box, comparing the contents with the invoice, marking each item off. "Your boxes are over there." He pointed with his pen.

"Ooh, goodies!" Jazz picked up a large box marked Priority Mail and quickly dispensed with the tape. She was soon opening bottles and jars, inhaling the rich scents with a near orgasmic thrill. "I'm in The Body Bakery heaven." She opened a small bottle of roll-on scent and tried it on her wrist, sniffing the fragrance. "This is great. Smell. It's called Cinnamon Crunch Cake." She held out her wrist.

"I thought you were going to cut back on the bath stuff." Krebs moved on to another box. "You have enough body wash and lotion now to last you for centuries. Still, considering your advanced age, maybe it is a good idea to stock up, just in case." He ducked the wad of packing paper lobbed at him.

"Ha, ha, very funny, *not*. I have cut back, but these scents are seasonal and limited editions, so I had to get them. Besides, I'm never at a loss if I need a last-minute gift for a friend."

"Ha! I asked you for some of your stuff when I needed a birthday gift for Michelle and you wouldn't give me any," he accused.

Jazz's gaze shifted away. She protectively cradled her booty as if guarding a small child. "Yes, well."

"You're a body wash and skin cream addict, Jazz. Pure and simple." He shook his head. "You're not happy unless you're surrounded by bottles and jars."

"Look at it this way. I'll never smell bad. Plus I can smell according to my mood, so you'll know how I feel before I even enter the room. Sometimes I want something sweet and subtle. Other times I can use something stronger and sexy. I'm set for every occasion," she stated.

"Plus Lia knows if she's ever cursed I am so there for her. And she can even pay me in product." She grinned as she reached for another box lavishly decorated with gold script. She didn't need to look at the return address to know the identity of the sender.

"Broom-Ex?" Krebs wandered over to Jazz and peered over her shoulder, reading the stylized logo printed on one corner of the box. "Now you witches have your own delivery service?"

"That's Thea's lame idea of a joke. Just because she doesn't want anyone to know she's a witch doesn't mean she won't use little hints like this," Jazz replied, setting the box on a chair and carefully opening it. As she lifted the lid, the contents popped up. "What on earth?" She started to laugh.

"What's so funny about a pair of shoes?" He thought over his question then backed up a few steps. "Or are they something I can't see?"

"They're magick."

"I see the real Fluff and Puff and they're magick." He backed up another few steps, just in case.

"That's because I fixed it so you could see them, so they couldn't pull any stunts on you."

"Yeah, like that ever stopped them," he muttered.

Jazz held her hand over the gorgeous dark gray stilettos that would tempt any red-blooded witch. "Reveal to he what I do see. Because I say so, damn it!" A shower of multi-colored sparks rained on the shoes.

"Shit!" Krebs stared at the open box as a pair of gray crocodile open-toed stilettos looked at him with yellowish-green eyes and fluttered their long lashes. Glossy red lips cooed soft sounds in his direction. "What the hell are they?" He backpedaled fast.

"According to Thea's note, they're named Croc and Delilah." Jazz scanned the sheet of linen stationary with an embossed seal at the top. "She found them in a boutique in Milan and thought they were perfect for me. Trust her to find the ultimate shoes. She knows how much I love stilettos."

"I've been to Milan and I don't remember any boutique selling shoes that are alive." Krebs remained at a safe distance. "Those aren't shoes! They're living, breathing crocodiles!"

"This kind of boutique doesn't cater to mortal trade and yes, they are crocodiles and shoes all in one. All the clothing and accessories sold there are magickal. You can pick up some incredible bargains there when they have their annual sale." She picked up the shoes and set them on the floor. She barely had her half boots off before the stilettos were on her feet. Their color had switched from gray to cocoa. She had to admit they fitted her like a glove—a glove that automatically changed color to coordinate with her dark brown jeans. She noticed even their makeup changed to go with the sepia-toned shade.

"Is that where the slippers came from?"

Jazz shook her head. "They came from somewhere else a lot darker and nastier. A place you don't even want to contemplate." She looked down, turning her feet this way and that to admire the stilettos that kept blowing kisses at her.

"Big surprise there." He also stared at the shoes. "They're awfully girly, aren't they? Not girly in shoe style, but in the way they act. Uh, Jazz?" He looked a little green around the gills. "Can you make them stop doing that?" That being the stilettos making their way closer to him and rubbing up against his legs.

"Okay, you slut shoes. Back in the box before Krebs runs screaming out of the room. Something tells me I'll have to put powerful wards around my makeup or you'll be in it." She slipped off the shoes and placed them in the box, ignoring their soft sounds of sorrow as they continued to gaze at Krebs with adoring eyes. Once off her feet they instantly returned to their original gray shade.

"Just as long as they don't try to eat my stuff." Krebs returned to his boxes. He barely masked the shudder that passed over his body.

"I'll do what I can to protect your virtue." Jazz didn't miss the lovesick expressions the shoes displayed toward her roommate. She made a mental note to sneak some wards around Krebs too. She doubted he'd appreciate waking up some night to find a pair of lovesick stilettos snuggled up next to him.

"It looks like you need some help carrying up your loot." Krebs headed straight for the box holding her scented spa goodies and left her to carry up the shoebox. "Although who knows where you'll put all this." He released a loud groan as he hefted the heavy box in his arms.

"All over my luscious body," she sang out, following him up the stairs.

"Okay, not an image I need because it will revisit me when Nick's around and he'll know what I'm thinking and probably try to eat me."

"Nah, he'll just settle for a nibble," she teased amid giggles from her new shoes. She hoped the shoes would back off on some of the girly stuff. She was positive the slippers would *not* be happy to meet her new footwear.

Fog rolled all around her, obscuring her view to where she could barely see her hands in front of her face.

She could think of only two cities that had fog this thick—San Francisco and London. So which was it? Even more important, when?

She didn't hear the sound of motorcars, but she could hear the faint clip-clop of horses walking across cobblestones.

It wasn't until she looked down that she noticed the Victorian-style evening gown she wore and knew she wasn't in her present century or even the last one. Gold silk with a low neckline that almost revealed her nipples, tiny sleeves and white gloves that reached up past her elbows. A jeweled bracelet winked at her wrist. The cold damp air seemed to make a path all the way through to her bones. She lifted her hand and found her hair pinned up in loose curls.

The stench of rotting garbage and offal caused her eyes to water. She pressed the back of her hand against her nose and inhaled the scent of lavender. But I don't like lavender, *drifted through her mind before she returned to more pressing matters. She grimaced as her shoe stepped in something damp and slippery. She fought for her balance and managed to remain on her feet. For once, she didn't mind that she couldn't see clearly, because she dreaded to think what might be around her.*

She stumbled along, looking for a hint of light, anything to show her she was going in the right direction where she might find assistance. She had no idea why she felt the need for protection, but the sense of self-preservation was strong within her. Along with the sense that she was being followed by something evil.

A sob traveled up her throat as she tripped and fell against a rough-surfaced wall that tore at her gown and her skin. She could feel blood dripping down her arm and the burn from bad scrapes.

Whatever was following her was growing closer. She could feel it! And she had no way to protect herself. She gathered up her skirts and quickened her pace, still taking care where she stepped not knowing what lay before her.

She moved swiftly along the lane, searching for the faintest hint of light that meant a street was there and hopefully a constable nearby. Except something black and forbidding swooped down around her and pulled her back into the inky fog with its sinister tendrils.

She opened her mouth to scream for help even as she feared no one would hear her. The heavy fog damped the sound, trapping her in a cocoon of terror. She knew even if her cries for help were heard, few would bother to intervene until after it was too late. Then they would converge on her body so that they could scavenge for whatever might be left.

Panic tasted sour in her throat as she whipped her body from side to side in a vain attempt to escape whatever trapped her against the damp stones of the building.

She whimpered. She felt like a small animal stalked by the larger predator who enjoyed playing with its prey. The reek of death was all around her.

All she could see was a larger-than-life figure of blackness with red glowing eyes and white fangs ready to attack

"Please, sir, no," she begged, hearing the accent of British upper crust in her speech. "Please, sir, I beg of you."

She had no chance to react as the pain streaked white-hot across her throat. A splash of red blinded her and then, she knew no more.

"No!" Jazz shot up in bed. She looked wildly from right to left, but the darkness prevented her from seeing the monster who'd visited her sleep and was probably standing in front of her. Fear laced her voice as she cried out, "Lights full!" She squinted as the lamps flared to life, the glare strong enough to chase away any shadows lingering in the corners. But they couldn't chase away the terror that left her body cold and shaking.

She was alone.

She pushed damp hair away from her face and scooted back against her pillows, her knees drawn up to her chin. She couldn't hold back the whimpers that escaped her throat and the panic that chilled her blood. The sweat that coated her skin felt like ice and her throat hurt as if someone had gripped it tightly. She was terrified to look in a mirror for fear she'd see bruises there.

She was positive what she experienced was too real to be a nightmare.

She wrapped her arms around her knees, resting her chin on them. It took her a few moments to register the soft crooning sounds beside her. She looked down to find Croc and Delilah on each side of her pushing their noses against her hip. From across the room she saw the area around the cage glow and Fluff and Puff pressing their faces against the bars.

"It's all right," she assured everyone as she picked the stilettos up and hugged them to her chest. They nuzzled her under her chin and cooed comforting sounds. "It's all right," she repeated, looking at the slippers who didn't look very reassured. The words echoed inside her head even as she thought of the enchanted broom resting under the bed and knew if the magick infused in the broom didn't stop the bad dreams, things weren't as good as she pretended they were.

Judging from the soothing clicks and whistles Fluff and Puff uttered back, they felt the same.

Chapter 4

"WHOA, WHAT HAPPENED TO YOU?" KREBS WINCED AS JAZZ entered his work area. "Sorry, that didn't sound too complimentary, did it? But you really don't look good. Are you sick?" He immediately gazed at his computer equipment for fear they'd start flying around the room as had happened in the past when Jazz was ill.

As Jazz had already looked in the mirror before venturing downstairs, she had a pretty good idea what Krebs saw and it wasn't a pretty sight. Since she'd barely slept after her nightmare she felt as worn and drawn as she looked. She'd even been too tired to bother with a glamour spell. The faded mint-green plaid cotton pants and solid green tank top she wore wasn't something she'd wear in public. After the night she had she didn't intend to leave the house in hopes of curling up for a nice peaceful nap later that day. Say, in an hour or so.

She headed for the coffeemaker Krebs kept nearby and poured a cup for herself.

"I didn't sleep very well." She winced at the understatement as she inhaled the rich aroma of Jamaican Blue Mountain before swallowing the hot liquid as fast as her throat would allow. She had a sad feeling caffeine wouldn't help her today. Memories of the nightmare still persisted in her brain. Strong enough that she'd taken the shortest shower in history because the shower scene from

Psycho kept replaying in her mind. She knew if the shower door had opened she would have released the scream of the century.

Krebs saved his work and turned in his chair. He smiled his thanks as Jazz topped off his coffee mug.

"You haven't been sleeping too good for a while," he ventured. "Is there a chance that something witchy is going on?"

Jazz shrugged. "Maybe, but I don't know why." After refilling her mug, she moved over to an empty chair and flopped down like a rag doll with her legs stretched out in front of her. She stared at her bare feet, feeling a sense of loss. The amethyst studded broom on her ankle bracelet winked back at her. She really missed her slippers, but they'd have to stay in the magickal cage until she could find out what really happened at the boardwalk.

Krebs followed the direction of her gaze. "You know, I really miss those little monsters."

She smiled. "I do too, but I have no choice but to keep them locked up until I can prove their innocence."

"Do you think you can do it?"

Jazz frowned in thought. None of her usual self-confidence was visible. "I'm going to do my best. It's not easy when they're not popular over there." She rubbed her forehead. The headache she'd woken up with hadn't gone away and she feared it wasn't going to go easily.

Once she'd gotten up she'd pulled the broom out from under her bed and cleansed it and her charms. She hadn't sensed anything in her rooms that could have caused the terror that woke her. But that didn't mean they hadn't sensed something.

"How have you been sleeping?" she asked.

"You know me. When I'm busy with a project I don't sleep too much." He turned back to his computer but didn't bring up anything on the flat-panel monitor that dominated the worktable. A soft beep and low hum announced an incoming fax just before pages spit out into the tray.

Jazz settled back in her chair, her elbow braced on the chair arm as she absently nibbled on a nail. She felt she knew her roommate better than most. And right now, she was positive usually wide-open Krebs was hiding something.

"All work and no sleep make Krebsie a cranky boy."

"It's more no sleep without the right reason that makes Krebsie a cranky boy." He grinned at her. "Not to mention waking up to find those shoes of yours in bed with me under the covers." His cheeks turned a bright red.

She snorted a laugh. "It could be worse. And you know what to do to take care of what makes you cranky." She waved a hand. "What happened to Miss Twit. . .uh, Laurette." She rolled her eyes.

"And *that* is why there is no more Laurette!" He pointed at her. "You called her a twit, you said she didn't have a brain, and worse."

Jazz felt a niggling sense of guilt since she knew he truly liked the airhead brunette even if she wasn't all that fond of someone who giggled non-stop. And here she thought that trait belonged to blondes. She shifted uneasily in her chair. "But I never said it to her face. I'm sorry if what I said about her caused you to break up with her. But think about it, Krebs. The woman thought that Voltaire was a French fashion designer and was convinced there's calories in water if you add ice to it." She held up her hands in an "I've made my point" gesture.

"Coming from someone who probably personally knew Voltaire."

Jazz ignored Krebs's twenty-millionth attempt to find out her true age. She was determined to have a few secrets, thank you very much!

"You deserve better." She softened her tone. "You deserve someone with brains, who has the intelligence to converse with you on all levels, is kind, and generous and. . ."

"And is drop-dead gorgeous," he added. "So I'm shallow? I'm a guy. It's allowed."

"The right woman for you is out there," Jazz said confidently. "Hey, if I didn't think of you as a wonderfully goofy brother I'd do you."

"Gee, such an offer." He brought up a computer file. His fingers flew over the keyboard. "Do me a favor and get out of here. I've got work to do."

Jazz pushed herself out of her chair and scuffed her way across the floor to the worktable. She ruffled his hair in the affectionate way of a sibling and dropped a kiss on top of his head.

"I mean it. Out," he said without any heat. His voice held more exasperation that she wasn't allowing him to work.

She carried her mug downstairs and headed for the kitchen in search of food. Normally, she loved the old-fashioned look of the ground floor with its antique furniture and stained glass windows. Today, she felt as if there was an unfriendly specter standing in the shadows observing her. After last night's nightmare it was easy to give in to the urge to probe those shadows. Jazz was brave, but she wasn't stupid. And right now, she considered all shadows her enemy.

As she scrambled herself a couple of eggs and warmed up a lemon-cream muffin in the microwave, she wished she had Fluff and Puff for company.

"Jazz! Get up here now!"

The panic in Krebs's voice had Jazz out of her chair and racing up the stairs to the second floor.

"What? What?" She looked around, fearing the worst.

"What are *they* doing in here?" He stared at the floor as if a venomous snake faced him.

Jazz followed the direction of his gaze and found the stilettos huddled by his feet. If she wasn't mistaken, Delilah was running her face all over Jazz's roomie's bare toes.

"Ick." She winced at his glare. "I set up wards to keep them out of here. I really did."

He shifted his feet, almost lifting them off the floor. "Get them out of here. *Please!*"

"What did I tell you?" She faced the shoes that didn't have one ounce of remorse on their faces. "No cuddling up to Krebs. You head back to the room, right now." She stamped one foot for emphasis.

Croc and Delilah lowered their lashes, sighed deeply, and left the room as slowly as possible, pausing every now and then to turn around and gaze lovingly at Krebs.

"The slippers are a pain in the ass, but I can handle them a hell of a lot better," Krebs muttered.

"At least Croc and Delilah won't expect expensive dinners," Jazz joked.

"Just please make sure they can't ambush me again."

"Let me get a few things." She headed upstairs to her rooms and picked up what she needed to strengthen the wards around Krebs's work and sleeping area. She didn't tell him that she had a hunch the sexy stilettos could get through anything to get what they wanted: Krebs.

After she finished she nuked another lemon cream muffin and refilled her coffee cup. The idea of going upstairs and dressing seemed like a chore beyond her capability.

She stared at the phone silently ordering it not to ring for her. She wasn't about to jinx herself now. She needed today to herself for some meditation, maybe a nice long nap and do some reading in her spell books to see if there was anything that would help her figure out why she was having these nightmares. For now, she was content to eat her muffin and infuse her body with more caffeine. By the time she finished eating, she felt better and the world around her even seemed a bit brighter.

"I know you're in there!"

Jazz dry-scrubbed her head, tangling her fingers in her hair as she buried her face in her arms on the table.

"I could have gone all day without hearing that voice," she muttered into her arms. "Even better, all year."

"Would it hurt you to come out here and check on me?" The voice grew even more strident.

Jazz took her time rinsing off her dishes and setting them in the dishwasher before she ventured outside. She paused on the edge of the yard, watching the dog snuffling along the edge of the fence. "Don't antagonize the neighbor's cat again," she warned. "And no digging holes, eating the flowers, or using the gazing ball for a toy." She recalled the last time she came out and discovered the dog had managed to bump the rainbow colored gazing ball off the man in the moon pedestal and was rolling it around the yard. She was only grateful that the neighbors on either side hadn't seen it. The dog offered her a goofy canine grin and returned to prowling the yard.

She lifted her face to feel the late morning sun on her skin. Since it was Saturday she could hear the faint tinny sounds of the carousel's calliope playing at the boardwalk and screams of children and adults on the roller coaster that partially rode over the ocean. The idea of walking over there for her favorite junk food and a ride on the roller coaster flirted in her mind. Even if she hadn't planned on leaving the house that day, thoughts of escaping still tempted her. She felt restless. She needed to find out what was going on, to bring out the bad dreams and whatever might be going on inside her head.

"Hello!"

"Oh, for Fates' sake," Jazz muttered, picking up her pace. She hit the keypad on the carriage house's exterior to activate the old-fashioned doors that slid open. "What are you yelling about now?" she asked, stepping into the dim interior.

"It's about time you got here," Irma muttered from the passenger seat of Jazz's T-Bird. "I want that." She pointed to the television/DVD combo set up for Irma's viewing pleasure.

Jazz stared at the screen that displayed a rerun of *Everybody Loves Raymond*. "Want what?"

Irma huffed. "Look at the mother's clothing. They're nothing like mine." She swept her hand over her navy blue print dress, beige nylon stockings attached to a plain garter belt, neat oxfords, and navy straw hat perched on her head. She looked like the 1950s woman she was the day she died. "I want to be dressed like her." She pointed at the screen.

"I want a day without you, but it looks like neither of us will get our wish, does it?"

Irma's slight growl told Jazz she hit her mark.

"You can go around looking as slinky as you like, but I have to be stuck in a long-gone era." Irma turned back to the TV. "Why can't you do one of those things?"

"Things?" Jazz wished she had brought her coffee with her. There were some days it wasn't easy to keep up with the ghostly woman.

"Yes, those witchy things."

"Define witchy things," Jazz said.

"Those things you witches do where you make something, or someone, look different." Irma crossed her arms in front of her plump breast. "Why can't you do that for me? After all, you went into that woman's house with your charms and spells and came out with a designer wardrobe."

"That was more her giving me her wardrobe. What you're talking about is an illusion spell." Jazz was impressed with Irma's idea. Not that she'd tell her, of course. The woman was impossible enough as it was. "So you want to dress like Raymond's mother."

Irma nodded. "Yes, I'd like to wear trousers because I'm sure they're more comfortable than a dress and a girdle." She shifted around in the seat.

"I don't think morticians bother stuffing the deceased into a girdle," Jazz pointed out, positive she'd be pouring bleach on her brain if she couldn't rid herself of an image of Irma wiggling her plump body into a girdle.

"I want to be dressed like someone in this century. Harold didn't approve of women wearing trousers, but there's no reason why I can't wear them now." She raised her chin. "But no denims. They're much too trashy looking and I don't want whatever you're wearing. Nothing skintight." Her gaze roamed over Jazz with cranky ghostly disdain.

"Just remember you're talking to the witch who could have you wearing a billowy blue and yellow suit and a red nose that squeaks." Jazz didn't believe in idle threats. To prove her point she sent an image of a clown, the stuff of horror movies, superimposed on the far wall.

Irma's white-gloved fingers tightened on her navy patent-leather handbag. "Now that's just mean. I thought once you were receiving regular sex from Nicky that you'd turn into a nicer person. Obviously, that isn't possible because I can't imagine he's doing something wrong."

"Take it to Judge Judy." Jazz felt the beginnings of a twitch behind her right eye. "Look, I didn't sleep well last night and I'm still not with it. I'll see if I can find an illusion spell that will work on you." She knew if she didn't at least make the attempt to placate Irma, the ghost would be in a royal snit for days and Jazz didn't have the patience to deal with her just now.

"Why shouldn't it?"

Oh yeah, arguing with Irma was just what she wanted to do. . .not!

"You're a ghost, Irma. You're caught between this world and the next. Regular magick doesn't work the same way on you. More's the pity," she muttered under her breath.

Irma's glare bounced off her before the ghost returned to her TV viewing. "I hope you don't plan on taking me anywhere today. There's a movie I want to watch later."

Jazz took it as dismissal and escaped the carriage house.

"And don't forget to come up with one of those illusion spells!" Irma called after her. "I've been wearing this horrid dress long enough!"

"Yeah, yeah, yeah." She escaped to the house. Irma's illusion spell would have to wait. She had some investigating at the boardwalk to do on Fluff and Puff's behalf along with heavy-duty cleansing in her suite of rooms. She knew that part of the job was going to take a lot more than Pine-Sol and Clorox.

After using cedar oil and charged water along with her favorite broom for sweeping out the negativity, Jazz was ready for a quick shower and change of clothes for her trip to the boardwalk.

She bypassed stopping for cotton candy or funnel cake and headed straight for the carousel. The enclosure was edged with gold curlicues and vividly painted scenes of mermaids, dolphins, sea serpents, and other sea creatures humans thought were mythical and Jazz knew to be all too real.

"Hey Hector," she greeted the Hispanic operator who she knew had Wereblood. The yellow vertical slit in his eyes meant that his Werenature had something to do with reptiles but since anything with scales totally put her off, she didn't pursue it. She'd just hope he wouldn't decide to turn during their conversation.

His scowl was an echo of Rex's. "Whaddya want?"

"How about some news about Willie? Have you talked to him lately?"

His hiss and snarl was worthy of his boss and his species. "We all know what happened to him. Those damn bunnies of yours ate him and you're protecting them when they should be destroyed. They broke the law. What'd you do to Rex to get him to back off? Give him a blowjob out behind the roller coaster?" he sneered.

Major *euww* moment there! "Yeah, like the slippers would eat a Were. They don't like Weres anymore than you like them," she argued.

He grinned, showing off yellowish-fangs that were definitely of the reptile family. Clear viscous liquid dripped off the fangs and sizzled when it hit the ground. *Ugh!*

"Give me a break, Jazz. Everyone knows those creatures eat anything and everything. What are you trying to say? That someone framed them? Give me a break, Tremaine. Willie's gone and one of those furry beasts coughed up his shirt button as proof where he went."

Jazz was tempted to say "Ms. Tremaine to you, bub," but she didn't want to see what would happen to a pissed-off snake that drips acidic venom.

"Which can come from anyone." She stared pointedly at his shirt that gaped a bit even if he had a concave belly. "In fact, it looks like you lost one somewhere."

Hector glided toward her. His breath was a little too rancid for her olfactory senses. Didn't anyone use mouthwash nowadays?

"Just hand over the bunnies and no one will get hurt," he told her. "Keeping them in that fancy magickal cage won't keep them safe forever."

While she wanted to wave her hand in front of her face, she settled for standing her ground.

"As I told you before, Fluff and Puff are protected by very old and very dangerous magick," she said in a low voice. "When Dyfynnog created them he made sure no one could ever harm them." *Other than the harm he cooked up to torture them since he was more than a little insane for close to three thousand years.*

"You think that scares us?" he sneered. "The laws are clear, Jazz. You harm one of us you die for it. No amount of magick can protect them and if you get in the way you won't find any protection for yourself either."

Jazz knew a threat when it was issued. Not that it bothered her. There was no way she was giving up the slippers because she knew they were innocent. And even if she didn't like reptiles, Were or not, she would still battle for their rights. Gloria Allred had nothing on a witch fighting for her bunny slippers' rights!

"Do us both a favor and get the hell out of here before I do something you won't like." Hector turned back to the machinery that ran the carousel.

"I intend to find out the truth," she declared to his back.

"We know the truth. They ate him."

Knowing she wouldn't get anywhere here, Jazz exhaled her exasperation and moved on to the next ride. But everywhere she went she was greeted with the same open hostility. As far as the Werecarnies were concerned, Fluff and Puff ate their friend and they deserved to be judged, convicted, and executed for it. She was grateful she didn't run into Rex, although she was sure the boardwalk manager would hear about her visit. Thanks to a Were that actually liked her, Jazz could still indulge in her funnel cake addiction without any problem.

"I never liked that Willie," Magda, a Werecat who ran the snack stand, confided as she handed over a large Diet Coke and a paper plate filled with a warm funnel cake dusted with powdered sugar. "That weasel clan doesn't have one good member."

"Is the clan large?" Jazz asked, nipping off a bite with her fingers and popping it into her mouth. She nearly moaned with joy as the flavorful treat gave her taste buds powdered sugar joy.

"Anything over two is too big for me. I'd say there's about fifty in the clan. There'd be a lot less if we could hunt them."

"I am so glad you're on my side." Jazz grinned before moving off. She knew the woman shifted into an Angora cat with beautiful silver fur echoed by the waist-length braid hanging down her back, but that didn't mean she wasn't afraid to get her claws dirty. Magda was known for her bloodthirsty nature. Thanks to her and her two daughters there wasn't one actual rat along the boardwalk except for two with Were-blood. Even they stayed out of Magda's way.

As she walked back to the parking lot, she decided to take a detour by the two-story building that sat at the end of the boardwalk. Since taking the stairs and carrying her booty wasn't going to work, she chose the old-fashioned cage elevator that creaked and groaned every inch of the trip.

"Some WD-40 would help," she muttered, struggling with the heavy grille door and squeezing her way into the cage.

When she reached Nick's office, she found the door ajar and the sound of a woman weeping inside almost hurt her heart. She set her food down by the door and slipped inside.

"There has to be a way you can help me!" The woman's voice was cracked and sounded tired.

"It's not that I can't help you, Mrs. Archer. It's that I feel some things are best left alone," Nick said, his tone soothing.

Jazz silently crossed the reception area and stood in the doorway. The woman seated in the guest chair was tiny with salt-and-pepper hair cut short. The hand lifted toward her heavily lined face was pink with visible veins and spots denoting her age.

Nick looked up, nodding his head. "It's all right, Jazz. Come in." He pushed a handkerchief into the woman's hand before leaning back against his desk. "Mrs. Archer, this is Jazz Tremaine. She's helped me in the past."

"I'm sorry if I'm interrupting something," Jazz apologized, walking inside.

"Perhaps you can help me persuade Mr. Gregory," the woman said, dabbing her eyes with the handkerchief.

"Mrs. Archer wants me to find her son," he said quietly.

Jazz immediately sensed the woman wasn't asking Nick to find a missing little boy.

"He was turned twenty-three years ago," he went on.

"I don't care that he's a vampire," the woman went on, clutching the damp handkerchief in one hand and a crumpled photograph in the other. Jazz could see the smiling face of a young man wearing a bright blue polyester shirt and brown polyester pants. She mentally cringed at the fashion disasters of the 1980s even as she remembered a few of her own hair tragedies back then. "I just want to know Ronnie is all right."

Jazz didn't miss the silent look of entreaty Nick shot her. He never was good with tears and those of a grieving mother with so much love in her heart were even harder. She crouched by the side of the chair, her hands resting lightly on the wooden arm.

"Mrs. Archer, do you truly understand what your son is now? That he isn't the young man you raised?" she asked softly.

The woman's head bobbed up and down. "Ronnie was leaving his night class when he was attacked by a band of rogue vampires. He was such a good boy. He was taking advanced accounting courses. He called me a week after he died and said that he wasn't really dead. He just had to tell me. He knew how hard I took his father's death only a few years before that. But he wouldn't tell me anything else." She dabbed at her eyes again. Her tears streaked a trail through her face powder. "But he still sends me cards on my birthday and at Christmas. All I want is to see him one time. To know he's all right. Someone at an occult shop I went to gave me Mr. Gregory's name and said he could help me."

"As I explained to you, Mrs. Archer, your son is no longer the young man you remember," Nick said.

Her sweet features hardened to a resolve Jazz could understand, even if she knew it wouldn't work on Nick. Her Cossack vampire was too stubborn. "I realize he might not be like the vampires in movies and on TV, but I also know he wouldn't be the monster so many are like. Present company excepted." She flushed in embarrassment.

Nick smiled. "No problem. But there's also the question of your safety."

"I'll sign anything you'd like absolving you of any liability; just, please, find him for me. Let me talk to him. Let me see he's all right."

Nick and Jazz exchanged glances.

She isn't going to give up and better she hire you than someone who will take her money and do nothing or worse, try to claim any vampire they can dig up is her son. And I'm here if there's a way I can help.

He nodded, easily reading her thoughts. He still took a few minutes before responding to Mrs. Archer.

"I can't guarantee that I'll be able to find your son." He held up his hand to halt her expected protest. "Yes, you told me everything you know about him, but some of the groups move around. I will start going out tonight and see what I can find. But you have to understand that he also has to agree to see you in a place of my choosing and I will be present for the meeting. I won't leave you alone with him."

Jazz rested her fingertips on the woman's bare arm, feeling the tissue-thin skin under her touch. "It's the best way if you really want to see him," she murmured.

"He wouldn't hurt me. I know that."

"My kind are predators, Mrs. Archer." Nick's voice suddenly turned harsh. "When we are turned we leave our old lives behind. Many times without a second thought."

She looked from Nick to Jazz then back to Nick again. "If I agree to your terms, will you find my son for me?"

Nick looked as if he wanted to still refuse, but Jazz silently willed him to say yes.

He looked as if the words he was about to say weren't the ones he wanted to say. "I will find him and see if he is willing to meet you."

After the woman left, Jazz returned to the hallway to retrieve her funnel cake and Diet Coke. A few words warmed up the cake and added ice to her Coke.

"Obviously Rex wasn't on the boardwalk." Nick slipped the check into his desk drawer and settled back in his chair.

""No, but his influence was there. No one wanted to talk to me about Willie." She perched on the chair Mrs. Archer recently vacated. "Most of them are convinced the slippers ate him. Sure, they're garbage disposals at best, but they'd never eat a Wereweasel. Even they have their standards."

"So you think Fluff and Puff were framed?"

"Definitely. But then what happened to Willie? Is he really dead or just hiding out somewhere?" She glanced up under the cover of her lashes. "Nick." She drew his name out in a loving coo.

"I'm not getting involved."

"But I'm helping you with Mrs. Archer."

"Only because you can handle mortal females better than I can."

"You're just afraid she'll cry again. So back to Fluff and Puff. The carnies will talk to you. They like you."

"And they don't like you."

"They don't like witches," she corrected him.

"No, I think it's more you." He suddenly groaned. "Why do I feel that if I don't help you clear Fluff and Puff you won't help me with Mrs. Archer?"

"Because it's something I'd do." She took a sip of her Diet Coke.

"I'll go talk to them, but don't expect me to hear anything."

"Thank you. When do you want to start looking for Mrs. Archer's son?"

"I'm going alone on that. From what little she knows I have a good idea he's in Luger's clan." Jazz made a face at the mention of a rogue band known for vampire violence and mayhem at every turn. "While your blood makes you safe from them biting you, that doesn't mean they can't try something else."

"Normally I'd argue that I can take care of myself courtesy of fireballs and such, but since it's Luger, I'll let you do the big bad vampire bit and go by yourself. Just call me when you get back. And I promise if Luger goes off and kills you I'll avenge your death."

Nick snorted at Jazz's declaration.

"I'd say send the slippers, but even then I think you'd be better off contacting the Protectorate."

Jazz grimaced. She wouldn't go to the Protectorate if her life depended on it. She polished off her funnel cake and crumpled up the paper plate, tossing it in the wastebasket before she stood up.

"I have some cleansing to do."

"Are you still having dreams?"

She nodded. "But I have a spell that should do the trick." She walked around the desk and dropped a kiss on his lips. Nick slid one arm around her waist, pressing his fingertips against the base of her spine.

"Maybe you just need to have company in bed," he murmured against her lips.

"Good idea. I have a cute stuffed teddy bear for that." She nipped lightly at his mouth while her palm caressed his chest. "But if you happen to dream about the boogieman, give me a call." She straightened up.

As Jazz walked through the parking lot she felt an unsettling sensation descend upon her. Normally, she'd put it down to Rex glaring at her, but it didn't feel like a Were's anger. It was something darker and more intense. And very personal.

Jazz was grateful she had eaten the funnel cake for energy as she worked on the cleansing spells for her rooms. By the time she finished her tasks she was positive she'd sleep peacefully for the next month. A long soak in the tub with the Jacuzzi jets going full blast and the scent of vanilla and cinnamon candles in the air was just what she needed.

She smiled to herself as she lay back against a soft terry bath pillow, stretching her toes toward the end of the tub and enjoying the hot water lapping around her body. The smile turned to a frown when she heard sounds coming from the bedroom. She didn't like the sounds of an irritated grumble that had to have come from either Fluff or Puff because she feared it meant they were plotting against her. They weren't happy with their captivity and no amount of reminders why they were incarcerated helped. She was tempted to shove the cage in a closet, so she wouldn't have to look at their accusatory eyes, but she knew she couldn't be that mean. It was tough enough on them being in the cage. The slippers preferred their freedom.

"If you guys dare to escape and manage to even nibble on one of my new designer shoes I will cage you in Krebs' locker at the fitness center for a month. Trust me, that will make where you are now feel like an exclusive resort!" she called out. "And I doubt he's cleaned it out since he joined there eight years ago."

"Wouldn't that be considered cruel and inbunny punishment?"

She lifted an eyebrow. "Inbunny?"

He shrugged. "I can't exactly call it inhuman, can I?"

She regarded Nick standing in the bathroom doorway, his shoulder braced against the doorjamb.

No one should look that good.

Nick's coffee-colored hair was slightly tousled as if he'd walked here instead of driven or teleported himself. With a lean body made for jeans and a dark green polo shirt, he looked like any all-American hot-looking guy she might meet while out dancing. Until she looked closer and saw the hint of fang, which said this hottie's normal body temp was a lot lower than a human's, even if his sexy quotient was way higher.

She didn't miss the faint hint of color in his face that indicated he'd recently fed. She didn't like to think about his eating habits, even if it was a fact she knew she couldn't ignore. Maybe because she preferred to chew her dinner than drink it out of a plastic bag. She was just grateful he didn't tap humans for his meals any longer. That was way too icky.

"It's usually polite to knock on a door before entering a lady's boudoir," she told him, just plain enjoying the view of the sexy vampire. She smiled as one of her spa rubber duckies quacked dismay at the facial mask that went from eyes to beak. Another one that resembled Mae West blew him a bubbly kiss while a Betty Boop ducky strutted her stuff.

"Krebs told me it was all right to come on up." He smiled. "Obviously, he didn't realize how you were occupied." His gaze settled on the curves of her breasts barely visible above the water line.

"Yeah, like that would stop you." Her inner snarky gargoyle whispered a suggestion in her ear that she followed up on. The scented bubbles drifting on the water's surface shifted, as first her bent knee appeared then her leg straightened out and arched upward, her toes in a perfect point. Nick's gaze was diverted to watch the opalescent bubbles slide down her wet skin.

A woman in a bubble bath. Gets 'em every time.

"And you're here because. . .?" she prompted.

"I thought we could go out tonight. Have dinner at a nice restaurant. Maybe do some dancing." The gleam in his eyes said if she was lucky there just might be two different kinds of dancing.

"I thought you were going out tonight to track down Luger?"

"It turned out not to be too difficult. The son is still hanging out with him and a meeting is set up for this weekend. That's why I thought we could have an evening out." His eyes darkened with a heat that reached all the way across the room.

"Umm, it sounds very good," Jazz purred, circling her ankle in the air, which kept Nick's gaze riveted on her bubble-dotted leg. "But that would mean dressing and going out when. . ." she paused for effect, "we could just stay in. I'm sure we could find something here to nibble on." She raised an eyebrow for effect.

Nick straightened up and walked into the bathroom. His fingers went to his shirt buttons, but before he could release them, the buttons slid free from the buttonholes on their own. He looked up, shooting Jazz a faint grin.

"Just couldn't wait, could you?"

She directed her gaze at his fly, her whisper a musical cadence as Nick's belt freed itself and the zipper rasped downward.

"Why exert yourself, darling, when I can do it for you," she purred. "Besides, this is a lot more fun." She scooted down to one end of the tub, sending her rubber ducky bobbing among the bubbles.

Nick shed his clothing in record time and tossed them to one side before heading for the tub. "Thank you for not ripping them off me."

"The thought was there, but I figured you might not be happy with me doing that. Honestly, just like a man," Jazz uttered a theatrical sigh, using a wave of her fingers to send his clothing upward and folding themselves neatly on a nearby vanity bench.

Nick hissed a curse as he eased his way into the steaming hot water. Jazz scooted back between his spread thighs, resting her back against his chest.

"See, isn't this better than going out?" She released a sigh.

"I never complain about having a naked witch in my arms."

She tipped her head back so she could look up at him. "Just as long as I'm the *only* naked witch in your arms, bud." She wiggled her fingers, sending multi-colored sparks into the air that rained down on them.

Nick's chuckle vibrated against her back. "The knowledge that you can conjure up witchflame keeps me in line."

"You'll never let me forget that, will you?" She wrinkled her nose.

"No, I won't." He stroked his fingers up and down her arms in a lazy pattern. "I almost ended up as a bonfire."

"No, I deliberately missed you. I just wanted to get your attention." She wiggled her hips backward and smiled at the hardness resting against her spine. "I wish you had brought up some wine."

"If I'd known you were in the tub I would have. Why not order some up?" He brushed his lips over the curved shell of her ear.

"Not a good idea. The last time I did that Krebs freaked out when he saw a wine bottle roll its way upstairs. And I received an additional two weeks from the Witches' Council since I was told I was using my magick more for personal gain than the better good. I just saw it as better than leaving wet footprints on the stairs. " She smiled when she felt Nick's hand trail down her arm then around to curve over her breast, his fingertips teasing the nipple.

"Then I guess we'll just have to go without, won't we?" He nosed aside a long curl that had escaped the untidy bundle of hair clipped on top of her head. "But then, when I'm around you I don't feel the need for. . .wine."

Jazz slid out of his arms and turned around to kneel in front of him. She picked up her bath pouf and a bottle of body wash. Nick barked a laugh when she squirted the body wash on his chest.

"I guess I should be grateful you didn't choose something ultra-feminine instead of," he sniffed the air, "chocolate." The grimace on his face told her he still wasn't too sure about her choice.

"Mmm, this isn't just chocolate," she purred, "but Decadent Chocolate Mousse." She leaned forward and licked the tip of his ear.

Nick's chuckle rumbled deep within his chest. "Why do I get the feeling that you wish it was real mousse?"

"Well. . ." She laughed softly, waving her hand in the air. Silver sparkles danced in the air around them like a glittery shower. "I could whip some up and," she swooped down, tonguing his ear again, "cover you with it then lick it verrry slowly off your chest," she gently scored said area with her nails, "then head lower." Her hand did the same until she encircled his cock.

Nick swore under his breath as she squeezed him with a feather light touch. "You do like to play with fire, don't you?"

"Once I mastered it, I did." She brought her lips back to his ear and blew on it gently. "And I think, in a way, you do too." She adjusted her body so that she sat on his lap, his cock grazing her pubic hair. A wiggle of her hips had him muttering curses in Russian. "Such graphic language for my tender ears, Nikolai Gregorivich. Especially when I intend to have my way with your body."

"And I would say you are doing an excellent job of it." His eyes burned with heat. He cupped her breast with his hand, her pebbled nipple nesting against the heart of his palm. He hissed another curse as she rose up onto her knees then slowly lowered herself down onto him. Her inner muscles tightened around him as she rotated her hips, making sure she could feel every inch of him.

Nick gripped Jazz's hips tightly, but didn't take over. He allowed her to set the rhythm, even if her slow pace was killing him. But he knew the end result would be more than worth it.

They stared into each other eyes, Jazz's lips parted as she panted lightly while she lovingly imprisoned him within the velvet vise of her body.

"I am yours and you are mine," she whispered, rising up slowly and lowering herself inch-by-inch, feeling the thickness of his cock rasp against her vaginal walls. She leaned in, kissing him with the same loving thoroughness.

"We are together always." Nick said words he'd said many times in the past, but only to Jazz, because she was the only one who deserved the vow. He arched up, driving himself deeper within her. She moaned in response, swiveling her hips in a movement guaranteed to shoot his blood pressure, if he had one, into another galaxy and beyond.

The energy between them grew so strong, Jazz's hair floated around her head as if shot through with electricity. The delicate lines of her face were taut with desire, her lips moist, full, and red.

As their mouths met, feeding on their desperate need for each other, their energies merged with a force that could have triggered an earthquake.

"Krebs asked if I wanted to come over and watch a football game with him this Sunday," Nick commented once he found the ability to speak again.

"He said he was going to ask you." If she felt anymore relaxed she'd be in a coma. "I hope you turned him down gently."

"No, I told him I'd come."

She twisted her neck to look up at him. "You're kidding?"

"Sure, why not? I enjoy football and I was flattered he asked me." He paused. "It helped me feel more. . ."

"Human?" She asked softly, idly stroking his chest.

Nick nodded. "As if he'd like to have me as a friend and not consider me a monster."

At the sound of pain in his voice Jazz reared back. "You are not a monster," she said fiercely. "And there is no way Krebs would ever consider you that way."

"Okay, I get the message." He pulled her back against him. "But for now, let's forget about your roommate and get back to us. I promise no more talk of monsters."

But she wasn't finished. She framed his face with her hands, her fingertips gently stroking the corner of his eyes.

"Agreed. No more talk of monsters, but there is something I want to know. Please tell me you're no longer having anything to do with the Protectorate," she whispered.

He gazed into her eyes. There was no surprise in his gaze at her question—as if he'd expected it. "I no longer have anything to do with the Protectorate."

She smiled with a hint of relief and leaned forward to kiss him. So why did she feel deep down that he was lying to her?

"Why do I make promises I don't want to keep?" Jazz heaved a sigh even as she breezed her way down the 5 freeway.

"That's one answer I'd like to hear," Irma muttered. "You're always making promises to me and never keeping them."

"Finding a spell to give you a new wardrobe isn't easy." Okay, she lied. It was easy once she realized where to look. She just hadn't bothered searching for it yet. She sipped her coffee then returned the mug to the cup holder a few words and a flick of her fingers had created in the car. "I was stupid to tell Dweezil I'd go see Mindy. Then the nitwit had the nerve to call me up at the crack of dawn to remind me of that promise. Ugh! That little elven bitch blew my car up."

"In case you've forgotten, I just happened to be in it at the time," Irma issued a tart reminder.

"No, I didn't forget, except you had a better chance of surviving the blast than the car did." She tried pushing the ghostly dog's head off her shoulder, but he refused to budge. She shuddered at the idea of the ectoplasmic doggy dribble covering her sweater, even if mortals couldn't see it. She glanced over her shoulder and quickly changed lanes as her exit came up.

Irma looked out the window. Since the day promised rain, Jazz had the top up. "I suppose we won't stop at the zoo or Sea World, will we?"

"Not a chance." Jazz made a quick left turn and followed the bay. "Although I wouldn't mind spending the night at the Del Coronado Hotel. You'd love it. They have a ghost there. Maybe the two of you could compare notes even if she's been around longer." Her attention was momentarily diverted by the appearance of Horton Plaza, which offered shopping and dining for everyone, even a shop-happy witch. She made a mental note to stop by after seeing Mindy. By the time she finished with the Barbie-like elf, she'd be ready for a leisurely meal and some retail therapy.

"You're not going to park in one of those enclosed garages, are you?" Irma shifted uneasily as she stared at a multi-storied parking garage.

Jazz wasn't surprised that Irma didn't want to be left in a parking garage. After Clive Reeves had tainted Irma and the car in a mall's garage, the irascible ghost was apprehensive of parking structures.

"There's a parking lot with an attendant near the business. You know I've increased the wards on the car since then and you have your dog."

"A dog that can't be seen by everyone."

"You wanted a dog. You got one." Jazz muttered a few words before she pulled into the parking lot entrance.

As the attendant approached her she knew he saw the typical California blonde in a skimpy dress instead of a redhead in tailored black pants and teal sweater.

"Sweet car," he said, keeping his eyes on what he thought was a *Playboy*-worthy bustline.

"Thank you," Jazz used a breathy voice to keep the illusion. "I really worry about my baby. You'll keep a close eye on her, won't you?" She ignored Irma rolling her eyes.

"No prob. I can park her right over there." He was so fixated on the fleshy mounds Jazz had to lean forward and pluck the ticket stub out of his hand.

"Thanks so much." She gave him her flashiest smile.

"Will you go before he melts at your feet?" Irma shouted.

Jazz ignored her and headed up the street with the purr of the T-Bird sounding behind her. She had no doubt the young attendant would treat her car right and she was pleased to know she was correct.

After all the times she'd been in San Diego, she couldn't remember visiting the historic Gaslamp District before and now wished she had the time to explore the many shops and boutiques in the area. It took some time, but she finally came upon the small building that she knew was protected by magick and only seen by preternatural beings. "Historic Cars" was written in elegant script over the door.

The interior wasn't anything like Dweezil's barebones office that blared techno punk music and didn't have anything there to comfort anyone who wandered in. Here, harp music soothed a visitor's ears and all the pieces of furniture were elegant antiques.

"Welcome to Historic Cars. Is there something I can help you with?" a woman who could be Mindy's twin said from behind a waist-high counter. Her blond hair was pulled up into a loose knot displaying her pointed ears. Instead of Dresden blue eyes like Mindy's, her irises were deep lavender. Just like Mindy she looked as if a stain or wrinkle wouldn't dare assault her clothing.

"Yes, I'd like to see Mindy."

She glanced at the flat screen monitor in front of her. "Do you have an appointment?"

"Tell her Jazz Tremaine is here. I'm sure she'll see me." She walked over to a small table she gauged was from the Regency period and studied a gold-trimmed porcelain vase centered on it.

The young elf kept her gaze on Jazz as she pressed a button on a console and whispered into her headset.

"Come this way." She disconnected her headset and led the way down a hallway until she reached the door at the end. She opened it and gestured for Jazz to enter.

Looking around Jazz saw touches of Mindy's heritage with artwork painted by elf artists and a freeform sculpture set on a credenza.

"Hello, Jazz." Mindy stood near a delicate desk. She wore a pink dress that flowed about her knees. "This is a surprise." She gestured to a nearby chair.

"You have a lovely office, Mindy." Jazz sat down and accepted the cup of tea Mindy handed her. She preferred getting down to business, but manners dictated she do the polite thing first. Elves had their own ways of conducting business, so Jazz had to follow their rules instead of her own.

"After my time with Dweezil I knew I wanted something elegant." She looked around her office with the pride of ownership.

Jazz sipped her tea and found the flowery taste a bit much for her, but she merely smiled and sipped again.

"Since I can't imagine you're here for a job or stopped by for a chat I imagine that Dweezil sent you."

"D doesn't send me anywhere. He asked me to talk to you."

Her blue eyes hardened to chips of ice. "He's a very nasty creature. I don't know why you care to deal with him. If you wanted to come work for me I'm sure we could come up with an arrangement beneficial for both of us."

"I don't think so, Mindy. I still haven't gotten past the fact that you blew up my car."

"Your destruction of the curse blew up your car," she corrected.

"Semantics. But it was a curse you set up." Jazz waved her off. "I'm just curious how a business so far south ended up servicing so many of Dweezil's prime accounts."

"I should have known." Mindy's lips widened in a smug smile. "It really hurt Dweezil, didn't it? He never thought that someone might find a way to cut into his business and offer the clients more."

"More, such as?"

"Such as private company business that is none of your concern, Ms. Tremaine." A tall man entered the office.

"My father. Eilemar," Mindy murmured, looking up to smile at her sire.

Whoa! Jazz realized she was looking at a tall man who could give Orlando Bloom's Legolas a run for his money. She kept her composure long enough to incline her head and issue a greeting.

"We do not steal clients from anyone. Our clients prefer a car service that offers them all the amenities they deserve," Eilemar told her.

Jazz had a pretty good idea what amenities he meant and not something any of Dweezil's clients would have gotten from her.

"As far as I'm concerned, you're welcome to them." She pushed herself out of her chair. "I came here as a courtesy to Dweezil. After all, it's whatever the clients want, isn't it? And business is business. But he is also upset because some of his workers have chosen to leave his employ and come to you. I was asked to speak to you about it and I've done just that."

"Tell Dweezil the next time he wants answers, he is to come himself and not send one of his witches." The elf's nostrils flared, the disdain in his voice making the word sound more like a curse.

For a second thunder rumbled overhead, which had nothing to do with the threatening rain and everything to do with Jazz's rising temper.

"And tell your daughter if she ever tries to destroy something of mine again I will turn her into a literal Barbie doll complete with Dream House," she said with a bright smile.

He straightened up. Eyes as blue as his daughter's turned hard as marbles. "Are you threatening us, witch?"

"I never threaten. And Mindy knows that." She glanced at the young elf before sweeping out of the office. "Good day."

As she walked out of the building, Jazz gave in to temptation and wiggled her fingers at the sign over the door. By the time she reached the corner, the script read Public Restrooms.

Not what she would have liked to have written on the sign, but she figured it wouldn't get her into trouble with the Witches' High Council. It really was for the greater good.

She pulled her cell phone out of her bag as she walked down the sidewalk and punched her speed dial.

"Whaddya want?" Dweezil's ground glass voice grated in her ear.

"My, aren't we chipper today? Honestly, D, would it hurt you to greet someone in a pleasant manner or is that beyond you?" She dutifully waited for his usual tirade to wind down. "I saw Mindy. Her father even sat in on the meeting."

"And?"

"And it's just as I expected. They're going to continue doing business as usual. My advice to you is to do what you do best. Beat them at their own game."

"What the fuck does that mean?" he screamed in her ear.

She winced and held the phone as far from her ear as possible. "It means part with some of that money you have stashed away, upgrade some of your vehicles, and offer some incentives to the clients you have left. Don't water down the alcohol. In fact, buy some of the pricy booze. Offer perks to your clients if they refer someone. Come on, Dweezil. You're good at putting someone out of business. You've done it in the past. You can do it again. If you want Mindy gone, work at it. But if I were you, I'd suggest a compromise. She can handle the business in the San Diego area and you keep to L.A."

"Why should I do that?"

"Because it can work for both of you if you do it right. Plus her father has a message for you. Next time do your own dirty work. And you know what? I may totally hate that sanctimonious elf, but I agree with him. I've done my part. The rest is up to you." She disconnected during Dweezil's rant.

"Shopping. Time for lots of shopping." She set off for her car and Horton Plaza with the words *charge it!* running through her mind.

Chapter 5

"WHY DID I PROMISE TO GO?" JAZZ STUDIED THE CONTENTS of her closet. Incomprehensible chatter sounded at her feet. She looked down. "No way you're leaving that cage to go with me." She continued to shake her head as Fluff and Puff babbled away. "Why? Maybe it has something to do with you two accused of eating a carnie and then there's the time you destroyed Thea's favorite *Hermes* bag. If she'd had her way, you two would have been turned into a couple of powder puffs."

She finally settled on a pair of dark bronze pants and matching jacket paired with a lacy tank top in a paler shade. She took her hair out of its tight braid and finger combed the spiral curls. Her moonstone pendant shone with a milky blue light against her breasts as she fastened the chain around her neck. The ring on her finger echoed the soft glow. Fluff and Puff hissed displeasure from their cage as she brought Croc and Delilah out of the closet and slipped them on her feet. The grayish shoes immediately darkened to a rich caramel shade to coordinate with her pants. Delilah winked at Jazz and blew her a kiss.

As she started down the stairs the doorbell rang and a moment later she heard Krebs greeting Nick.

"You've got a great collection here," she heard Nick say.

"I'm just glad that more of my favorites are finally showing up on DVD," Krebs said.

"*Attack of the Puppet People* was fantastic." Nick slid the DVD case back into its slot.

"Oh no, don't tell me." Jazz walked into the large family room that housed every electronic toy a grown man would love. "You love all those old sci-fi movies too?"

"And horror films." Krebs grinned, turning to Nick. "Jazz groans anytime it's my turn to choose a movie for our movie night."

"The last time was a double-feature. *The Monolith Monsters* and *The Mole People*. But that's okay. Next time it's my turn and he's going to have an evening of soppy chick flicks." She laughingly bared her teeth at Krebs.

"I thought that after the game Nick might want to watch my latest find." Krebs sorted through his DVDs and pulled out a slim case. "We're talking a real classic here." His eyes danced with laughter.

Jazz gasped in horror when she saw the title. "Give that to me!" She snapped her fingers. Except her command fizzled the moment her power hit the case that refused to move from Krebs's hands. She muttered a second more powerful command, but it also failed.

"*Her Past Indiscretions* starring Jasmine Taylor." Nick grinned, reading the case. "A young factory girl is seduced by the owner's son and becomes the talk of the town because she has his baby. 1929. Oh yes, I remember this one."

"Did you honestly think after I spent cold hard cash to get this baby that I wouldn't find a way to protect it?" Krebs smirked at Jazz. "Blair set up an awesome protection spell for the DVD *and* the case. She said there's nothing you can do to this gem."

Jazz glared at Nick who was collapsed on the brick red sectional laughing so hard he sounded as if he was wheezing, except she knew there was no way he could wheeze.

"You need to look for another silent classic titled *The Gilded Cage*," Nick suggested. "Jazz played a kind hearted prostitute in a New Orleans bordello who falls in love with a wealthy playboy client who kills her because he doesn't want his socialite fiancée to find out about her. She wore a lot of black lace in that movie."

Jazz opened her mouth but all that came out was a squeak. "I would have starred against Valentino if he hadn't died," she finally managed to say.

"Wow, Rudolph Valentino? So tell me, Jazz, just how old does that make you?" Krebs asked.

"Do not tell him!" she ordered Nick, horror coloring her voice. "I swear, Nick, if you say one word you will literally end sunny-side up."

"Let's just say she looks incredible for her age," Nick replied.

Jazz shot one last glare at the DVD before checking the contents of her purse. "Do not think this is over. I'll find a way to get that DVD. I've got to get to Thea's book signing. She'll be impossible to deal with if I'm late. Enjoy your football game, boys."

"Hey! No way they can be down here!" Krebs yelled. "I thought you said they were locked up."

Jazz followed his gaze to the coffee table where a bowl of chili cheese dip resided with taco chips and a couple of beer bottles along with hungry looking Fluff and Puff poised over the bowl.

"Bad bunnies," she scolded, rounding on them. "How did you get out of the cage?" She pointed at them. "Bunnies been bad. Bunnies are sad. Do what I say without fail and return to your jail. Because I say so, damn it!" A tiny squeak erupted from one slipper's mouth before they disappeared in a puff of smoke. "That cage was reinforced by a powerful wizard. They shouldn't have been able to get out of it," she groaned.

"But if they got out of there once, they can again," Krebs said. "And they love chili cheese dip."

"If they happen to get out, and you allow them to eat that dip, their cage is going in your room tonight," she said, pausing long enough to drop a kiss on Krebs's cheek.

"Who allows?"

"Enjoy doing the guy thing," she whispered in Nick's ear after kissing him with a great deal more warmth than the kiss she'd given Krebs. The stilettos sighed loudly and flashed Nick their sexiest smiles. "Down girls," she commanded, but the shoes ignored her.

"Enjoy listening to Thea go on and on about her glamorous life."

She wrinkled her nose at his teasing. "I'll drink lots of wine at dinner." She waggled her fingers at the men as she left the house.

Krebs picked up his beer. "Uh, Nick, I wasn't sure if you could drink beer and I wasn't sure where to buy the other that you. . ."

"Other liquids are no problem for me."

"It's nice you could come over. I guess you didn't want to go with Jazz."

"Getting hit with one of Jazz's fireballs would be preferable to spending a few hours with Thea." Nick accepted the bottle of beer Krebs held out and watched the man drop into an easy chair.

"That bad, huh?"

"I can take only so much of Thea. Preferably at a great distance." Nick sipped the yeasty brew.

"I met her once and I admit that was enough for me." Krebs winced.

"She's been known to eat unsuspecting men for breakfast." Nick leaned back into the couch, resting his ankle on the opposite knee. "And I don't mean that in a good way either."

"Literally, I'm sure. I've also met Stasi and Blair and they're nothing like Thea."

"Or Jazz," Nick pointed out.

"You must have met some of the others. What are they like?"

"I haven't met them all but the ones I have are all unique," Nick said. "Each has her own special talent."

"The ones I've met sure aren't what I pictured witches to look like. Of course, neither is Jazz."

Nick grinned. "You were thinking black dresses and pointed hats, warts on the chin and nose? Maybe a hint of green skin?"

"Not that far. The witches on *Charmed* are sexy looking too, but Jazz is still in a. . ."

"Cauldron all her own?"

Krebs almost snorted his beer. "Yeah, that works. Just

like you." He eyed Nick's black boots, well-worn jeans, and gray T-shirt announcing that he was a night person.

"What? You thought we all wear capes and tuxedos and spoke with a Hungarian accent? I was born in Old Russia, Krebs. There are still some ancient vampires who believe in always wearing black and displaying a lot of affectations, but most of us prefer to blend in the best we can. Since my work with the Protectorate meant I also had to spend time among mortals, it was best I retain more human-like qualities."

"You were with that group for a long time, weren't you?"

Nick nodded. "Centuries. We have always believed in policing our own, because we knew the mortals couldn't do it."

Krebs rubbed his chin in thought. "I didn't really believe in any of this until I met Jazz and learned what she was and what was around me. I knew it was going on. It's like an unspoken secret, but I guess it's only when you face it that you realize the truth. And hope you don't end up as someone's midnight snack. No offense."

"None taken." Nick cradled his beer bottle between his hands. "You shouldn't have to worry about that. You are under Jazz's and my protection. Plus, if anyone did hurt you I'd say that Jazz would happily tear that creature apart. She's very loyal to her friends," he murmured.

He watched Krebs fiddle with the television controls. The feeling that more was going on than appeared grew stronger. "So tell me, Krebs, why exactly did you invite me over? It can't be just because you want company to watch a football game."

"No hidden agenda. I thought since you're involved with Jazz, we could take some time to know each other better." Krebs sat back with his legs stretched out in front of him.

Nick smiled, deliberately displaying his fangs. He was impressed that Krebs didn't look away or wince.

"Uh," Krebs hesitated then forged on. He looked down at the beer bottle in his hand as if it held all the secrets of the world. "You can't tell Jazz what I'm about to tell you. At least, please don't say anything to her at this time. Because she'd probably find a way to lock me up in that cage with the slippers, if not worse."

"Is this something that involves her?"

"No." He took a deep breath. "Well, yeah, sort of. Come to think of it, just maybe."

Nick usually felt comfortable around mortals, but the ones he felt most comfortable with were cop mortals. Krebs was proof that everyday mortals were a whole different species.

"Which is it?" He already feared the worst.

"All of the above," he admitted. "I don't know if Jazz told you I design Web sites for. . ." he searched for just the right word.

"Members of the supernatural community," Nick provided.

"Yeah." Krebs picked up his beer and swallowed half the contents. "One of my clients is Leticia who runs a vampire dating service."

"I know of her and her service. It's very popular among our kind." It didn't take much for every light to blaze to life inside Nick's brain. He really didn't like what he was thinking either. The look on Krebs' face confirmed his suspicions. "Are you saying you've met her outside of e-mail or the telephone?"

"We've met for coffee a couple of times," Krebs explained, heading into the kitchen and returning with two more beer bottles.

Nick groaned at the ramifications of such a meeting. "I thought you had promised Jazz you would keep your interactions to e-mail and the phone only when you dealt with vampire clients? In fact, any preternatural client."

"E-mails went to IMs and she asked if I was willing to meet her for wine or coffee and we'd talk about a new business she was thinking of starting. All very innocent."

"Innocent, yet you never said a word to Jazz." Nick sensed Krebs was talking about way more than a couple of hours at Starbucks.

"Hell, no, I didn't tell Jazz! I like my body parts exactly where they are." He looked down and grimaced to find Fluff and Puff nibbling in the dip again. He shooed them away and one of them snarled and almost took his fingers off but moved aside. Nick's snarl was more effective as each snatched a taco chip and instantly disappeared again. Krebs guessed they returned to their cage before Nick followed up on his silent threat. "You know what would happen. I tell her about meeting up with Leticia and I could find my dick in place of my nose and vice versa."

Nick winced as the word picture popped into his mind. "She is inventive with her curses and Blair is even more creative. But you must know humans and vampires aren't exactly friend material."

"Why not? I mean, other than pretty much going out only at night and the drinking blood thing, your kind isn't all that different from us."

"We're very different than you. We're predators by nature, Krebs," Nick said softly, realizing that even after all the time Krebs spent with Jazz the mortal was still pretty clueless about supernatural beings. "I'm not trying to make you feel uncomfortable, and I'm aware of Leticia who has always, well, behaved herself. But she is still not someone you could turn your back on. She's walked this earth a long time, done things you couldn't even imagine."

"Hey, no one's perfect!" He held up his hands. "Maybe a massive understatement, but we sat there and talked for hours. And not once during that time did I see her as a vampire. I only saw her as an intelligent and beautiful woman."

Nick's mind reeled at what could have happened that night. Along with what would happen when Jazz found out and he knew that she would. He wondered if this wouldn't be a good time to take a vacation far far away. And Jazz would have every right to throw a fit when she found out.

"When Jazz finds out, rearranged body parts will be the least of your worries. I'm sure she explained to you why she felt it was best you restrict communication to non-face-to-face."

"And that's why I was hoping you could help me out." Krebs worked steadily on his second bottle of beer. Nick worried if the mortal continued in this manner he'd be totally wasted by the time the game started. He also worried about the glint in Krebs' eyes and the way his voice softened when he spoke Leticia's name. It was apparent that the mortal was well and truly hooked and Nick doubted she had to use one speck of her power to mesmerize him.

Oh yeah, he could see that Krebs was heading for major trouble. From a vampire he was clearly falling for and from a witch who was going to be furious with him for falling for said vampire. The idea of space travel was looking better all the time.

He picked up his bottle of beer and tipped his head back to take a hearty swallow. While he couldn't get a buzz from the alcohol, he could enjoy the taste.

"We're talking rock and a hard place for you," he began.

"That's why I thought maybe we could all go out together and Jazz could see Leticia the way I do."

Nick ignored the other man's hopeful expression. "Are you talking about a double date?"

Krebs nodded. "It wouldn't have to be dinner since it wouldn't be easy for you and Leticia. Maybe spend an evening at a club where we could all feel comfortable."

Nick closed his eyes. "I'll think about it." He held up a hand to stave off Krebs' response. "Only think. And let me give you some advice. Don't tell Jazz about meeting with Leticia until I can figure out how you can tell her and you *will* tell her."

Krebs sighed with relief. "Thanks, man."

"Don't thank me yet." Nick finished his beer and started on the second bottle.

"What in the hell?" Krebs stared at the bowl of dip that was now down on the floor and disappearing at a rapid rate.

"Irma's damn dog." Nick growled at the bear-like animal that happily barked at him.

"Ghosts can eat?" Krebs couldn't take his eyes off the chips now going the way of the dip even if he couldn't see what was consuming them.

"Apparently this one can." Nick raised his voice. "Irma, come get your dog!"

"She went with Jazz." Krebs fought a rapidly losing battle for his beer bottle.

A moment later, an intense stench filled the air.

"*Augh!*" He gave up the bottle and covered his nose with his hands

"Outside now!" Nick ordered. While he didn't have the power Jazz did, he was able to give the dog a mental push toward the kitchen door where the dog flashed through in his escape to the back yard.

"That is disgusting." Krebs's voice sounded nasal as he pinched his nostrils shut.

"Until now I have never been so glad not to have the ability of breathing," Nick muttered, fighting to keep from laughing, but he soon gave in.

Krebs glared at him then ended up following his mirth.

"You can't say I don't provide an interesting time," Krebs choked, heading for the kitchen and replacement beers.

Nick grinned. He liked Krebs a lot. And he could see why Jazz was protective of her friend. But he really didn't want to be around when she learned of their conversation today.

❖ ❖ ❖

"Oh dear." Jazz stared at the building that resembled a warehouse. She looked around, expecting fireworks exploding overhead and thankful to find none. She was well aware of Thea's temper when she didn't feel she was given the adoration she felt she deserved. "This is not good."

"Will you have her sign a book for me?" Irma asked, as Jazz climbed out of the car.

"I'll pick up the audio version."

Jazz crossed the parking lot and almost lost her balance as the stilettos cooed and abruptly turned her in the opposite direction as a man walked past her.

"Do not even think about it!" she hissed a warning then looked up at the man who knew how to wear a pair of snug jeans. "Oooh, he is cute. But you can't go chasing men." Croc pasted a pout on her glossy lips while Delilah exhaled a pained sigh as they turned Jazz back in the correct direction.

As she walked toward the entrance, Jazz conjured up a membership card for the warehouse and walked inside. She looked around briefly then followed the signs advertising author Thea James was signing her newest historical romance.

"I loved *Be Mine Alone*," said a woman standing in front of the cloth-draped table heaped high with hardcover books. Two poster-size reproductions of the book cover flanked each side of the table. About fifteen women stood behind the woman waiting for Thea to autograph her book. "Colin was your best hero yet."

"Thank you." Thea dipped her head, a smile on her red-glossed lips. Her sleek raven's-wing hair was swept up into an intricate knot with rubies displayed at her ears and around her throat. Large eyes the shade of a deep blue topaz echoed her smile. It was no wonder her red silk suit screamed power in all caps. Her manner was that of a queen receiving her due. "I was quite fond of him myself."

So was Fiona since she was the one who fooled around with Colin back in 1787, Jazz thought as she remained in the background in order to enjoy the show. If nothing else, Thea knew how to put on a performance worthy of a literary diva.

At one point Thea looked over and noticed Jazz. Her face lit up and she gave a quick wave of her fingers.

Once the last fan left the table, Thea jumped up, grabbed her Prada bag, and hurried over to Jazz.

"It is *so* good to see you!" She hugged her tightly. "This place is a warehouse," she whispered.

"A lot of people shop here and it looks like a lot of your fans do too," Jazz whispered back.

Thea drew back slightly. "I'm usually offered coffee or my favorite wine and Belgian chocolates at my signings," she said in a low voice. "Here I was offered a Coke in a paper cup." She wrinkled her nose. "And my publicist said this is what goes on."

"I'm sure it's not that bad," Jazz assured her, even as she knew her sister witch only too well.

Thea considered herself the queen of historical romance who should be treated as such.

Thea stood back and scanned Jazz from the top of her head to her toes. "You're wearing the stilettos!" she exclaimed. Croc and Delilah looked up and cooed at her. "Aren't they wonderful? The minute I saw them I knew they were meant for you. And so much nicer than those nasty slippers of yours," she added in a low voice. Both Croc and Delilah blew out girly raspberries. "I got a pair of gorgeous drag-on-skin boots when I picked these up for you."

Jazz considered herself lucky she hadn't been the re-cipient of the boots. Fate knew what Fluff and Puff would have done to them. The stilettos always managed to stay out of bunny jail range. She'd even seen a hint of fear cross their faces when they were in the vicinity of the slippers.

"Well, thank you for the shoes," she said, even as she found herself spun around and steered toward the exit. "Don't you have anything to do?"

"My time is up and I'm out of here." Thea was a witch on a mission as they headed for the exit. "I made dinner reservations for us at a lovely restaurant the hotel concierge recommended."

Jazz increased her pace to keep up with Thea.

"Please tell me you brought your sexy roommate's Porsche and not that ghastly Thunderbird of yours," Thea said, just before they arrived at the car.

"I heard that! And I'm not ghastly," Irma announced.

"Let's all be ladies here," Jazz said, shooting a warn-ing glance at Irma.

"Did you get the audiobook for me?" Irma asked, ig-noring Thea.

"Yes," Jazz lied, digging deep inside her bag and pulling out the package.

Thea shook her head as she pulled her cell phone out of her bag. "I'll call the limo service I use."

"Irma can sit in the back."

"The trunk you mean."

Jazz wished she'd stayed home and watched the football game with Nick and Krebs even if she considered football an appalling waste of time.

"Sit, Thea," she ordered. "Irma, in the back. What's the name and address of the restaurant?"

It was no surprise that the restaurant was elegant and catered to the wealthy. Since she knew Thea would be picking up the check, she chose all her favorites.

"How is the curse elimination business going?" Thea asked, savoring her martini. "You really should try this. It's called the Abra Cadabra."

Jazz chuckled at the apt name. "No thanks. I'll stick with my double fudge martini." She held up her glass. "Although I was tempted to try the Haunted Bride cocktail. I may have to come back here just to try each one of their selections. As for the business, I did end up with a fantastic designer wardrobe, shoes, and bags courtesy of breaking a curse on a Hollywood wife. She had a walk-in closet even you would envy. And I managed to help a little boy whose older sister cursed him into spitting up beetles." She swallowed her giggle as the waiter who was approaching them abruptly made a 180-degree turn. "What about you? Are you still seeing that Italian *comte?*"

Thea shook her head. "Lorenzo is very much last year. Especially when I caught him in bed with a Russian supermodel."

Jazz winced in sympathy. But she also knew Thea's recuperative powers when it came to the opposite sex.

She bounced back pretty quickly, but if the man did Thea wrong, there was a good chance he didn't escape unscathed. Thea was considered one of Blair's best customers for revenge spells.

"Just as long as you made him suffer," Jazz said.

Thea smiled. "He'll also make a wonderful character in a future book. Not as the hero, of course."

"Other than Lorenzo, what's been going on with you?"

"I've been working on my new book along with handling this book tour." A smile from Thea had the waiter instantly returning to take their order. The man was so enthralled with Thea that he didn't write a thing on the pad and Jazz wondered if they'd get the right food. "And the writing hasn't been easy lately," she said in a low voice.

"You can't be running out of ideas yet. I thought we all had fodder to keep you going for decades." Jazz surveyed the basket of rolls and chose one along with a pat of chilled butter.

"That's not the problem." Thea examined her French-polished nails with more care than usual. She dredged up a smile. "Still, let's talk about you."

Now Jazz was convinced something was wrong. Thea never asked anyone about what was going on with them. Not when she could talk about herself.

Jazz leaned slightly across the table. "I have been experiencing bad dreams," she murmured.

"Nightmares are nothing unusual."

"These are." She recounted the more chilling dreams, feeling the same anxiety as she did when she woke up after the dreams. She picked up her glass and swallowed the rest of her drink, but the alcohol only intensified her unease.

Thea was quiet for a moment, tapping her fingers against the tabletop. "It sounds like your dreams are induced by magick."

"Gee, ya think? I may not have figured it out right away, but it did come up later on. And nothing I've done has worked. No amount of cleansing, warding against dark dreams, you name it."

"Have you done any searches to determine who cast this spell against you?" She glanced down, idly eying her broomstick charm on her ankle bracelet. It was no wonder the stone in her charm was the extremely rare and expensive red diamond.

Jazz shook her head. "Deep down I didn't want to consider someone was controlling my dreams. I preferred putting it down to eating too much junk food before bedtime."

"Or perhaps you didn't want to think the curse eliminator could be cursed." Thea smiled at the waiter as their salads were placed before them. She approved her choice of wine and waited until both glasses were partially filled and the waiter left them to their food. "You've had a busy time what with vanquishing Clive Reeves." She tactfully ignored Jazz's grimace. "You have Nick back in your life and you still work for that horrid creature. If I were you, I would make a list of anyone who could have it in for you." Her laughter was pure music. "Oh my, perhaps I should start writing thrillers. This could be exciting." She quickly reached in her bag and pulled out her BlackBerry, quickly tapping in some notes.

"This cannot go in a book, Thea," Jazz protested. A heavy feeling in the pit of her stomach told her it wasn't a good idea no matter what the literary witch thought.

Thea paused and saw the panic on Jazz's face. She made a face and put her phone away. "You're right. This could be something very serious. What can I do to help?"

Now Jazz was convinced this was either a crazy dream or Thea had had a partial personality transplant. She was also touched by her offer, but knew she would have to refuse. Only the victim could fight a curse leveled on a witch.

"I'd be grateful if you come up with any information on how to find the one casting the curse," she said.

"You do know that your best bet is The Library."

"I was hoping I could bypass that experience, thank you very much."

"The Librarian still doesn't like you?" She correctly pronounced "the" with a long "e" as was ordained by the pompous Librarian heading the otherworld library.

"Still? He's never liked me."

"He doesn't like anyone." Thea waved a hand in dismissal. "He should have been retired centuries ago. The antiquated rules that allow a wizard with such an imperious nature to remain in that position are ridiculous."

"He has friends in high places."

"And I'm sure they're all as fusty and domineering as he is. Don't worry, sweetie, I'll help you find a way." She reached over and patted Jazz's hand.

"Okay, this is so not you. What is going on?"

Thea concentrated on her salad. "I told you. It's just a problem with my work-in-progress. All writers go through it."

Jazz knew better. Thea had been penning stories for hundreds of years. At first using a man's name when women weren't thought to have the mental capacity to have an imagination and later under a variety of pseudonyms as she wrote penny dreadfuls, westerns, pulp fiction, and later on, historical romance that shot her skyward in the romantic fiction genre. She also knew if Thea didn't want to divulge her problems, she wasn't going to say a word even if Eurydice, headmistress of the Witches' Academy and head of the Witches' Council, demanded an explanation. Thea's stubborn nature was as strong as Jazz's

"Come to Moonstone Lake for the next full moon," she urged, feeling her sister witch's need to center herself as strongly as her own need for that grounding.

Thea shook her head and looked away. "I have my book tour," she murmured.

"Then come for Samhain. You can surely do that. You haven't celebrated with us for years," Jazz reminded her.

"I'll see what I can do." Thea's reply was non-committal.

While Jazz wouldn't think twice about forcing an issue, she also knew it was a lost cause with Thea. "All right, then let's forget about what could be my curse and your writer's block." She forked up goat cheese and romaine. "Tell me about your trip to Milan." Luckily, that was enough to brighten Thea's face and have her talking a mile a minute.

For the rest of the meal Jazz only had to enjoy her dinner and listen to Thea's latest adventures.

By the time she dropped her friend off at her hotel, the two women were relaxed and each had momentarily forgotten about their worries.

"How long are you staying in Los Angeles?" Jazz asked.

"I leave for San Francisco in the morning. I have signings there for the next four days then up to Seattle and New Mexico where I'm the keynote speaker for a romance writer's conference." Thea air-kissed her cheek. "Let me know what you find out about your curse. Of course, that could take a while, since I'm sure you have a long list of people not happy with you."

Jazz groaned at the idea of even making out a list. "Let's just say there's a few who could head it. Safe journey." She air-kissed back.

And released a huge sigh once she was on the freeway heading back to Santa Monica with Celtic Woman's *A New Journey* playing. Even if the vintage T-Bird didn't come with a CD player, it was no trouble having one installed. Jazz still recalled the mechanic almost in tears as he added the equipment to the classic car. He told her she was ruining the car. She considered she was updating it.

"May I come out now?" Irma asked, exhaling noisily.

"Of course."

Irma immediately appeared in the passenger seat. "What did she mean about you having bad dreams?"

And here Jazz hoped to keep that to herself. "I'm giving up Thai food before bedtime. It's nothing."

"There are times you don't lie very well. This is one of them." A lit cigarette appeared between her white-gloved fingers then just as quickly disappeared when Jazz flicked her a warning look.

"I'll make a deal with you. You give up the Lucky Strikes. I won't lie to you."

"I smoked Lucky Strikes when I was alive and I don't intend to give them up just because I'm dead. Besides, you'd still lie to me," Irma pointed out.

"Then we'll never know, will we?"

Jazz thought she was off the hook, but she should have known the ghost had a different agenda.

"So have you found an illusion spell for me, so I can have a more up-to-date wardrobe?" she asked just as Jazz's feet crossed the carriage house's threshold.

Jazz made a face. "Tomorrow. I will hit the spell books tomorrow," she promised.

"I'll hold you to that!" she shouted even as Jazz beat it to the house.

Jazz heard the murmur of male voices as she passed through the kitchen. She snagged herself a glass of wine before heading for the family room. She waited a moment, listening to what was playing in the background.

"Men and sports," she murmured, swallowing some wine first. "Hello boys," she said throatily, sauntering into the room.

Jazz's first thought was that Krebs looked guilty about something and her second thought was that Nick knew why Krebs looked guilty. She made a mental note to torture the information out of him when they were alone.

"How was dinner?" Krebs asked.

"Very posh. Very nice." She settled on the couch next to Nick, twisting around to drape her legs over his thighs. He smiled and slipped off her stilettos, making sure to gently place them on the floor. They started to make their way toward him with air smooches but he stared sternly at them until they moved back to where he put them. "How was the game?"

"28–0. What does that tell you?" Krebs leaned forward and grabbed a taco chip.

Jazz lifted her head as she heard bumping sounds upstairs. She had a pretty good idea where they were coming from. "Did Fluff and Puff behave and not come back?"

"What do you think?" Krebs said. "But it was only once. I think they were afraid of Nick."

She shot back more wine. "Obviously the standard spells aren't holding them in the cage well enough. I'll strengthen them tonight."

She sighed as Nick's hands kneaded her feet, rubbing the tension out of her limbs. "This is good. Don't stop. Maybe I'll have a good night's sleep."

Nick's massage paused at her words. "Are you still having bad dreams?"

She wiggled her toes to tempt him into continuing. "It happens."

"Not for you."

"Says the man who can sleep like the dead." She pushed herself up and swung her legs around to rest her feet on the floor. She reached across Nick and picked up her shoes. "It's been a long day. I'm for a hot bath and bed." She didn't look at him as she left the family room.

"Don't forget we have that meeting with Mrs. Archer tomorrow night," Nick called after her.

"I'll be there." Her voice drifted back.

Krebs raised an eyebrow as he glanced at Nick. "Is it me or was there an 'I'm off to bed and don't follow me' added in there? I admit there's been mornings she's admitted she hasn't slept well."

Nick didn't look pleased by her words. "Dreams have meaning," he said slowly. "Some good. Some not. And with some there are reasons that have nothing to do with bad food." He tipped his beer bottle upward and finished the contents then stood up. "I guess I should get going. Thanks for having me over." He held his hand out to Krebs who accepted it.

When Nick reached the sidewalk he looked up to the third floor where a few lights gleamed behind the blinds. He could hear the angry chatter of the slippers and soft cooing sounds probably coming from her new shoes. He turned away and headed up the street.

On his way back to his apartment, he thought of Jazz and her nightmares. Especially the one where she was convinced he had torn her throat out. He'd put it down to nothing more than a bad dream. But she'd mentioned in an off-handed manner that there had been bad dreams since then. Now he wondered if they were connected.

And if that was the case, then it had nothing to do with bad food or even watching a scary movie, although it was doubtful there was a scary movie made that would freak out Jazz. No, whatever caused her nightmares had more to do with magick.

"Do you never pick up your phone?" Jazz sauntered into Krebs's work area, a coffee cup in one hand and a custard-filled donut in the other. With her hair tied up in a pony-tail and wearing a cream-colored lace-trimmed shirt over black leggings, she looked like a ballet dancer. Her bare feet sported bright red nails that matched her fingertips. "Janelle called three times this morning alone!"

"Damn," Krebs muttered. "What did you tell her?"

"That you were involved in a project that was taking more time than you estimated. I don't like to lie, Krebs." She stuffed her donut in her mouth and used that hand to thump the back of his head leaving behind a smidge of chocolate frosting.

"Ow!" His hand flew up to defend himself. He looked at his fingers then licked them clean of the frosting. "I haven't figured out yet how to let her down gently."

"I think she's already realized that because she said, and I quote, 'tell that scum-sucking bastard he can just melt in a lake of acid,'" Jazz said. "Along with some other insults I didn't quite catch, but I think had something to do with cutting something off and feeding it to her goldfish. She hung up before I could grab a pen and ask her to repeat them."

"Maybe I should send her flowers."

"I think the only flowers she'd want to see are the ones adorning your casket." She frowned at the splash of color by his computer. "What are these?" She picked up the colorful glossy brochures.

He hunched down in his chair. "Nothing important. Just something I picked up."

"Uh huh, you just happened to walk by *three* different boat brokers and they pushed these brochures on you." She fanned them out and shook them under his nose. He batted them away impatiently. "I can't believe this, Krebs! You're thinking of buying a boat? Why would you do that?

I get seasick just looking at the radio-controlled models in the pond in the park. Crossing the Atlantic from England was a nightmare for me! And we're talking a voyage that lasted months!"

"You know I like going out on the water and renting a boat gets expensive. Plus I could use it for entertaining clients," Krebs mumbled, still refusing to look at her.

"Clients? Most businessmen schmooze with their clients out on the golf course. Oh wait, that's right! They can't go out in the sun! Krebs, half of your client base can't go out after dark and many of those have an inordinate fear of water. And no way you should be dealing with them face to face. Don't you think a pool would be better for your human clients? At home entertaining is quite the thing. Something nice and cozy?" She pulled herself up to sit on the table, swinging her legs back and forth. "Weekend barbecues with the neighbors. Romantic evenings out by the pool, although I hope you'd only do that when I'm not around. And I strongly suggest you don't ask Janelle over. She'd probably try to drown you."

"Get off the table and no, a pool would *not* be better. If you want to swim, the beach is only a few blocks away. Go with me when I go surfing and you can swim all you want."

"You go surfing at dawn! Thank you so much, *not!* And I burn easily so I'd burn even more out on a boat along with getting seasick before you even left the dock. Plus I'd have to use so much sunblock I'd slide right out of my bikini."

"And I'd complain about that?"

"Mind out of the gutter, Krebsie." She snapped her fingers in front of him. "Back to putting in a pool, which would be so much nicer. Even relaxing. Especially if you include a spa in the deal. Maybe one of those rock waterfall spas or a pretty lit fountain in the middle of the pool? You've wanted to upgrade the backyard after the you put in the new patio last year, so why not upgrade to a pool?"

He frowned at her. "And you'd contribute to it?"

"I paid my share of the patio costs."

"Yeah, after I threatened to make you a witchy star on *Judge Judy*," he reminded her.

Jazz rolled her eyes. "Like you would have done that."

"But you didn't want to push me into it, did you? Plus what exactly would you contribute to this pool other than pushing Mr. Hickman into cardiac arrest if he looks over the fence and sees you out there in a bikini?"

She tapped her chin with her forefinger in thought. "Oh. . .my rubber duckies. They'd have all that open space to swim in instead of my tub and they'd love to be out there in the sun."

"Do you mean they're re. . .?" A panicked look washed over his face. He waved his hands in front of him. "You know what? I don't want to know."

"Could you honestly expect anything that Blair gave me not have a speck of magick in them? Besides, they're harmless. They like to hang out by the tub." Jazz returned to perch on the table, but further down. "Even with the new patio we still have more than enough yard for a pool and spa and plenty of grass left over. Less for you to mow since you don't want a gardener."

"I like the exercise. Plus, I've always wanted a boat," Krebs confessed. "My family spent a lot of time out on the water when I was a kid and I miss that."

Jazz knew that Krebs and his upper-crust, very socially conscious family had parted company when he wouldn't attend Harvard and join the family business. After a time partying in the rock 'n' roll scene, Krebs found his niche in computer Web site design where his unique style caught the attention of the preternatural community. He hadn't lacked for work since.

"A pool would be cheaper than a boat, would add to the value of the house, and you wouldn't have to find a boat slip," Jazz said, coming up with what she hoped were her best arguments.

"I can have a day out with my buddies, drinking beer and doing some fishing."

Jazz slid off the table. "Boat salesmen are like car salesman. Remember what happened when you bought the Porsche? You had to call me to get you out of there because you felt trapped. If you've got a boat salesman working on you getting that bigger and better boat, I might not come to your rescue," she warned.

"I didn't feel trapped by that Porsche salesman. He was just talking about add-ons I didn't need!" he called after her.

"Wuss!"

"I wasn't the one who gave him that cold sore!" He returned to the computer code scrolling down his screen. "And she calls me nuts."

"I heard that! Next time you're trapped by a Porsche salesman you're on your own!"

Chapter 6

THE SUN FELT WARM ON HIS SKIN, PROVIDING A COMFORTING *heat he hadn't felt in centuries. While he could go outside during the day when the sky was overcast, he couldn't be out when the sun was this intense. How was it possible for him to stand outside in the bright light of day without bursting into flame?*

He took stock of his surroundings and felt even more confused.

If he didn't know better he'd swear he was standing in the middle of the street in a suburban neighborhood complete with little white fences around lush green lawns, SUVs and mini vans parked in driveways, basketball hoops and bicycles littering the yards. While the houses were obviously expensive, they were also abodes for the all-American family.

"If you want a ride to school, Kirk, you need to get here now." A blond-haired man wearing a navy suit and carrying a briefcase walked out of the house Nick stood in front of. He headed for a gleaming silver BMW parked next to a white minivan. Nick could see a hodgepodge of sports equipment filling the back of the van.

Surfer dude all grown up, Nick thought to himself.

"Hey, you! Didn't you forget something?" A woman wearing a white polo shirt and black jeans hurried out carrying a travel mug. She handed it to him along with a kiss while a boy of about ten ran out and climbed into

the passenger seat of the BMW. A little girl who could-n't have been more than three toddled outside and clung to her leg. The woman looked down and laughed, swing-ing the girl up to settle her on her hip.

Nick stared at the woman feeling as if someone had punched him hard in the heart. Her copper-red hair was cut in a short easy-care style and her moss green eyes showed no hint of makeup. Her delicate features were alive with happiness and love for the man she faced. Nick was used to seeing magick sprinkling around her; now he saw nothing but a sunny aura that smacked of mortality.

Witchy Jazz had turned into a soccer mom.

She's happy, *a voice whispered in his ear.* She doesn't need her magick and she doesn't need you.

"No." His body shook with sorrow. "No!" He reached out, wanting to pull her away from the man who had one arm around her. "Jazz! Jazz!" But she didn't hear him as she and her husband shared a pas-sionate kiss and their son yelled, "Gross!" and made gagging noises.

"No!" Nick literally flew out of his bed, falling against the chest of drawers. He still felt the pain in the vicinity of his heart as he pulled himself to his feet and clung to the wooden top.

Images were seared on his mind's eye. Jazz looked happier than he'd ever seen her before and the love she showed the man who was obviously her husband shim-mered all around them.

She had a normal life. A life without magick. A life without him.

If Nick's heart still beat, it would have ached with a pain that could tear through his entire body.

When he made his way back to his bed, all he heard was the seductive voice whispering in his ear that Jazz was in a life that didn't include him.

The thought was the stuff made of nightmares.

Nick still felt unsettled when he picked up Jazz that evening.

"Wow, if I didn't know better I'd say you didn't sleep well." She peered closely at his face as she settled in the passenger seat of his Jeep Wrangler.

"It's been a busy time."

"How is this meeting going to be handled?"

"I'm picking up Mrs. Archer then we head to the Full Moon. The pack leader is letting us use the meeting room in the back."

Jazz wrinkled her nose at the mention of the all night café that catered to Weres. Normally, vampires and Weres didn't do well together, but Nick had managed to have a cordial relationship with the pack leader that owned the café and enjoyed using the facility for neutral ground. "If anyone there humps my leg, I'm outta there."

"I feel sorry for anyone who'd even try."

He felt her gaze on him and knew she was trying to figure out why he wasn't his usual self. There was no way he'd tell her about his nightmare or how it left him feeling.

The idea that Jazz could have a future without him was unsettling. But he knew it was possible.

Witches and vampires. Never the twain shall meet.

"Please tell me Luger isn't going to be there," Jazz said. She stuck out her tongue.

"I doubt he'll allow Ronnie to go without him."

"Ah, trust issues. Have you ever done this before? Hooked up a mortal with their vampire family member?"

He shook his head. "A few have approached me, but I was able to persuade them it wasn't a good idea."

"Yet Mrs. Archer somehow slid past your power of persuasion." She drew a deep breath. "She's a mother who wants to see her son again, but she has no clue that he's no longer that person." She was quiet for a moment. "What about you? Did you want to see your family again after you were turned?"

Nick shook his head. "My parents were told I died in battle. If I had gone to them they would have seen me as a monster and tried to kill me. Flavius explained it was best I go far away and that's what I did."

Jazz momentarily thought of the time she and her sister witches were banished from the academy and her first thought was to return to her family, but she knew it was impossible. By then, she wasn't the girl her parents had raised, so, frightened and unsure what to do, she and the others made their way into a world they were unfamiliar with.

"Some decisions are difficult," she murmured, looking out the window. She felt the brief cool touch of Nick's hand on her hand and felt the comfort he offered.

It turned out Mrs. Archer lived in a sprawled-out apartment complex geared for retirees. Jazz obligingly climbed into the back, resting against the window with her legs stretched across the seat.

"So my boy will be there?" Mrs. Archer asked, clutching her purse tightly in her hands. Her arthritic knuckles looked white.

"His sire promised me that he would be there." Nick didn't add that no one went against Luger's wishes without repercussions.

Jazz wondered what Nick promised Luger to agree to the meeting. She knew little of the vampire, but what she knew was that he believed in rage and violence of the first order. She feared the kindly woman would learn a very hard lesson that night.

The Full Moon Café was a '50s style diner designed to look like a train's dining car. While it looked appealing, for some reason humans were prone not to stop there while the Weres enjoyed the hearty fare served 24/7. Jazz popped in now and then since they brewed a mean cup of coffee.

Coby, the pack leader, stood behind the counter looking at the newcomers with a black flat stare that was offputting at best. At about five-foot-seven, he had the wiry strength that was even more pronounced when he was his furry self. Jazz figured his salt-and-pepper hair was an echo of what color he'd be like during the full moon. Four Weres occupied stools at the counter while the booths remained empty. The four didn't bother looking their way, but there was no doubt they knew exactly what had just walked in. Jazz wondered if they were here for backup in case something happened, and if that was the case, she'd be grabbing Mrs. Archer and diving under the nearest table.

"Coby." Nick nodded his head in greeting. "They here yet?"

Coby shook his head. "Luger just called and said they'd be here in about five minutes." He stared at Jazz. "I suppose you want coffee?"

"Yes please." She put on her bright polite smile. She knew since she stood on neutral ground her spells were forbidden, but that didn't mean she wouldn't be ready in case something happened. Sometimes a witch's gotta do what she's gotta do. And Jazz liked remaining in one piece a lot more than following rules. Witch blood didn't bother Weres the way it bothered vampires, so she was fair game. But she also knew Coby was tough on his pack and anyone who disobeyed his rules was dealt with in a less than pleasurable manner.

Coby picked up a large mug and filled it with a dark brew. He glanced at Nick and Mrs. Archer. The former nodded and the latter looked uncertain.

"Would you prefer tea, ma'am?" Coby asked in a voice that was almost gentle.

"Yes, thank you." Her reply was barely a whisper.

"If you want to go on to the back room, I'll bring them in." Coby pulled out a couple more mugs.

"Thanks." Nick guided Mrs. Archer toward the rear of the diner.

"He's very polite," she whispered to Nick, unaware she was easily heard by preternatural hearing.

Jazz noticed that Coby watched the woman with what she felt was sorrow.

"She's going to regret tonight," he muttered, pouring coffee into another mug and fixing up tea the British way by warming the mug before pouring more hot water and adding a tea bag.

Jazz sipped her coffee, grateful for the caffeine jolt to her system. "I think she knows that, but she still intends to go through with it."

Coby shook his head. "My old lady kicked me out my first full moon. Seems she couldn't handle it." He looked as if he wished he hadn't made the confession. He shook it off. "Maybe you should introduce Nick's client to your ghost. The lady looks like she grew up in the 1950s."

"So did you."

"Yeah, well" He placed the mugs on a tray along with a small container of sugar and another with lemon wedges. Before he picked it up, he topped off Jazz's mug from the coffee pot. "You wanna take this in with you?"

"Sure." She figured he didn't want to face the hopeful mother again. She picked up the tray then paused. "Do you know Willie who works at the boardwalk?"

"Ferris wheel? Some. He's come in here a few times." Coby's expression told her he didn't think much of Wereweasels. "That's right. Your magickal bunny slippers were accused of eating him."

"They didn't do it!" She was getting damned tired of defending her slippers, but she knew if she didn't, no one would.

He shrugged. "No fur off my nose if they did. His kind isn't what you like to be around too much, but I guess Willie did okay working for Rex. At least he stayed out of trouble."

"If someone mentions seeing him would you give me a call?" She conjured up a business card and placed it on the counter.

"No guarantee that will happen, but if I hear of something I'll let you know." He picked up the card and slipped it in his shirt pocket.

Jazz carried the tray to the back room where she found Nick and Mrs. Archer seated across from each other at a small table. Nick spoke softly and she guessed he was explaining how the meeting would be handled.

"Here we go," Jazz said brightly as if she was the hostess entertaining guests. She handed Nick his coffee and set out the tea for Mrs. Archer.

"I didn't realize. . ." Mrs. Archer stared at Nick's mug.

"Coffee seems to be something we can't give up." Nick smiled.

"They're here." Coby looked in the open doorway then walked away.

Nick stood up and walked around to stand by the elderly woman, resting one hand on her shoulder. Her expression was hopeful.

Jazz stood to her other side.

The first man to appear was well over six feet, dressed in a black suit and tie. White-blond hair flowed down to his shoulders, highlighting white skin that hadn't seen the light of day in centuries and eyes so blue they almost blazed a cold fire.

"Nikolai." He inclined his head in a polite greeting.

"Luger."

"My boy?" Mrs. Archer started to stand, but Nick's hand kept her seated. She silently implored him.

Luger stared first at Mrs. Archer then at Jazz, who remained stone-faced, and finally turned his gaze to Nick.

"I thank you for agreeing to this meeting," Nick said formally.

"It is not a good idea."

Nick said nothing since he agreed.

Luger stepped aside to reveal a slightly built man who would never stop being in his early twenties.

Jazz easily sensed the lack of humanity in the elder vampire. It was the same with the younger one. She knew the elderly woman would see only the boy she raised.

"Ronnie?" Mrs. Archer's voice was hushed, expectant. Her face shone with joy. She held out her arms, but he didn't go near her.

"Mom, you shouldn't have tried to find me." He sounded weary.

"I had to know you were all right." Her smile wavered then disappeared.

"I'm fine, so please go."

"But. . ."

He shook his head, slashing his hand through the air. "I'm not the same, Mom! You're better off thinking of me as dead."

"You're not dead!" She stood up, this time Nick not bothering to restrain her. "You are my son."

He continued to shake his head, still keeping his distance.

Jazz felt the pain in the other woman's heart; the sorrow that overwhelmed her that her baby boy was no more.

"Please, Mom, you've seen me, so will you go and not bother me again?" Ronnie asked.

Mrs. Archer drew a deep breath. "Are you happy?" She whispered it as if she was afraid of the answer but compelled to ask anyway.

Ronnie looked at Luger then glanced away. "This is my existence now." For a second his eyes glowed red and his fangs dropped, but she didn't shy away.

Luger gave a crisp nod.

Ronnie ventured toward his mother, his movements stiff and uncertain while Mrs. Archer stepped forward with outstretched arms. Nick remained on high alert.

The top of the woman's head reached Ronnie's chest as she wrapped her arms around him tightly.

Jazz wasn't sure what caught her attention first but she knew that Nick and Luger also felt that something was very wrong.

"I will always love you," Mrs. Archer said.

Just that quickly, Ronnie hissed, his eyes turning red again, but nothing more. He reared back, a look of horror on his face, before his body turned to dust and drifted to the ground. Mrs. Archer stood there, a wooden stake gripped tightly in one hand. She looked down at the dust with grief shadowing her eyes.

Nick's body was a blur as he moved to protect her.

Luger also stared at the pile of dust that had once been one of his younger vampires but made no move to retaliate.

"I had to save him," Mrs. Archer whispered, lifting her head to gaze at Luger. "He was already dead and I needed to know he wouldn't be out there hurting people."

"She is under my protection," Nick declared.

Luger chuckled. "You are brave, madam. If anyone else but you had done this deed, they would have been dead before they could blink. I will miss Ronald, but I will not strike back. Sometimes a mother has rights a sire does not." He was a dark blur then the doorway was empty.

Nick helped Mrs. Archer to her chair and urged her to take a sip of her tea. Her hands shook so badly he had to hold the cup for her.

"I couldn't let him be the way he was. I know he was a good boy, but when I saw him, I saw that his soul was truly gone," she murmured, dropping the stake to the floor. "That's when I knew I had to do it. I read what to do in a book."

Jazz edged her way to the open doorway where Coby stood near the counter. The other Weres watched her with shadowed eyes. She flashed them a slight smile.

"Um, does anyone have a Dust Buster out there?"

Guessing why she was asking for one, Coby sighed and turned to the waitress. "Get out the Dirt Devil. But you," he turned back to Jazz, "have to clean up your own mess."

"Just because witches have brooms doesn't mean we use them for that particular purpose," she muttered, accepting the handheld vacuum.

A half-hour later, Mrs. Archer was back in her apartment and after assuring she was all right, Jazz and Nick left.

"She's stronger than she looks," Jazz said, settling in the passenger seat.

Nick rested his hands against the steering wheel but didn't bother to switch on the ignition.

She turned and looked at him. "You knew she was going to destroy him, didn't you?"

He nodded. "I guessed it."

"But why kill her son?"

He continued to stare out through the windshield. "Because he was her only son and was as lost to her as the husband who'd died years ago. She wanted to properly mourn him, not think of him out there looking for prey. She wanted to save him since he would never again have a normal life." His lips momentarily twisted into a grim smile.

"Nick?" She leaned over, covering his hand with hers, gently stroking his fingers, and lending him her warmth. "What's wrong? There's more to it than what you're saying."

He wouldn't look at her as he slid his hand away and reached for the key in the ignition.

"Just that Luger was right. She is a very brave woman." He put the Jeep into gear and drove out of the parking lot. He was silent all the way back to Jazz's house, but before she climbed out of the vehicle, he leaned over and gave her a kiss that was rich with hunger. Before she could invite him inside, he pulled away and drove off the second she was out of the Jeep.

"I'm sorry, Esme, but I honestly don't see how I can help you," Nick told his newest client. And how he hated saying that to someone who could clearly pay his fees. Business had been slow lately. Not that the bank cared about that when his mortgage payment was due. While the Protectorate had wanted to pay off his mortgage as payment for his assistance in destroying Clive Reeves, he turned down the generous offer that he knew would have held too many strings. He preferred to remain independent of the vampire organization that he knew was going through a great many shakeups after Reeves destroyed Nick's sire and mentor, Flavius. Nick's sire had been a ruling force in the group and now his spot was open to many. Nick knew no one could fill Flavius's seat. He feared whoever took it would not have the strength to do what was right.

Nick was used to the fact that not too many of his clients could pay his usual fees. The woman facing him, however, could pay his rates ten times over.

"Surely, there is a way you can help me. I need to see my daughter. I want to know she's truly safe." She looked distressed.

Nick studied the vampire facing him. She was well dressed, wore expensive jewelry, and was well-fed judging by the healthy tint to her skin—although he knew more vampires were going the spray tan route nowadays. She shifted in her chair, sending out a seductive cloud of perfume that he was positive Jazz would recognize. His hexy witch was well versed in all the female stuff that eluded the male mind. He sent out a small wave of power, trying to guess Esme's age, but for some reason wasn't able to gauge her actual age. He wondered why she felt the need to shield herself. He had a feeling if he wanted to know the truth, he'd need some help. Luckily, he knew just who to contact.

"When our kind is turned and leave behind human family members, we must literally leave them behind."

"I know that, but I want to see her for myself. Know that she's well," she said angrily. "They keep her locked up in that house like a prisoner, so there's no chance of my even getting a glimpse of her."

Nick nodded. "Let me talk to someone who might have a few ideas," he said as he reached for the phone. One ring later he heard a familiar voice. "Hey." His tone softened and then grew crisp when he noticed Esme's interest. "I have a client in my office who has a problem that you might be able to help out with. Any chance you can come over and talk with her?" He chuckled. "Sure, usual payment." He hung up. "My colleague will be here in about fifteen minutes."

"She?"

He nodded but volunteered nothing else. He'd sensed the female's interest in him the moment she stepped inside the office. He was positive if he'd returned that interest, his desk would have been instantly cleared of everything but their two bodies. Maybe it happened in books and movies, but he didn't consider it a good professional move for a private investigator, even a vampire one. And especially for one hooked up with a witch who could conjure up witchflame with a snap of her fingers.

Luckily, it wasn't long before he felt the shift in energy that meant Jazz was on the boardwalk. Not too long after he heard the faint whir of the old-fashioned cage elevator grind to a stop on his floor.

"You know, while you might be a total night person, I'm not." A whirlwind called Jazz swept into his office with a Venti Starbucks cup in her hand. She stopped short at the sight of the beautiful vampire seated in the client chair. Her narrowed gaze rose to meet Nick's amused one. "And I'm here because?"

"Jazz, this is Esme. Esme, Jazz Tremaine."

Esme's lovely features tightened and her fangs dropped. "A witch!" she spat out the word like a curse.

"Wow, you figured that out all by yourself?" Jazz sipped her drink. She was used to vampires hating her. Not that she understood it, since she was such a cute and cuddly witch.

"Ladies," Nick hastily intervened. He didn't want to think how this would go if either one got out of hand. There wasn't enough space for him to take cover. "Jazz, why don't you have a seat?" He glanced at a chair set nearby, but she promptly hopped up onto a corner of his desk, her legs swinging loosely. He should have known better.

"So, Esme, what's your problem?" Jazz asked, continuing to sip her drink.

The vampire took a moment before she replied. "I have a daughter that is taken care of by my family. I've always made sure she is provided for as long as I have access to see her, but now they take my money and refuse to allow me to enter the premises. They've had the grounds warded to bar me entry."

"The way I understood it, you vamps leave all mortal family behind once you've been turned," Jazz commented. "That it's safer for you."

"That's true, but my daughter is very precious to me."

Jazz looked her over with a sharp gaze that missed little. "In essence, you're dead to her. Why not let her think that? You're going to outlive her anyway."

The woman's glare was strong enough to cut her to the bone. "Clearly, you aren't a mother."

"I thought since you have an easier time moving among humans than we do, that you could check out the house and Esme's family for us," Nick interrupted.

Jazz didn't look away from Esme's face. "Address?"

Esme rattled off a BelAir address that Jazz immediately filed in her memory.

"I'll check it out today and get back to you tonight." Her smile held a hint of the same toothiness the vampire's did. "Say nine o'clock?"

Esme rose with the innate grace all vampires possessed. The whisper of silk was the only sound as she extended her hand to Nick. "Thank you." She merely nodded at Jazz and left the office.

Jazz didn't move from her perch, deliberately not saying a word for a few minutes.

"How many lies did she tell you before I showed up?" she asked.

"What makes you think she lied?" Nick settled back in his chair, propping his feet up on the desk surface.

She rolled her eyes. "Duh! The woman wouldn't know the truth if it bit her. Plus, she's heavily shielded. She probably has more than one charm on her. I'd say one charm to hide her true age and another one to hide her thoughts. You couldn't read her properly, could you?" She arched an eyebrow in question. She nodded. "Which is the real reason why you called me. Honestly, Nick, couldn't you see past the face and boobs?"

"I never noticed." But his pious expression didn't fly with her.

"Oh sure." She reached into her jeans pocket and pulled

out a card. She dropped it in front of him. "I'm making it easy for you. Just a healthy reload, if you please."

Nick picked up the Starbucks gift card. "Why do I feel as if my idea of a healthy reload and yours is completely different?"

"Then let me make it easy for you." She leaned over, jotting down numbers on a piece of paper and pushed it toward him.

Nick winced. Thanks to Esme, his bank account would be healthier than it had been in some time, but if he continued paying for Jazz's Starbucks addiction, he'd be broke in no time. "Done."

"Thank you," she cooed, hopping off the desk.

"You're not staying?" He eyed her form-fit jeans and body-hugging sweater.

"I just got in from driving a group of drunken gnomes to a bunch of parties. I'm tired, my ears are ringing from crazy gnome jokes, and I reek of gnome ale. I want a shower. You're on your own, lover." She stopped long enough to stretch across the desk and drop a kiss on his mouth. "I'll check out the address and will be back here before nine."

"Before Esme shows up," he deducted correctly.

"She can't be trusted." She headed for the door.

"Because she's a beautiful woman?"

She looked over her shoulder, her hand resting on the doorknob. "Because she's a liar. I don't like liars." She blew him a kiss and walked out.

"I wonder if all men have so much trouble with their women," Nick muttered, turning to his computer and typing in Starbucks' Web site address. He had a gift card to reload and he knew Jazz wouldn't be happy if it wasn't done by the time she showed up that night.

"Talk about major real estate," Jazz muttered, staring at the 1920s Mediterranean-style mansion enclosed by an eight-foot wall with security cameras mounted along the top and the closed gate that had a speaker box attached to one side. She parked back far enough on a side street facing the house that the security cameras wouldn't see her. "Who exactly lives there?" she mused.

"What did Jonathan tell you?" Irma asked from her spot in the passenger seat. "You had him use his computer skills, didn't you?"

"First thing this morning. The property owner's name is hidden under corporate shells." She tapped the steering wheel with her fingertips.

"So how do you expect to get in?" Irma asked, attempting a nonchalance that didn't work with a 1950s dress, white gloves, and pearls. "Are you going to try one of those spells that makes you look like someone else? Maybe you could pretend to be a maid? I would think a house that size has day help."

"Yeah, that'll happen," she muttered. "The last time I was a maid was 1872. Longest day of my life."

"A day? You could only last one day? I'd hate to see what your room looks like now if you can't keep a cleaning job for one day."

Jazz waved her hand for silence. "Forget my being a maid."

"Then what do you plan to do to get past that gate? I heard dogs and it sounded as if they run free on the property," Irma laughed. "You'll never get inside. Not unless you make yourself invisible, walk through that wall, and escape the dogs. What if you send the dog in there? He might be able to distract them long enough for you to sneak in."

"Right, like a ghost dog would attract their attention." Jazz clicked her nail against her teeth as she studied the elaborate dwelling a bit longer. Her smile brightened up as she turned to Irma. "Fine. You said you want to help me and *you can* walk through walls."

"Uh." Irma's gaze shifted from Jazz's smiling face to the house. "How do I know you won't drive off and leave me there?"

"Easy." Jazz grimaced and shoved at the ghostly furry head resting on her shoulder. "He's going with you and, as you suggested, distract the dogs in there." She tried pushing the massive head away, but he wasn't moving. The lack of a backseat didn't matter to a ghost dog. "Euww!" She gagged as she felt the chilled rush of dog tongue across her face.

"He likes you." Irma beamed, a proud ghost doggy mom.

"He can like me just as well from a distance." Jazz frowned at the dog before turning back to Irma. "How about it? Do you want to do some spy work?"

Irma's faded eyes lit up. "What do I have to do?"

Jazz leaned against the door and thought for a moment. "Be my eyes. Be my ears. Find out what's behind the walls and return without fear."

"That's a spell?" Irma's voice drifted off as Jazz snapped her fingers in front of her and she disappeared from the seat, the dog following her a second later.

"Now why couldn't she do that when I wanted her to?" she muttered. "Ugh! Bad dog! Bad! He couldn't do that before he left the car!" She cupped her hands over her nose. "How can a dead dog have such terrible breath and gas problems?"

Within ten minutes Jazz was wishing she'd stopped at Starbucks. Then she remembered that sipping her favorite latte would mean the urgent need for a bathroom.

After twenty minutes, she was impatiently tapping her nails against the steering wheel in time to the music coming from the radio.

"What are you doing in there?" She huffed a sigh.

"What a beautiful house!" Irma appeared as quickly as she had disappeared.

"*Ack!*" Jazz jumped. "I should have hung a bell around your neck."

Jazz glanced at the dog who looked entirely too happy. "I gather he was able to find some new friends?"

Irma scrunched up her nose. "I think her name was Willa."

It took a second for Jazz to comprehend. "You mean he—"

Irma nodded. "You wouldn't think it was possible, but he found a way." She patted the dog's head.

"So anyone looking outside would see one of their guard dogs humped by something they can't see?"

"Exactly. Now, don't you want to know what I found?"

"So you did find something?"

"Besides glorious furnishings out of a Jean Harlow movie that I wouldn't mind having for my room once you have it set up for me, I found a lot."

"Spill."

Jazz's grin grew wider by the second as Irma gave her a detailed report of the secretive house.

"Tonight is going to be soooo fun."

Chapter 7

"SO YOU'RE TELLING ME YOU FOUND SOMETHING IN LESS than a day?" Nick asked that evening when Jazz breezed into the office wearing an emerald silk babydoll top, black narrow-legged pants, and a cloud of Michael Kors. Her croc stilettos had turned themselves into sexy green slides and her hair was piled high in loose curls that put her close to Nick's six-foot height. He watched the moonstone drop earrings caress her cheek and thought about doing the same.

"What can I say? I'm good at what I do." She dropped into the client's chair. She held up one hand, palm up. "My fee?"

"Once I know what you came up with." Nick's head snapped upward. "Our client is early."

"Why am I not surprised?" Jazz stood up and moved to Nick's chair then stood up again. "No, you sit here and I'll take my usual spot." She perched on a corner of his desk.

"How good is your information?"

"So good that I'm probably going to royally piss off your client."

"What?" Nick's head swung from Jazz to the door as it opened and Esme walked in. Her warm smile for Nick dimmed when she saw Jazz.

"Nick," she murmured. "Ms. Tremaine," was uttered in a much cooler tone.

"Esme." Jazz's smile worried Nick.

"Were you able to see my daughter?"

"How old are you, Esme?" Jazz asked.

The vampire stiffened. "That is a very rude question."

"Oh please," she waved her off. "I'm 719 years old. Do you see me acting coy about it?"

Esme crossed one silken clad leg over the other, hiking her already short skirt up another few inches. A faint hit of displeasure tightened her lips when she realized Nick didn't notice.

"I don't see what my age has to do with this. All I hired you to do was find me a way in to see my daughter. Is this normal with your office?" She turned to Nick.

"Fine." Jazz ignored the snub. "Then tell me this. How does a vampire who's obviously using a shielding charm so no one can find out the truth about her have a living breathing daughter? Because. . .fiddledeedum, fiddledeedee, give me what I need to see." She snapped her fingers; Esme yelped as something crawled up under her silk top. "Aha." Jazz leaned forward and plucked up what appeared to be a scarab. She placed it on Nick's desk and slammed his paperweight on it. Multi-colored sparks flew around and magick shifted in the air. "There, that's better."

"Nothing like another dent in my desk," Nick muttered before turning to Esme. It only took a slight push of his power against her. "You implied you had been turned only a couple of years ago."

"I'd guess more like a couple hundred years," Jazz interjected a little too happily. "Which means either you have a child who you happened to turn. . ."

"Which has been illegal among our kind since 1735," Nick added.

"Or. . ." Jazz paused, "the child you claim is yours isn't. And since the sweet little girl in that house is living and breathing and barely six years old, I'm going for she's not yours."

"She is!" Esme's fury erupted. "She is the last of my line and I will *not* allow *them* to raise her."

"Who are 'them,' Esme?" Nick asked gently.

Jazz remained quiet, allowing Nick to do what he did best. She likened it to her being the bad cop and his being the good cop. She made a mental note to do this duet again.

Esme's beautiful features turned ugly. "*His* family. They have my line prisoner since I was first turned because that was the only way they could control the money and control me." She leaned forward. "The child in that house is my descendant, daughter of my daughter and so on. Each generation has been raised to marry a man in their family. And in each generation that girl dies within six months of the birth of a daughter with her trust fund going to her husband, therefore, his family. The trust fund for the baby is now under the control of her father." Her dark eyes flared with fire. "They have used powerful magick to bar me from the premises. The girl is tutored at home and is watched over carefully. I refuse to see this girl meet the same end."

"And you can prove this?" Jazz asked, still skeptical even if she could sense the truth in the female's voice and manner.

Esme's fingers trembled as she reached inside her small silk clutch handbag. Jazz's attention was briefly diverted from the subject as she wondered where the vamp had found the exquisite bag. "I can prove the Hastings wives all died before their first anniversary. I just can't prove it was murder. With their money, due to *my* family's wealth years ago, and the social connections they have fostered over time, they have been able to cover it up each time. The little girl in that house is named Ashley. I don't want to read her obituary twenty years from now."

I believe her. Jazz knew Nick could easily read her thoughts. While she didn't normally like his invading her mind, this was a time it was necessary.

So do I, but I don't see what we can do about it.

Your all-precious Protectorate?

They only deal with vampire problems. The family members are mortal.

Mortal with powerful magick. I felt those wards a block away.

"What is it?" Esme spoke sharply, looking from one to the other.

Nick nodded at Jazz, indicating she speak.

"Tell me something, Esme. Why did you marry a wizard all those years ago?"

"I—" She lowered her head, seeming to choose her words. "I didn't know he was a wizard at the time. I was mortal then and all I knew was that he was handsome, charming, and he loved me." She plucked at the delicate silk bag resting in her lap. "My father saw it as an advantageous match and I was envied by all my friends."

"So when did you learn he wasn't what you thought he was?" Nick asked.

"I knew he wasn't what he appeared to everyone, but I had no idea magick existed. Then one night we gave a ball and a handsome stranger attended. One who flattered me, hung on my every word, and made me feel beautiful," she said wistfully. "I had no idea he was a vampire and I was to be his next victim. Vincent rescued me from my crypt that first night I arose and he vowed to teach me what I needed to know to safely exist as a vampire. I wanted to return to my family, but he said it wasn't possible. I refused to listen. I wanted to see my daughter and I went to my family home. Frederick, my husband, thought at first I was a ghost and threw magick at me. When he realized I was of the undead he showed his true self. He needed money and my family had a considerable fortune. He warded the family properties against me to ensure I never approached them again. I remained nearby only to learn that my daughter grew up to marry a distant cousin and not long after her daughter was born she died in a riding accident." Her lips twisted. "It was no accident."

"Is there a reason why only daughters have been born?" Jazz asked curiously.

Esme shook her head. "It is only speculation on my part. Due to an eccentric aunt centuries ago who felt women should control their lives, the major part of the fortune was passed down through the women in the family and not the men. They could direct the funds if the girl is underage, but once she is of age, the money is hers. When she marries, it does not pass into the husband's hands unless she dies and there is a daughter."

"Was a solicitor used for all the paperwork?" Nick asked.

Esme nodded. "Frederick's family firm. His father and mine were classmates at University."

"So Frederick's descendants have played fast and loose with your money all these years?"

"What I have learned about Frederick's family over the years is that they value the power money gives them more than anything else. But in the last 150 years my family's fortune has been steadily dwindling as they have found ways to tap into the principal. I fear if they manage to control my latest descendant's marriage and ultimate death, the fortune will be completely gone. As will my family."

"Unless this girl produces a daughter. Which considering what you're saying it sounds like they use magick to ensure a daughter is born in each generation," Jazz mused.

Esme nodded. Her earlier hostility toward Jazz appeared to have subsided. "After I married I was given a special tea to drink every evening. It wasn't until after I. . ." she closed her eyes, "I became a Daughter of the Night, Vincent assisted me in obtaining a sample of the tea. The leaves were infused with magick to produce daughters only."

Nick glanced at Jazz.

"What?" She held up her hands. "Don't look to me for answers. I'm not the herbalist expert."

"But you can find out."

She mentally sifted through names as to who would know or give her a direction to look. "I'll see what I can learn."

She was definitely upping her consultant fee.

❖❖❖

Jazz looked out the window but only saw the rain sliding down the windows.

"What a perfect night to stay in," she murmured, taking two large mugs of hot chocolate out of the microwave and handing one to Krebs. She popped in a bag of microwave popcorn and set the timer.

"I've got the DVDs alternated between your choices and mine," he told her, spooning a large dollop of marshmallow crème on top then added to hers. He picked up both mugs.

"I'll be in as soon as the popcorn is ready." She dug out a box of cinnamon red-hot candies and added it to the stash of chocolate and the empty bowl waiting for the popcorn. She was looking forward to a night of hot cocoa, popcorn, candy, and tacky movies. "Which movie is first?"

"*The Thing from another World*," Krebs called back.

"Perfect." She was tempted to ignore the phone as it pealed a demanding ring, but it just wasn't in her. All Caller ID told her was that it was a wireless caller. "You better not be Dweezil," she warned.

"Not even close," Nick said tersely. "I think we have a situation."

"A situation as in. . .?"

"As in Esme. I'm on my way over to pick you up."

Jazz stared at the microwave that just beeped. "It's raining."

"As opposed to the Wicked Witch of the West, you don't melt."

"And it's cold out there." She pulled the bag out and poured freshly popped popcorn in the bowl. "We have movies. Wouldn't you rather come over and watch *The Thing from Another World* with us?"

"Definitely, but this is more important. You've got four minutes, Jazz." He hung up.

"Damn it!" She took a deep cleansing breath. "Krebs, I guess you're on your own tonight." She dropped off the snacks and headed upstairs. She knew if she wasn't ready on time Nick would drag her outside in her favorite Happy Bunny pjs.

"When are you going to tell me what's going on?" she asked, gratefully accepting the Venti mocha latte Nick handed her the second her butt was planted in the passenger seat of his Jeep Wrangler. At least the man knew what would help in the way of bribery. "I hope this thing doesn't leak."

"Hasn't yet. Make sure the lights are in our favor and no cops can sense me." He pressed harder on the accelerator.

Jazz's stomach tightened. She didn't know a thing and it already didn't sound good. "What is going on with Esme?"

"There was a message on my voice mail from her. She said she found a way to get onto the property and intended to make things right." He hit the freeway on-ramp well over the speed limit.

Jazz gripped her cup in one hand and hung on to the strap over the door with the other. Her lips moved silently, the words weaving spells that kept them safe and off the California Highway Patrol's radar—she didn't intend to end up a splat on the road.

Nick pulled through the open gates to the Fielding family home and skidded to a stop in front of the front door. He killed the engine.

"Can we go home now?" Jazz asked. "I left my stomach about ten miles back."

"Come on." He climbed out, oblivious to the pouring rain.

She yelped as the cold rain soaked her within seconds of exiting the Jeep. "Rain go bye-bye, keep me dry," she muttered. The bubble overhead stopped the rain except for still drenching her feet. "The door's open," she said unnecessarily, as they headed up the steps.

"Yeah." His black leather duster swirled around his calves as he moved past the threshold.

"Wait a minute!" She ran after him with the intention of asking how he could enter without invitation. The moment she stepped inside she had her answer.

An invitation wasn't needed if the master of the house was no longer living.

"Esme!" Nick's roar echoed off the high-ceilinged entryway as he strode across the tile floor.

Jazz didn't spare a look at the Monet gracing one wall or the Lalique vase centered on a small table. All she noticed was the smell of death and baneful magick tainting the air so strongly she could barely breathe. She feared what she would find in the room Nick entered, but she didn't consider herself a coward.

"What in Hades have you done?"

She flinched at the fury in Nick's voice. "At least he's not yelling at me," she muttered, picking up her pace.

When she reached the drawing room she realized Nick was actually keeping his temper at a low simmer compared to what it could be.

"Oh no." She found her legs couldn't support her as she slowly lowered her body to the floor in a kneeling position. "No." If the smell of death and magick was strong in the entryway, here it was suffocating. She choked on the stench and the magickal residue coating the walls.

Six bodies littered the antique Persian carpet with blood splattered everywhere. Not one face was recognizable because each was torn off.

Jazz was afraid to swallow for fear she'd throw up instead. But the dead bodies weren't bad enough. The sight of Esme seated on a nearby love seat with a tiny girl's limp body in her lap was downright chilling. Blood coated her silk pants and top with tiny drops even marring her exquisite features, but by the faint smile on her face she didn't care. Nick stood over her, the look of a dark avenging angel.

"How did this happen?" he demanded in a low voice that chilled Jazz to the bone.

"Your colleague said she was able to learn about the house using her ghost partner. I found a way to use a ghost to enter the premises," Esme said coolly. "While the walls were heavily warded, it seemed there were many weak spots in the house. They had grown too complacent."

"Fine, you didn't like them, but did you have to kill them? Kill the girl? An innocent in all this?" Jazz gasped, staring at the lifeless body drooped in Esme's arms and finally seeing the twin marks on the girl's neck and one tiny drop of blood on the flawless skin. "What kind of monster are you?"

Esme turned her head and smiled. "Ashley isn't dead." She tenderly stroked the girl's hair. "She's merely asleep. She will wake up soon and she will have no fear of dying."

Nick stiffened. "You turned her." If possible his voice turned even colder. Jazz looked at his icy features and saw a Protectorate enforcer.

She looked up, her lips still curved in the faint smile that hinted at a madness that had to have been simmering underneath but she had managed to hide well. "She's safe now. No one will ever take advantage of her."

The realization struck Jazz like a mighty blow. She pressed her hand against her stomach. "How could you do that? She was a child! And what you've done will *keep* her a child. She has no chance of becoming an adult, of finding love, of having a full life!" she shrieked at the vampire.

"And she will never die," Esme said in a level voice.

"You know our laws, Esme," Nick stated flatly. "You turned an innocent. A child. You will die. And she will die because she cannot be allowed to exist like this."

Esme shook her head. "There are no enforcers here and you wouldn't allow that to happen. You know what I did was right."

Jazz stumbled to her feet and lurched her way toward the love seat. She couldn't keep her eyes off the delicate features of a woman who thought nothing of sentencing a child to such a horrid fate. "There is *nothing* right about what you did and you have to pay for this crime."

Esme continued to smile and shake her head. "I thought you two would say that, so I came prepared."

"No!" Jazz shouted just as the other woman raised her hand then threw something to the floor. A puff of oily smoke erupted, sending Jazz and Nick stumbling backwards. "Be gone!" she shouted, but by the time the smoke dissipated, it was too late. Esme and the child were gone.

Nick took off in a blur of speed.

"Great, leave me with the bodies!" Jazz took off after him but she knew she couldn't catch up. She stopped at the open front door.

A few minutes later, Nick returned. Anger rolled off him in waves.

"She had help," he muttered, brushing past her.

"Do you have any ideas how we're going to explain this to the police?" she asked. "They're not going to believe our story about an insane vampire, some nasty magick, and all these dead bodies."

"We're not calling the police." Nick continued back to the drawing room.

"Then who—?" Jazz followed him. The minute she saw his expression she knew what his answer would be. Her stomach dropped into a freefall. "Oh no, not *them.*"

"I already called it in and a unit will be here in about five minutes."

She walked over to the stairs and sat down. "Maybe they were lying, cheating scum, but there had to be a better way to deal with them."

"After all these years, Esme felt there was no better way." Nick spun toward the door as a faint sound of heavy-duty engines sounded outside. "They're here."

"Oh boy. Protectorate lackeys. I'm such a lucky witch."

"Behave," he warned her, heading for the door.

"I always do." She groaned silently when Nick opened the door to a tall man dressed in black leather including fingerless gloves. His heavy bulk easily filled the doorway and he had the sort of face children ran from. He was also not one of Jazz's favorite vampires.

"Wow, Reinhold, look at you!" she gushed with all the enthusiasm of a rabid fan. "You're all fierce and dangerous dressed up in black leather like a *Matrix* wannabe. There's just one hitch with that look. I've got to say you're no Keanu Reeves."

The man easily stood six-foot-seven and was pure muscle. The fact that he had been a vampire for almost 1000 years meant power rolled off him like a living thing. Jazz heard he had been a solider in the principality of Galicia where he died in battle and awoke as a vampire. His bald head, mashed-in nose, heavily scarred bull-terrier features, and dogged personality made him the perfect enforcer for the Protectorate.

Jazz hadn't seen the big bad, not to mention highly insane, vampire in about 140 years and as far as she was concerned she didn't care to see him for another 140.

"The bitch witch." His growl would have sent the most ferocious Were running. "I should have known you would have something to do with this mess. Wasn't it enough you caused Clive Reeves' mansion to implode and end up in the fires of Hades? Did you have to make sure an entire family was destroyed? Amazing that no matter where you go you end up in a bloody mess. Literally."

"Ah, ah, ah. . .no names." She wagged her forefinger at him. "Didnt your mother teach you any manners where a lady is concerned?"

"I don't see a lady here and I ate my mother's bones for breakfast."

Nick walked past and grabbed Jazz's errant finger that had begun to glow a dark red. He lowered the digit before something happened. "The bodies are in the drawing room," he said tersely, cocking his thumb over his shoulder. "I checked the rest of the house and there's no one else here."

Reinhold nodded and jerked his head. Four men, also dressed in black leather dusters over black leather skintight pants and leather shirts, walked past him.

"Clean-up crew?" Jazz asked.

"She does not belong here," Reinhold told Nick with a curl of a thick upper lip. His matte black eyes shifted in her direction.

"Trust me, I fit in these surroundings a lot better than you do." She tried for the same curled lip but couldn't get the right effect. "And I'm not dressed as if I was ready to do some B&E in the local neighborhood like some vampires I could mention."

"Will you be quiet for just one damned minute?" Nick murmured in her ear before turning to the enforcer who looked as if he wanted nothing more than to tear Jazz into tiny pieces. "They are the last of their lineage, so no one will be looking for them."

Reinhold nodded. It was clear he didn't like Nick any more than he liked Jazz, but at least he was moderately civil to the vampire.

"The director will want a report from you by next evening," he said.

Nick nodded. He turned away when his name was called and he returned to the drawing room.

Reinhold's smile when he stared at Jazz wasn't the least bit pleasant. "You stink of magick," he growled.

"Gee, and here I thought my new perfume had one thinking more of spring rain," Jazz drawled. Her smile remained fixed but her moss-green eyes betrayed a cold hard steel that echoed the large vampire's gaze. "But better to stink of magick than of death."

He leaned in until they were nose to nose. "You've always been a pain in the ass, witch. Too bad no one thought to drown you at birth."

Jazz almost reeled from the fetid stench of his breath, but she refused to show any weakness. "Do us all a favor and greet the dawn."

Reinhold took another step further into her personal space. "I could tear out your throat before you could scream."

"And be dead a second later from my blood," she reminded him, wanting to think he wasn't serious with his threat but pretty positive he was.

"Nothing more than an old wives' tale." His eyes glowed a dark red as he moved another step forward, his fangs dropping.

A blur flew between them and Reinhold found himself tossed across the entryway. His body slammed against the wall, leaving a deep crater in the wallpaper. The air rumbled as if an earthquake was looming.

"You will never threaten her again," Nick stated in a low deadly voice. "The next time you do you will not live to see the following moonrise."

Reinhold jumped to his feet. "I never knew a witch could lead you around by the balls, Gregorivich." He used Nick's original surname. "Maybe it's better you're no longer an enforcer, after all." With a last killing look at Jazz he walked into the drawing room.

"Well, thank you. . .*whoa!*" Jazz yelped as her arm was almost yanked out of its socket as she was dragged outside so fast she couldn't come up with enough breath to utter a spell to keep her dry. She winced against the rain coming down in an icy sheet, soaking her in seconds.

"You just can't let it go, can you?"

"He started it," she muttered, cringing at the sound of tired resignation in his voice. She didn't mind if Nick was mad at her, but she didn't want him disappointed.

"And you're not five years old," he reminded her, not slowing his pace even as her heels literally slid across the wet slick surface. "Reinhold would have torn out your throat without a second thought."

"And died from ingesting my blood. Too bad we can't have his death without mine." *Shut up, Jazz. You're making matters worse.* But, as usual, she was ignoring the good gargoyle in her brain—the one that tried to keep her on the right track even when she tended to veer off.

Nick stopped so quickly Jazz slammed into him. "Fates preserve me," he muttered. He rounded on her, his forefinger pointed at her like a teacher reprimanding an errant student. "Let's review Vampires 101. We don't need our fangs to tear out our victims' throats." By now, his fury turned his eyes a glowing red.

Jazz tried to step back, but the fingers bracketing her wrist wouldn't allow her any room to escape.

"Got it. It's just that he's so nasty and what happened in there was so. . ." she realized she couldn't come up with a good enough description without comparing it to all the major slasher movies thrown together in one gory bloody mess. She turned green and pressed her hand against her stomach. "I don't feel so good."

Nick swiftly pushed her toward the Jeep and sat her down, gently pushing her head down to her knees.

"Better I throw up here than inside where *Herr* Reinhold can see me," she muttered, pulling in deep breaths. She waved a hand around. "Okay, better now." She slowly lifted her head.

"You didn't blink an eye at the carnage at Clive Reeves' mansion, yet you're ready to drop from seeing six bodies." Nick kept his hand resting against the back of her neck.

"Yeah, well, there was a lot more blood in there and since I was pretty much the cause for what happened at the mansion I couldn't go all girly there." She suddenly moaned. "How can you handle it? All the blood, I mean? Why didn't you go all fangy?"

"I fed before I left."

She straightened up more, his hand falling away. "You knew we'd find them all dead, didn't you?"

He looked at the house, his gaze distant in thought. "I had a gut feeling we'd find something bad."

"Bad? Bad is my hairdresser giving me bangs. Bad are Fluff and Puff finding my wand and waving up unimaginable spells. What we found in there was horrific. Was so ghastly that. . ." she shook her head. "I think I just experienced my nightmare for tonight and I didn't have to go to sleep to have it. I'm not sure if that's good or not."

Nick looked up and noticed Reinhold standing in the doorway. The vampire's dark expression wasn't much different than before.

"I'll be right back." He headed back to the house.

Jazz watched the two vampires. While it was tempting to use some magick to eavesdrop on their conversation, she didn't want to do it only to discover they were discussing the number of body parts found. Nick's expression had darkened and his features looked as if they had been carved from stone. He appeared to snap something to Reinhold then walked away, his body straight and tall. Reinhold watched him leave, a definite sneer on his face.

"Whatever it is I didn't do it," Jazz said as Nick moved closer. She yelped as he picked her up and tossed her fully into the passenger seat.

Without saying a word he started up the engine and navigated his way around two large black SUVs parked in a wide V.

"What did he say to you?"

"Nothing you need be concerned about," Nick said, tight-lipped.

Jazz sighed. She glanced over her shoulder and watched Reinhold still standing in the doorway. She might not know what the two vampires had said to each other, but she did know she liked the chief enforcer even less than she had before, and she'd hated him before.

"What are they going to do in there?" She figured Nick would answer that question.

"You don't want to know," he said tersely. "But they'll basically make it all go away. By the time the clean-up team finishes their part of the job no one in the neighborhood will ever know any murders occurred in there. The house and grounds will be put up for sale and life in the neighborhood will go on as before."

"The Protectorate will make sure no one finds out a vampire killed a wizard and his family," she murmured.

"And the enforcers will hunt down Esme."

"And destroy her."

"And the child."

"That is so not fair," she argued. "She's only a little girl."

"It is fair, Jazz. Otherwise, she will be six years old forever. As she grows in power she won't be able to handle the restrictions of her looks versus her age. I've seen it happen before and each time the young vampire grew insane because there was no way for the creature to deal with what went on. It's absolute cruelty to allow a vampire to exist in such a fashion."

She nodded. "Like Kirsten Dunst's character in *Interview with a Vampire*."

"It's the way of our world, Jazz. Just as there are things in your part of the world I don't agree with."

"I haven't eaten a child in centuries. My oven is for Toll House cookies only." Jazz picked up her Starbucks and wrinkled her nose at the cold taste but knew the caffeine would help. "Maybe Esme can elude them."

Nick cocked an eyebrow. "I was an enforcer for over eight hundred years, Jazz. There isn't any way she can elude our kind for too long. We're trained to track without stopping." He made his way to the freeway.

Jazz thought of the stack of classic horror and sci-fi movies waiting for her at home. After the last couple of hours they didn't sound as appealing as they had before.

"You know, sometimes it would be nice to have a nice normal life," she murmured. Since she was looking straight ahead, she didn't see the brief look of pain cross Nick's features.

Chapter 8

JAZZ FOUND HERSELF IN A WORLD FASHIONED OF SHADES *of gray ranging from pale ash to a deep charcoal. She turned in a tight circle, but could find no point of reference or any landmark to give her any idea where she was. For all she knew it could be the middle of the day or middle of the night. She had no idea why everything seemed not only dark but also unclear as if she was viewing her surroundings through clouded eyes.*

The faint outline of wraith-like figures moved around her, looking as if they floated through the thick ash-colored air. The silence unnerved her the most.

"Hello?" She reached out to touch one of them, and then looked down to see that her arm was the same non-color as the beings that glided around her. Her hand was partially covered by a dark sleeve of what appeared to be some kind of robe made of a coarse fabric that chafed her skin. It was nothing like her favorite plush robe that she liked to curl up in on cold winter nights.

"Where am I? What's going on? What are you? What am I?" she called out, but received no answer.

Frustrated by the silence from the others, she moved forward and discovered she seemed to be floating off the ground as they were. "Whoa, what in Fates is going on here?" She turned and found a familiar figure hovering nearby. "Nick!"

She flinched when the man, wearing a matching robe, turned toward her. It was Nick, yet not him. His skin was the same ashy gray as the other individuals around her. But what well and truly frightened her were his eyes. His beautiful eyes—the ones she likened to the color of the Irish Sea—were dead.

"Where are we? What is this place?" She started to touch his arm then drew back. She hated herself for her reaction, but this. . .creature in front of her was Nick.

His smile was sad and that alarmed her as much as his reply. "We're shades, Jazz. We lost the battle against Clive Reeves and now we are doomed to spend eternity with the others." He gestured with outstretched arms to include the shadowy figures that drifted aimlessly around them. No one looked at them. It was as if they didn't exist to the shades either.

That was when she noticed the rank odor that lingered in the thick air. It seemed like something tangible that she could taste as well as see and smell. She knew immediately what it was. A miasma of death surrounded them tainting the world she once saw in brilliant colors of the rainbow. Now that universe was nothing more than tints of gray and a dirty hue of white.

She turned her head, seeing a three-story building that stood a short distance away. The gothic architecture was all too familiar and through the fog were tiny dots of red along the base of the building. What chilled her blood, if that were possible, was the hazy outline of a man standing before an upstairs window.

"No." The word was a brief exhalation of air. "No." This time the word came out stronger. "He can't be alive.

*We killed him. He was draining your blood and I
screamed for justice for all the victims. That's when Irma
showed up and. . ." She paused to take a breath then realized she didn't need to because she wasn't breathing.
But it was the look of sorrow on Nick's face that caused
her the most pain.*

*"I'm sorry, Jazz, but that wasn't what happened. He
succeeded. You fought him so hard, but he fought back
harder. You made him so angry he killed you then he
drained all of my blood. He mixed our two bloods together, and with it he became stronger than ever. Now
he can never be destroyed." His sad words bounced
around inside her brain. "The hardest thing I ever had
to do was to lie there and watch you die and not be able
to save you."*

*She shook her head, denying what she heard. She re-
fused to believe what she saw around her. "No. This isn't
real. It's just another nightmare." She stepped back from
his outstretched hand. She was positive that if he touched
her she wouldn't be able to continue to deny his words
and they would take on a horrifying truth. "This is
wrong." As she turned away she looked at the mansion
again and viewed the monster she was positive she saw
die now looking down at her. And smiling. "You bastard!" She started running toward the house even if it
felt as if she was slogging through a thick goo. When her
feet touched the patio she suddenly bounced off something and fell back onto her ass. Caught up in her fury,
she tried again only to slam against the invisible shield
that refused to allow her to get any closer. She looked up
and saw Clive Reeves sneering at her—as if he felt all the*

fury and frustration in her body. He held up a crystal goblet filled with a ruby colored liquid and silently toasted her before lifting the glass to his lips.

"You will never win! Never!*" She screamed so hard and long her voice soon gave out. "Never!"*

"Jazz."

"Never!" She lashed out with her fists, connecting with solid flesh. A muffled *oomph!* reached her ears. Images of the man who caused her death continued to haunt her and she fought even harder.

"Jazz! Jazz!" Her hands were held in a vise-like grip that almost crushed her bones. "Wake up! You're having a nightmare. Come on, sweetie, wake up."

Her eyes popped open to find Krebs seated on the side of the bed, still holding on to her hands. A faint bruise was already coloring his cheekbone. She could see the slippers huddled in a corner of their magickal cage watching her with fear darkening their eyes. Even Krebs appeared uneasy as swirls of fear magick colored the air.

She pushed her damp hair away from her face, feeling the slickness of sweat coating her skin and the smell of horror on her. When Krebs was confident she was fully awake, he released her hands. She held them in front of her, relieved to see them a healthy pink color but trembling violently as if her nightmare still affected the nerves.

"I. . ." She struggled to find the right words to explain the terror that still bounced around inside her head. She pressed her fingers against her temples as if the pressure could drive the memories out.

"You were screaming the house down. I was afraid of what I'd find when I got up here." He rubbed her back and shoulders lightly. "That must have been some nightmare to spook you like that."

She thought of the colorless world her nightmare showed her. And the idea that Clive Reeves still lived while she and Nick. . .She swallowed the sob that threatened to travel up her throat.

"What happened, Jazz?" Krebs asked gently, folding his arms around her.

She shook her head then rested her forehead against his shoulder. "I'll never eat nachos before bed again," she muttered, wishing she could come up with a better lie. She was reluctant to tell him about her nightmare for fear it would return.

"Yeah, try again. I've seen the junk you eat before bed and nothing before has caused you to wake up screaming much less look like death warmed over." He paused. "Could your nightmare have anything to do with what you and Nick did last night?"

She grimaced at the memory of what she'd seen in the house. A memory she didn't care to have again, nor would she make Krebs suffer by sharing it with him. "I'm sorry I woke you up." She looked at the windows across the room. The open blinds afforded her a perfect view of the boardwalk in the distance where old-fashioned streetlamps dotted the walkway.

Nick.

Jazz had an intense desire to know that he was all right. That he wasn't the *thing* she saw in her nightmare.

She pushed herself off the bed and ran to the bathroom.

"What are you doing?" Krebs asked.

"I need to see Nick." She ran cold water over her wrists and splashed it on her face. She ran her fingers through her tangled curls and grimaced when it didn't make it look any better. "I have to know he's all right."

"Jazz, it's after four in the morning. I realize that's late afternoon for him, but still. It's dangerous out there."

She shot him a look as she walked out of the bathroom. "And that's a problem because—?"

"Fine, he's a super night person." He stood up. "But you're not going alone. I'll drive you over there."

She shook her head. "I can drive or even walk over. I'm sorry enough I woke you up."

He shook his head in an *it doesn't matter* gesture. "Look, you're rattled after your nightmare. I'd rather you stay home and calm down, but I know better than to try to reason with you. Still, you shouldn't be driving. Let me get my keys and I'll meet you downstairs." He left the room and headed downstairs.

Jazz heard the squeaks and chatter from the slippers.

"Everything will be all right," she promised them as she headed for the door even if she didn't know how she could keep a vow that she had trouble believing.

Jazz was impatiently hovering by the back door when Krebs walked into the kitchen now wearing jeans and a T-shirt and carrying his car keys. He eyed her with a faint frown. "Uh, are you going in your pjs for a reason?"

She looked down at her dark pink flannel pajama pants with Happy Bunny scattered over the surface stating *"Cute but psycho. It all evens out"* and a long-sleeved solid pink thermal T-shirt. The idea of changing her clothes was the last thing on her mind. She needed to see Nick fast and with her emotions in a turmoil casting an illusion spell wasn't a good idea. Fates knows what she'd end up wearing.

"Only ones out at this hour are early morning fishermen and they won't care," she said heading for the door. Her need to see Nick grew stronger with each moment.

Irma looked up from the Tyrone Power movie she was viewing when Jazz and Krebs entered the carriage house. The dog woofed a welcome as Jazz climbed into the passenger seat of Krebs's Porsche.

"Where are you going?" she called after them but not receiving a reply. "Is something wrong?"

"Everything's fine," Jazz lied.

With no traffic Krebs made good time reaching the boardwalk parking lot and Jazz was out of the car like a shot.

"Call me if you want me to pick you up later," he called after her, receiving a wave of the hand over her head that she heard him.

"I'll be fine. Thanks!" She turned around to run backwards and blew him a kiss then turned back around.

Jazz picked up speed as she ran toward the building. A locked front door didn't deter her as she gripped the handle. "Open says me, damn it," she muttered, pushing her power through the lock. Once she heard the click she pushed it open and raced for the stairs that descended to what had been a Civil Defense Fallout Shelter during the 1950s and Nick had fixed up as his lair. A shot of power on the heavy-duty locks released the steel door that opened with little fuss. Inky darkness greeted her and she could sense Nick's presence in the apartment.

"Light in hand, light to lead, light to see where I must be," she whispered, holding out her hand palm up. A small flame hovered over her palm giving her enough illumination to avoid the furniture as she made her way to the rear of the apartment where Nick's sleeping quarters were.

She paused to gaze at the man sleeping on the bed. Silence was heavy in the room, but it didn't bother her. She knew there would be no sound of his breathing or even snoring. What she needed was the comfort of seeing him. It brought a relief so strong she almost fell to her knees. She headed for the bed, lifting one side of the sheet and sliding in.

"Jazz?" Nick's surprised murmur was music to her ears as he turned over to face her.

She smiled, happy she'd arrived before he slipped into the true sleep of the undead that came at dawn. While Nick didn't need to rest during daylight hours, if he used his powers the night before, he needed those hours to recuperate. This would be one of those days.

"I needed to see you," she murmured back, wrapping her arms around him. She felt his smile against her lips as he kissed her. Now she felt complete.

"Nice surprise to see you," he murmured sleepily.

"I had a nightmare about us," Jazz said then stopped as she felt him slip from her. There were no windows in the apartment; no way to tell her the sun had finally peeked its way over the horizon. She only needed to feel the literal dead weight in her arms. Nick would be in this vulnerable state until sunset. She felt a tear track its way down her cheek and fall onto Nick's bare shoulder.

"Something's happening, Nick," she continued talking even though she knew he was beyond hearing her. "It's bad. I just know it. And I don't know what to do." She rested her cheek on his shoulder. "I'm so scared that we won't survive this. I want you to tell me we'll make it."

Jazz closed her eyes and was soon able to doze off. She knew this time, with Nick's arms around her, she would sleep without bad dreams.

Coffee. I need coffee. Jazz's eyes opened on that thought. She still lay curled around Nick, but he didn't stir. She slid out of bed.

"Time to go," she said softly. She leaned over, dropped a kiss on Nick's lips, and used a small flame to make her way through the dark apartment. She secured the steel door after her and the same with the building door. Before she ventured further she cast an illusion spell so that anyone seeing her would see jeans, T-shirt, and tennis shoes instead of her pajamas.

She barely walked fifty feet before a familiar voice stopped her in her tracks.

"Any reason why you think a guy can get it up when he sees you wearing Happy Bunny pajamas? I know my dick likes something a lot more sheer."

I couldn't have coffee and a muffin before facing him? Or better yet, not see him at all, she mentally asked as she turned around. She could see that Rex hadn't changed since their last meeting. If anything he looked, and smelled, even more disgusting. And if she wasn't mistaken, he was wearing the same clothing.

It was bad enough only the preternatural kind would notice the odd smells of some creatures. To a human being Rex would only appear to be a pretty ugly guy with hygiene problems. Just as her illusion spell wouldn't fool him, she saw his true form as well. Repulsive.

Rumors were he had a drop-dead gorgeous girlfriend, however.

Hm, maybe the girlfriend literally was dead. Now that concept she could see, no matter how gross the idea was, because she couldn't imagine a living female wanting anything to do with him. Her chest rose and fell with her deep sigh.

"What do you want, Rex?"

"You off my property."

"It's not yours." And that she could say with surety since she'd once had Krebs do his own computer magick and check out the boardwalk ownership the first time Rex ordered her off *his* property. The corporation name didn't sound like it belonged to a Were-pack and since she could smell that Rex didn't seem to be able to afford a good body wash, she doubted he could afford the payments on the popular piece of property.

Still, she also knew that appearances could be deceiving, which was why his grin had her mentally backpedaling. An angry Were meant teeth and claws.

"Funny thing, Rex. Until you stopped me I was on my way home. So I'll tell you what. You go do whatever you do, like maybe take a long hot shower with plenty of soap, and I'll head home. Deal?" She brought up a bright smile she didn't feel.

His eyes narrowed and when he spoke, there was a dark rumble in his voice that meant danger.

"I want those fucking slippers. *Now.*"

"You promised me time to look for Willie and that time isn't up," she reminded him, while mentally reminding herself she had to do some serious work on finding the Wereweasel. "And even then you have no right to take them into custody. There's a council to deal with them, and you know how cranky they get if someone thinks they can usurp their job."

"That's not a problem. I've contacted them about the matter. As far as I'm concerned, time's up, so be prepared for the Ruling Council to show up any time now. Have good day, Jazz." With that missile he turned around and walked away.

Jazz took several deep breaths to calm her racing pulse. "Shit. Shit. Shit. Shit. Shit." While she wanted nothing more than to race home, she knew she had to appear calm, cool, and collected. Unfortunately, at the moment, she was none of the above. She had to act as if nothing was wrong. Which was so false it wasn't funny.

Instead, she was swiftly crossing the boardwalk's parking lot in her Happy Bunny pjs, her heart crawling up her throat, and her blood pressure at an all-time high. All in all, her morning wasn't starting out well. Not that the night before had been all that much better.

"I should give those little monsters a real scare and hand them over to the Ruling Council," she muttered, even as she knew she wouldn't give in to Rex's demands. She was determined to keep Fluff and Puff with her until one of the members of the Ruling Council showed up at the front door with an official order stating she had to give them up and even then she'd stall the magickal authorities as long as she could. The thought was enough to have her picking up her pace.

"Don't answer the door today," she said, barging through the back door and collapsing at the kitchen table. She flicked her fingers at the door, watching the lock engage itself.

"Right now you look like you need medical attention. I've never seen your face so red." Krebs poured her a mug of coffee and set it in front of her. "What did you do, run all the way home? I told you to call me to pick you up."

Jazz gulped down coffee and picked up a piece of buttered toast from Krebs's plate. "Rex went to the Ruling Council about Fluff and Puff." She was at the point she wasn't sure whether to be mad as hell or frightened out of her wits. The Council tended to do that to her. The Witches' Council was bad enough, but the Ruling Council was even scarier, because their word was law for everyone and they didn't believe in a Court of Appeal either. For some, they were judge, jury, and executioner all in one.

Krebs got up long enough to pop more bread in the toaster. "What's so terrifying about the Ruling Council?"

"They oversee all of us. The Witches' Council takes care of only witch issues, the Protectorate enforces vampire law, and then there's the Weres, the elves, the. . ."

"Okay, I get the message." Krebs held up his hand. "So this Ruling Council is in charge of everyone."

Jazz nodded. She got up and rummaged in the refrigerator, pulling out a jar of black raspberry preserves.

"There's seven members and if a member of one group breaks the law against someone in another supernatural community it's up to the Ruling Council to pass down judgment." She pressed her hand against her stomach.

The word for the day is queasy.

"Judgment as in. . .?"

She nodded. "If you're declared non-guilty you go free. If you're guilty you're destroyed within five seconds. There's no appeal process with them."

"Whoa, you guys really don't fool around, do you?" He shook his head. "But I thought you said nothing can be done to the little guys. That they have some big bad magick that protects them."

"They do, but the Ruling Council overrides all magick." She sipped her coffee and racked her brain. Why was Rex pushing so hard? "If I provide you with a name, can you find out about someone?"

"Sure. Just give it to me and I'll run some searches."

Jazz snagged pen and paper and wrote out what she remembered.

"I promise not to make fun of your next three girl-friends," she vowed.

The look on Krebs' face had her wondering if there was something going on she wasn't aware of. If she wasn't so freaked about the slippers she would take the time to pull it out of him. *Inquiring witches wanna know.*

"Six." He knew her well.

"Four."

"Five, including the woman I'm seeing now."

Aha! She knew there was something going on. "That makes six."

"Do you want the information or not?"

Jazz knew her computer skills were limited to e-mail and online shopping. Anything more complicated required Krebs and she didn't have the time to read *Internet for Dummies*.

"I won't continue to push for a pool," she threw out.

"Four girlfriends and no whining for a pool."

She stuck out her hand. "Deal. And I don't whine."

Krebs sighed as he accepted it. "Something tells me you're still getting the better part of the deal." He took the paper and stood up. "I'll see what I can come up with."

"Thank you. Krebs. I love you." She made kissing sounds.

"Yeah, yeah, yeah." He waved the paper over his head. "Just don't bug me by asking if I've found anything yet."

Once Jazz finished her quick breakfast, she headed upstairs to interrogate the slippers.

"I want you to tell me the truth now. Did you or did you not eat Willie?" She stared into the two bunnies' eyes, desperate to see the truth written there. But she also knew her slippers were excellent liars.

Fluff chattered away with Puff adding on to it. They admitted a few minor wrongdoings that night, but nothing that required consuming a wereweasel.

Jazz sat down on the floor, tucking her legs under her. She pressed her palm against the cage bars, feeling the strong magick hum against her skin. "I swear if you're lying to me, I will give you up to Rex right this very minute and not wait for the Ruling Council to show up."

Puff bounced up and down, his chatter high-pitched.

"Then where did the button you coughed up come from?" She listened closely to Fluff's explanation.

She raked her fingers through her hair then conjured up notebook and pen. "Okay, things I should have asked sooner, but we'll go through it now. Let's go through this all over again and I want everything. Tell me exactly where you went that night and where you found the button." Jazz took notes of the slippers' movements and once they finished their story, she put the notebook on the bed. She went into the bathroom and took a quick shower, then dressed.

"With everything else going on I've got to say your timing sucks," she told them. "But if I can help it, no one will take you away. You'd better hope I can find Willie before someone shows up. They don't waste much time, you know." The slippers blew raspberries as she slipped on the stilettos, which turned a dark plum color to match her tunic style sweater draped over navy pants. She sniffed and looked down at the shoes. "Did you ladies use my Michael Kors perfume? Honestly, Delilah, you're wearing my Nars lip gloss!" For a minute she was sorely tempted to toss the perfume and makeup-stealing shoes into the back of her closet, but they did look good on her feet and felt as if she was walking on air. "I'm such a girl," she muttered, realizing the comfort of the stilettos was good for her soul right now.

When she reached the second floor she paused by the side of the house that was left open for Krebs' work. The energetic sounds of the Beach Boys flooded the open space and an exasperated "Don't call me, I'll call you," drifted out toward to her.

"Okay, okay." She spun on her toes and went downstairs instead, listening to the stilettos chatter about their plan to take the tub away from the rubber duckies. "Stay out of the tub," she ordered. "Even Fluff and Puff know better than to take them on. Those beaks aren't on them just for decoration, you know."

As Jazz crossed the backyard, she idly visualized a pool and spa taking over one corner. Just because she promised not to continue begging for a pool didn't mean she couldn't dream about one.

"A spa and pool would be so cool, because I say so, damn it!" she whispered, flicking her fingers at the section. The air shimmered for a moment before a hewn-rock pool and spa replaced the lush green lawn. She stopped for a moment to admire her handiwork before sighing and recalling nosy neighbors that might look out their windows. "Pool and spa go away, come again some other day, because I say so, damn it!" Just as fast, the lawn was back to its green splendor and the pool and spa were history.

When Jazz entered the carriage house, she found Irma seated in the easy chair she'd gotten her now that she was free of the car when she wished, the dog sitting beside her, his massive head draped over the chair arm. A curl of smoke wafted upward.

"Krebs will not be happy if he walks in here and smells cigarette smoke," Jazz announced. "And that he can smell."

Irma's cigarette disappeared in the wink of an eye and she waved her hand to dissipate the smoke. "You'd think if he can't see me he couldn't smell the smoke," she grumbled, giving Jazz a ghostly evil eye.

"If he had his way no one would smoke within a hundred miles of the Porsche he loves more than life itself." She paused to look at the TV screen. *"What are you watching?"* She almost turned her head upside down to understand better what was on the screen. She almost shrieked when she realized just what it was.

"It's called *The Naughty Nymphs*. I thought it was a fantasy movie, but it wasn't long before I realized it wasn't, but once I started watching it I found myself unable to change the channel," Irma explained, keeping her eyes forward, while absently stroking the dog's head. "I'm trying to figure out how the men and women can do that without damaging something. Or that." She pointed at the screen. "How is that physically possible without hurting something important?"

"TV off," Jazz ordered. There was no way she was watching a sex film with the ghost! "It's a good thing I pay the satellite dish bill because there's no way I'd want to explain to Krebs you were watching a pay-per-view X-rated movie."

"I couldn't find anything to watch."

"You have how many hundreds of channels to watch along with stacks of DVDs and you claim you have nothing to watch?"

Irma shrugged. "Well, nothing that looked interesting. Where do you intend to drag me off to today?"

"This is purely a visit." Jazz perched herself on a nearby chair she usually sat in when she watched a movie with Irma.

"You never visit me." Her lower lip took on a decided curl.

"I stayed up all night with you for that *Die Hard* marathon," Jazz argued.

"That was a month ago. The only time you come out is when you're going somewhere."

"At least I don't make you stay in the carriage house all the time." She pulled up a stool and sat down. "Besides, I'm out here with good news."

Irma looked skeptical. "Good news for you or good news for me?"

"So suspicious!" She waved off Irma's distrust, brilliant sparks floating off her fingertips. She looked over at a nearby table piled high with magazines and clothing catalogs. "Do you have an updated outfit in mind?"

Irma's expression switched from suspect to hope. "Do you mean. . .?"

Jazz nodded. "I think I have the right spell to provide you with a new wardrobe."

Irma mentioned a woman's clothing catalog that lifted up from the table and floated toward her. Jazz took it from the chair after it settled through Irma's ghostly body.

"Page forty-three," Irma whispered.

Jazz opened to the correct page. Her initial fear that Irma had chosen something so inappropriate she'd gag just looking at the picture was replaced with relief. The pants and coordinated knit top was in a dusty rose shade that would complement Irma's skin tones and full figure. She placed one hand over the outfit, while the other hovered over Irma's shoulder, and closed her eyes.

"New clothes and style you wish. All modern as can be. Ask and you shall have what you require from what you see. I request this be done now because I say so, damn it!"

"Oh my!" Irma twittered, as a shower of sparks rained down then swirled around her in a multi-colored tornado. The dog barked and backed off quickly, his head down and hind end up as if thinking it was playtime. "What's happening to me?" Irma shouted.

"I hope you're getting new clothes," Jazz muttered, now fearing the ghost would appear to her naked and that was a sight she so didn't want!

"You *hope?* Do you mean you don't know for sure that this will work?"

"No spell is perfect!" Jazz started to worry as she realized the sparkling tornado didn't dissipate as quickly as she thought it would. She suddenly had a vision of Irma trapped eternally in the magickal tornado and she would be the cause of it. The ghost would never let her forget it either. "Oh boy, this isn't good at all."

The tornado seemed to whip faster around the chair. "No, it's not! *Help!* I'm getting dizzy!"

"Quiet!" Jazz ordered the dog that now raced around the carriage house barking his head off. He skidded to a stop and plopped his butt down on the floor. He stared at the tornado with a fascination only a canine could show.

"I feel all tingly," a voice erupted from the tornado that was finally slowing down and sliding off until it disappeared altogether. Irma still sat in her chair, but the navy print dress, white gloves, and straw hat were now replaced with the pants and top from the catalog. And her gray hair had been restyled in a short stylish cut. Her Tangee lipstick was gone and a rose lip color was in its place while a more natural looking blush highlighted her wrinkled cheeks.

"Wow, I do good work!" Jazz crowed, conjuring up a full-length mirror. With the magick infused in the glass Irma easily saw her new image.

"This is what I look like now?" Irma asked, stood up, and turned this way and that to get a better look at herself.

"You're looking at a new millennium, Irma." Jazz couldn't stop grinning. "From now on all you have to do is see the image of an outfit and you can wish it on yourself. The only thing I ask is that you don't start wearing spandex or too many sequins. Actually, no sequins at all."

"What about the holidays? Everyone wears sequins that time of year."

Jazz had a feeling if she didn't give in now she'd be haggling all day. "As long as you're not covered with them."

Irma's smile was ear to ear and if Jazz wasn't mistaken, there was a hint of tears in her eyes. Nah, she had to be mistaken.

"Thank you. I was very tired of that same old outfit. I felt as if I was still living in *Father Knows Best*." She named a popular television show from the early 1950s. She walked toward Jazz with her arms outstretched.

"Boundaries!" Jazz squeaked, backing up. There was nothing ickier than a ghost walking right through a body.

Irma dropped her arms. "I forgot. Your body doesn't feel very good to me either when I walk through you," she admitted. "But I'm still so grateful you did this for me."

"You're welcome." Jazz smiled back. She looked at the dog that appeared to be more morose than usual.

Considering his mastiff face looked mournful most of the time, it wasn't easy to tell when he was happy. Except the slobber factor was more extensive. A flick of her fingers provided a bright red collar around his neck complete with ghostie dog license hanging from it. He perked up at the feel of his new finery and barked a thank you. "Just don't drool anymore in the car. Or on my clothes. Or in the carriage house." Even as she spoke, she saw strings of ghost doggie dribble slowly drip to the floor and immediately wrote off her plea as a lost cause.

She looked at Irma who was now busily studying the magazines. "Uh, don't switch your wardrobe too often," she warned. "This is all new to me and I'd hate to think you'd end up with ten different outfits on at the same time."

"It's just nice to have a change." Irma ran her hand over her hair. "Although I do wish you'd done something with all these lines and wrinkles. Can you work on a spell for that now that you have the clothes figured out? And what about coloring my hair. Not a trashy red like yours. Perhaps a tasteful ash blond or warm brown." She returned to her magazines. "Do you think Botox would work on a ghost?"

Jazz sighed. "The woman never stops."

Chapter 9

"WAY TO GO, MY FAVORITE SON!" JAZZ SHOUTED, HUGGING *her sweaty and dirty son. A tiny girl with a copper red ponytail that matched her mother's, wearing dark green shorts and a print sleeveless top, stood by Jazz's leg. "You kicked the winning goal!"*

"Mom!" He wiggled free, looking about as embarrassed as a ten-year-old boy could look. "Besides, I'm your only son."

"Oh yeah, that's right. Twenty-two hours of labor will do that to you," she teased, resisting finger combing his hair back from his forehead. Moms of sons could get away with only so much and her baby boy was at the age where public displays of affection were a death sentence.

"Way to go, sport!" The man beside her was tall, blond-haired, and gorgeous. He wore an artfully faded plum colored polo shirt tucked into a pair of jeans. He picked up the boy who resembled him all the way down to the broad grin and spun him in a circle. "You take after your old man."

"The coach said we're all going out for pizza, okay?" He looked from one to the other.

"Go and have fun." He pulled his wallet out and handed him a few bills. "Just don't OD on the arcade games, okay?"

"Thanks! Love you both!" He ran off to join his teammates.

"Mommy! I wanna go too," the little girl whined, hug-

ging Jazz's leg so tight it was amazing she didn't cut off the circulation.

Jazz looked down and smiled at the daughter who was her very own mirror image. "Sorry, sweetie, but this is your brother's day. How about you, me, and Daddy go out for our own special dinner, how is that?"

At that moment a pair of warm arms encircled her from behind and pulled her back against a body that smelled warm and inviting. She melted back into his embrace.

"Are you sure there's not someone we can fob her off on? Think what kind of dinner we could have with no kids around for a few hours?" he whispered in her ear.

"A dinner that wouldn't include food, I'm sure," she murmured, feeling that familiar tingle deep within her body.

He rested his chin on top of her head. "I might feed you. . .eventually. Thank you for two fantastic children, my love."

She followed the direction of his gaze, watching Kirk climb into an Explorer with his best friend, Ryan, right behind him. She and Ryan's mother joked the two boys may as well be twins since they were never far from each other. While four-year-old Melissa "Missy" was already promising to be a handful.

Jazz quickly thought back over the last twelve years. Who knew life could be so fulfilling? She had a wonderful husband who could alternately make her laugh with joy and scream with pleasure. She had two children who made each day a joy to wake up to. She had everything a woman could want for a perfect life.

Just then a shadow seemed to pass over the trio as if a cloud drifted across the sun. She turned her head and looked *toward the edge of the soccer field where a stand of trees edged the park. A tall figure stood there, leaving no doubt in her mind that his attention was focused on them. Even at this distance she could feel his eyes on her, dark, intense, and with a passion that robbed her of her very breath.*

Jazz couldn't see his face from that distance, but deep inside she knew what he looked like as if he stood right in front of her. He had hair the color of her morning coffee, eyes the greens and grays of a storm-swept sea, and the heart of a warrior. He was a man who loved with the fervor of one who knew that love was meant to be cherished like a rare treasure. She could feel her heartbeat increase and her skin turn warm as if he physically touched her.

"Hey, you okay?" Her husband's voice pulled her from the stranger's influence.

She shook off the spell and tipped her head back, offering him a bright smile. "I'm fine."

They walked back to the minivan that any busy mom needed when she had two kids and everything from soccer to ballet lessons. Her husband draped his arm across her shoulders while Missy skipped along beside them, chattering about where she wanted to go for dinner, which alternated between McDonalds, her favorite Chinese restaurant, and IHOP. Jazz could only resist the pull to look over her shoulder for so long. When she finally did turn her head the figure was gone and she experienced a sense of loss she couldn't explain.

You don't need him any longer, *a husky feminine voice whispered in her ear.* Look at the wonderful life you have. You're much better off this way and you know

*that, don't you? As a mortal, you have much more than
you ever did before. You can have all this and more, if
you wish for it.*

As if the words were a wake-up call, Jazz struggled to
open her eyes then wished she hadn't.

"Ow!" She pressed her fingertips to her forehead in
hopes of pushing the headache right out of her skull. Jazz
didn't get too many headaches, maybe every twenty
years or so; but when she did get them they were doozies
and this one was off the charts. She sat up, gingerly rubbing her temples. "Oh for Fates' sake, it was only a
dream about being mortal. There's no reason for me to
wake up feeling as if I was one," she muttered with an ir-
ritable sniff as she crawled out of bed.

As she passed the cage, Fluff and Puff growled and
snapped at her while the stilettos squeaked in fear and
backed away from her.

"Hey!" She hopped out of the slippers' biting range,
wondering why she couldn't understand their angry
chatter. "Knock it off! You know you won't be released
until I can prove you didn't kill Willie." She stumbled
into the bathroom and turned on the shower faucets. She
knew the medicine cabinet wouldn't yield any aspirin,
so she'd beg some from Krebs after she drowned herself under a spray of hot water. "Oh, this is bad." She
made the mistake of looking at herself in the mirror.
There was nothing like ruining her morning with puffy
reddened eyes and blotchy skin to go with the killer
headache. Not a good way to start a day and even worse
when she'd planned a shopping trip. Victoria's Secret's
big semi-annual sale began today and she planned to be

there when they opened their doors. There was nothing like big discounts and sexy lingerie to perk a witch up.

Jazz's head hadn't stopped pounding by the time she dressed and applied makeup since her illusion spell seemed to be on the fritz.

"Do you have any aspirin?" she asked Krebs when she stumbled into the kitchen.

"Aspirin? Don't you have a witchy remedy for headaches?" He didn't take his eyes off his BlackBerry as he worked his own form of magick on the keypad.

"Nothing that works for this one." She opened the cabinet by the sink and pulled out a bottle. She tossed a couple of tablets back with a chaser of coffee and pulled a microwaveable breakfast of eggs and pancakes out of the freezer. "Anything we need while I'm out?"

"Nothing I can think of." He returned to his texting.

"I'll pick up something for dinner." The microwave dinged and she pulled her meal out. She forked the eggs into one of the pancakes, folded it, and ate it like a taco.

"You do remember you have something like twenty computers upstairs with much bigger screens than that one?" She stood at the counter eating her breakfast and watched his fingers fly across the BlackBerry's keys.

"I'm texting a guy back East."

"Oh yeah, that makes a lot of sense." She swallowed more coffee.

Krebs paused and looked up, this time really seeing her. "Did you have a nightmare last night?"

Jazz froze with the folded pancake halfway to her mouth. Her thoughts ran a mile a second as she tried to relive her night.

"It wasn't a nightmare as in dreaming monsters were trying to eat me or tear me apart. The dream I had was almost nice. It was more what my life would be like if I was mortal with the husband, two kids, and a minivan. Not a scary moment there. But then I wasn't wearing shorts, so I don't know if I had any cellulite." She ignored the memory of the shadowy male figure standing among the trees and reached for her coffee mug and polished off the contents before refilling it. "All that happened was that I woke up with a killer headache." She glanced at the brightly colored coffeepot-shaped clock on the wall. "Off to the mall. Victoria's Secret waits for no one."

"Don't forget to leave something in the stores for others," he advised.

"I'll try to restrain myself." She let herself out the back door and headed for the carriage house. "Irma, where are you?" She walked in and noticed the interior was silent with no sign of the irascible ghost or her ghost dog companion. Jazz couldn't even find a hint of ectoplasmic drool or doggy poo on the garage floor. Not that she was complaining, but it wasn't like Irma to wander far from the carriage house even if there were days her newfound freedom went to her head. "I'm going to the mall and if you're not here in two minutes, I'm leaving without you!" When she didn't receive an answer she shrugged her shoulders and climbed in her car.

As Jazz backed the classic T-Bird out of the carriage house, she realized this was the first time in more than fifty years she was alone in the car. There was no argument over radio stations, the smell of cigarette smoke in the air, or someone telling her she was driving too fast. And no ghostly dog hanging his head over her shoulder.

She should have enjoyed the drive, but even with the radio playing it seemed too quiet. She planned to leave later in the day for Moonstone Lake for the full moon ceremony. She wondered if Irma wouldn't be accompanying her this time and what had the ghost in such a snit she was avoiding Jazz.

Jazz parked the car outside of Nordstrom and left for the store entrance. She was still feeling more than a little wonky from the dream trickling through her mind every so often and hadn't thought to cast the illusion spell over the car. And she still couldn't figure out why the slippers and stilettos acted so odd toward her.

"Sure, Jazz, as if they haven't acted strangely before," she muttered, pushing the heavy glass door and entering the kingdom that offered her idea of therapy.

When Jazz left the mall several hours later she was loaded down with bags and nursing some tired credit cards. She juggled the bags as she used her cell phone to call a local pizza place to arrange a delivery to the house. She knew she'd be home in plenty of time to accept her mushroom and beef pizza and Krebs's Canadian bacon and pineapple pizza. The fact that her son in her dream was going out for pizza hadn't eluded her thoughts.

"I should zap all of you to the car," she muttered, quickly grabbing a heavy bag as it started to slip from her fingers. She started to move forward only to find her path blocked. Since the section of the parking garage was a bit dim, she could only see the outline of a man's body covered by a hooded sweatshirt and baggy jeans that looked as if they hadn't been washed in months. The *eau de* trashcan preceding him confirmed it.

"Gimme your wallet." His face was pockmarked with acne scars, and eyes cold and dark as he showed her a wicked-sharp knife. He looked her up and down, his tongue flicking out to lick his lips. For a mortal he showed a distinct lack of humanity.

Here she'd had a beautiful day shopping and this jerk was trying to ruin it! Not if she had anything to say about it. "Bad timing, slick. See all these bags? I just left the mall and I left it broke. You should have tried to rob me before I went in."

He sneered and poked the knife at her. "I said gimme your wallet, bitch."

"Bitch? Big mistake, scumsucker." She dropped the bags and threw out her hands. Except instead of the expected whoosh of a fireball or even nasty sparks, there was nothing. "Big bad boy turn into a toy, because I say so, damn it!" Again, there was nothing. Not even a tiny fizzle. A cold lump settled in the pit of her stomach.

"Very funny." He lunged forward, the knife almost sticking her in the stomach with the wicked point.

"Hey! This is so not good!" She danced to one side, wildly looking around for some help, but couldn't see a soul. She threw the bookstore bag at him figuring the weight of the magazines and paperback books she'd indulged in would take him down, but he easily dodged the flying bag that burst on contact with the ground and scattered her purchases everywhere. When she tried to conjure up a fireball nothing happened. "What in Fates' sake is going on?"

Before Jazz could react, the man lunged forward and grabbed her shoulder bag and pulled it away, almost dislocating her shoulder in the process. Pain shot through her shoulder as she again tried to fight him with magick, but nothing happened. She felt a brief sense of victory when she managed to score his skin with her nails.

"Bitch!" Before she could escape, the back of his hand connected with her face with stunning force. As she fell to the ground he hopped forward and kicked her in the stomach while his fists and feet rained down on her head and body.

Lights out was her last thought, as everything turned black.

Jazz's first thought was that her latest nightmare surrounded her with pain that had invaded every cell in her body. Her second thought was that this pain was way too real to be a nightmare.

"Jazz?" The male voice was familiar and music to her ears.

Jazz moaned as she tried to open her eyes but discovered they would only part a bare slit because it hurt too much.

"Hey you," Krebs whispered with a relieved smile on his lips.

"What happened?" She almost cried as she listened to her garbled words. Oh yeah, the pain was mega-real as it streaked across her face.

"You were mugged, babe." He sat gingerly on the edge of the bed. He wore a wrinkled gray T-shirt and jeans and his hair stuck out in all directions as if he'd used a lawn mower on it. The scariest part was the look of fear in his eyes. "Hey." His voice softened as he carefully brushed her hair from her forehead. "Did someone with bad *mojo* go up against you and you lost the battle?"

She started to shake her head but agony spiking her skull warned her it wasn't a good idea. "No, it was some really bad-smelling thug with a knife who wanted my money." Tears pricked her eyelids. "He hit me and kicked me, Krebsie. And it hurt. . .a lot."

Krebs looked up as a doctor wearing rumpled blue scrubs walked in with a medical chart in one hand.

"I'll be honest with you, Ms. Tremaine. You are one lucky lady," he announced, glancing at the chart. "We thought your cheekbone was broken, but only the skin was split. That can easily be stitched up. You also have two black eyes, a pulled tendon in your shoulder, a bruised kidney, some sprained ribs, and your assorted cuts and bruises. You're fortunate to even be alive. Bastards like that usually do some even more serious damage. You could have ended up in a body bag."

"I should have been able to take him down," she whimpered, struggling to sit up and allowing Krebs to help her. "Nothing worked on him."

"You look like a savvy lady, Ms. Tremaine," the doctor said. "It's best not to fight someone like that. He was probably high on drugs and when they're like that, they don't stop to think; they just react. It's always best to just give them your purse and live to tell about it." He made some notations in her chart. "We'll get that cheek stitched up, prescribe something for the pain, and there's no reason why you can't go home after that. I'd suggest you see your own doctor within the next few days."

Jazz liked the idea of going home where she could wallmail Lili and see if she could suggest something to take the pain away. And to think she used to bitch about cramps and headaches!

"Thank you, Doctor." Krebs held her hand tightly.

"What's wrong with me, Krebs?" Jazz whispered, once they were left alone. "I tried to shoot him with a fireball, but it didn't work."

He shook his head. "I don't know, baby, but if anyone can find out why it's you."

She swiped at her wet cheeks with her fingertips. Krebs pulled a tissue from a box on the table and handed it to her.

"I guess it's a good thing my blood's the same as a mortal's or they'd want to send me off to one of those creepy science labs and dissect me," she whispered, accepting the tissue and carefully dabbing her eyes.

"I called Nick and told him what happened."

A spark of life brightened her eyes as she looked around, but once she realized the vampire wasn't nearby, the spark died a quick death.

Krebs shook his head. "He didn't think it was a good idea for him to come inside." He lowered his voice. "I don't think he'd fed recently. He said he'd pick up the car for you and get it back to the house."

"I want to go home." She couldn't believe she was whimpering. She hated women who whimpered, but right now she felt like a major wuss. "I want my own bed and my own pillow."

"We'll go as soon as they finish up with you. I promise." He dropped a kiss on her forehead and gently combed damp strands of hair away from her face.

Jazz considered herself a strong woman. One who could put up with pretty much anything that came her way. She'd battled all sorts of ugly creatures in the past and present. She worked for Dweezil, for Fates' sake!

But feeling as if a big rig truck had driven over her then backed up to run over her again, and the humiliation of vomiting on the doctor's shoes after she received five tiny stitches in her cheek, pretty much finished what was a ghastly day.

"I feel awful," Jazz moaned, as the nurse later wheeled her out to the parking lot and helped her into Krebs's Porsche. Luckily, the local anesthetic they'd injected in her cheek meant she didn't feel the stitches right now, but she was certain when it wore off she'd be feeling them big time. The doctor had also given her a painkiller for everything else and she should be flying high. Instead, she felt sick and miserable.

"You'll feel loads better once you're tucked into bed." He paused. "You don't feel like hurling again, do you? No offense, but I just had the car detailed."

She managed a soft snarl. "I'll try to give you a two-second warning." She looked out the window and saw the full moon hanging gently in the sky. She should be in Moonstone Lake with Stasi and Blair. Instead she spent the night feeling as if she had been turned into a pincushion. She closed her eyes to shut out the calming picture of the gentle night that was only making her feel more depressed.

She fell into a drowsy state during the drive back to the house. Krebs parked the car outside the carriage house. Jazz blearily stared at her T-Bird parked inside and wondered what happened to Irma since she wasn't anywhere in the building. She couldn't see the dog either. Feeling groggy from the pain meds, she imagined Irma taking the dog out for a walk. Now that would be a real Kodak moment.

"What in Hades' name happened? How could she have been injured?" Nick appeared near the car. A touch of fear darkened by anger crossed his sharp features as he looked at Jazz's battered face.

"Nick!" Feeling better just seeing him, Jazz jumped out of the car and ran to him, leaping up and wrapping her arms around his neck and her legs around his waist. "It was awful! This really smelly, nasty guy beat me up! And he took my new Dooney and Bourke bag! I want you to find him and fang him really good," she ordered with bloodthirsty relish. "I bet you can still find his scent on me, so you can track him down. Turn him into mincemeat, okay? Take all his blood but don't turn him because I'm sure he'd make a really disgusting vampire. But make him really suffer first. Make him cry like a baby and beg for mercy then tear his throat out."

She was so lost in her murderous thoughts she didn't see the revulsion cross Nick's features just before he dropped her and stepped back. Jazz yelped as her butt connected hard with the cement driveway. Great! That was one of the few body parts that wasn't hurting before.

"You're human!" he exclaimed.

"Huh?" Not her best moment, but the drugs had totally messed up her thought processes.

Nick retreated another step. His features were still twisted with a pained expression she'd never seen before. "You smell of blood."

"Well, duh! I just got out of an ER and the creep beat me up! And he tore my favorite top." She stumbled to her feet and swayed before she caught her balance. She started toward him but he backed up more with his hands up, palms out as if to ward her off.

"Don't come near me." Nick shook his head violently. "Your blood doesn't smell of magick. It's human. You're mortal." He pronounced the word as if it was a curse.

Jazz froze at his words. "No, it can't be. *I* can't be. I'm just beat up and messed up because of the drugs they gave me. Doctors in the emergency room love to give pain meds by the dozen. It's just an off day for me."

His eyes briefly flared red as his fangs dropped. He waved his hands in the air as if he could spell her away from him. "I can't be here. I can't be around you when you're like this. I'm sorry." He walked backwards then quickly turned around and strode off without looking back.

As Jazz watched him leave she seemed to shrink within herself. She stared into the patch of darkness that Nick had disappeared into. "And here I thought being attacked was my nightmare," she whispered, ignoring the tears streaking her cheeks and her nose running like a sieve. She was the epitome of the sad waif with her tangled hair, the tiny black stitches bisecting one cheek, her smeared makeup, and torn clothing. The sassy witch had never looked, and felt, as wretched as she had that night.

And now she felt as if a piece of her heart had been torn from her. She swiped her sleeve across her nose.

"I feel awful, Krebsie." Her chin trembled with the onslaught of more tears as her body swayed from side to side.

"I know, babe. Come on." Krebs put his arms around her and guided her toward the back door. "Let's get you cleaned up and tucked into bed. You'll feel a lot better after you've had a good night's sleep."

"Can I have hot cocoa with tiny marshmallows to help me sleep?" Jazz asked in a plaintive voice as she stumbled along beside him.

"Sure, you can. Anything you want."

"With real milk and real cocoa and not the packet hot cocoa you use with water and stick in the microwave?"

"Made from scratch."

"And cinnamon toast with lots of butter and cinnamon sugar on it?"

"Thanks for asking for something I can manage." He kept his voice soft and soothing as they went inside the house. "Once we've got you in bed I'll fix you some hot cocoa with miniature marshmallows and a plateful of cinnamon toast."

"Hello? What happened to Jazz? Is she all right?" Irma called out from inside the carriage house, but her questions went unanswered. "When Nick picked me and the car up at the mall he only said she was attacked by a mugger and he had to go to the hospital. Helloooo!"

Chapter 10

"I DON'T UNDERSTAND HOW THIS COULD HAVE HAPPENED to her. She looks terrible!"

"Well, of course she does. She was robbed and beaten! Anyone who'd gone through what she had would look bad. Although, she does look worse than I thought she would. She looks like a black and blue patchwork quilt."

"None of this makes any sense. Normally, she could take care of a sleaze like that guy without a second thought. He should have been in the emergency room having his body parts reattached, not her ending up with all those cuts and bruises. And stitches! What happened that she couldn't do something to heal herself?"

Jazz kept her eyes closed as she mentally demanded that the voices go away, but she knew that wasn't about to happen. She groaned as she silently evaluated a body she refused to believe was hers. No doubt about it, she was in a serious world of pain. And now she was dreaming that two women were talking about her. Lifting her eyelids proved to be a real chore and hurt like hell as the morning light assaulted her eyes. The only things that kept her from screaming were the women sitting on the bed.

Stasi and Blair perched on either side of her, their legs stretched out in front of them, each cradling a mug of coffee in their hands. The aroma of the rich brew with the tantalizing scent of chocolate and mint was sheer heaven to her nose.

"I thought I was dreaming." She almost gagged on her words. When did a cotton field end up in her mouth? Oh yeah, Krebs had forced a pain pill down her throat after he helped her undress and get into bed before he went off to fix her hot cocoa and cinnamon toast. She had barely finished her comfort treat when she closed her eyes and floated off to the land of Nod. "I am so glad to see you! But what are you doing here? What about your shops? You can't afford to leave them." She started to shift her body to give hugs but quickly realized any movement promised pain along with refusing to down-right cooperate.

"What? You think you can end up almost killed and we wouldn't come down to make sure you really are all right? No offense to Krebs, but we were not about to depend on his assurance that you're still in one piece. Plus, there's no problem in closing the shops for a few days. Our customers will appreciate us more if we're not easily accessible," Stasi said. She took one arm while Blair took the other and they gently helped Jazz sit up amid a bunch of "ows" and "oophs." She reached over to the night table and picked up a third mug and handed it to Jazz.

Jazz stared at the blue plastic cup with a special lid on top as if it would reach up and bite her. "A sippy cup? You're giving me a sippy cup?"

"Trust me. With a mouth that looks like you had major amounts of collagen pumped into it, you'll prefer drinking your coffee this way." Blair looked ready to cry. "Oh honey, how did this happen?

"I have no clue." Jazz started to shake her head then realized what a bad idea that was when the world spun around like an out of control Tilt-A-Whirl. She took a tentative sip of her coffee and discovered the sippy cup was an excellent idea for her cut and bruised lips. "This creep wanted my money and I told him his timing sucked since I was coming out of the mall. He wasn't all that amused. I tried to send the mugger a fireball and nothing happened. He was ugly and smelled bad and he started hitting and kicking me. And he took my new Dooney and Bourke bag too." Her friends offered the appropriate sympathy for her loss. She swallowed the tears that threatened to erupt. "Then when Krebs brought me home from the hospital, Nick didn't want to be around me. He said my blood smelled mortal. That my magick is gone." Her whimper was sad enough that any woman would think that chocolate had been banned worldwide.

Both witches exhaled shocked breaths. Blair leaned in and hugged Jazz. "Pain! Pain!" Jazz yelped. The other witch backed off a bit with an apologetic smile. Stasi settled for stroking Jazz's fingers and crooning softly over the broken nails and badly chipped nail polish. She conjured up a nail file and buffer and began repairing the damage.

"You need some poultices and some healing spells to heal the cuts and draw out the bruises," Blair said, climbing off the bed and heading for the wall left blank.

"I tried wallmailing Lili last night but nothing happened." Jazz rested her head on Stasi's shoulder, watching her smooth the ragged nails. Her witch sister murmured comforting words as she worked. "I think the wall is broken."

"It works fine," Blair said after uttering Lili's name, which appeared on the wall in graceful cobalt calligraphy.

Jazz was stunned as she stared at a wall that still appeared blank to her while Blair spoke to it and waited for a reply.

"Is Lili answering her?" she asked, sounding listless as she looked.

Stasi nodded. "Blair told her what happened to you and asked her what we can use to heal your injuries," she whispered.

"Then why can't I see it?" But she already knew the answer. Nick had been right about her last night. The wall was still magickal, but she wasn't.

Blair's expression wasn't hopeful when she returned to the bed. She climbed back to her spot beside Jazz.

"Lili said our spells won't work since Jazz isn't magick right now. If she was here she could heal Jazz, but she can't leave the hospital right now. They're short-handed due to a flu epidemic. I know she would come in a heartbeat if it was life-threatening. And she said to use white vinegar to draw out the bruises."

Jazz's spirits sank even lower. "Great, add a little oil and herbs and I'll smell like a salad. I'm hurt and not on my deathbed, thank the Fates. You know what? I think I'll just remain in bed with the covers pulled over my head until this all goes away." Then the horror hit her. "But what if it doesn't go away?" She sat up straight, swiveling from one to the other. The pain in her head and body was dizzying, but she did her best to ignore it. "What if I'm like this from now on? What if I remain mortal? I won't be able to work as a curse eliminator or drive for Dweezil. Okay, that's not a total bad thing since he's more sleazy than a slug, but the pay is so good!"

Stasi and Blair didn't have any answers for her, but they were there with their warmth and comfort as Jazz burst into noisy tears that weren't about to stop any time soon.

"Why don't I run you a nice hot bath?" Stasi suggested once the tears started to taper off leaving Jazz with pasty skin and a red nose. She helped Jazz off the bed and steered her toward the bathroom. "It won't get your stitches wet, and you can relax with the Jacuzzi jets running."

"A bath would be good," Jazz replied in a small voice, allowing herself to be guided and seated on the commode while Stasi filled the tub and poured in bath oil that smelled like berries and mint.

"My magick can't be gone forever," Jazz went on, staring off into space. "It must have something to do with my nightmare."

"You had another nightmare?" Blair asked, standing in the doorway. "You said in your last wallmail they were happening, but since you hadn't mentioned it again we thought they had stopped."

"I wish they had. This last one was different. I dreamed I was mortal with a husband, two kids, and a minivan, and look what happened? I woke up mortal. I just didn't realize it at first since I hadn't done anything that required magick. Something like this had to have been formed by magick. So if it's because of the dream, the effects can't last forever, can they?" She appealed to her friends.

"Of course they won't," Stasi soothed, helping her out of her pajamas and gently brushing her hair before coiling it on top of her head and carefully pinning it in place. "You sit there and soak and after your bath I'll help you wash your hair. Just remember not to touch your stitches with a wet hand."

Once Jazz was in the tub, Stasi returned to the bedroom and searched through the closet for clothing that would be comfortable against Jazz's injuries and easy for her to get into.

"This is bad, Blair," she whispered.

"I know." Blair crouched by Fluff and Puff's cage. The bunny slippers wore their most innocent expressions and anyone who didn't know any better would think they were blameless of the accusations that had been leveled against them.

Crushing the T-shirt and cotton lounging pants in her hands, Stasi dropped down to the bed, the clothing falling to her lap. "What happened? How could Jazz lose her magick just like that?"

Blair shook her head. "I don't know. This makes no sense at all. She said she dreamed about having a mortal life and then she wakes up actually mortal. I can't think that the Witches' Council would have done this to her as some sort of punishment. Besides, they always believe in giving warnings first and Jazz didn't mention being in trouble with them. At least, nothing lately."

"And when you think about it it's not a stunt that Eurydice would do. She's threatened Jazz and many of us in the past, but no, I can't see her behind something like this. Magick is so much a part of our lives and now she's lost that and we have no way to help her." Stasi absently smoothed out the wrinkles in the shirt she had just crushed. "It was scary enough when Krebs called to tell us Jazz had been badly hurt, but now seeing and hearing her. . ." she took a deep breath. "She's. . ."

"I think the word you're looking for is pathetic, which is so not Jazz," Blair said and Stasi nodded.

Stasi's sunny brown hair framed her face as she looked down at Jazz's turquoise soft cotton T-shirt lying in her lap. With her heart-shaped face, brown eyes, and fair skin she looked like dark-haired Alice. And with power that gave Cupid a run for his money she was in her own form of Wonderland. She made good use of her romantic nature in the lingerie shop she owned at Moonstone Lake. Blair preferred anything retro and owned a shop that carried everything from vintage Madame Alexander dolls to 1950s dinette furniture. Both shops in the small mountain village were popular with the skiing tourists during the winter and fishing and hiking tourists in the summer.

"Nick's right, Blair," she whispered. "I don't sense a speck of magick in Jazz."

"I know," Blair said quietly, sneaking a snack to Fluff and Puff, then offering a treat to the stilettos that sidled up on either side of her with worried murmurs on their lip-glossed mouths.

"I better get in there before she decides to drown herself." Stasi disappeared into the bathroom long enough to leave Jazz's clothing on the counter. When she returned to the bedroom she found Blair standing before the wall, reading messages written in different colors as word of

Jazz's plight reached the other witches. She'd put out the word of a witch-in-need and the "sisters" had responded in force. When the entire class of 1313 had been banished from the Witches' Academy, they were left adrift in the outside world to make their way or die trying. Over the centuries they never lost touch with each other and banded together when it was necessary. The original banishment was only supposed to last 100 years—as long as they behaved. 700 years later they were still wicked and still banished.

"This hasn't happened to any of us before," she said. "And no one has any idea how Jazz's magick could have been taken from her just because she dreamed she was mortal."

"Which has to mean someone caused this with magick," Stasi said in a low voice. "There's no way it couldn't have been done without someone wielding a powerful spell."

"Krebs said she's had nightmares for some time. She's positive they're caused by magick, so this is definitely part of it."

"Well, if someone wants her to suffer they found the perfect way to do it." Blair waved her hand, wiping the wall clear of messages. "Jazz without her magick is not the Jazz we know and love. She's nothing more than a hollow shell."

"Maybe it's like a twenty-four-hour bug and she'll wake up to be her old self tomorrow."

"And maybe Johnny Depp will show up at the front door and ask me to have wild monkey sex with him."

"Honestly, Blair, you're so negative!"

Jazz's scream had them racing into the bathroom. She had a towel wrapped around her wet body as she leaned over the counter and stared into the oval mirror hung over the sink.

She turned to them, her expression wild with horror. Her ear-splitting wail bounced off the walls.

"I have a zit on my chin!"

"Nikolai Gregorivch, you are the vilest, most heartless vampire I have ever had the misfortunc to know! How could you abandon her in her time of need? How could you leave her when she needed you most? What were you thinking?" Blair's fury almost melted Nick's eardrums. He regretted answering his cell phone without checking Caller ID first.

"Hello, Blair. How are you? I'm doing fine, thank you for asking," he said, walking down the sidewalk with a fluid stride. Even though it was late at night and he was walking through a section of L.A. most people would avoid during the day much less after dark, he was left unmolested as if the lurkers sensed he was a bigger predator than they could ever hope to be. "To what do I owe the pleasure of this call?"

"How I am is nothing compared to what Jazz is going through right now." She sounded as if she wanted to come through the phone and tear out his throat. Considering her magickal gifts had to do with revenge, it wouldn't take much for her to do just that. "Do you know what she did today?"

He pushed down the sorrow that welled up. "I'm sure you're going to tell me whether I wish to know or not." He had to keep his emotions in check or he'd be as bad as Jazz was. Leaving her the other night tore a piece out of him, but he had no choice if he wanted to hang on to his sanity. Jazz had stood there, scratched, stitched, and bruised looking so hurt he felt her pain as acutely as if it had been his own.

This time Blair's fiery curses did blister his ears.

He looked straight ahead and saw what he was looking for. "Blair, great to talk to you, glad you had a safe drive down here, but I've got to go. Let's do lunch." He switched off the phone in mid-rant and clipped it to his waistband.

The trio of young men lounging by a seedy bar could have been triplets in their baggy jeans and hooded sweatshirts. But it was the middle one that interested Nick. It only took a visit to the crime scene and finding the man's scent, plus the necessary time, to track him down. If there was something Nick prided himself on it was his hunting skills.

"You looking for anything special?" his intended victim asked while the other two melted into the shadows.

Nick smiled, allowing his fangs to show and his eyes glow a deadly red. "I think I've found it."

"Being mortal sucks. I don't like it," Jazz moaned the words she'd used all day until Krebs retreated to his work with mumbles he not be disturbed for *anything*. Stasi and Blair were this close to running out of patience. "Fluff tried to bite me through the cage bars! The stilettos slid under the bed and refused to come back out. I can't see Irma, although maybe in a way that's a good thing, but it's not the same. And I bet I stepped on the dog, but I couldn't tell."

"That dog is something else," Blair muttered. "The hairy monster tried to hump my leg."

"He's done a lot of that lately." Jazz sighed. "Not that I know anymore."

She picked through the box of candy until she found a Bordeaux brown sugar cream and nibbled on it. "I have a zit that's almost as big as my chin. And I gained four pounds in one day!" She plucked at the waistband to her lilac plaid cotton pants then rearranged the hem of her solid lilac fleece hoody over her tummy that she was positive was podding out big time. "There has to be a way to banish this spell before I turn into a balloon!" Her words were garbled from the chocolate mint truffle she next stuffed in her mouth. "And look at this! Nothing. It hasn't glowed once!" She gently stroked the moonstone ring she wore on her right ring finger. The milky blue stone usually glowed a faint ethereal light in response to her touch. Now there wasn't even the faintest of flickers. Her chest rose and fell with the deep heart-rending sigh of the emotionally suffering individual.

"I still say it's some sort of curse." Stasi looked up. She sat on the floor using the coffee table to hold the books and scrolls she'd checked out of The Library where she'd spent a good part of the day and most of the evening. Even though it was past two a.m., the three women were sprawled in the family room with Stasi reading while Blair and Jazz watched DVDs. Jazz idly leafed through a few spell books she asked Stasi to bring back to her since she knew The Librarian would allow Stasi anything while he would have lent Jazz only grief. She quickly discovered that her new mortal brain couldn't assimilate the magick infused in the paper, how-ever, and she finally shoved the books aside.

"Great, a curse hits the curse eliminator. How ironic." Jazz started to pick up another chocolate, but Blair snatched the white See's box away. The battle was short-lived when Blair caused the box to disappear into thin air. "Where did you find The Library's realm?"

"It was in the center of a lovely botanical garden that featured a fishpond filled with these gorgeous carp," Stasi said absently, studying her books. "I'd love to go back and see more of the gardens."

"Terrific. You get a pretty fishpond. I get an X-rated bookstore or the county dump for an entrance," Jazz grumbled. "Even more proof how much The Librarian hates me."

"Maybe if you were nicer to him," Stasi suggested.

Jazz thought about the notion for a second and just as quickly discarded it. "Nah, he'd just hate me more." She swiveled around to glare at her friends. "And why didn't you tell me Dweezil called? Not that I really care, but it would be nice to know what's going on in my own house."

"How did you find out?" Stasi had the deer-trapped-in-the-headlights look.

"Duh! Caller ID."

"I told him you're sick."

"I can imagine that went over well." By now Jazz was just plain depressed. "Since he never gets sick he doesn't believe anyone else does either."

"I wasn't about to tell him you had become mortal."

"Oh, no way." Jazz looked around her for a snack but couldn't find anything within easy reach and she was too lazy to get up and root around the kitchen for something. She decided maybe it was better she taper off since her stomach was feeling a bit wonky after all the chocolate she'd eaten. She might have to ask Krebs for some Alka-Seltzer. "The entire supernatural community would know what happened to me in no time. He's a worse gossip than Minerva."

The other two witches were very familiar with the tarot card reader based in Capistrano who managed to ferret out closely kept secrets and broadcast them faster than the Internet. No one with something to hide went anywhere near the woman.

"I mentioned you had a very bad rash all over your face due to a spell gone wrong. He said to call him when you get your looks back. That if you looked that bad you wouldn't be of any use to him right now anyway."

"That's Dweezil. All heart. I bet he won't even spring for a get-well card. Actually, come to think of it, for all I know his kind doesn't even have a heart. You know, if my magick doesn't come back I'll have to find a job and we all know I don't do well with mortal jobs. I don't want to stand in a store entrance greeting people! Or ask someone if they want to upsize their order! I can't do that! I need my life back!" she wailed.

Jazz flopped back down on the couch, hugging one throw pillow against her chest and another stuffed under her head, her tangled hair looking as if it hadn't been brushed all day—which it hadn't—and her bare feet dangling over the side. She hated to look at her feet since her ever-present gold ankle bracelet with the amethyst studded broom charm had vanished. It was bad enough that she required a nasty smelling cream for a zit that she swore was expanding by the second, but when her ankle bracelet abandoned her during her time of need it was downright heartbreaking.

She hated to think what she'd wake up to in the morning.

Blair took up the other side of the couch, but she'd thoughtfully covered her feet with fuzzy socks so her ankle bracelet wasn't visible.

"Is that a rash?" Jazz curled her body upward to peer closely at her bare ankle. She scratched the patch of red scaly skin then scratched harder. "Does anyone know what psoriasis looks like?"

Stasi and Blair exchanged telling looks over Jazz's bent head.

"I wonder if you don't have some kind of odd magickal virus and all we can do is wait for it to work its way out of your system," Stasi said.

"Then why doesn't Lilibet know there's a virus targeting witches running around? Or am I the lucky witch. . .non-witch. . .to get it?" Jazz was well on her way to earning an Oscar nod for her portrayal of the most pitiful witch-turned-mortal in history.

"Did The Librarian have anything to say about all this?" Blair asked as she filed and shaped her nails.

Stasi grimaced. She didn't look at Jazz as she muttered. "Just that it couldn't happen to a better witch."

Jazz whimpered and buried her face in her hands. "He's not a wizard; he's a nasty troll with an evil sense of humor. He knew some of the spell books you checked out were for me and the only reason he let you take them was because he likes you. If I'd been able to go in there, he would have turned that damned hourglass over and told me I have an hour in a dark, smelly, and moldy alcove with who knows what scurrying around. And now it's only going to get worse for me. Do you know what I saw in the mirror when I was in the bathroom?" She paused for maximum effect before sobbing, "Crows feet! And then I found this!" She held something up between her thumb and forefinger.

Blair leaned over to get a better look. "Is that what I think it is?"

Stasi's mouth dropped. "It can't be. It's not possible."

"It is exactly what you think it is." Jazz nodded. "A gray hair!"

"Well, you are seven hundred and—"

"Do not even go there, Stasi!"

"What if we talk to the Witches' High Council," Stasi suggested. "Eurydice might know of a solution. I can't imagine she would allow this to happen to any of us."

"She'd probably agree with The Librarian that I deserve this like some horrible punishment. You know what? I'm done. I'm going to bed and if I'm really lucky I'll wake up in the morning and discover all of this was part of my nightmare." She peeled herself off the couch. "And if I ever get my magick back I'm tracking down that mugger and I'm turning him into a warthog. Then I'll turn him into disgusting slime and pour him into a bucket and ship him to Nick." She slowly climbed the stairs. "As for fang face Nick Gregory, he sucks big time! I hope he drinks tainted blood that turns him into a hobgoblin! A really ugly foul-smelling hobgoblin that needs to be banished to the Under Earth." With each ascending step, Jazz's revenge plans turned more gory and bloodthirsty. By the time she reached her room, Nick had been sliced, diced, and stuck in a crematorium. Both Stasi and Blair released sighs of relief when the door closed on Jazz's ranting. They dreaded to think what else she'd come up with.

"I'm not sure which is worse. Jazz as a mortal who's so wretched it's downright scary or her getting her magick back and going on the warpath," Blair said. "At this rate, no one will be able to live with her."

"I hate to admit it, but I'll be relieved when we return to Moonstone Lake." Stasi pulled a scroll toward her and began scanning words written in an archaic language. "None of what happened makes sense, Blair. She has a dream about living a mortal life and then wakes up mortal. While I'd still like to call this a virus, it's just too easy to say that. Plus, if that's the case, then the idea of this happening is frightening. That would mean if it happened to her, it could happen to any of us. . ."

Blair reached down, sorted through the books, and chose one. She wrinkled her nose at the musty smell that rose up as she turned the pages of a book that was easily a thousand years old. "Oh yeah, not a good thing and something Lili definitely needs to be made aware of. Maybe she can come up with a vaccine for it."

"Only if it does turn out to be a virus and not a spell."

"Just as Jazz said, a curse against the curse eliminator." Blair exhaled a deep breath. "But if it's a spell, who cast it against her and why? This isn't some everyday spell your ordinary witch could cast. Something like this is very complicated and it would involve a lot of power. Probably even a wizard's power and possibly even someone's blood to make the spell work right. If that's the case I don't look forward to whoever cast it against her because Jazz won't care how many years are added on to her banishment when she goes looking for payback. She'll turn that person into a microbe that can still see and feel. And that's only if they're lucky."

Jazz didn't turn on the lights when she went into her bedroom. No way she wanted to see her pitiful self. She knew her ponytail was falling out of the scrunchie she'd haphazardly jammed it in and her hair felt dry with split ends; her clothing was so rumpled it looked as if she'd slept in it for a month; and she was positive the zit on her chin was expanding to the same massive proportions she imagined her body was doing. She was convinced by morning anything was possible. She could even imagine she'd wake up looking and smelling as disgusting as Tyge Foulshadow. Thanks to his dirty deeds at Clive Reeves' mansion where Nick was almost destroyed and she would have ended up the maniac's pet, he had been sanctioned and banished to his world, wherever that was. All she knew was that it wasn't a realm she cared to visit.

She didn't bother brushing her teeth or washing her face. In her frame of mind, she didn't want to look at her disgusting self in the mirror and she didn't care who she might offend with halitosis or gross out with her bad skin. Without even undressing, she crawled into bed and pulled the covers over her head.

"With my bad luck I'll dream I'm married to Dweezil and we have three million little Dweezils." She choked on her words.

As she drifted off into a self-induced tortured sleep, breathy words laced with a hint of evil laughter floated through her head.

You're not as invincible as you thought you were, are you, little witch bitch? What a shame I couldn't make your time of mortality last longer, but I hope you enjoyed your adventure. But don't be too complacent, my dear. There's no reason why it can't happen again. And next time your new adventure could last forever.

An eardrum-piercing scream from upstairs was their first warning.

Stasi sighed as she poured herself coffee and topped off Blair and Krebs' cups before sitting down at the table. Syrup-drizzled waffles sat in front of each of them. "Oh dear, it's gotten worse."

"I don't even want to think how much worse it could be." Blair shuddered.

"You two have it easy. I have to live with her. Unless you want to take her back with you. Maybe it would be a good idea for her to get out of L.A." Krebs looked ready to bolt from the room.

"Don't even think about it," Blair warned him, easily guessing his thoughts. "I'm more than ready to make sure you can't leave that chair. And she's not leaving here until this virus or spell or whatever it is is broken."

Krebs half stood up to make sure Blair hadn't followed through on her threat. Seeing her expression, he dropped back down in his chair and returned to his breakfast.

"I'm back! I'm back!" Jazz raced down the stairs with the speed and noise of a toddler heading for a loaded Christmas tree. She danced into the kitchen with that same type of energy. "Cup to me!" she sang out, giggling when her *Wicked* cup floated toward her. She held the cup high in a victory motion while dancing around on her tiptoes showing off a gold anklet with an amethyst-studded gold broom dangling from the chain. Her hair flowed down her back in perfect shiny copper waves and there was no sign of the skin imperfections she suffered from the day before.

Stasi, Blair, and Krebs erupted in loud cheers laced with major sighs of relief.

"I'd say it had been part of my nightmare, but seeing you two here shows it wasn't."

"Which means it had to have been a virus and just needed to work itself out of your system!" Stasi jumped up and hugged her with Blair following.

"All I know is that it was the longest two days of my life." Jazz dropped into a chair and smiled at Krebs as he slid his plate toward her and got up to make another waffle.

Blair leaned forward and gazed into Jazz's eyes. She frowned as if she saw something that shouldn't have been there. "It wasn't a virus."

Stasi looked at her. "Why not? What do you see, Blair? It's the perfect explanation for what happened to Jazz."

"I don't care what caused what happened. All that matters is that I no longer have a zit the size of Australia on my chin and that rash is no longer growing up my leg," Jazz declared. "And I'm going to find that bastard that beat me up and turn him into an amoeba."

"I don't know, you were kinda cute as a mortal," Krebs chimed in. "Dismal, for sure, but cute." He looked from one to the other as they all scowled at him with the fury of three witches. His hair stood on end as the power wrapped around him. "*What did I say?*"

"He'll never have a clue," Jazz said.

"It's not his fault," Stasi, ever forgiving, added.

"He's a man," Blair summed it up.

"We missed the full moon." Jazz followed Stasi and Blair out to Blair's sage green Explorer.

"The good thing about the moon is that it returns every month and the lake isn't going anywhere." Stasi hugged her tightly. "This month we were meant to be down here with you in your time of need."

Jazz smiled at the magick warming her through and through. Stasi's magick dealt with love and comfort and that was what she was offering now.

"I'll be up for Samhain," she promised. "Nothing will keep me from coming up for that."

"Of course, you will," Blair replied. "The town is going all out this year with decorations for the fall festival and activities for the children. They even want to set up some haunted tours and turn the village into a ghost town."

"Which is ironic since the ghosts don't like to come out during that time of year even if the veil of non-living and living is thinnest then. I'll be surprised if any will show up for the tours or walk the streets, more's the pity," Blair said.

"Just as long as not too many of those little darlings in costume don't sport warts on their chins or noses and wear pointy black hats," Jazz said with a long-suffering sigh. "I really hate the mortals making us look like a nasty cliché."

"Nowadays it's more Disney princesses or wizards or robots," Blair said. "Although I understand the Anderson triplets want to be the Three Stooges."

"Then they'll be going as themselves," Stasi murmured, thinking of three boys who were trouble with a capital T. Their mother was a big customer of Stasi's or she would have wrapped the little fiends in a magickal cage long ago. Bogie, her Chihuahua mix of magickal descent, tended to disappear the moment the boys came anywhere close to the shop. And not disappear such as hide in the back room, but literally disappear into thin air.

"Thank you so much for being with me," Jazz murmured, hugging each one tightly. She fought back tears that still wanted to flow too easily. "I wouldn't have handled the last couple of days as well as I did if you hadn't been here."

"If that was handling it well, I hate to think what you would have been like if you turned into some kind of mess," Blair teased, hugging her back. "Besides, someone had to be here to take the See's candy away from you. I never saw anyone put away that much chocolate in such a short time."

"Don't worry, I had a mega stomachache to show for it." Jazz grimaced.

"Tell Krebs he's welcome to come up for Samhain," Stasi told her.

"I'll let him know." Jazz stood back and watched friends who were closer to her than her family had ever been. A part of her mourned their leave-taking, even if she knew she would be seeing them again in a matter of weeks. But a part of her was also glad she could get back to her life.

"What is going on out there? Land sakes, can't anyone tell me what happened?" Irma's plaintive voice rang out.

"Well, I did want all of my magickal life back." Jazz trudged up the driveway to the carriage house.

Irma sat in an easy chair that Jazz had provided for her. A variety of magazines lay on the small table in front of her while the TV/DVD combo was tuned to the Game Show Network. Now that the specter was free of the T-Bird, she demanded more and more luxuries to make her un-life in the carriage house easier. Jazz was waiting for the day Irma would want the apartment overhead fixed up for her use and a dog house set up in the backyard.

"Blair said she came out to tell you what happened to me and why I couldn't see and hear you," she said, vainly trying to push away the dog that pushed his massive ghostly weight against her legs. He released a wet slurping sound and wandered outside. "Don't eat the trees," she warned him. "Krebs can't believe the damage you did to the southern magnolia."

"She said some hooligan had robbed and beaten you." Irma peered at Jazz's face that was now unmarked courtesy of Lili's healing poultices, which were now able to work. Stasi had zapped away the stitches and the poultices took care of the other cuts and bruises. She felt a little sore, but still worlds better than she had before. "She also said you couldn't see me that day because your magick was gone, but you didn't know it at the time."

Jazz headed for the ottoman that matched the chair and sat down. "It's been a harrowing few days," she spoke a major understatement.

"I'm just glad I could be told." The ghost sniffed. "It isn't nice to be stuck out here and unable to know what's going on. Just because I'm dead doesn't mean I don't exist on some sort of plane. That nice Jonathan could have come out here to tell me what happened to you even if he couldn't see me. Or you could have come yourself even if you couldn't see or hear me. It wouldn't have hurt you, you know."

Jazz stared at Irma's expression. If she didn't know better she'd swear that the ghost had been worried about her.

Irma leaned forward and patted her hand on Jazz's knees. Unfortunately, her hand sunk right through leaving a sense of cold in Jazz's skin.

"Perhaps what happened to you was meant as a message from someone in your witchy world, you know. Think of it as a way to make you think about how you've lived your life." She settled back in her chair, her gray waves gleaming in the dim light floating through the carriage house windows. She smiled at the dog that returned to the carriage house carrying a tree branch and sidled up next to her chair and sat down, dropping the branch in front of him. "What you've done and perhaps what you should have done."

Jazz's head shot up. "What did you just say?"

"Does no one listen to me? I said. . ."

Jazz thought back to the dream, words she thought were part of that dream.

What if they weren't a dream? What if the person behind her nightmares was actually talking to her? Not just a message, but a threat.

"That's it!" She jumped up from the ottoman. "Irma, I could kiss you!" Knowing it wasn't possible, she didn't. But she knew what she could do.

"Where are you going?"

Jazz didn't answer. Her mind was already going a mile a minute as she hurried back to the house.

Once in her room, Jazz picked up the books Stasi had checked out for her. While the spells hadn't meant anything to her before, they did now and in a short matter of time she discovered what she was looking for.

"I should have Stasi look for my reading material all the time," she muttered, opening a large wooden chest and pulling out the materials she needed. She sat cross-legged on the floor with many silk pouches in a variety of colors scattered before her. Scents swirled around her causing her to sneeze as she sorted out what she needed and sprinkled herbs into a small iron cauldron. Once she had added the right amounts, she would take her cauldron downstairs to brew slowly on the stove. With luck, the watery surface would reveal what she was looking for.

She wiggled her toes, feeling the chilly air wrap around them. A moment later, her feet were covered with crocodile that turned soft and warm like slippers. Even the three-inch heels had disappeared. Croc smiled at her, displaying teeth that should have been terrifying but weren't, and Delilah cooed, batting green shadowed eyes and pursing red-tinted lips. Which was even stranger since crocodiles didn't really have lips. They weren't Fluff and Puff, who still refused to have anything to do with her even if her magick was back, but Croc and Delilah offered her their own form of calm. She stroked their heads with her fingertips and listened to their soft sounds of contentment.

Jazz spent the next two hours taking out a pinch of this and a pinch of that and carefully placing the necessary ingredients in the center of a square of cream-colored silk. With each new herb, an aromatic scent rose in the air to surround her.

Once she finished, she picked up the square by each corner, murmuring "air" for one, "fire" for the second, "water" for the third, and "wind" for the last. After tying the bundle with a silken cord the same color as the square, she carefully carried the cauldron and bag of herbs down to the kitchen.

A half hour later, the charged water bubbled on the stove and she dipped the silk pouch into boiling water.

"Show me the one who haunts my sleep. Show me the one who hides away deep. Show me the creep. Because I say so, damn it!" She rolled her eyes at her less than stellar spell, but pretty soon the water swirled in a minia-ture multi-colored whirlpool. She bent over the cauldron, staring into the contents, waiting to see the face of the one who was doing his or her best to ruin her life and sleep.

The water's surface smoothed out and she waited for the face of her enemy to appear.

"Show me!"

Except instead of a face appearing in the water, the water suddenly started to bubble upward and turned into a waterspout, emitting fumes that burned her eyes and nose and was strong enough to blister the paint off the walls.

"*Augh!*" She jumped backwards, holding her hands over her face but the smell still seeped through and filled the kitchen.

"What the hell?" Krebs skidded into the room. His face was a sickly green. "What are you doing? I could smell that all the way upstairs!"

Jazz held her breath as she ventured forward to take a quick peek inside the cauldron. The contents were a thick nasty-looking yellowish-green oil that told her she wouldn't learn her tormentor's identity anytime soon. Plus she'd be spending hours cleansing her cauldron. She wasn't about to get rid of it just because a spell backfired on her. She'd also need a biohazard bag for the mess in the cauldron because it wasn't something she could pour down the sink without the drains melting or worse, turning the neighborhood into a swamp.

"Wow. Whoever is behind this is really good."

Chapter 11

"WHAT DO YOU MEAN IT WON'T BE EASY TO GET RID OF the smell?" Krebs followed Jazz into her room. She threw open all her windows in hopes the fresh air coming in would cancel out the stench that seemed to permeate the walls.

"It's the gross results of a bounceback spell," she explained. "I wanted to know who was behind the nightmares, but it seems that person sent up a counterspell in case I went looking for them."

"I thought you guys used mirrors or something when you ran a search." Krebs looked down and blanched as the stilettos tiptoed their way around his feet, practically wrapping themselves around his legs even as their nostrils appeared closed. Obviously, shoes had smellers too. "Scrying. That's the word I was looking for."

"*You guys?* Sheesh, Krebs, it's not like we're a witchy mafia or something. Even if we do have our own form of enforcers and the don is more a pompous witch who could scare the toenails right off you." She finally took pity on him and shooed away the shoes. Croc released a lovesick sigh, while Delilah pouted her way back to the closet. "Plus what happened is proof it would have been much worse if I'd used a scrying glass."

"What can be worse than the house smelling like a toxic landfill?" He used his fingers to pinch his nostrils closed but quickly realized that breathing through his mouth meant the smell had a distinctive taste. He gagged and released his nostrils.

"Believe me, you don't want to know."

Jazz walked around the room spraying air freshener. She stopped when she realized the baby powder scent made the counterspell reek even worse.

"Can't you spell it gone or something?" Krebs gagged on the new reek.

She shook her head. "After what happened with the search spell, I can't take a chance. It should be gone in about twenty-four hours or so."

"*Or so? Should?* You mean it could be what? Forever?"

She thought about it. "I don't think so. Most bounce-back spells last no more than twenty-four hours, but I don't know how extensive this spell is."

"Jazz!"

"I'll pay for a hotel room."

He looked as if she'd finally lost her mind. "There's no way I'll leave windows open with all my computer equipment at risk. I'll wear a gas mask if I have to."

"I can strengthen the wards around the house so nothing, not even the neighbor's cat, can get past," she promised. "You'd be miserable wearing a gas mask, not to mention it's a really bad fashion statement."

"Oh that's right; they had them during World War II, didn't they? How did it feel wearing one of them, Jazz? Or did your witchy powers mean you didn't have to worry about gas?"

Jazz uttered a low snarl as she started to pull clothing out of the closet, but soon realized the smell had invaded there too. She had a bad feeling she was in for a day of heavy-duty cleansing throughout the house. And not with Lysol either.

Krebs muttered the words "insane" and "why me?" as he pulled his cell phone off his belt as it played *Surfin' USA*. "Hi." His voice softened as he turned away.

Jazz paused in her rummaging to look at her roomie as he walked through the door. There was no doubt his voice had gotten quieter even if he was further from her. Witchy powers didn't mean superwoman hearing. And if Krebs was acting so private with his phone call that could only mean one thing. . .

"Who's the woman?" she murmured, tapping her chin with her forefinger. "And why do I now think that my making a deal not to pick on his girlfriends could turn into a mistake on my part?" The thought again popped up that it would only take a few words and a flick of the fingers to ensure her hearing every word of the conversation that now aroused her curiosity even more. Except with the bounceback spell so strong in the house she dreaded to think what could happen. "And it would be invasion of his privacy," she whispered to the stilettos. "And not nice to boot. Still, what if she's totally wrong for him and he's thinking with his little brain and not the big one. As his very good friend I should look out for him." Before she could give in to her urge to chance an eavesdropping spell, Krebs closed his phone and turned back to her.

"I—uh—was wondering if you and Nick would like to go out on a double date Thursday night?" he asked, but not meeting her gaze.

Jazz's radar went on high alert. New woman. Krebs wanting to do a couples thing that he's never suggested before. Even more telling was that he wasn't looking at her.

"A double date? With Nick? It's not as if he isn't housebroken and hasn't gone insane and bitten someone in centuries, but he's still not someone most humans want to party with," she reminded him.

His lips tightened. "Look, I thought it might be fun for all of us to go out. Do you want to do it or not?"

"Sure, it could be fun." But her suspicion level still hovered in the high digits. "So who's the lady?"

"Someone new." He still refused to look at her.

"How new?"

"Just new. What is this? An inquisition? Damn it, Jazz! You just turned my house into a noxious dump and now you want to play good cop/bad cop all by yourself? Give me a break here!"

Defensive. This was very much a new thing with him, so she must be special in his eyes. Now she was even more curious to meet the mystery woman. "Uh, no, I was just curious. We women are like that."

He took a deep breath. "Sorry. It's just that. . ." he shook his head. "Let me know what Nick says. Don't worry; I know he can't eat." He wrinkled his nose. "I'm going out to pick up a couple, or ten, cases of the strongest air fresheners I can find."

A few moments later, Jazz heard the growled rumble of Krebs' Porsche rolling down the driveway.

"If she had called you on the house phone I could check Caller ID," she muttered, heading for the phone and tapping out numbers. "There are days I really hate having a high moral compass."

"I'm sure there are more than a few who would disagree with that statement."

She smiled at the sound of Nick's voice warm in her ear. "I was hoping you were awake."

"I'm writing up a report for a client. What's going on?"

"It seems Krebs has a new woman in his life and he asked if we wanted to double date this Thursday night. It should prove interesting. Witch, vampire, two mortals. We'd be a well-diversified group. What do you think, Nick?" she asked when she didn't hear anything.

"What did he tell you about her?"

"Just that he wanted to make it a foursome. Why?"

"Nothing. Just curious, I guess. Thursday is fine."

"He left to run an errand, so I'll let you know the time as soon as I find out." She paused. "Is everything okay?"

"Everything's fine; I've just been busy. I picked up a couple of new clients the other day."

Jazz dropped to the floor by her bed and sat cross-legged leaning back against the black and white comforter. The question tripped off her tongue even as she dreaded asking it and dreaded even more the answer she feared she'd receive. "Were Esme and the girl ever found?"

"Yes."

She so didn't want to ask the all-important question that had to follow his reply, but that had never stopped her before. "It was Reinhold who found them, wasn't it? And he destroyed them."

"It's Protectorate business."

Let Nick think a cold and clipped voice would stop her from probing further, but she already had confirmation of what she knew deep down had happened. It still sent icy shivers through her body.

"I'll be the first to admit that what Esme did was wrong but we're talking about a child, Nick. It's horrible that such innocence needed to be destroyed."

"We're talking about a child with the strength of five adults. A child who could have a temper tantrum and kill without a second thought." His words bit into her flesh like tiny knives. "She was one of the undead, Jazz. Her soul was gone. She died when Esme turned her into a feral animal."

She touched her stomach that felt queasy all of a sudden. "Oookay, I am really sorry I asked."

"And I'm sorry I put it that way to you, but you've been around long enough to know it's the way of our world. Not a pleasant one, but necessary."

"Reinhold always enjoyed that part of your work," she said quietly before she exhaled a deep breath. "So, on to a lighter topic. Thursday night. The four of us doing whatever couples on a double date do."

"Haven't you ever been on one?"

"No." But she hesitated too long to sound believable.

"When and who with?"

Jazz winced at the steel coating his question. She was never so grateful she'd called Nick instead of going by his office. This was a conversation she didn't want to have face to face. Come to think of it, this was a conversation she didn't want to have at all.

"We were broken up at the time." *You decided the Protectorate was more important than me.* A petty thought, yes, but even after two hundred years it was a grudge she held close to her heart.

"Which time?"

"It was a long time ago and you don't know him." She really should learn to keep her mouth shut! "Besides, I can't imagine you were living like a monk during those times." She winced as her internal gargoyle whomped her upside the head.

"We're talking about you, Jazz," Nick reminded her.

"And I don't intend to go any further unless you're willing to share. So let's just let this lie for now and I'll see you on Thursday." She quickly disconnected the call. "Men! It's all right if they tomcat around, but if you have one teensy weensy innocent date they act as if you had a rip-roaring affair." She scowled at Fluff and Puff as they chattered their defense of Nick. "And those statements you two are making are proof you're guys." She wrinkled her nose at the stench that hadn't left the room and seemed even worse when mixed with fresh air and baby powder scented air freshener. "Ugh! I need to do something about this."

Before she could move a step the phone rang. "He better not be calling to demand the name of the guy I dated. A name I don't even remember much less what the guy looked like," she muttered, reaching for the receiver, "then he can think again. What now?"

"Jazz?"

She froze at the sound of the soft feminine voice. Definitely not Nick.

"Hello, Mindy." Jazz wasn't known for having a cautious nature, but this was one time she'd do her best to listen more than talk. "Don't tell me. You managed to buy out Dweezil." Oh yeah, there was that mouth again.

"I realize I'm not your favorite person," Mindy said.

"Gee, ya think?" She almost bit down on her tongue. "Sorry. It hasn't been a good day."

"I'd like to explain something to you. I was angry with Dweezil. I asked him to make me a partner. I offered to buy in and the money could have gone a long ways to expand the service. Buy new vehicles and increase the garage space. Instead, he laughed and said no elf would do anything more than make him coffee."

"That sounds like D, all right. So what do you want from me?"

"I know my father could have been a lot crueler to you the day you were at our office," Mindy said. "And you would have had every right to be the same back to him, but you weren't and I thank you for that. He's. . ." she seemed to search for the right word, "difficult at times."

"Fine, we were polite to each other. Why are you calling?" she asked.

"My father wants to drive Dweezil out of business. I just want to run my car service my way," she said softly. "But my father feels you've been helping Dweezil more than you claim and that you were even before you came down to our offices."

Jazz thought of the curse that almost blew up her car. "What is he doing?" She heard a muffled sound as if Mindy turned away from the phone.

"Someone's coming, but you need to look to the past," she whispered. "What is haunting you is from there." She hung up.

"Wait a minute!" But Jazz yelled too late and Mindy was gone. She snarled at the receiver as if the inanimate object had been the harbinger of troubling news. Which, if she rationalized it right, it had. "Cryptic much? Look to the past. Gee, only 700 years to sift through." When the phone rang again she fostered the hope that Mindy had a change of heart and was going to tell all to make it easier for Jazz.

"Are you up for a road trip?" Nick asked.

Jazz thought of the smelly house, her stilettos huddled in the closet because they hated the smell as much as the rest of them and Fluff and Puff weren't too happy with the horrible odor either.

"Absolutely."

"I'll be there in ten."

"Doesn't anyone say good-bye anymore?" She tossed her phone down and ran for the bathroom. The good thing about having her magick back was that she could easily get ready in ten minutes.

"You going to tell me what died in your house?" Nick asked, as he steered his Wrangler toward the freeway on-ramp. He wore what Jazz called his scary, but incredibly sexy, vamp garb. A black silk button-down shirt, black leather pants, and his black leather duster along with black sunglasses finished the daunting look. "I haven't smelled anything like that since London in the 1500s."

"It was the result of a bounceback spell. I tried finding out who's behind the nightmares and got a smelly house instead." She sipped the mocha espresso Nick had thoughtfully brought her. Something she appreciated a lot more than flowers. Unless it was her favorite chocolates. They ran a very close second to anything loaded with caffeine.

"No wonder Krebs was carrying a case of air freshener into the house."

"And Mindy called me. It seems it's more her father who wants Dweezil driven out of business."

"He doesn't know Dweezil very well, does he? He prefers driving others out of business."

"No kidding. But then she said something that makes me wonder just who all knows what's going on with my nightmares. She said if I want to find out who's behind what's going on with me I need to look to the past."

"That was her only hint?"

"I could have used a few more. Such as what decade or even what century, but she hung up before I could ask her any questions."

"And it's not as if you haven't made your share of enemies over time."

"Not enemies. Just people who didn't agree with me." She eyed the southbound lanes sign. "So where are we going?"

"How does Laguna sound?"

"Nice, but if you wanted a cloudy beach we could have stayed home."

"Not if you're looking for a sneaky Wereweasel named Willie."

She sat up straight and turned toward him. "You found Willie? How did you find him?"

"Coby had put the word out and called me this morning that one of his people spied Willie in a Were club down in Laguna." He made a quick zigzag around a slow moving sedan.

"Coby? I gave him my card. Why didn't he call me?"

"Don't pout," he teased.

"It's the witch thing. He trusts a vampire more than a witch. And I'm not pouting. It's my lip plumping lip gloss." She quickly uncrossed her arms and settled her expression in something less. . .pouty.

Nick grinned, but he knew better than to say anything more.

"Coby better not get cursed anytime soon, because he won't get any help from me," she muttered returning to the comfort of her espresso. "And you *will* buy me lunch."

"Shouldn't you be the one buying *me* lunch since I'm the one taking you to Willie, which is your problem, not mine?"

Jazz shuddered at the idea of patronizing one of the underground cafés that offered an iron-rich menu alongside one more palatable to her taste buds.

"Take me out to lunch at a restaurant of my choice and I promise you a night you will never forget." Her fingers danced along the length of his thigh until they reached the button fly. She smiled at the hardness that grew under her fingertips.

"Deal."

She smiled at his prompt agreement. Men were so easy!

Normally, Jazz loved browsing through the many shops and art galleries in the funky beach town of Laguna Beach. But Nick abruptly turned up a steep road framed with small colorful bungalows set on either side of a street that was so narrow it could barely accommodate vehicles going in opposite directions. She twisted in her seat looking at the picture postcard view of the ocean behind them.

"He's up here?"

"No, but I think I have a tail and if I do, I want to lose them before we reach our destination. And don't turn around either."

"Oh please, like I don't know Super Spy 101." She pulled down the visor then frowned. "No mirror?"

"You look fine and you look too obvious doing that anyway." He made a quick turn up a twisty road that was even narrower than the one they had been on.

Jazz rested her head against the headrest and glanced toward the side view mirror.

"Why do they always drive those huge SUVs with heavily tinted windows? Talk about obvious." The answer hit her as soon as she finished her question. "Since there's no reason for government authorities to be after us, it's got to be vampires. Why are they following us? Or are they following you? Okay, this just isn't acceptable. Show to me what I cannot see. Show to me who these people be. Because I said so, damn it!" She flicked her fingers over her shoulder. A shower of dark purple sparks traveled through the air until it hit the black SUV behind them. At the same time the windshield momentarily cleared showing her the driver. "Ugh! It's Reinhold."

"I thought so. He prides himself on never losing someone he's tailing," Nick said grimly.

"Yeah, well, his perfect record is about to be marred." Jazz bared her teeth. She closed her eyes to better concentrate. "Big bad vamp about to get his due. Big bad vamp won't have a clue. Big bad vamp up for something dire. Big bad vamp has four flat tires. Because I said so, damn it!" This time she turned around and pushed her power toward the vehicle behind them. The moment the power hit the SUV all four tires deflated and it shuddered to a stop. She squealed with glee and clapped her hands. "I am so good."

Nick chuckled as he sped up, making several turns before he headed back down to the Pacific Coast Highway.

"So do you guys have your own version of Triple A?"

"They'll be here soon and Reinhold will be pretty pissed off you did that."

"I thought about seizing up the engine too, but I guess that would have ticked him off more."

"Definitely."

Jazz looked at the elegant hotel Nick slowed in front of. "Good place to hide the Jeep." She allowed the parking valet to help her out.

"An even better place to hide a Wereweasel." He climbed out and tossed the keys to the valet as he walked around the Jeep's hood. He laced his fingers through Jazz's and steered her through the lobby.

"He's hiding *here*?" She eyed the two-story high waterfall that dominated the lobby, expensively dressed women who were bleached, Botoxed, and lipoed, and the men who paid the bills. She imagined spending a long weekend here with Nick where they didn't leave their suite. The idea grew more appealing by the minute.

Nick nodded as he headed for the bank of elevators. It only took a bit of vamp power to ensure they had the elevator to themselves.

"Coby managed to obtain the suite number."

"A suite? That scuzz is staying in a suite? I can't see him making that much more than minimum wage. How did he afford all this?" She eyed the discreet sign advertising the rooftop restaurant and its elaborate brunches along with another sign detailing spa services. Oh yes, she wanted to stay here for a while.

"I guess we'll have to ask him."

"Since you're already dressed like the darkest of dark I guess you'll be the bad cop while I'm the good cop. For once I want to be the bad cop," she groused.

He hugged her close to his side. "I promise not to ruin your fun. Just go for the out of control witch."

"I can't believe he's staying here," she muttered, feeling the plush carpet beneath her feet as they walked down the long hallway. "Someone must be footing the bill and I'd like to know who."

Nick stopped at the suite double door. "You ready to go all witchy on his Were ass?"

Jazz thought of her precious Fluff and Puff incarcerated in bunny slipper jail. "Oh yeah." She rapped on the door.

"Who is it?" The voice on the other side was squeaky.

"Housekeeping," Jazz trilled, pushing her face so close to the spy hole all Willie would get was a nose and part of one cheek.

"You were already—" The door opened a crack, which allowed Nick not to have to destroy it.

"Hello, Willie," Jazz purred, gliding into the suite with Nick on her heels. She didn't have the all-black vamp look or fangs or red eyes, but she did have a couple of aces up her sleeve. She had the resources to turn him into one nasty looking slug if she didn't get the answers she wanted. "Fancy finding you here. I wouldn't imagine you to be one for a luxury hotel. Or do you come here for the heated stone massage? It's obvious you don't make use of any exfoliation treatments." She made a face at the tufts of dark fur that sprouted over the collar of his grimy T-shirt and covered his arms.

Willie's looks suited his Wereweasel heritage perfectly. He was a bit shorter than Jazz, small and wiry with sharp features that betrayed his feral nature. With a narrow face and black beady eyes, Willie looked every bit the weasel. His gaze darted between Jazz and Nick as he slowly backed up. When he turned to escape through another room, Nick was there before him, blocking any chance of retreat.

"I wouldn't make her any angrier if I were you," Nick advised, keeping his stance relaxed with his hands folded in front of him. "The lady's had a rough morning and she's already done some serious damage to an SUV."

Willie blanched. "I haven't done anything wrong."

"Did we say you have?" Jazz wandered around the large parlor, wrinkling her nose at the piles of dirty clothing left on a chair and one end of the couch. She hoped a very big tip would be left for the maids because they deserved it if they had to deal with a disgusting slob like Willie. The wide-screen TV showed a soccer game that was thankfully muted. She paused long enough at the wet bar to fix herself a sparkling water and grabbed a bag of peanuts since she was feeling a bit peckish. No reason why Willie's benefactor shouldn't pay the high price for her snack. "Funny thing, Willie. Rex said you were dead." She opened the peanuts and tossed a few into her mouth.

He inched his way backwards. "Really? Huh. Well, you can see I'm not." He stopped short when he found Nick again behind him. "So you can just go."

"Do you know what else Rex said, Willie?" She advanced on him and Nick's speed meant the sneaky Wereweasel couldn't easily escape.

"No." He didn't take his eyes off her.

She had wished she'd worn a kick-ass outfit instead of her favorite dark purple yoga pants and matching hoody and purple leather flip-flops, but it seemed she was still able to give off the dangerous witch vibes that made Willie nervous. She pretended to examine her nails, which had black and gold sparks dancing off the tips. Willie watched them with the horrified fascination of a victim watching a deadly cobra sway back and forth in front of him before striking.

"Rex said my beloved bunny slippers ate you," she said in a conversational tone. "Now while I admit my babies aren't as well behaved as I'd like. And yes, they have eaten more than their share in hot dogs and funnel cake in the past, we both know they wouldn't eat someone like you," she speared him with her meanest gaze, "now, would they? I mean, no matter what, they do have their standards. So tell me, Willie, would they come after you?"

"No." He made it sound more like a question.

"So what if one of them coughed up a button that allegedly belonged to one of your shirts." She was so getting into this wicked witch *shtick!* "It's easy enough to plant a button somewhere. Maybe slather it with some powdered sugar or honey that would attract them." She moved closer to Willie then stepped back a pace since he didn't smell all that great. She guessed the multi-room suite had more than one bathroom, but it seemed the Wereweasel hadn't availed himself of the tub or shower. What was it with some of the Weres and their disdain of basic hygiene? Totally gross!

"So tell me something, Willie. Why would anyone accuse Fluff and Puff of killing you, which means an automatic death sentence for them, when it turns out you're alive and living pretty well in a pricy hotel suite in Laguna Beach?" She tossed the last of the peanuts into her mouth and finished her sparkling water.

"I don't know!" He flinched when Nick planted a hand on his shoulder as Willie tried to move away from her.

"Who put you up in this suite, Willie? Who's paying the bills?" She snapped her fingers, the sparks flaring brightly in his face. He flinched and closed his eyes. "Who got you out of town so Fluff and Puff would be accused of eating you?"

"Nobody."

"You're a very bad liar."

"I don't have to talk to bitches like you! Ow!" He howled as Nick's hold on his shoulder tightened to the point of pain. He sank to his knees but Nick didn't let up.

"You might want to remember you're talking to a lady, Willie," Nick said quietly. Whatever he next whispered in Willie's ear leached the last of the color from his ratlike features. "Think you can help us out?"

He tightened his lips and shook his head. There was no doubt that it wasn't just stubbornness keeping him silent. Fear was doing a good job of it too.

Nick looked at Jazz. *He might be afraid of you, but it looks like he's even more afraid of whoever put him up here.*

This was one time when Nick talking inside her head was a good idea. She mentally uttered a sad farewell to the brunch offered in the rooftop restaurant.

"Okay, no more Nice Witch. You're going back with us, so we can prove to Rex that you're not dead and Fluff and Puff are off the hook." She grabbed his wrist and pulled.

"I can't leave!" He dug his heels into the carpet, but it was so thick he merely slid as she dragged him across the room toward the door. She glared Nick an *are you going to help?* look, but he just smiled and stood with legs apart and arms crossed in front of his chest.

"Oh yes, you can. Nick, if he tries to escape again, do whatever you need to do," she ordered, figuring he could at least do that.

"I'm serious, Jazz. I *can't* leave!" Willie bracketed her wrist with his hands in a vain attempt to free himself, but she was having none of it and just gripped him harder.

She quickly discovered the Wereweasel might be small and wiry, but he was strong. And pure unadulterated fear added to that strength.

Jazz ignored his fear and focused on getting the creature to the door. "Just move it!" she snarled, pulling so hard it was amazing she didn't dislocate his shoulder.

"Uh, Jazz." Nick frowned as they reached the door. "Maybe—"

She slashed the air with her free hand. "No, this bastard is going with us to prove that Fluff and Puff are innocent." She grabbed the doorknob and twisted it. "And I'm going to grind this truth right in Rex's face. With my foot if I have to!" She ended with blood-thirsty relish.

"Jazz!" Nick's warning shout was uttered a bare second before the door exploded under her hand. The three were thrown backwards, Willie's slight body tossed across the room to slam against a wall and fall to the carpet, lying there like a rag doll.

Jazz sat up coughing and waving her hand in front of her face to dissipate the smoke. "Ugh! What was that?" She stared at the door that didn't look as if it had just turned into a prop from *The Towering Inferno*.

"You're the one with a degree in magick; you tell me." Nick moved swiftly over to Willie. "We have a problem."

Jazz groaned as she maneuvered herself to her feet and slowly made her way to Nick's side. She stared at Willie who not only lay still, but his head was twisted in a direction that wasn't physically possible when his legs were lying in an opposite position.

"This is not my fault."

Nick moved rapidly to the door, checking the un-marred surface with his palms then cracked it open and looked out.

"No one noticed the noise?" she asked, still aware of a ringing in her ears and the smell of sulfurous smoke stinging her nostrils.

"Not when the explosion was caused by magick." He eased the door closed and turned back to her. "Someone meant to keep Willie in here. Anyone else could come in and out, but he couldn't leave."

Jazz dug in her bag and pulled out her cell phone.

"I don't think it would be a good idea to call the police," Nick said.

"Forget the cops. I want proof for Rex." She snapped several pictures.

He remained in his crouched position by the body. "We can't leave him here."

"Except whatever magick was on that door won't let him out."

"He's dead, Jazz. I don't think the spell will stop him now." He stood up and started to bend down to sling the body over his shoulder when Willie's form turned hazy. When the mist disappeared light brown fur replaced skin and he was a fraction of his original size.

"He looks better in his furry form than human," she said.

Nick picked up the critter and stared at Jazz's leather tote bag.

She didn't need magick to know his intent. "Oh, no, you don't. There is no way you're putting that *thing* in my bag. This is a Prada for Fates' sake!"

"We need to get it out of here and do it without using magick," he said quietly. "Do you have any better ideas?"

While Jazz excelled in her role as Wicked Witch of the Southland, she couldn't win the battle of the glares with Nick.

"Fine, but we're wrapping it up. There's no way I'm dumping this *thing* in there without a lot of covering." She stalked to the closet and pulled out a plastic laundry bag. Once the body was dumped in the bag and Nick tied the top, she wrapped the bag in a hand towel that proved to be almost as large as a bath towel. "And someone's buying me a new bag, because no way I'm using this one after this. First my Dooney & Bourke bag is stolen, now this. I can't keep anything nice!"

"Send the bill to Rex." Nick took her red leather shoulder bag from her, rolled the weasel in the towel, and carefully tucked it inside before handing it back to Jazz.

Instead of slipping the straps over her shoulder, she used her fingertips to hold it out as far from her body as possible.

Nick made a quick pass over the door and furniture with a towel and slipped a *Do Not Disturb* sign over the doorknob as they left.

"Say 'thank you, Nick,'" he said as he sped up the highway.

"I'm supposed to thank you for putting a dead weasel in my Prada bag?" She gagged as she deposited said bag in the backseat.

"How about for finding Willie for you, which means the slippers are off the hook?"

"You didn't find Willie. Coby did. And now I'll have to explain to Rex why Willie is dead."

"Call me crazy, but something tells me that if there was a chance Rex knew Willie was actually alive, he wouldn't have expected him to come back."

Jazz released a deep sigh. "While I didn't like that time I was mortal, at least it was a bit saner—except for the blotchy skin, dry ends, breakouts, and crying jags." She was silent for a moment. "You really hurt me that night," she said softly. "I was so upset and I was in so much pain, at least I was when the painkillers wore off, and when I asked you for comfort you treated me as if I had the plague. Considering the emotional wreck I was then, your timing totally sucked."

Since she was still looking out the window she didn't see the pain and regret briefly cross his features.

"You asked me to go after the man who mugged you," he reminded her. "You wanted him torn into pieces. That doesn't sound like comfort to me."

"It was my way of wanting comfort."

"There are some things we can't control," Nick said quietly.

Jazz's memories of her days as a mortal blended with the odd dream of her being a mortal complete with husband, two kids, and a minivan—and probably even a dog in the backyard.

She had no idea that Nick's thoughts closely mirrored her own, but that his feelings were tainted with something much darker.

Chapter 12

"AND I'M SUPPOSED TO BELIEVE THAT'S WILLIE?" REX stared at the towel and plastic wrapped bundle Nick dropped on his desk. The small office behind the carousel smelled of popcorn and cotton candy and was neat as a pin, which surprised Jazz since she expected a space that would rival the looks of a pigsty. She didn't even see a stray sheet of paper on the filing cabinet.

Jazz pulled out her cell phone and brought up the photographs she'd taken. "Don't even try and claim this isn't Willie. Because if you lie about it, *I'll* be the one going to the Ruling Council. Instead, do the right thing and let them know that Fluff and Puff didn't eat Willie."

Rex picked up a pen and poked the body with it. The furry critter rolled over onto its other side. "What in Hades' name did you do to it?"

"Someone else made sure he wouldn't leave that hotel suite alive. Someone I think you know." Nick leaned against the wall. "A lot of magick in that room, Rex, and none of it was witch magick."

"I know a lot of people, vampire." Rex smirked.

Jazz knew this was the last place she wanted to stay for too long. "Make the call," she advised, picking up her bag that she privately vowed would be going into the trash as soon as she got home. Considering what the contents had been for even a short while, she couldn't in good conscience give the bag to charity.

Nick remained in his spot as Jazz reached the door.

"I'll make the call once Willie's pack leader confirms this is him." The boardwalk manager pushed the bundle off his desk and into a wastebasket.

"I'm serious, Rex. Don't wait around for his pack leader. You make that call now, because I don't think you'll want me to make it." Jazz was proud of her parting shot as she exited the office.

"Vampire." Rex's voice stopped Nick from following her.

Nick looked over his shoulder.

"There's things going on here even you can't control and you can't always protect her."

"Meaning?"

"Meaning, if you really want answers look to your own nest." Rex's smile didn't hold any humor.

Nick's expression darkened. "We should have a talk one day."

"Yes, let's." Rex bared his teeth indicating that was the last thing he wanted to do.

Nick barely closed the door behind him before Jazz had hold of his duster lapels. "Okay, what was the supernatural testosterone war in there about?" she demanded. "Stuff like that gives me a major headache."

"Nothing you need to worry about."

She rolled her eyes. "Oh sure, don't bother your empty head about it, little witch. Let the big bad vampire deal with it. Puleeze!" She started to stalk off then changed her mind. "Mindy said the source of my problems, which I take to mean my nightmares, could be found in my past and now Rex is saying you need to look to your own nest which, as far as I'm concerned, is pretty much the same thing. That makes me think the two are connected and Willie was nothing more than some sick pawn in this whole thing. What reason is there to stash a scummy Wereweasel carnie in an exclusive hotel and then set up a magickal bomb in the door so he can't leave? Rex was really fast to accuse Fluff and Puff of eating Willie while everyone knows he could really care less if the carnies take off as long as someone else took their place. He was pushing big time for the slippers to be destroyed and it was pure luck I could talk him into not going to the Ruling Council right away." She forgot what had been inside her bag as she pushed the straps up over her shoulder.

"Or maybe not luck. Maybe he didn't go to them," he murmured, walking along with her. "It's easier to threaten you with the Council and then only go to them if you fought him for too long. He was positive you wouldn't find Willie and then he could go to the Council to demand that Fluff and Puff be destroyed and that would be that. It's a known fact the slippers are precious to you."

"I always knew I didn't like him," she muttered. "He really needs to go. Do you think Coby would help?"

Nick shook his head. "Wrong pack. Plus Rex is the alpha in his pack, so the only ones who can help you are the Ruling Council."

Jazz spun around, her hand outstretched, but Nick grabbed it in time.

"No magick!" he ordered, almost crushing her fingers with his strong grip.

"Willie's dead! He won't mind if he explodes in a gross smelly mess all over Rex's office!" She didn't look happy at being thwarted.

"No, but the Witches' Council will. You're already walking a fine line with them after Clive Reeves. Don't make matters worse until we discover who's behind the nightmares and everything else going on," he advised.

She reluctantly lowered her arm. "Okay, for now. But his time is coming." She glared at the building as if that could level it.

Nick gazed up at the sky. "I have a client showing up a little after dusk, so I need to get going. I guess I'll see you Thursday night."

Jazz nodded. "That's the plan. And I still haven't been able to find out who the mystery woman is." She studied her nails. "Ugh! I need a manicure to get the weasel gunk out from under them. Good luck with your client." She stood up on her tiptoes and kissed him on the mouth.

"Don't you want a ride back to the house?"

She shook her head. "Don't worry about it. The walk will do me good."

Nick stood in the shadows of the building and watched her cross the boardwalk. More than one man paused to watch her graceful stride.

"Perhaps you do need a normal life," he whispered, as he headed for his building.

"What would impress Krebs's new girlfriend?" Jazz murmured, studying the contents of her closet and pulling out various pieces of clothing with comments "too slutty," "too witchy," "not sexy enough," and "why did I keep this thing?" She tossed the last item to one side. In the end, she settled on a teal silk slip dress edged with matching lace. "Okay, girls, you need to behave tonight," she told Croc and Delilah as she slipped them on. They obliged by changing to a matching shade of teal. Jazz had settled for putting her hair up in a mass of curls that drifted down her back. She studied her reflection in her full-length mirror, turning one way and then the other. "Yes, very nice."

Chatter from a corner of her room caught her attention. She looked at the magickal cage that still held Fluff and Puff. The bunny slippers were a lot more subdued lately, which kept her life a little quieter and saner. She thought it had to do with the fear someone from the Ruling Council would show up to take them into custody. Guilt assaulted her for not freeing them as soon as she got home, but she had to admit knowing where they were and that they had no choice but to stay out of trouble kept her from telling them that she found proof that they hadn't eaten Willie. True, she first found him alive and well, but now he was dead due to a booby-trapped doorknob. Still, they had nothing to do with it.

"Forget it. I'll channel Scarlett O'Hara and think about it tomorrow." She took one quick check of her lip gloss before she picked up her evening bag and left the room. As she descended the stairs, she heard the chime of the doorbell and the faint sound of a woman's voice along with Nick's. She warmed at the sound of the latter and froze at the sound of the former. "Don't tell me.

Please don't tell me." She quickened her pace, almost running down the rest of the way. When she reached the bottom of the stairs, she almost skidded on the Italian tile floor.

Nick, dead sexy in charcoal slacks and a silk shirt that echoed the color of his eyes, stood by a woman wearing dark red silk pants and a black lace tank-style top along with a jacket that matched her pants. She gave eternal beauty a whole new meaning. Black hair was fashioned in a short sassy cut that framed delicate features and belied a core that Jazz knew for a fact was strong as steel. Eyes a deep cobalt blue watched Jazz with an expression she couldn't easily read. If Jazz didn't know better she'd say the woman was nervous, which couldn't be the case at all.

"Good evening, Jazz," she spoke with an accent that wasn't easy to identify. Understandable since the woman had lived in many countries over her five hundred years of existence.

"Leticia." Jazz's tone was noticeably cooler. Her gaze hopped over to Nick and what she saw there didn't make her any happier. She prided herself that she didn't need a scorecard to know that Leticia was Krebs's date and that Nick appeared to already know this. Krebs stood on the other side of the woman watching Jazz with the wariness of a mouse watching a cat. "I didn't realize you and Krebs were seeing each other outside of business," she said carefully.

Leticia looked up at Krebs with a warmth that transformed her face from porcelain beauty to something almost human. She stood with her head reaching his shoulder.

"We started to get to know each other through e-mails and phone calls when he first worked on my site," she explained. "We thought it would be nice for the four of us to go out. It's good to see you again, Jazz."

"And you, although, it's been some time." She decided not to mention that World War I was going on at the time. A part of her wanted to rant and rave that this was wrong, very wrong. But another part looked at Krebs's face and saw something she had never seen before.

Her very mortal roommate was in love. Honest to Fates love. The only trouble was, he was in love with a vampire.

"So? What are the plans for tonight?" she asked in a voice that came out higher pitched than expected while she pasted a smile on her lips. She deserved an Academy Award for this performance.

There was no missing Krebs's sigh of relief or the warm approval in Nick's eyes.

She kept her smile in place even if it felt a bit forced.

"We have time before the limo shows up. Would anyone like some wine?" Krebs played the perfect host.

"You knew about this?" Jazz hissed, as she and Nick moved toward the family room.

She can hear you.

Jazz mentally slapped herself upside the head. *He told you that day you were over here for a football game, didn't he?*

He did.

And you didn't tell him what a really bad idea this is? You know him better than I do. Do you think he'd listen?

No, but that shouldn't have stopped you. Leticia's on an eternal liquid diet. Krebs loves his steak rare. They both might be night people, but it's for different reasons.

It's only an evening out, love. Even with us present as buffers they might discover they're not meant for each other.

Jazz studied the sparks that had nothing to do with magick between the couple.

Somehow I don't think that's going to happen.

As the evening passed she realized the two were perfect for each other. Leticia shared Krebs's taste in music, or at least pretended to, and her roomie had never looked happier. Considering the number of women Jazz had seen him with over the few years they'd known each other, she liked seeing this side of him as the enraptured male as the foursome spent the evening at an upscale club. She even gracefully handled Nick's knowing looks.

It wasn't until she and Leticia retired to freshen their lipstick that Jazz felt comfortable enough to say what had been in her mind all evening.

"Krebs is very special to me," she said, as she sat down in front of the vanity mirror.

"And to me," Leticia said.

"Then you will understand if I say that if you ever hurt him or try to use him for a midnight snack I will do everything in my power to make you suffer." Jazz's tone was bright as she dusted her cheeks with a golden blush.

Leticia's eyes met hers in the reflective glass. "I wouldn't have it any other way."

Jazz's internal detector told her the vampire was speaking the truth. "You really do care for him."

"Very much. Jonathan is the first man to treat me like a real woman for hundreds of years. He doesn't care what I am or what I've done in the past. Do you realize how freeing that is to someone like me? It's as if I've been given a whole new life."

Jazz didn't have to think about her answer even as she reminded herself that Leticia seemed to prefer Krebs's real name instead of the nickname Jazz dubbed him with. "Yes, I can," she murmured. "I'm sure you'll understand that I'll always worry about your association, but I'm glad that you and Krebs found each other. He's a great guy and deserves someone special."

"Thank you." She smiled. "I love your shoes. Milan?"

"A friend gave them to me." She looked down to see Croc sneezing as she nosed the plush carpet. Delilah somehow managed to add another layer of mascara to her inch-long eyelashes, although Jazz had no idea where the stiletto hid her makeup. "They're not my usual style, but they are fun to wear."

"I used to have an ermine makeup case until she ate all my lipsticks and regurgitated them during a date."

Jazz burst out laughing. "And I thought it was bad when Fluff and Puff drank three bottles of my body wash and burped bubbles for a week."

"I guess I was lucky with the lipsticks."

Leticia returned her lipstick to her small evening bag and turned on the bench to face Jazz. "I hope you don't mind that Jonathan told me that you have been suffering from odd dreams."

"In a way, yes, I mind, but since my nightmares woke him up a time or eight, I can understand. Plus, it seems

others have been finding out somehow." She thought of
Mindy's advice and even Rex speaking up.

"And you feel they're magickally induced?"

Jazz nodded. "But that's the best I've been able to
come up with so far."

"Sometimes old grudges rise up to the present." She
appeared to pick and choose her words.

Jazz frowned. "Look to the past."

"That's a good way to look at it. Parts of our world
are in turmoil now what with Flavius gone and
Angelica taking over as director of the Protectorate,"
Leticia went on.

Jazz was positive her blood had turned to ice.
"Angelica?" The name felt thick and sluggish on her
tongue. "I thought she was still somewhere in Europe."
*Even another galaxy was too close if Jazz had anything
to do about it.*

"Why, yes, didn't you know? I would have assumed
that Nick told you. Vincent, the previous director, had
been in charge for the last 400 years. Many felt it was
time for him to step down. That his ideas were too antiquated for many of the members. When Angelica challenged him for his seat and had enough backing from
others, he had no choice but to retire. With Flavius gone,"
she hesitated, "well, there was no one left who was truly
strong enough to fight her."

"It sounds as if you don't like her any more than I do,"
Jazz commented.

Leticia stood up and smoothed down her jacket with
her hands. "Let's just say if she was on fire, I'd break out
the marshmallows."

Jazz grinned. "Leticia, I can see we'll be the very best of friends."

She was pleased to see Krebs's look of delight when the two laughing women returned to the table and Nick's wary puzzlement when she shot him a look fit to kill.

"If you'll tell me what I did wrong I'll apologize," he murmured in her ear as he held her chair out for her.

"Something tells me you'll be groveling a long time for not telling me that Angelica found a way to gain more power," she murmured back. "And now I know why you were so furious after Reinhold spoke to you. He told you about Angelica, didn't he?"

Nick glanced at Leticia and Krebs whose heads were together as they shared their own private conversation.

"We'll discuss this later."

"Yes, we will." She reached for her glass of wine then drew back when she realized her hand was trembling.

Angelica, an ancient powerful vampire, might have a name that made one think of an angel, but she was as far from the celestial being as she could get. Jazz considered the female vampire a bloodthirsty boogeyman.

Angelica was well known for her beauty, great intelligence, and an insane thirst for blood that outshone even the infamous Elizabeth Bathory—the notorious serial killer of the late 1500s who enjoyed bathing in her victims' blood. While Elizabeth Bathory was punished for her crimes, Angelica always escaped scot-free.

Jazz was aware that Angelica had also been involved with Nick at one time. Even though it had been before he and Jazz met, it still galled Jazz that he had once, and probably way more, bumped uglies with the evil-spirited vampire whose soul was as black as her non-beating heart.

Krebs shot Jazz a wary look then raised his eyebrows, looking upward. Nick's muffled laughter had her sending her senses outward and realizing there was a rumble of thunder overhead.

Damn it! Mother Nature will have me scrubbing out all her rainbow pots for the next five hundred years!

It was enough to stop her trembling and allow her to pick up her wine glass without the contents sloshing all over her hand. The thunder was silenced as abruptly as it sounded.

Since Nick had walked over to the house, Krebs offered to drop him off at the boardwalk and Jazz decided to go with Nick.

"I had a lovely evening, Jazz," Leticia told her as Nick helped Jazz out of the back of the limo.

"I did too," she said sincerely, realizing this was one female vampire she not only liked, but she could see as a friend.

Thank you, Krebs mouthed in her direction.

"Why do I feel as if you're not along for my esteemed company?" Nick asked as they reached the boardwalk

In deference to the chilly sea air, Jazz wrapped her shawl tighter around her shoulders. Her heels clicked an angry staccato on the weathered boards.

"Why didn't you tell me that Angelica had left her den of malevolence and returned to this side of the world?" she asked in a voice that was too sweet and conversational to be sincere to cynical vampire ears. It also had an edge to it that was painful to a vampire's ultra-sensitive ears.

"Maybe because I knew you'd have the exact reaction you're having now." He easily kept up with her swift pace. Her smile didn't fool Nick one bit. He was positive his sexy witch was spitting mad and it didn't have a thing to do with Krebs dating Leticia. While there wasn't a hint of thunder and lightning overhead, thank the Fates, there was that nasty black and purple cloud swirling around her that indicated a whopping temper tantrum if he didn't handle this right. He kept one eye on her hands. If she pulled up a fireball he wanted to be out of range before he went up like a Roman candle.

A push of power had the heavy glass doors blowing open with ease as she entered the building and the elevator door opened without anyone pushing a button. Nick decided it was safer to just follow her. Besides, the view was damn good. The witch had a very sweet butt, not to mention the way the flirty hem swished around her thighs even if that purple and black temper haze obscured some of the view.

He barely made it inside the elevator car before the grille snapped shut and the elevator moved downward with an off-balance jolt—all without a finger touching one button.

Even the heavy steel door leading to his lair opened with ease as Jazz marched past it with Nick close on her heels. Even then he was almost smacked in the face with the door as it started to swing shut. He hissed a curse and shielded his eyes with his hand as she waved her hands and lights flared with noonday-bright glare.

"There's a reason why I have a dimmer switch," he growled, dialing back the lights to a more reasonable illumination.

"But the truth looks so much better in the light of day, don't you think?" She made her way to the kitchen and opened the refrigerator door. She grimaced at the bags of blood that almost filled the interior and reached beyond the bags to pull a bottle of wine out. She found a wineglass in a nearby cabinet. After filling the glass, she took a seat on the couch.

"I don't lie to you." He sprawled in a nearby chair.

"But you do choose not to reveal all the facts, which the way I see it is another form of lying." She sipped her wine.

"Maybe because I didn't think this was the kind of news to just dump on you."

"What? Were you going to ease into it? It's been a couple of weeks since Reinhold told you. You've had plenty of time to find a way to tell me." Her fingers tightened around the stem of the glass. She had no idea her lipstick stood out in stark contrast against her pale features or that her eyes deepened to a darker moss green than usual. "Honestly, Nick, you knew I'd find out sooner or later. There are no secrets among any of our kind. And this piece of news is a big one. Maybe I'm a lowly *witch*," she spat out aware of the majority of the vampires' opinion of her kind, "but I do know that a woman hasn't ever been named director of the Protectorate because it's been your typical old boys network for how many thousands of years? So for Angelica to climb to the top of the bloody heap means she held some pretty strong cards that ensured the post was hers. I'm not stupid, Nick. Angelica has never done anything for the greater good of the vampire race. All she's ever cared about is herself, and she doesn't care who she destroys along the way. Clive Reeves was a rank amateur in the psychopath community compared to her. And if Flavius had still been here, she would have found a way to destroy him too. How many humans has she killed over her years as a vampire? How many vampires has she managed to destroy in her quest for power? And what the fuck did she do to you all those years ago to linger in your spirit as if she still has some kind of hold on you?"

Nick's head snapped to the side as if she'd physically slapped him.

"Yes, Angelica is now the director of the Protectorate and even sits on the Ruling Council. Yes, Angelica is most definitely someone to avoid at all costs. And yes, Angelica and I shared a past I'd rather not revisit. And you knew that long before I even knew you. Subject closed." The red in his eyes echoed his words.

She took a large swallow of her wine. "Oh ho, so that's it. You did the unthinkable, didn't you? You left her. Her kind would prefer to do the leaving or tossing out in pieces because I just bet that's her habit." She kicked off her shoes and sat back, tucking her legs under her.

Nick's eyes were riveted on the way her short skirt slid up her thighs. He wasn't sure if she deliberately flashed him a hint of her thong panties or if it was accidental. Either way, he wasn't complaining.

"If we are careful we can live a long time," he said slowly. "And no matter what some may think, our kind is a small number compared to the rest of humanity. It's natural for us to run into each other throughout the years. And not all of them are pleasant encounters."

"But you still deal with the Protectorate," she pointed out. "And don't tell me you don't."

"I told you I don't work for them."

Jazz nodded. "Yes, you did tell me that and we both know you lied to me because when we were at that house the first ones you called were the Protectorate enforcers."

"Because they're the ones who deal with a clean-up of that nature!" he snapped. "Damn it, Jazz, why do I feel as if I'm on trial here? Because I didn't tell you about Angelica being named director? The last hour is proof why I didn't say anything. I knew you'd have a fit about it and so you are."

"Perhaps it has something to do with the fact that even though I never met her years ago she tried to have me killed! To this day, I don't even know why." She abruptly snapped her mouth shut. She dropped back against the couch with her head resting against the cushions as she rubbed her temples. "And this is exactly why I despise her. She doesn't even have to be in the room for us to fight." Something niggled the back of her brain that she couldn't put her finger on. The harder she tried to focus on it the more it eluded her. She finally gave up before she ended up with a mammoth headache. "Something's very wrong about her."

"That's nothing new." He relaxed in the chair now that he felt assured he wouldn't end up a victim of spontaneous combustion. "Besides, why ruin the rest of the evening with talk of my past when we can focus on the present?"

"You have a one-track mind, vampire."

"Only when it comes to a certain witch." He could easily match her snarl for snarl.

Jazz's eyes still glittered with torrid green lights as she slowly rose to her feet. The stilettos squeaked a protest when she bent over and picked them up, settling them in a corner of the couch with a pillow over them. She straightened up and walked the short distance to the chair. She straddled his lap and slowly sat down.

"Is there something you don't want your shoes to see?" Nick asked.

"More like I'm not one to want an audience." She fingered the buttons lining his shirtfront.

"This is a new shirt," he murmured, watching the flash of her red polished nails sliding between two of the buttons.

One rip had the buttons flying everywhere. "Buy another one." She rubbed against his thigh with sensuous feline grace as she effectively shredded his shirt then went to work on his slacks. She raised up long enough to push his slacks and boxers down to his ankles. She deliberately ignored his cock rising up to bob a happy hello at her.

"If you'd let me up, I could kick them off," Nick murmured, slightly raising one foot.

"Now, why would I do that when I have you in my power?" She leaned forward to nuzzle his ear then nibbled on the lobe. "And I do," she whispered with a dart of her tongue. She smiled as he shuddered. The subtle abrasion of her silk thong rubbing against Nick's thigh soon had her labia pink, plump, and damp with arousal.

Nick's nostrils flared at the musky scent of her while a pinpoint of red appeared in his dark eyes. "Power can shift before one is aware of what's going on." He lifted his thigh enough to increase the pressure against her. He slipped his hand under her dress, unerringly finding the tiny mole that dotted the area just above her pubic hair.

Jazz gasped softly at the lightning flashing through her body, but she wasn't about to allow Nick to have any say in this sexual adventure.

She leaned forward until her lips brushed his ear. "You have something to fill. But you must remain still. And if you're a very good boy, you will get quite a thrill." She smiled as she stopped before completing her spell.

"You little witch." Nick's grin grew wider.

"Beep beep, beep beep, take us where Nick sleeps. Because I say so, damn it!" In the wink of an eye, they were sprawled on Nick's bed. Before Jazz could say anything more, Nick had shifted them so that she lay under him.

"Very nice," she whispered in a breathy voice that literally dripped sex. "You didn't even need to use any vampire tricks on me."

He dipped his head and ran his lips along the curve of her throat. While he didn't need to breathe, he could still detect the rich scent of her perfume mixed with the potent musk of her skin and arousal, which he found even more intoxicating than human blood. He felt ready to burst into spontaneous combustion as she feathered her fingers over his cock with a touch that teased but didn't deliver.

She lifted her hands and cupped his face and kissed him with a heat and passion that started up that spontaneous combustion idea again. Her tongue tangled with his, darting here and there, leaving behind the taste of the wine she'd drunk at the club. At the same time, she angled her body just right to rub her breasts against his chest until he felt the pebbled points of her nipples stroking his skin.

Nick watched Jazz as a red-polished nail outlined her areola, then lightly scored her skin, leaving the faintest of pink lines behind before fading to nothingness. Nick couldn't keep his eyes off her activity when all he wanted was to rear up and bury himself inside her. He didn't think she could torture him any more until she ran her finger down her middle and further down to slide between her lips, lightly touching his cock at the same time. When she held the digit up the skin was shiny with her juices.

"You just may have found a way to kill me," he said hoarsely.

"Then what a way to go." She ran her finger across his lips. His tongue flicked out to lap up what she left behind. As he did that, Jazz lightly raked her nails down his chest until she reached the place he wanted her to touch, but as if reading his thoughts she veered away, gently running her nails back up his chest.

"You have always been the only one for me," Nick admitted.

"You existed many years before we first met," Jazz murmured, showing a vulnerability she rarely revealed.

"And no one has ever affected me the way you do." He tucked a lock of hair behind her ear. "My existence is whole with you."

She exhaled a soft "oh!" "Damn it, Nick, if you make me cry!" She punched him in the chest but without any heat or anger.

"Then only cry in pleasure," he whispered in her ear,

combing his fingers through the crisp coppery hair until he reached his goal. She was wet and plump with desire.

Nick closed his eyes, allowing all the heat of desire to race through him as Jazz moved her lower body against his erection.

Just as Nick was positive he would implode from all the sensation rolling through his body, Jazz lifted up as he bore down. He felt himself swell even more as she swiveled her hips and rocked back and forth slower than he would have liked. Normally he would have wanted nothing more than to grab her by the hair to kiss her senseless as he fucked her into another century. But he'd seen another side of Jazz. One she rarely allowed to be seen. His hexy witch needed romance. He slowed his movements, dropping his head to nuzzling her ear, stroking her lips with his tongue, and murmuring compliments.

"Do you know how good you feel to me?" he murmured, grazing his teeth over her throat. The fact that she allowed him without threatening dire consequences if he broke the skin told him how trusting she had become that night. He moved his hips in a lazy rhythm.

"Maybe as good as you feel to me? All hard but covered with this velvety skin. I can already feel the tremors begin inside me," she said. So could Nick as he felt her inner muscles tighten around him. He only hoped she'd come soon or he'd definitely go up in flames. He groaned as a fire seemed to build up inside him. She chuckled. "Hmm, my very own vamp vibrator."

"Let's talk about how good you feel to me." Maybe he could survive if he did some talking of his own. "Wet and tight. Hot molten. . ." his words were cut off as her mouth covered his with a kiss that was even more stirring than the previous one. Heat poured off her body and mouth turning her into a witchy furnace that threatened to incinerate him. Flames he would gladly welcome as long as Jazz was a part of it.

Nick felt the tension overtake his body and knew it wouldn't be long. But before that could happen, Jazz laughed softly and slid out from under him and flipped around to kneel by his thigh. Nick cursed in Russian at the untimely interruption until Jazz leaned down and covered his cock with her mouth.

Nick closed his eyes as he dug his fingers into Jazz's hair as her mouth moved up and down on his cock. It was a feeling he couldn't have described if his existence depended on it. He felt her warm fingers cradle his sac, rolling the velvety skin between her fingers. He lay there and allowed himself to just *feel*.

Before he knew it he felt the familiar tightening of his lower body and knew it wouldn't be long before he would be lost to his body.

"Not this way," he whispered, pulling her up and over him to settle on his cock. With a desperation that echoed his own, she nibbled on his lips and quickened her movements until he felt his orgasm tear through him.

It wasn't until he finished that he realized he could once again move. Jazz stood up and disappeared into the bathroom. She returned with a damp cloth and cleansed him.

When she stood up she smiled down on him. "Your ego doesn't need to inflate anymore by my telling you what a fantastic lover you are and everything you mean to me," she said softly. "But you know me. I don't want to think that Angelica can mess with our lives. And especially mess with you. So if you ever keep something like that from me again I will bite it off," she informed him.

Nick winced. He had no doubt she would do it, too.

Chapter 13

"COME ON, JAZZ. IT'S AN EASY JOB FOR TONIGHT AND SINCE it's last minute I'm charging a double rate," Dweezil told her before she could barely get out a hello. "I've got a high-profile client who wants you to pick her up at her house at ten and take her to the Velvet Trap." He mentioned a vampire club that was so exclusive it was not only filled with higher echelon members, but membership was by invitation only. He then rattled off an address in Holmby Hills, one of the priciest neighborhoods in L.A. "I got a great deal on a Bentley, so you'll be taking that. But if you get even a tiny scratch on it, it's coming out of your pay."

Jazz jotted down the address. "I'm driving a vampire?" They were her least favorite clients since they tended to get fangy after they partied for a while. And vampires didn't like witches what with their blood being poisonous, so it wasn't as if they could snack on the driver. She also found them lousy tippers. "Who's the client, Dweezil?" She frowned as she heard the dial tone. "If he's hanging up before he tells me who she is then it's not a good thing. Or he knows it won't make me happy. I opt for both options."

But the idea of her share of the double fee kept her from calling Dweezil back and telling him she couldn't do it because she had to wash her hair.

When she arrived at the garage that evening, she found more than the usual number of dwarves bustling around several new limos in the bays.

"Hey, Kurdilir, I thought you were working for Mindy," she said, greeting the lead mechanic who walked up to her with a slight waddle on his short legs.

"I was, but her old man laid us all off," he grumbled, shifting from one short leg to the other like a mini Sumo wrestler. "He said if he's giving work to anyone it'll be his own kind. Seems Santa laid off a bunch of his elves, so Eilemar hired them. Yeah, like a bunch of toymakers know how to change a tire or bleed brakes. Asshole will be out of business in no time." His slightly pushed in features scrunched up even more. "Dweezil heard what happened and offered us our jobs back."

"Please don't tell me you took less pay." She knew her skinflint of a boss only too well. If Dweezil thought he could get a bargain he'd take it in a heartbeat.

He shook his head. "The guys who stayed behind weren't doing all that good a job, so he was glad to have us back, so I fought for an increase for all of us and actually got it. The only thing he'll admit he doesn't know is how to service a car, so he'll pay if he wants the vehicles in perfect running order. He purchased a few new vehicles from a police auction." He gestured toward a champagne colored Bentley that gleamed like a rare pearl under the lights. "She's ready to go, gorgeous. The bar's stocked with plenty of AB neg."

Jazz still hated that she'd be driving a vampire. But the idea of driving the luxury car was overriding any apprehension to do with her unknown client.

She looked toward the office and found the interior lights on dim. She'd already noticed that Dweezil's Jag was noticeably absent from his slot in the garage.

"He said he had an errand to run." Kurdilir noticed the direction of her gaze.

"Uh huh, and I bet he left five minutes before I arrived. The coward. Is Grevia still working here?"

The dwarf shook his head. "Some vendor came in and totally freaked out when two of her fingers fell off. Seems there's some zombie support group that will help them find peace, so he sent her there. He hasn't hired anyone new yet. That's not making him too happy since he doesn't like dealing with people."

"No kidding." She caught the keys Kurdilir tossed toward her and headed for the Bentley. "Say, would you guys mind washing the T-Bird while I'm gone?"

Kurdilir's face broke out in a broad grin. Unlike many of the drivers, Jazz shared her tips with the mechanics and even paid them to hand wash and detail the classic car.

"You know I hate those little perverts doing unspeakable things to me!" Irma wailed from the passenger seat.

"Ignore her," Jazz told Kurdilir as she tossed him her key ring.

He grinned. "No problem there. It's the dog who's hard to ignore. He tries humping us."

"He seems to do that a lot." Jazz sketched him a salute and took off for the Bentley with Irma's protests and the dog's barks ringing in her ears.

"Finally, D did something right." She settled into the heated leather seat with a blissful sigh. She familiarized herself with all the bells and whistles then took off.

Jazz enjoyed driving through Holmby Hills since it boasted some of the most exclusive pieces of real estate in the state. While she had no desire to live in the elite area, she liked visiting.

"I wonder if the celebrities around here know they have a vampire in their midst or if they consider it part of the charm? Maybe it makes the property values go up," she muttered, slowing down to identify herself at the gate guarding the home then rolling through as the gate slowly slid back. She parked in front of an antebellum-style mansion that could have been transplanted from the Old South. "Wow, Scarlett O'Hara goes west." She climbed out of the limo and climbed the stairs to the front door. Elegant carriage lamps on either side of the double doors flickered as if lit by candlelight instead of electricity.

"I'm from All Creatures Car Service," she told the stone-faced butler who answered the door and she could have sworn his face literally was made from stone.

He merely inclined his head and gestured for her to enter. "Madam is in the drawing room." He indicated she follow him.

Jazz was surprised since the client was usually ready to go when she arrived or complained that Jazz was late even if she was early. Vampires had no sense of time except for their own idea of what it should be.

The minute she stepped into the drawing room she realized just why Dweezil hadn't given her the name of the client. He had to have known Jazz wouldn't drive her anywhere but to the local landfill.

The woman stood amid eighteenth-century antiques that suited the Southern mansion exterior. Her dress, however, was pure twenty-first century with a slit in the neckline that reached her waist and hinted at the full swell of pale-skinned breasts. She wore a deep purple velvet figure-hugging gown that Jazz would have killed for, except she knew a hole in the dress where the non-beating heart resided would totally ruin the fabric. Still, she liked the idea of planting a stake in this creature's heart and then she'd just shop and find the same gown. The vampire's long nails were polished a matching purple that glowed almost black in the dim light. At the moment her fingertips rested on a rare Lalique kneeling nude figurine, a gold ring with a red black opal winking on her right hand. A pendant was the same color.

The woman with burnished golden hair that flowed down to her waist in loose waves stood barely five-foot-one, but the power that radiated from her was strong enough to push Jazz back a step. The witch focused on keeping herself grounded because no way was she going to allow this particular vampire to push her around.

"Good evening, Jazz." Her accented voice that boasted of European roots was lyrical, pure music to the hearer's ears, and complemented a face that rivaled a seraph's. Her eyes matched the rare red and black opal she wore with its shades of black, red, gold, and blue in its unlimited depths. While the uncommon stone held fire, Jazz only saw coldness in the woman's eyes. A vampire who lost all traces of humanity centuries ago. If she even had any to begin with.

"Angelica." Jazz ignored the ball of ice that formed in the pit of her stomach. While there was more than its share of animosity between the witch and vampire society, there were still rules that had to be followed. One of them was that Jazz was prevented from bringing up a whopping big fireball, so she could put the bloodsucking bitch's lights out.

Well, she could do that, but there'd be Hades to pay and her present year's probation with the Witches' Council had more than six months left to go.

Damn it!

"I understand you're going to The Velvet Trap," she said, keeping her voice as formal and remote as she could even if fury filled her to the marrow.

"Yes, I am." The vampire's dark eyes studied her as if she was an insect under a microscope. Probably not all that far from wrong either since Angelica considered the entire world her own private hunting ground.

"Congratulations on advancing to the position of director." The words tasted like ashes in her mouth. Miss Manners would be proud of her since it was the last thing she wanted to say when *die bitch die* was more to the point. "I understand after the death of Flavius, the previous director felt it was time to step down and you were there to take over. How fortuitous."

Angelica smiled as if there was no implied insult in Jazz's words. "Thank you. I know you don't mean it, but I appreciate that you are gracious enough to offer the words. Yes, with Flavius gone it's been a very sad and trying time for so many of us. Vincent's power was weakening and he felt it was time to take a much needed rest."

Jazz didn't bother to return the smile. Good manners only went so far and she was pretty much at the end of her rope.

"If you're ready to leave," she said, wanting out of the house that she imagined smelled of death even if all she detected was the rich scent of gardenias.

Angelica moved with a sinuous grace she must have been born with, although a few thousand years can give one a lot of practice.

Jazz once heard a rumor that Angelica had been one of Cleopatra's most trusted handmaidens. Jazz figured she was the one to hand the Egyptian queen the deadly asp, if not actually press it to her breast. Maybe not even at the queen's direction. Jazz wouldn't put anything past the vampire.

Angelica stood very still, watching Jazz. The witch was glad she'd dressed accordingly in tailored black fine wool pants, a cream colored silk tuxedo styled shirt, and a black wool jacket. She had pulled her hair back in a French braid, threading a black silk ribbon through the braid. She'd left the stilettos home and opted for black half boots. Now she wished she was wearing something more lethal.

Angelica moved past with the glide inherent in vampires. The stone-faced butler stood by the door with a black velvet hooded cape in his hands. She allowed him to drape it over her shoulders then waited as he opened the door for her. She swept out of the house with the grace of a queen. Jazz followed feeling more like the court jester.

Jazz released a sigh of relief once the passenger door was closed behind Angelica, who was ensconced in the backseat with a Waterford wine glass of AB neg in her hand.

She realized her luck wasn't holding when the privacy window was lowered.

"Is there something you need, Angelica?" she asked politely, the perfect chauffeur.

"No, but since it is just me back here I thought I'd leave it down and we could chat. It's so rare for me to find someone who has the strength to do what you have done. You don't mind, do you?"

"No, of course not." She was positive her nose grew a good half-inch. She decided this was a lie best said rather than the truth she would have preferred spouting. The last person she'd want to chat with was the monster sitting in the backseat.

"You were quite the heroine in saving our kind at Clive Reeves' mansion several months ago," Angelica said, running her fingertip along the rim of her wine glass. "I understand you also returned to the property to cleanse it."

Jazz's stomach tightened at the memory of the night she came way too close to losing her life. Along with that memory was a quick replay of her dream where she and Nick were the shades haunting the property and Reeves still lived. "It had to be done," she replied. "I don't think anyone wanted him to return and harm more vampires. Also his destroying a member of your council couldn't have endeared him to you. I understand Flavius was respected by many." She felt a bit of satisfaction when she saw Angelica's lips tighten. Proof that the vampire and Flavius, who truly cared about his kind, must have been at odds for some time.

"Yes, but I can't imagine any witch who would be so foolhardy as to brave Clive's lair even with the prospect of ending up in his dungeon as you had. You were very lucky you weren't killed in the process." Her musical laughter was off by just a hair. The tone was enough to set Jazz's teeth on edge.

Ending up in his dungeon. Her fingers tightened on the steering wheel until her knuckles turned white. "Yes, well, some of us don't like bullies." She felt her head and jaw aching with the tight rein she kept on her temper.

"A bully is only a coward who needs to be shown who's really in charge." Angelica sat back and crossed her legs, revealing a pale expanse of leg up to her thigh. "That is why every society needs an alpha. I've always believed our sex is much stronger than the males. That we know how to run things properly."

Like you? Jazz exhaled a deep breath. She was positive by the time the evening was over, she'd have a massive migraine. For a witch who rarely suffered a headache, lately she was sure making up for it.

Ending up in his dungeon. The words rolled over in her head as she drove through Beverly Hills until she pulled up in front of a modernistic building built in the 1930s with *The Velvet Trap* written in stylized script on the canopy that led to the street. A valet ran forward and opened the rear passenger door.

"Return for me at four and not one moment earlier or later," Angelica instructed without looking at Jazz, now relegating her to nothing more than a servant.

"In case you change your mind and wish to leave earlier just call the car service number and press Star 6. That will page me," she said, keeping her eyes forward.

"I'm sure I won't."

Jazz waited until the door was firmly closed then rolled forward. Her first inclination was to burn rubber outta there, but the last thing she wanted to do was attract attention or allow Angelica to realize she had gotten to her.

Ending up in the dungeon. "That bitch! And I bet she knows exactly what happened down there and not the story Nick and I agreed would be told to the Vampire Council, which wasn't everything that happened." She made her way through the streets to the freeway. The vehicle responded to her touch with a burst of power.

Jazz wanted nothing more than to heap a mountain of curses on the bloodsucking bitch, but that would only get her into so much trouble with the Witches' Council she'd never escape the fallout.

Her first thought was to call Nick and tell him what Angelica said, but considering the mood she was in she knew she'd say something she shouldn't. Plus, she realized that while she was angry, she also felt very unsettled from her conversation with Angelica even if the vampire had done most of the talking.

"And no way this little witch is going to go to big strong macho vampire for help when there's no reason she can't handle this herself," she muttered, making a quick U-turn when she saw a Starbucks. There was something about a Venti cinnamon dolce latte that helped her think more clearly.

By the time she had two lattes and sat through what was advertised as a spine-chilling thriller that turned out to be a yawner, she picked up an Angelica who appeared downright merry.

I wonder whose vein cheered her up so much. Jazz had made sure the privacy screen was up before she returned to The Velvet Trap and luckily for Jazz, it remained up for the trip.

When she arrived back at Angelica's house and opened the rear passenger door she heard a snatch of Italian before Angelica snapped her cell phone shut and tucked it into her small evening bag.

"You are very good driver, Jazz," she said as she stepped out of the Bentley. "So many I've encountered tend to have a heavy foot on the pedal or brake too abruptly. I will let Dweezil know I was very pleased with your service." She placed her folded fingers in Jazz's hand and walked up to the open front door that the stone-faced butler stood by.

Jazz's fingers tightened on the small roll of bills that Angelica left there. She didn't need to count it to know she had never received this large a tip, not even from the lascivious Tyge Foulshadow. The idea of dropping the money to the ground lingered in her mind for about two seconds. She knew the bad taste the money left in her mouth would disappear once she turned it over to the Witches' Benevolent Fund. There was no reason witches down on their luck should suffer because she wanted to indulge in a witchy temper tantrum.

As she left the property in the rapidly appearing dawn, the pinkish light gave the Southern-style mansion a decidedly creepy look as if ghosts of Confederate soldiers would soon descend on it.

"I really can't stand that woman."

❖ ❖ ❖

The balcony overlooked a lush green expanse of petit gazon, *or Louisanagrass, and beyond that was a row of cypress and oak trees, laden with Spanish moss damp with moisture.*

But instead of the scene giving her peace, she felt mind-numbing terror as she stood barefoot on the white-washed wooden planks that were wet with blood-flecked liquid. Her white gown, made of fine lawn, looked like a sack hanging on her emaciated body with its distended belly that twisted and turned with signs of impending birth. Her broken nails dug into the wood as she clutched the railing while pain rolled through her body. She gazed outward, her hope growing as weak as her body as the one she prayed to return wasn't in sight.

"Let us in, ma petite," *the male voice was husky, cajoling even as the knock on the door was made with a heavy-handed fist that promised pain more horrific than what went on within her body.*

Her stomach clenched with fear as she saw the door shiver under the pounding. The door may have been of solid cypress, but that didn't mean it wouldn't eventually give in to the madman's fury.

"You are very sick, chérie. *Please come here and unlock the door. We need to help you before the babe arrives. Let us in. Allow the midwife to attend to you."*

She knew the last thing he wanted was for a midwife to attend her. He could sound so sweet, so tender. But his hands were hard and calloused, made for violence, not tender caresses. There was an excellent reason why he made many trips to the slave markets in New Orleans. Slaves tended to die when the lash was laid too heavily on their bodies and he preferred to be the one to mete out the punishment. She knew he wouldn't hesitate to use the lash on her if she defied him for much longer.

She cradled her belly with her hands, feeling the rolls and bumps of her child who was so eager to be born. It was a time when she should be eagerly awaiting the arrival of her baby. Instead, because of the man on the other side of the door, she feared it wouldn't live long outside of her womb and she would soon follow her child into the afterlife.

"No, my little one, it is too soon." Her eyes burned with her tears as she scanned the grounds, looking for the only one who could save her. "We must wait." She cried out as the pain wrapped around her belly. She gripped the French door, the remnants of her fingernails breaking under the force. When the pain receded, she collapsed against the door, panting heavily.

"You bitch! I will not allow you to do this!" The roar on the other side of the door left her trembling with fear even as the door seemed to bow under his blows. "You cannot lock me out of my own room. Let me in now or suffer the consequences."

She licked her chapped lips and tried to remain upright even as her legs threatened to give way. But she knew if she collapsed she wouldn't be able to get up again. It was the twenty-third of the month and he promised to be back by then. All would have been well, but her husband found the letter his brother had written to her. A letter speaking of love and passion, his joy at the impending birth of their child, and that he would come to take her away from the hell she'd lived in and the devil who tormented her.

Luck had been on her side. If she hadn't been feeling ill that noon and spent that time resting in bed, she would have been downstairs and incurred her husband's wrath where she wouldn't have had a chance to escape. Instead, her maid had just enough time to warn her, so that she could bar the door from the man who had left her with cuts and bruises too many times over the five years they'd been wed.

"Your papa is coming," she whispered to the child eager to join the world. "We must wait for him to arrive. He will protect us." But she knew by the increasing pain that wasn't possible and that she would be dead before her lover could reach her. There would be no warm and loving family life in another city where they would be safe. She always knew she wouldn't escape, but the dream of doing so had kept her going during the dark nights.

She started and looked over her shoulder as the crack of an axe striking the door soon sent pieces of wood flying. A tall man wearing a white linen shirt and riding breeches stood in the doorway. He held a whip handle in one hand. For one brief moment the flash of a pale face appeared behind him then seemed to disappear back into the dark hallway.

"Eve!" She spun around to look out over the lawn, spying the man she'd been waiting for riding toward her. There was no mistaking the love and light on his face, just as she saw the darkness and hate on her husband's features as he stalked into the room. The miasma of hate and violence roiled around him like a dark cloud.

"Please, don't." She backed away. "The baby is coming." She hoped he would show compassion for the child. It was quickly apparent he wouldn't.

"You shall bear no bastard, bitch, even if I have to cut that babe out of you," he growled.

She blindly felt behind her for the balcony railing, sensing the wood against her back.

"I beg for your mercy." While she hated him with every fiber of her being she would do anything for the child. She could hear the shouts and sounds of boots pounding up the stairs. But looking into her husband's eyes she knew her lover would be too late.

"Philippe, no!"

Eve looked past her tormenter and gazed at the man she had loved since childhood but lost when her father sold her to Philippe to settle his gambling debts. Philippe had always envied anything his brother had and his acquiring Eve as his wife was the ultimate triumph in his eyes.

He looked over his shoulder. His features darkened further as he stared at the man who shared his blood, but he had no more feeling for him than he had for his hunting dogs. "If you want her so badly, brother, I suggest you run fast."

Neither lover had an idea of Philippe's intent until it was too late as he quickly scooped her up into his arms and dropped her over the balcony.

Eve's screams mingled with the cry of horror from her lover as he rushed to the railing. At the moment her body hit the stone pavement below and before her life force abandoned her she saw the shadow of a man following her.

She had no idea that when the man she loved so dearly landed beside her, his hand flung out as if to touch her. But even in death they were fated to be kept apart.

❖ ❖ ❖

Jazz awoke feeling as if every bone in her body had been pulled in a different direction. No wonder, considering what her dream self had done to herself. She cupped her hands over her face to stop the hyperventilation, but it took some time for her breathing to return to normal.

She lay back down, forcing herself to relive every moment of the dream, once again experiencing the horror, fear, and helplessness of knowing there would be no reprieve for a woman guilty of nothing other than being forced into a brutal marriage and finding love elsewhere. And having no way to escape that terror except through death.

"There's something I'm missing," she whispered to herself. Even though she hated the idea, she mentally replayed the dream once more, slowing it down and pausing as if viewing a DVD. In time, what eluded her became viciously clear. The flash of light behind Philippe finally turned into a face that was familiar to her. The face of an angel coupled with the soul of evil. A woman who had a smile on her face, as if she knew the young Eve would soon meet her death.

Angelica.

Jazz forced her dream-battered body out of bed and limped her way to the bathroom for a long hot shower.

"I don't care how powerful she is, the bitch has got to go."

Chapter 14

"THE BITCH HAS GOT TO GO."

Nick looked up from the paperwork strewn in front of him. How he hated living in a millennium that demanded more forms by the moment. Yet, at this minute the thought of filling out the forms seemed a lot more appealing than dealing with Jazz, even if his saucy witch looked damn hot in black leather jeans and a black knit top highlighted with a lilac Pashmina shawl draped artfully around her shoulders. Her copper red hair was pulled back in a mass of spiral curls spilling down her back. He noticed her crocodile stilettos had decided to match her shawl instead of going for basic black and if he wasn't mistaken they wore lilac eye shadow. His nostrils flared at the rich scent of something light and floral. It figured her choice of fragrance would be lilac too.

"Nick!" That one sharp spoken word brought him back to the present.

"I thought you hated the B word."

Jazz dropped into the chair across from him. "I do, but when we're talking Angelica, we're talking bitch with a capital B. She's behind the dreams."

Nick rubbed his forehead. Vampires weren't supposed to feel stress, but then most vampires didn't deal with a snarky witch with attitude either.

"Angelica has much better things to do than find a way to give you nightmares. Directors of the Protectorate don't have time to make one witch's sleep miserable."

She peered at him sharply. "It's just not me and you know it." She settled back with a smug smile when he sat up straighter. "Krebs has had odd dreams too and so has Irma."

"I've had a few," he admitted.

"Such as?"

"Just the usual." *Such as a sexy witch ending up with a white picket fence lifestyle or his taking her life in a violent manner.*

"Like any of us would have usual nightmares. If we did, my biggest nightmare would be standing in the middle of the mall without credit cards or finding out Starbucks went out of business." Jazz absently stroked her tiny Kate Spade bag. "Or I'd somehow end up with every curse I've eliminated. And some of them weren't all that pleasant." She considered her words. "Actually, none of them were. Especially that rash on that guy who was engaged to six women at the same time. You remember, the one where they all ganged up on him," she reflected.

"You didn't eliminate that curse."

"Only because he really deserved that rash and I told him so." Jazz took a deep breath. "But back to the blood-sucking bitch."

Nick rubbed his temples. "Jazz, no name calling."

"Oh come on, I'm speaking the truth." She drummed her fingertips on the chair arm. "Any ideas who she'd use to conjure up your basic terrifying nightmares? It's got to be a wizard." She wrinkled her nose as if something smelled bad.

Nick grinned. "You're not blaming a witch for this?"

She shook her head. "Not after I really thought about it. A witch would get to the heart of it. Zap you once good and strong. Not lead up to it. We don't go in for torture when we can do it all at once and have it over with." She stopped, thinking of her last nightmare. The fear and pain that went with it. Someone wanted her to suffer and suffer was exactly what she did. "Besides, I had a nightmare that featured Angelica."

Nick shook his head. "Just because you heard she's back in town you dreamed about her? Isn't that a bit much?"

"Not when this witch drove that vampire to The Velvet Trap the other night and she first acted like my new best female friend then relegated me to the role of servant. Probably because she was in her role as high muckety muck of vampires." She idly examined her nails. Nick noticed even they were polished a shimmering lavender and looked a little too sharp for comfort.

"And once again, why would she want to bother with you?" He knew playing devil's advocate here was dangerous since he was only too aware of Jazz's feelings toward Angelica. Not that the head vampire was one of his favorite people. He had his own issues with Angelica and would have to deal with them on his own. Not something he would say to Jazz either, because knowing her, she would want to do her thing whether it was a good idea or not. Her sense that Angelica could have something to do with her nightmares was something he'd also thought of, but he wanted to be wrong. Except now Jazz was thinking the same thing.

"Even with her 'let's be best friends forever' crap, we both know I'm not her favorite witch," she admitted.

"What do you expect? You piss off the vampire community on a regular basis."

"And you don't?"

"No, I piss off the witch community." A hint of a grin lifted the corner of his lips. It was soon echoed on Jazz's mouth until it blossomed into a full smile.

"Gee, with our charming personalities people would think we were made for each other." She leaned over to take a look at the paperwork on Nick's desk. He shot her a warning look and pushed it together into a pile and off into a drawer.

"Is that the only reason you showed up here? To tell me you think Angelica is your nighttime boogievamp and you want me to head over to her house and call her out?"

"If that was the case, I'd rather go over there at high noon on a hot summer day and call her out. Although, you really do owe me for getting you out of Clive Reeves' mansion before you bled out. I took care of Clive, so it seems fair that you take care of Angelica." She conveniently forgot her vow that she wouldn't ask someone to take care of her problem for her.

"Do you have any idea how old she is?"

"I know she's been around as far back as Cleopatra. And for all I know she crawled around wearing a saber-toothed tiger skin and had a really ugly high forehead." She stood up, wrapping her shawl more tightly around her. "I do know that in my dream I saw her gloating face as my husband broke down my bedroom door, strode in, and in front of the man I truly loved tossed my pregnant body over the balcony railing."

Nick flinched. "Jazz—"

She shook her head. "I believe Angelica has her blood-stained fingers in this dream pie and I intend to prove it."

"The last time you tried to search out the source you ended up with a house that smelled like a toxic dump. What if the next time you end up mortal for all time?"

"Then I'll just have to find another way, won't I?" She exited the office with a dramatic flourish.

His blood may not flow through his veins, but he was positive his blood pressure was at an all-time high. And while peace and quiet returned to his office once Jazz was gone, Nick didn't feel all that serene.

"Why do I feel she's going to get into trouble and I'll have to find a way to extricate her," he muttered. His eyes fell on a chunk of obsidian on his desk that doubled as a paperweight. It had been a gift from Flavius many years ago. "You should still be among the undead, my friend. If you were here you would be the new director, not that venomous bitch."

At least he hadn't told Jazz that he agreed with her assumption. Once Reinhold told him that Angelica had risen to the position of director he felt that she had something to do with the unsettling dreams he and Jazz were having. If there was something Angelica did well, it was hold grudges. She held a very major grudge toward Jazz. And a much bigger one toward him for leaving her. And even with their battles over the centuries, he always returned to Jazz while he refused to return to Angelica.

He picked up the phone and tapped out a number he never thought he'd call.

"We need to talk," he said when Reinhold's growl sounded from the other end of the line.

"This is a curse, right?" The bleached, liposuctioned, and ultra-thin blonde who Jazz sensed was already a plastic surgeon's dream client was dressed more like she was in her early twenties than her mid-thirties. Her strapless hot pink dress barely covered the essentials with the tiny shrug sweater with pink and silver threads to add to her "let's go clubbing" look.

Jazz looked out over the deck complete with chaise longues, tables, and umbrellas. She doubted the deck was used for anything but parties. The woman's spray tan was proof she didn't use the sun for color.

She stared at a deck overlooking Los Angeles that could have been considered for *Architectural Digest*—except for the frogs and slugs that covered the wood. Bullfrogs and their smaller brothers hopped around on the tables while fat slugs crawled up table legs and chairs and chaises. One extremely large bullfrog sat in the center of the deck and erupted a deep froggy growl. What sounded like thousands of coyotes howled from the foothills.

"My neighbors are trying to get me to move," Sofi "with a fi, not phie" moaned, wringing her hands as she stood behind Jazz as the witch surveyed the animal kingdom. "They say I'm a nuisance. I didn't do this!"

"But you know who did." She turned around, studying a room that was so white it hurt her eyes. The only hint of color was a large abstract painting over the fireplace that was equally eye burning in glossy shades of red, black, and, you got it, white.

"Denny Masters," Sofi spat out the name. She reached over to a small table and picked up a black envelope. Her name was written in elegant calligraphy in silver ink.

The minute Jazz took the envelope she felt a hint of magick covering the envelope. The black cardstock inside was even stronger, although she sensed it was a lot stronger before Sofi opened the card.

You claim to be looking for a prince, bitch. Here's your chance.

"And the minute you read the words the frogs and slugs appeared," she said.

Sofi nodded. "They just popped up everywhere!"

"Scorned lover?"

She shook her head. "Not a chance. The guy wouldn't even be my thousandth choice. He was a disgusting hairy prick. I told him I'd rather have a. . ."

"Prince," Jazz finished for her. "So he found a way to give you that chance." She swallowed her sigh. She *really* hated dealing with curses from the rejected. They were always gross and messy. "Okay, let's see what's really out there." She took a deep breath—she always hated anything slimy—and stepped outside. When the frogs retreated from her she knew that they recognized just what she was. "Show me what you are."

"What is it?" Sofi demanded.

Jazz waved her hand, indicating she wanted silence. She walked around the deck, stopping every so often to examine a frog—*euww!* And checked out a few slugs.

"This is a good one," she said, once she returned to the house.

"But you can get rid of it," Sofi demanded. "I was told you're the best."

"I am the best, but this isn't your everyday curse. It wasn't set up as a curse, but as a powerful spell."

"Meaning what?" Sofi tottered around the room on her four-inch Christian Louboutin peep-toe pumps.

"Meaning I banish curses. Only the one who cast a spell can remove it."

"But I don't know who did this!"

Jazz winced at the shriek that assaulted her eardrums. "Actually, this spell is set up for *you* to remove."

"Me? I don't know anything about magick. That's why I hired you."

Jazz shook her head. "The spell needs you to do it."

"But how do I find out what to do?"

"It's easy." She just knew this wasn't going to go well. At least she'd received her fee up front. Maybe there wasn't a curse to eliminate, but she still had to work at figuring out what happened. She picked up her bag.

"So what do I do? I'm not moving! This is a prime piece of real estate!"

"You don't have to move, Sofi," Jazz said, heading for the front door. "Just remember your fairy tales."

"Fairy tales?" Sofi shook her head. "Who remembers fairy tales?"

"You have the Internet, right? Look up *The Frog Prince*," she advised. "It will tell you how to get rid of the frogs and slugs and I bet once they're gone the coyote howls will disappear at the same time."

She noticed that Sofi was busily typing away on her laptop as Jazz exited the house. She'd barely seated herself in the T-Bird when she heard an ear-splitting shriek from the house.

"What was that?" Irma's cigarette disappeared in a puff of smoke. . .literally.

"I guess Sofi with an 'i' found out what she needs to do to remove the spell. There was no curse in there. And the only way she can remove the spell is to kiss every frog hopping around on her deck. She told a guy she wanted a prince and that's what he sent her. An army of frogs and a whole mess of slugs."

"It sounds like she needed someone from pest control instead of you."

"Not with this." She put the car into gear and backed out of the driveway. She looked through the windshield and saw Sofi pacing back and forth in front of the bay window, her hands moving and lips moving just as frantically as she spoke on her phone. Jazz guessed she'd called the spurned suitor in hopes of finding another way to end the spell. She was pretty sure anyone who laid out serious money for a spell that complicated wasn't going to take it back just because Sofi asked him to.

"How many frogs were out there?" Irma smoothed her hands over her gray tweed wool pants that she'd paired with a soft blue sweater. Jazz was grateful the woman was willing to dress her age. Even Irma's blush was changed to a rosier shade that matched her lipstick. The ghost was making good use of the fashion magazines Jazz picked up for her. Even the dog had stopped terrorizing Mrs. Sanderson's Pepper, or at least was doing it when she wasn't around.

"More than I cared to count. I've got to say I was impressed with the intricacy of the spell." The sports car picked up speed as Jazz roared down the winding road. "Whoever did it knew just how to get to this woman."

"Except you didn't banish anything so you weren't paid."

"Oh, I was paid and she's heard enough gossip to know not to stop payment on the check. Besides, I figured out how she could end the spell. That took work."

"If you truly wanted to work you'd find a way that I could have food and drink. I do miss my pink squirrels and brandy Alexanders." Irma looked about as forlorn as a ghost who'd been dead for the last fifty years could look.

"You can change your looks and hair. Isn't that enough? You're not Pinocchio, Irma. I can't make you into a real woman. No matter what, you're still dead. There are some things you can't do." There were times she hated being so blunt, but she felt it had to be done. And this was one of those times. Not to mention she didn't want cracker crumbs everywhere. Plus, then she'd probably want the dog to have the ability to scarf down his share of real Milkbones.

"No kidding. Although, you'd think there would be some kind of dating service for us."

A lit Lucky Strike appeared between Irma's fingers then disappeared when Jazz uttered a warning growl.

"There's a dating service for vampires, so why not for us? I'm sure I'm not the only ghost wandering around," Irma went on.

A dating world for the living challenged. Oh no. Next thing Jazz knew Irma would be talking about sex and Jazz would have to claw her eyes out to keep the images from bombarding her brain.

"Be happy with what you've got, which is a hell of a lot more than you had six months ago. You even have a dog now. If you want to do something then do something for him. Give him a name!"

"He hasn't told me what his name is yet," Irma said primly. "It's not like he came with a collar and name tag."

"In a sense he has a new life now. Maybe he wants a new name to go with it. Find out what he wants to be called."

"Good idea." Irma appeared lost in thought as Jazz exited the mountain road.

Jazz slowed the car as she spied an official looking vehicle parked at the Full Moon Café and then confirmation of what shouldn't be inside the restaurant, but somehow was. She made a quick and very illegal U-turn, and headed back to the diner's parking lot. She parked next to the car that caught her attention.

"Why does it smell like wet dog around here?" Irma wrinkled her nose.

"That's nothing new to us thanks to your new pet." Jazz climbed out of the car.

"We should have brought the dog." The ghost looked around with a worried frown.

"Trust me, even dead, he wouldn't like it here." She walked to the entrance.

When Jazz stepped inside she heard the pounding sounds of Steppenwolf's *Born to be Wild* coming from the jukebox and a stocky man wearing a rumpled suit seated at the counter nursing a cup of coffee. Coby stood at the other end, staring at his customer with his usual flat black stare. The other man looked up at Jazz.

"Hey, it's Jazz the witch," Detective Larkin grinned. "What're you doing here?"

Jazz's gaze flipped to Coby, who wasn't saying a word, then back to the sheriff's detective. "More to the point, what are *you* doing here?"

"Having a cup of coffee." He gestured to the cup in front of him along with a plate with a half-eaten apple pie slice on it. "Can we have another cup for the lady?"

"She's no lady," Coby growled, literally, as he reached for a mug and filled it.

Jazz had encountered the detective when Dweezil was framed by Mindy and the authorities almost seized his business. While the man knew magick and supernatural creatures were around, he preferred to ignore the fact. Jazz showed him it was better not to disregard anything unusual.

She took a seat at the counter, murmuring her thanks for the coffee.

"Didn't you feel anything when you came in here?" she asked in a low voice.

The detective shrugged. "Like what? It's getting late and I wanted a caffeine fix. The place was open and it looks clean. Okay, I felt a little odd when I got out of my car, but like I said, I needed some caffeine. It's been a bitch of a day. How about you? Doing your witchy thing? Oh, want some pie to go with that coffee? It's pretty good."

Jazz looked at Coby instead. "Your wards are strong. I could feel them, so that's not it. And he's never been here before?" Coby settled for a quick jerk of the head.

Detective Larkin looked from one to the other. "What's going on here?" He shifted his arm so that his jacket lapel rolled back revealing his weapon.

"Forget that." Jazz flicked her fingers so that the jacket closed up again. "It wouldn't work here anyway."

"He didn't hesitate outside and just walked in," Coby finally said. "This isn't good for business. They'll smell him from a mile away."

"You have something against cops?" Larkin was now the steely-eyed lawman.

"Okay guys, no bumping up the testosterone count." Jazz put her hands up in a "stop it" motion. "This is more your thing than mine," she told Coby. "Why can't you explain it to him?"

"It looks like you know him. You do it." He placed a slice of pie in front of her and walked away.

"What the fuck is his problem?" Detective Larkin glared at Coby's retreating back.

Jazz forked up a bite of pie and almost groaned in bliss. Someone knew how to make great apple pie. She took another quick bite and set down her fork.

"Remember our talk about witches and vampires?"

"Yeah, that they're more real than I'd like to think. You proved that at Clive Reeves' house when you blew it up."

"I didn't destroy the mansion. Magick did that." She took a drink of her coffee and found it as dark and strong as she had the last time. "There's a lot more out there than witches and vampires and trolls and ogres and pixies."

"Okay, okay." He held up his hand. "Just spit it out."

"Your word skills are atrocious. Here's the deal. The Full Moon Café is aptly named because the main patrons here have a special ritual during the full moon." She waited for realization to kick in. Instead, she got a blank look. "Full moon. Ultra hairy. Big teeth. Don't you ever watch horror movies?"

"I'm more into sci-fi. I've seen *The Day the Earth Stood Still* hundreds of times."

Jazz exhaled a deep breath. "Werewolf." A growl erupted from the kitchen. "If you don't like the way I explained it, you should have done it yourself! Besides, it's not my fault he got past the wards."

"Werewolves, yeah," Detective Larkin snorted. "That's what my wife turns into every twenty-eight days." He laughed at his own joke. "Witches, okay. Vampires, I'm still working on, but Werewolves are a bit much. No way."

"Big way." She raised her voice even though she knew it wasn't necessary. "Coby, you have to come out here and convince the man."

"I'm not some pet you can trot out to show off to the neighbors," Coby muttered, walking out of the kitchen.

"I came in here out of the goodness of my heart," she ignored the snorts from both men. Terrific, now they bond! "so I could make sure that everything was okay and I even try to explain to the detective why he shouldn't be here and all I get is crap."

Detective Larkin looked at Coby as the man placed his hands on the counter. "Fuck!" He almost fell off the stool as Coby's facial bones shifted and lengthened to a snout, his eyes changing to an eerie yellow while his canines lengthened, and fur sprouted along the back of his hands. Larkin stared wide-eyed at the man whose face was now more wolf than human. He jerked around to Jazz. "What's next?"

"This café is considered neutral territory. Consider it Switzerland for all creatures if they need it, but it's mostly a hangout for the Weres," she explained. "The café is also heavily warded against humans. If any human stops here, they get an unsettling sensation and move on. Except for you." She glanced at Coby who'd returned to his human façade. "There has to be some Were-blood in him, no matter how diluted."

"I don't sense any," Coby muttered, still uneasy at the uninvited presence.

"Were you ever bitten by an animal?" she asked the detective. "Maybe when you were a child."

"Trust me, I'd know if I ever changed into a hairy beast under a full moon," he grumbled.

"Work with me here," Jazz urged.

"Yeah," he said reluctantly. "My grandma's dog bit me when I was six. I hated that little monster after that. No offense," he said to Coby.

"What kind of dog?"

"Pekinese. Grandma loved that ball of fur. He showed up on her doorstep one night and she took him in."

Jazz and Coby exchanged glances. "Could be," Coby said. "A blood test would prove it. I've heard of Weres in that species, but we don't see too many. There were rogues among the small breed some years ago."

Larkin started to back away a few steps until Jazz froze him with a flick of her fingers.

"No running out now," she said. "It would be a good idea for you to find out."

"You're saying my kids could become. . .dogs?" He looked so horrified that Jazz wanted to laugh.

"It sounds like you only got a trace of his saliva in your blood, and it could have remained dormant all these years. Maybe your being around supernatural creatures more brought it out. Just let Coby take a small sample of your blood and we can find out. And I'll unfreeze you if you promise not to run away."

He looked horrified at the idea. "But what if I'm what you said I am? A damn Pekinese?"

"Honestly, Larkin, all that's happened is that you entered a Were establishment when you shouldn't have been able to. That means you have a form of magick in your blood and it sounds like a tiny drop of Were-blood. With all the magick flying around L.A. it's no wonder your dormant Were-blood was activated."

"My life was perfectly sane until I met you." He glared at Jazz.

She pooh-poohed his statement. "Come on, admit it, your life was downright boring until I showed up."

"Just get the blood sample, Jazz," Coby ordered, holding out a small vial and sealed packet with a syringe.

"I'm not all that fond of blood. Whether it's mine or anyone else's." She took the vial and packet between her fingertips

"Surprising considering who you hang around with."

"I promise I won't hurt you," Jazz told the detective.

"Fine, I do need to know." He took the items from her. "My kid's diabetic. I probably can do it better than you can. What about an alcohol swab?"

"Weres don't catch diseases and I bet you've never even had a cold," Coby said in a flat voice that matched his eyes.

"I was the only kid in my class with a perfect attendance record," he muttered, efficiently drawing his blood then handing the vial to Jazz who took it with her usual girly distaste. She quickly handed it off to Coby.

"Wait here." He disappeared into a back room.

Detective Larkin shook his head. "You're telling me stuff that I only knew from fairy tales and horror movies."

"Funny you would use that comparison," she muttered, returning to her coffee and pie just as the detective did. "I know this is information overload for you while we've all lived with it for years."

"How many years?" He sipped his coffee.

"Enough." She wondered what it was with men and needing to know a woman's age. But then she spent a lot of time with men who wouldn't see 300 again.

"He has enough Pekinese in him to allow him past the wards," Coby announced, returning to the dining area. "Your pups won't be affected, because it's not strong enough."

"Pups, great." He flushed at Coby's look. "Sorry. This is new for me. So what does this mean?"

"Nothing more than what you had before, other than you now know about us and I won't throw you out if you come in again," Coby admitted. "We don't bother each other in here and no arrests are made. There's no human law here, Detective, only Were law. And I enforce that."

"Does that mean her boss comes in here?" Larkin asked.

"Hell no."

Jazz snorted a very unfeminine laugh. "Dweezil's choice of drink isn't caffeine."

Larkin dryscrubbed his face. "All because my grandma's damn little yapper bit me." He turned to Coby. "And I guess since you don't want your. . .lifestyle. . .getting out, I don't need to worry about this new hitch."

"You don't."

Jazz polished off her pie and finished her coffee. "What an evening. I go from dealing with a woman who's going to have to kiss probably a thousand frogs and slugs to get rid of them to finding out my favorite sheriff's detective is a Were." She beamed.

"Kiss frogs?" He held up his hands. "All I wanted was a damn cup of coffee."

"Come on, sit down." She patted the stool next to her. "Coby can explain the Were community to you." She disregarded the Were's glower.

By the time Detective Larkin, on information overload, left the café, Jazz's veins were happily humming from several cups of coffee.

"So what happened when you found Willie?" Coby cleared the counter of plates and cups, except for Jazz's.

"I'm sure Nick told you."

"He did, but I'd like your opinion. He might have been a Wereweasel in the strict sense of the word, but he was still one of us."

Jazz related the events starting with their arriving at the luxury hotel to the booby trapped doorknob that set off the explosion that killed Willie and ended with their visit to Rex's office to drop off the body.

"Knowing Rex he dropped Willie in the trash rather than hand him over to his pack leader," Coby said. "Willie didn't tell you who set him up at the hotel?"

"He was pretty nervous about that, which has to mean it was someone with power." She fiddled with her mug handle. "And I think it's tied in to me."

"I told you to look to your past," he reminded her.

"Yeah, yeah, but I have a lot of past to consider." She froze as she considered what had been going on the past few weeks. None of them good. "Except some things seem to. . ."

"Show up unexpected?" Coby said drily.

"What do you know?"

"No more than you. Only hunches. And my hunch says what's going on in your life has to do with your past." He busied himself fixing fresh pots of coffee.

"Except why are you concerned about l'il ole witchy me?"

His sudden grin lightened up his harsh features so much that Jazz thought he was pretty darn cute. Not her type even if she knew he'd have a blast up at Moonstone Lake with all the mountain trails to explore. Still, anyone who shed fur, could end up with fleas, and saw nothing wrong in licking their privates wasn't her idea of a fun companion.

"Why? Because Weres and witches have that old feud?" he said.

"We're the misunderstood race." She picked up the sugar packets and laid them out in a row. No artificial sweeteners found here. "Come on, Coby, be a pal and give me a few hints on what and where to look." She had an idea who he was talking about, but she wanted to see if they were talking about the same one.

Coby poured himself a cup of coffee and walked around the counter to take the stool next to her. "There are a lot of changes going on in our worlds. Some good. A lot of them not so good."

"I can think of a few of the latter," she muttered, remembering dreams that were better left unrecalled.

When he looked up at her his eyes revealed the yellow of the wolf and teeth elongated as he exposed the predator side his soul revered. "Let this old wolf give you a piece of advice."

"I'm open to anything." Oh boy, was she! There were days she felt as if she was flying without a broom.

"There's a funny thing about dreams created by strong magick. Some night you just might land in a nightmare that turns into reality with no hope of waking up."

Chapter 15

"YOU'RE FREE, GUYS. I'M JUST SORRY I DIDN'T LET YOU out sooner." Jazz sat on the floor and released the spell holding the cage closed. She laughed as Fluff and Puff scampered out of the cage and slid up her body to smother her with bunny slipper kisses along with their chattered thanks. "I knew you didn't kill Willie and now everyone knows it." She decided she wouldn't tell them that in a sense she was the one who killed him. No reason to get into that. "Just do me a favor. Don't wander off on the boardwalk anymore. At least not for a long while." She knew their promises were pretty empty. The slippers loved exploring the area too much, but she hoped they'd at least keep a low profile.

Some night you just might land in a nightmare that turns into reality with no hope of waking up.

Coby's words replayed through her mind too many times since the previous night. She had been hesitant to go to sleep the night before and tonight was even worse. She wore her favorite pajamas for the comfort factor, a cup of steaming hot chocolate flavored with peppermint syrup sat on the night table, and *I Married A Witch* with Veronica Lake played on the TV.

Croc and Delilah huddled together as the slippers raced all over the room, reacquainting themselves with every corner. Fluff found a bit of licorice root under the

bed and hauled out his booty. Puff scooted over to try to
steal a taste, but Fluff wasn't having any of it. Things
were back to normal.

Jazz sat cross-legged on the floor, pleased to see her
babies so happy and glad that she was able to prove
their innocence.

She would have felt downright content if it hadn't
been for Coby's words haunting her thoughts. She'd left
the diner feeling more uneasy than she had before.

"I settled the problems between Dweezil and Mindy.
I solved the case of the missing Willie. Oh wait, that
doesn't sound right, does it," she said to the slippers. "I
didn't even go ballistic when I found out Krebs is dating
Leticia. So if I'm on a roll, why can't I prove that Angelica is behind the nightmares? I know it has to be her."

*Think about it, dummy! You're not fighting her on her
turf.* Her mental gargoyle smacked her upside the head.

When the truth hit her, it hit with a vengeance.

"That's it. Why didn't I think of it before?" She took
a deep breath, closed her eyes, and raised her hands over
her head. The air thickened and swirled around her with
magick sparkling through her aura. "Beep. Beep. Beep.
Beep. Bring Irma, Nick, and Krebs to where I sleep. Because I say so, damn it!" She clapped her hands so hard
they stung from the contact. When she opened her eyes,
she found the three in front of her, one of them in all his
freshly showered glory. "Not good! Not good!" She
waved her hand, providing Krebs with a pair of pajama
pants and even making sure he was dried off.

"How the hell did I get here?" he demanded,
looking around.

"I was getting ready for bed," Irma groused. The spirit was dressed in a floral print flannel nightgown and had old-fashioned curlers in her hair. A smidge of cleansing cream dotted her nose. "Although it would be easier if I had an actual bed."

Krebs turned at the sound of Irma's voice. "And how come I can see her when I couldn't before? Hey! Boundaries!" he barked, when Irma's gaze centered on his lower half.

"I fixed it so you can see her and the dog from now on," Jazz explained.

"Why do I get the sense you have a spell up your sleeve," Nick muttered, looking just as disgruntled as the other two.

"Because I do." She gestured for them to be seated. "And I need all of you to help me."

"Even non-magickal me?" Krebs looked pleased. "Wow, I'm part of the Scooby gang."

"I could have told you long ago I was necessary," Irma stated. "After all, you couldn't have defeated that horrible Reeves person without me."

"Yeah, yeah, yeah, broke the curse, did your thing, we all survived." Jazz waved it off.

"But this is a lot more dangerous," Nick said, seeing the intent in Jazz's eyes.

She nodded. "I've gone about this the wrong way. I tried to find the person when all I had to do was backtrack through the dream realm."

"Do you realize how stupid that is?" Nick exploded with a force that had the vase on a nearby table teeter back and forth until Jazz sent out a protection spell to keep it from falling off. "The dream realm is made up of trails and paths that can lead to nowhere. It's meant to mislead anyone who enters it. Once you're there there's no guarantee you can leave."

"Wait a minute, there's a dream realm?" Krebs piped up. "And it can trap you? That doesn't sound good." He backed up a step then halted when Fluff and Puff slid around behind him, snarling and nipping at his ankles.

"None of that," Jazz admonished the slippers. "This is all new to him." They backed off but stayed within nibbling range.

Nick shook his head. "There are too many disparate energies here. It will create a chaos that won't be easy to manage."

"A chaos that had already begun when someone messed with our dreams," she argued. "All we'll do is unravel those threads and make them right. At the same time, we'll confirm Angelica is behind this. . ." she ignored Nick's shake of the head, "and take care of her at the same time."

"And you need me for this, why?" Krebs looked over his shoulder to find Fluff and Puff still on bunny slipper duty.

"Because you're human. Which means I have witch, vampire, ghost, and human energy." She gave a *voila* gesture.

"This sounds like fun to me," Irma said, rubbing her hands with glee. "I do love getting involved."

"Sure, you do. You're already dead, so you don't have to worry about biting the dust. Neither do you." Krebs's gaze slid past Nick.

"You'll be protected," Jazz assured him.

"Says the witch who almost ended up as some monster's sex toy," he muttered.

"If Jazz said you'll be protected, you will be," Nick said quietly.

"Says the vampire who only worries about silver, wooden stakes to the heart, and bright sunlight. Okay. Okay." He held his hands up in surrender. "I've wanted to be a part of all this, so if it means putting my life on the line, so be it."

"Since you brought us here, I gather you intend to do this now," Nick said.

"No time better than the present. Plus, if there's a nightmare in the offing for any, or all, of us, we'll be safer this way." Jazz jumped to her feet and rummaged through the hidden room in her closet. The four stones she carried glowed from within.

"We'll sit in a circle," she instructed, pointing to where she wanted them and placing a crystal in front of each and the fourth crystal in front of the empty spot she would occupy. Each crystal picked up a different color. "The crystal will hold your energy. When we return the crystals will dissolve."

"And?" Krebs stared at his crystal as if it was a snake ready to strike.

Jazz tapped the top of his head with her fingertips. "You're dating a vampire, Krebs. Get used to the strange and unusual." She took her place between Nick and Irma, grabbing hold of their hands, although it was apparent she couldn't hold onto Irma firmly. She closed her eyes and visualized the shadowy realm they would be entering and hoping to find a place safe enough for them all. "Between here and there, we sleep the slumber of innocence. Between here and there we dream what we wish for. We ask to leave here for there. To venture to that place that offers us what we wish for. Because I say so, damn it!"

She felt Nick's grip tighten as the air around them darkened and swirled in a funnel cloud worthy of Dorothy leaving Kansas for Munchkin Land.

"What is it with you and all this dust and dirt?" Irma cried out, her words lost in the wind that shrieked in their ears.

Just as quickly, the magickal tornado stilled and the silence was as deafening as the screeching wind had been.

Jazz opened one eye and then slowly opened the other. The first thing she noticed was that Irma's hand that had only been a mist through hers was now as solid as her own.

"I'm real here!" Irma squealed. "Oh, I like this realm."

"You wouldn't if you stayed here too long," Jazz said.

Their surroundings were layers of shifting colors, blues sliding to lavender and deep purple, reds with orange on the edges, and greens moving into yellow. What they sat on looked, and felt, like jagged stone.

"What is this?" Krebs whispered.

"The dream realm," Nick whispered. He flinched as a golden orb appeared in the distance then slowly rose to hover over them. "What we wish for." He looked upward at the image of a noonday sun.

"Oh my." Irma looked around her with interest then giggled when a pie with cherry juice leaking through the latticed crust raced past her.

"At least she dreams of pie," Krebs muttered, even as the shadowy figure of a shapely woman sauntered past him.

"We don't need this." Jazz concentrated on keeping her mind blank even as the image of Hugh Jackman floated in front of her.

"Yes, we don't." Nick stood up slowly, reaching down to help Jazz and Irma to their feet.

"So what do we do now?" Krebs turned in a tight circle.

"We look for the right realm." Jazz held up a small purple crystal. "Good dreams. Bad dreams. Scattered sleep for all. We seek the one who brings darkness and fear to our slumber." The crystal uttered a tiny peep and floated off her palm. "No matter what happens, don't wander off," she warned. "Stay together and if something flies in your face, ignore it. If what looks like a face stares at you, don't look in its eyes and don't speak to anything but one of us."

"Oh yeah, this is getting better all the time." Krebs sidled up to Nick.

"Follow the bouncing crystal." Jazz headed off with Irma behind her, Krebs and Nick taking up the rear position.

What with having no point of reference, Jazz felt as if they were walking in circles even if she knew they were walking in a straight line. She knew they were going in the right direction when the peaceful pastel layers of color surrounding them started to darken in color.

"Something's following me," Krebs whispered.

"It can't hurt you as long as you don't look at it and make it real."

"Do me a favor and next time you do something like this, find another human." Krebs started to bat at something flying around his head, but Nick reached forward and stayed his hand.

"Not a good idea," he advised. "You never know where they've been."

"It's getting darker," Irma observed.

"Keep your eyes on the crystal." Jazz not only saw the darkness descending on them but sensed another kind of darkness in the air itself. The air around them turned shades of black, purple, and deep blue. "We're entering the nightmare realm. It can get dicey."

"Dicey she says," Krebs muttered.

Voices sounded around them. Curses at the world in general. Pleas for mercy. Groans of pain and worse rent the air.

They all jumped when screams surrounded them.

"We're close to our destination." Jazz had no solid evidence where they were other than her intuition.

"Jazz, look to the right," Nick said suddenly.

When she did, she saw an arc of a deep mustard color that appeared to be an entrance.

"Wagons ho," she murmured, veering off to the right. As they reached the arc they could hear the faint sound of chanting and the smell of sulfur and nasty-smelling herbs permeated the air. "This is it."

"What do we do, dear?" Irma whispered. Anticipation lit up her face. "I don't think hitting whatever is in there with my purse will work. Plus, I don't have my handbag with me."

Jazz reached out, allowing only her fingertips to graze the shades of yellow. She wasn't surprised to find the entrance unprotected. After all, who of their own free will would dare cross into the nightmare realm?

"Protect us and shield us from what is inside." She looked back at her little band. She in her *café au lait* thermal pajamas, Irma in her flannel nightgown and curlers, Krebs in his soft flannel pajama pants, and Nick, the dark and brooding vampire, in a black T-shirt and matching jeans since he literally belonged to the night. She really wished she'd worn a pair of slippers because the rock strewn floor was hell on her bare feet. Not that she would have brought Fluff and Puff here.

"What do you mean you can't sense her?" A familiar voice bounced around the rocky interior. "I thought you have always been able to keep tabs on her."

Jazz looked back and shot Nick an *I told you so* look.

"She isn't in her quarters." Another familiar voice to Jazz's ears and one she hadn't expected to hear.

"Did you try the vampire's lair? She's probably fucking him," Angelica sneered.

"I find nothing."

"You are no good to me unless you can finish the job!"

"I'll finish you, you fangy bitch," Jazz growled under her breath, starting to move forward then stopped. It didn't take a brain to know that barging into the cave wouldn't do much other than probably end her life and those with her.

She led the way as they crept their way along the rock walls.

What we have ahead of us is not good. Nick's voice echoed inside her head.

Nothing new there, but I'm not letting either one of them win.

Why doesn't that surprise me? She heard his chuckle.
I'll do my part, but can you make sure that Krebs is safe?
You shouldn't have brought him.

I needed a mortal to ground the spell and he was the closest one.

Don't tell him that or he'll pout for a month.

No kidding.

Do you have a plan?

Yeah, kick some vamp and wizard ass. She took a deep breath and forged ahead.

When Jazz entered the large chamber, she found long wooden tables filled with various beakers and glass jars filled with contents she didn't care to further investigate. A large ornate leather-bound book of spells sat open on a carved ebony bookstand. The man who resembled a living skeleton wearing a dark blue robe stood at one end of the chamber facing an image of Angelica reflected on the stone.

The only good thing about the scene in front of her was watching an old enemy get his butt handed to him by a furious Angelica.

"This final dream spell is important," Angelica ranted. "You must make sure she cannot wake up from it and I want it to look as if Nikolai Gregorivich is to blame for her death. That way both of them are taken care of. Considering his feelings for her, it will be assumed he killed her in a fit of anger."

"What about the mortal in her house?" The wizard that Jazz knew as Dyfynnog, a powerful wizard with a sadistic streak and the owner of Fluff and Puff until Jazz *appropriated* the slippers from him. Since she had proof he had abused the bunny slippers in such a way the elder wizards would have gotten involved, he chose not to demand their return and Jazz promised to stay out of his territory and he out of hers. Now it appeared he'd found a way around that vow, so she was determined to put a stop to it. . .and him.

Unfortunately, her temper got the better of her.

"Because of your nasty little spells, I haven't had a good night's sleep for weeks!" she shouted, stepping into the chamber and throwing down a fireball that exploded near one of the tables. Luckily, the flame fizzled out as soon as it struck the floor, otherwise, the table would have gone up in flames.

Dyfynnog spun around. "How did you get here?" he demanded, a snarl on his lips. "This realm is protected." He raised a gnarled hand; the palm etched with arcane magickal symbols that pulsed with his anger.

Krebs would have backed up, but Nick kept a hand against the middle of his back and pushed him forward instead, while Irma looked around in wide-eyed wonder.

"You are so busted!" Jazz was too lost in her anger to think exactly what she was facing; as in a 2,000-year-old wizard with more power in his fingernail than she had in her entire body. But Jazz was on a roll and she knew she had right on her side.

He pointed his finger at her, a strange reddish-orange light streaming from the tip. "You took my property!"

She was quick enough to dodge from it, while the light shone through Irma's body.

"I *rescued* them from your abuse. While you ruined my sleep, sent me disgusting nightmares, and had me dreaming I was driving a *minivan!*" She continued to advance on him, but kept an eye on him to make sure he didn't make any wrong moves. "Not to mention giving me the *worst 48 hours of my life* by making me mortal!"

The wizard looked at the three behind her. "Vampire, spirit, and human. So that is how you entered the realm. But do you think they can protect you?"

Jazz chanced a quick look at the stone wall that had harbored Angelica's image. Naturally, she was gone. She'd probably left the moment she saw Jazz and her crew. It didn't matter. She'd find a way to get the bloodsucking bitch too.

"You have broken so many laws among all our communities that you deserve to be destroyed a million times over," she declared, making sure to keep a potions-covered table between him and her.

Dyfynnog sneered and shot a blazing blue light toward Irma. The ghost's mouth opened in a silent scream of horror. At the same time her image wavered and appeared to melt.

"*No!*" Jazz threw out her hands, instinctively sending a blast of cold power toward the light instead of Irma, deflecting the stream to one of the tables, detonating a bottle of bubbling mustard yellow liquid. The boom was loud enough to injure ears and the smell acrid enough to burn their nasal passages. Only Jazz's quick thinking sent a protective bubble around the other three.

"I told you, this battle is with me," she growled, moving toward him. "Who thought this up? You or Angelica? Who found who? Something tells me Angelica, because while you have a totally insane sadistic nature, you aren't inventive enough to think about fooling with peoples' dreams. That sounds more like something Angelica would come up with," she said, removing the protective bubble.

"What did she promise you, wizard?" Nick asked. "What did she say you could have if you invaded my dreams, twisted my darkest thoughts?" His fangs dropped and his eyes turned a deadly red as he moved slowly around the other side of the room.

"Stay with me," Irma could be heard whispering to Krebs.

"Oh yeah, you make a great shield," he muttered.

"*How?*" Nick roared.

Dyfynnog looked down his nose at Nick with all the disdain a lofty wizard could impart. "You are *nothing* to me, vampire, but I must say your deepest fears were interesting." His gaze turned sly.

Nick's face seemed to have turned to stone.

Jazz's gaze shifted from one to the other. She could feel the abrupt change in the cavern's atmosphere and it wasn't good.

"What smells so bad in here?" Irma walked over to one of the tables. Her nose wrinkled up as something foul drifted up out of a beaker.

"You don't want to know." Jazz watched the war of wills between vampire and wizard and knew if she didn't step in quickly, the battle would intensify to something none of them would be able to control. She knew what Dyfynnog was like. She had studied his nature and habits for some time before she had crept into his castle one late night to rescue a pair of bunny slippers that had been magickally created for his own dark-natured fun and games. From the day she liberated Fluff and Puff from their torture chamber, the slippers had been loyal to her and she had vowed to keep them safe. She just knew if she lost the battle here, Dyfynnog would take back the slippers and they would suffer unimaginable trials under his machinations.

It's always up to the witch, she fussed and fumed.

She had no idea what she would do. No idea what would work against someone this powerful, but that hadn't stopped her before.

What do you intend to do? Nick's words inside her head were calming in their own way.

Hell if I know. I'm flying without a broom here. She took a deep breath and just spoke from the heart.

"Four stand together. Four stand apart. All invincible in their own way. Ye must do as I say. No appeal on your part. No vengeance." She spoke in a voice that throbbed with a fury she knew she couldn't unleash. "We leave ye alone. Ye leave us alone. And harm shall come to none. But if ye enter our worlds again, ye shall suffer one-hundred-fold as ye have made others suffer." She held up her palm, displaying a tiny flame the same color as the amethyst that winked from the broom charm that dangled from her gold ankle bracelet. The flame slowly grew in size until it spilled out over her hand. "*Leave us alone!* Because I say so, damn it!" She pursed her lips and blew the flame toward him. It floated in the air until it rose up and wrapped around Dyfynnog in a blanket of cold fire.

"You can't defeat me!" he shouted, waving his arms in a vain attempt to dispel the flames.

"You're finished, Dyfynnog. You've escaped punishment too many times. This time your crimes include mortals and spirits. Your elders won't like that." Jazz deliberately turned her back on him and walked toward Irma and Krebs. "Let's go." Nick obligingly took up the rear.

"Your day is coming, witch!" Dyfynnog screamed after her from his prison of flames.

She stopped to give him one look. "You know what? I've heard that for years now and I'm still walking around. While you. . ." she flung her hands outward. The legs under the tables collapsed and beakers and bottles slid onto the floor, breaking and releasing their contents, "have nothing."

"That flame won't keep him prisoner forever," Nick said as Jazz led them out of the nightmare realm.

"No, but it will slow him down until I can report him to the wizard elders. Then they can deal with him."

"He tried to turn me into goo," Irma grumbled, pausing long enough to tighten one of her curlers.

"He's good at that." Jazz stopped and indicated they form a circle with hands clasped. "

"We're not going to go back and find ourselves in the wrong bodies, are we?" Krebs asked. "Things can happen!"

"You'll return to your body and with luck, you might even find yourself in your bed." She took a deep breath. "We have seen. We have defeated. We ask the Dream Master permission to leave this realm and return to our own. And we ask that the one who has tainted his realm be punished for his misdeeds. Because I say so, damn it!"

Jazz felt Nick's hand tighten his grip as the same tornado seemed to lift them up and return them to her room. When she opened her eyes she found only she and Nick present.

"I feel like Dorothy returning to Kansas! It's good to be home!" she heard Krebs shout from the room below.

Jazz laughed and grabbed Nick, tumbling them both backwards onto her bed.

Fluff and Puff screeched a welcome and scampered up the bed and swooped over them. Croc and Delilah were right behind them.

"I'd say they know what you did," Nick said, fondling Puff's ears. The slipper practically purred from the attention while Fluff snuggled under Jazz's arm. The stilettos tried to find their way into his lap, but Jazz rescued him and warned them to behave themselves.

"I think they've always been aware of Dyfynnog even when he was far away." She scratched Fluff's head between his ears. "Maybe now that link has finally been dissolved."

Nick rolled over onto his side, keeping Puff cradled against his chest. Both slippers now hummed from contentment. He reached over the two furry heads and two crocodile ones to cradle Jazz's cheek in his palm.

"He'll do his best to discredit you," he murmured.

"He can try." She knew she sounded cockier than she felt inside, but her hatred for the evil wizard was still simmering strong inside of her. "Another reason why I wanted witnesses."

"No supernatural court would accept the word of a mortal," he reminded her. "Especially when the charges are against someone like Dyfynnog."

"He tried to dissolve a spirit and that other spell would

have destroyed all three of you. I should have taken video," she mused. "Did you see his face when I deflected that stream against Irma? I thought he'd have a stroke. Too bad he didn't."

Nick shook his head. "You took a chance."

"And I won."

"No, you didn't. You merely built a wall between you that one day he'll scale and he'll come after you." He set Puff down on the black and white comforter and sat up.

"Aren't you staying?" Jazz felt high with success. Her blood was thrumming with excitement and she knew the perfect way to celebrate her triumph.

"No, I need to get back." He stood up with fluid grace. He walked around the bed to drop a kiss on her lips that started out light then deepened. When he lifted his head, she felt the heat racing through her blood.

"Are you sure?" she asked archly.

For a moment, a hint of regret darkened his eyes. "Yes. Be proud of yourself, Jazz. You vindicated Fluff and Puff and you stopped Dyfynnog from creating any more bad dreams."

"But Angelica is still at large." She rolled over onto her back, allowing Fluff and Puff to slide over her prone body. Croc and Delilah had left the bed and tried to climb their way onto her dresser.

Nick returned to the bed and leaned over her, a hand planted on either side of her. "Be very careful, Jazz. She's not one to trifle with and she holds grudges for centuries."

She shrugged off his warning. "I don't want to trifle with her. She might have great fashion sense, but I still want to see her as a huge pile of ash."

He straightened up.

"If you don't have anything going on tonight, wouldn't you rather go out?" she asked, feeling the need to celebrate. "Find a fun club for some dancing." She smiled and shimmied her shoulders as best she could what with the footwear all over her.

"I'll call you later." Nick kissed her again and left the room.

Jazz lay on the bed, knowing she wouldn't hear Nick's footsteps on the stairs. If she hadn't strained her ears she wouldn't have even heard the soft click of the front door as it opened and closed.

"The man definitely needs some fun," she murmured, hugging the slippers to her as she drifted off to sleep.

Epilogue

JAZZ HAD BARELY CLOSED HER EYES ONLY TO FIND THEM popping open as she stood barefoot in her lilac robe on a cold stone floor facing a much too familiar ornate table with stern-faced witches seated across from her. The most daunting was the witch who was seated in the center.

Oh, this is not good.

"You take chances, young Griet of Ardglass," Eurydice declared in a voice that echoed off the stone chamber.

If Jazz thought Eurydice was daunting, a more irritating sight was a chair off to her left. The woman seated in it looked much too smug as she smiled at Jazz, revealing a hint of fang. Her velvet gown was blood red, low cut, and dropped to her ankles, revealing a pair of red high heels that Jazz might have coveted if she wasn't positive they were as tainted as their owner. A blood red ruby ring sparkled on her ring finger with a matching stone embedded in a gold pendant that bisected her cleavage.

Oh yes, this isn't good at all.

"Our association with the vampire community is tenuous at best, but your accusation that the director is guilty of a magickal crime goes beyond the pale," Eurydice went on.

"She started it," Jazz muttered, earning a silent warning from the headmistress of the Witches' Academy and head witch of the Witches' Council. She knew the next time wouldn't be a warning. Her lips would be zipped shut. Perhaps permanently if she wasn't careful.

"And you know if a wizard targets others you must inform the proper authorities. Not take matters into your own hands. Dyfynnog would then be reprimanded and placed on a watch list."

Her jaw dropped. "A *reprimand?* I was almost killed, as were my friends! He arranged to have Fluff and Puff accused of murder. He almost destroyed a harmless ghost who never did anything to him and all they'd do is slap him on the back of the hand?" No way she'd let Irma know she called her harmless. The spirit would find a way to whomp her for that comment. "So he had a grudge against me. Fine, keep it against me and not bring in others. He didn't play fair."

"Wizards never play fair." Eurydice's nostrils flared. "Still, your actions could have created a turmoil between the witches, wizards, and vampires. For that, you shall be punished."

"I am glad to see you understand what needs to be done." Angelica spoke up, the smile on her face innocuous, but Jazz could easily smell the bullshit behind it. Jazz idly wondered what the vampire bitch would look like with a fireball on her head.

"And it shall." Eurydice's smile was equally unpleasant.

For a moment, Jazz was worried that the head witch had read her thoughts then she realized the woman was speaking to Angelica.

The vampire settled back in her throne-like chair, waiting for the hammer to drop on Jazz's head. Jazz hated the vampire with a fire that sent her blood boiling and the idea that the bloodsucking bitch would be present for her punishment was beyond unthinkable.

"Thank you for coming, Angelica."

The vampire's smile dimmed. "But I thought I would—" She disappeared in the wink of an eye. Her displeasure at not being there to see Jazz suffer lingered in the air like a bad smell.

Once Angelica was banished back to her world, Jazz unfortunately opened her mouth. "Why couldn't I sense it was her behind it all?"

"You are still a young witchling with much to learn," Eurydice informed her. "Especially in the area of thinking before acting."

"And if I'd thought too much we all would have been dead in that cavern. Even with your edict we would be banished with only the power we had at the time; mine has grown over the years! I still should have known what she was up to."

Eurydice looked at her as if she looked at a small child that amused her. "Reasons for everything. But you still do not have as much power as you would have had if you had not transgressed. That you risk your life for your friends is admirable, Griet. But you risked a tenuous link we have forged with the vampires and that we cannot allow. Therefore, fifty years has been added to your banishment." She flicked her fingers at a plumed pen, which wrote across a scroll. "And I advise you to remain out of Angelica's sight for some time."

"That I'm more than willing to do as long as she stays out of my way too." She was relieved her punishment wasn't worse and she had to wonder why not. Of course, she could tell that Eurydice didn't think too much of the vampire any more than she did. So maybe she should count her blessings.

"Life for you and your sister witches will be not easy. Things are brewing. I suggest you watch yourself carefully, young Griet, and don't appear before us for some time."

If Jazz expected to be zapped back to her bed, she was sadly mistaken.

This is that nightmare where I walk naked through the mall and not a credit card to my name.

She still wore her lilac robe, but now the hood covered her hair. She gritted her teeth not to shift back and forth on a stone floor that was freezing to her bare feet.

Jazz stared straight ahead. Power the likes of which she'd never seen before wrapped the ten throne-like chairs that lined the red carpeted dais. Two wizards, two witches, one of whom was Eurydice, two vampires, one of which was Angelica and so not a good thing for Jazz, two Weres, and two Faeries sat there with a tall vampire on one end and a Were on the other. Torches flared to life along the stone wall, adding yellow-orange light to the dark room.

The vampire bared his fangs at her and the Were merely stared at her as if she looked like a nice snack.

She stood in the presence of the Ruling Council.

Remembering her training, Jazz slowly inclined her head, making sure to bow to each member. Forgetting one was a slight that usually meant a limb chopped off.

"I do hope this means this *child* will be properly punished." Angelica was the first to speak. Her dark eyes gleamed red with malice and more than a hint of bloodlust.

"You were the one to call us together, Angelica." An ancient vampire named Mazcot idly inspected long yellowed nails. Jazz noticed his fangs were equally yellow.

"If anyone wanted to bring the witch before the Ruling Council, it would have been us," one of the Weres spoke up. "After all, she did destroy one of us."

"The spell used to destroy the Wereweasel was not of Griet's making," Eurydice corrected him.

Angelica turned to the two wizards. "She killed one of your own. Dyfynnog was a great and powerful wizard. Why aren't you demanding her death?"

Jazz practically ground her teeth together to make sure she didn't open her mouth and say the wrong thing and end up burned to a charcoal briquette in seconds. With all the suffocating power in the room it would be way too easy to happen. But then, Jazz wasn't known for keeping her mouth shut.

"Dyfynnog was a sadist of the first order," she argued. "He didn't work for the good of the magickal community. He preferred inflicting pain and death on those who didn't deserve it. He enslaved creatures, forcing them to do his bidding."

Angelica smiled, allowing a hint of fang to show.

"Ah, yes, your precious little slippers. The ones who have been accused more than once of eating either magickal or mortal."

"There was no proof they ate that squirrel!" Jazz barely held back her snarl. "They're not dangerous. They just get into mischief sometimes. But I keep them under control."

"How lovely, the uncontrollable witch controls equally uncontrollable slippers," Angelica sneered. "I demand Griet be tried for her attack on the great wizard Dyfynnog and her crimes against magick."

Jazz felt her legs turn to liquid. Talk about an automatic death sentence! Out of the corner of her eye she noticed Reinhold's broad smile.

"Griet of Ardglass, why did you seek out Dyfynnog and attack him?" Eurydice asked.

She wet her lips and forced her brain into gear.

"I didn't purposely seek out Dyfynnog," she said slowly. "I was looking for the one who was behind a series of nightmares and a plot to accuse Fluff and Puff of eating a member of the Were-pack. It wasn't until I confronted Dyfynnog and Angelica that I knew just who was behind it." She faced the cold-faced vampire with a steel resolve she didn't wholly feel inside.

"Lies!" Angelica half-rose out of her seat. "How dare you!"

"How dare you!" Jazz retorted, forgetting her intention of remaining calm. "I don't even know you and you worked with Dyfynnog to ruin my sleep, a spell was cast to rob me of my power for forty-eight hours, and you fixed it so Fluff and Puff had to be put in bunny jail! So if we're keeping score, I'd say you're way ahead on the bad meter." She froze the minute the last words left her lips. *Open mouth, insert both feet and the slippers too.*

Both wizards turned to face Angelica, whose normally translucent skin was a mottled shade of red and purple.

"Is this true, Angelica? Did you work with Dyfynnog?" Pithias, the eldest wizard asked in a breathy creaky voice.

"I did not know it was a crime for a vampire to be-friend a wizard."

"It is if you use that friendship to attack members of the magickal community," Eurydice said. "We must work together, Angelica. You know how important it is for us to remain united."

"Griet does what she wishes," Angelica argued. "If any-one doesn't understand the meaning of united, it is she."

"Is this personal, Angelica?" Jazz asked. "Because I honestly don't understand why you despise me so much. After all, look at all you've done. You're now the direc-tor of the Protectorate. The first female to ever attain that right. So why would a lowly witch such as myself be considered a threat to you?"

Angelica sat up straighter in her chair. "You're right, you're nothing to me." For a moment, red flared up in her eyes. "But your actions have worried many of us. Bringing you here shows that I am merely doing my duty by bringing those deeds to light."

Eurydice fingered the large emerald ring that graced her slender fingers. "Are you intending to file charges against Griet?"

For a moment it looked as if Angelica would grind her fangs down to nubs. "No," she said finally and very re-luctantly. "Although I would like there to be a warning given."

"That shall be done." Pithias agreed. He turned to his counterpart and a silent conversation took place. After the second wizard nodded his head, Pithias turned to face Jazz. "Griet of Ardglass. While your manner of dealing with your foes could be considered unconventional, I

must say that you show a strong loyalty to your friends
and the need to protect those who might not be able to
protect themselves. It is strongly suggested you do not
meddle where it is not safe. If there is to be punishment,
that will be left to Eurydice." He nodded toward the head
of the Witches' Council who inclined her head in response. "Angelica, as one of our leaders, you must remember that we all hold ourselves to a much higher
standard. While your dealings with Dyfynnog may have
been beyond reproach." He glanced at Jazz who started
to open her mouth then clapped it shut. "We still must
be cautious."

Angelica's smile was as cold as her non-beating
heart. "The director of the Protectorate is invulnerable
to any sanctions."

"Not so," Fergus, one of the Weres spoke up. He
glanced at Jazz and waved his hand.

"But—" Just like that Jazz was back in bed.

"Damn it!" She pounded her pillow. "And just when
it was getting good too! I wanted to see her get what's
due her."

That would not be a good idea. Eurydice's voice rang
loud and strong in her head. *Just be grateful that you
were spared.*

So that means I don't have to write I will not try to
kill Angelica *one million times?* She winced as pain
flared against the back of her head as if someone had
thumped her.

*Be grateful no one cared for Dyfynnog and they all knew
what he was truly like. And for once,* behave yourself!

The head witch left her head as easily as she had entered.

Jazz jumped out of bed and dressed in record time.

"I can't believe we're all still in one piece," Krebs greeted her as she danced into the kitchen and hugged him

"Neither can I." She poured coffee into a travel mug. She stopped to glance at paperwork littering the table. One printed word stood out and she squealed, hopping into Krebs's arms and hugging him tightly. "Thank you! Thank you!"

"Don't think the spa is just for you. I'll be using it too and I'll expect you to be totally gone when I have company over." He laughed. "But I still want your input in what we want for a design."

"Yes, yes, yes, and the duckies will be sooooo happy. They get cramped in the tub sometimes. They can use the sun." She kissed him on the cheek. "And I promise they won't invite over their friends."

"You know what? After what I saw last night, I'll pretty much believe anything. Are you sure he'll be up after last night? It's daytime, you know," he told her, knowing exactly where she was heading.

"He'll be up." She wondered if he had been called before the Vampire Council for his part in defeating Dyfynnog. Angelica hadn't said anything about Nick, but Jazz knew the fangy shrew wanted to create trouble. If Angelica did manage to make trouble for Nick then Jazz would get all witchy on the female vampire, no matter what the Ruling Council said.

When Jazz entered the carriage house she found Irma cooing nonsensical words to the dog whose tail wagged madly while Irma used a grooming brush Jazz had conjured up for her.

"How about a trip to the boardwalk?" Jazz asked.

"I'm sure Sirius would like that." Irma beamed.

"Sirius, huh? The dog star." Jazz skimmed her hand over the top of the dog's head. He looked up and panted happily as if he enjoyed the pampering. "It suits him." She waited as Irma and Sirius climbed into the car. "It's a gorgeous day and we're going out to enjoy it."

"I only wish you could have killed that evil woman and man. What he did to me was very unnerving," Irma confessed. "It was as if his hands were all over me."

"Okay, not a picture I need to have in my head," she muttered. "But I agree with you. I wish I could have killed them too, although Dyfynnog was the only one in the cavern and killing Angelica's image just wouldn't have been the same. And if I did kill them, I'd then be dead. Those two have connections in high and evil places I don't. I'm hoping what happened there will have others on alert and maybe Angelica and Dyfynnog's power will suffer for what they did." She revved up the engine while Queen's *Another One Bites the Dust* blared from the radio.

Jazz left Irma and Sirius on a bench at the edge of the boardwalk where they could enjoy the ocean view while she hurried toward the two-story building that housed Nick's apartment and office for his private investigations work.

The moment she stepped into the lobby, she felt a shift in the energy. Nick was in the building. And she was positive he knew she was coming.

For once, the elevator behaved as she ascended to the second floor.

She stood in the open doorway, holding a sultry pose. "Don't you look all Sam Spade." She kept her voice low and sexy.

Nick sat behind his desk with his feet propped up on the scratched surface. As if he knew of her intent, he wore dark slacks, a white shirt, and suspenders. A battered fedora sat rakishly on his head. "Hey doll," he growled. "You look like trouble on showgirl legs." Nick leaned back his chair, allowing his gaze to roam over her. There was no doubt he liked what he saw.

Jazz perched herself on the edge of the desk.

A blur of movement was Jazz's only warning before she found herself in Nick's lap.

"Isn't it amazing what happens when we work together?" She looped her arms around his neck. "Specifically, I didn't end up in jail and neither one of us ended up in trouble."

"Only because no one liked Dyfynnog all that much." His hold on her tightened, bringing her closer to him. "So what do you think? You think a vampire like me and a witch like you can. . .?"

"There would have been a time I'd tell you not on your unlife, but I feel generous today. Still, you know it won't be easy," she warned him. "I've got Irma and the slippers. And even if Dweezil makes me crazy I won't give up driving for him. And I want romance."

Nick grinned. "Anything else?"

"You know if we were in a fairy tale, there would be only one ending." She lowered her face until her lips brushed his.

"And what would that be?"

She laughed merrily and threw her hands up sending a shower of pink and gold sparkles down on them. "That we'd live happily ever after."

Acknowledgments

WRITING IS A SOLITARY BUSINESS, SO FRIENDS ARE important. Those friends that understand you best are real treasures. I couldn't have done it without the help and support of some fantastic people.

My husband, Bob, who understands that I "hear" voices in my head.

My mom, Thelma Randall, who always told me I could do it.

My agent, Laurie McLean of the Larsen/Pomada Literary Agency, aka, Batgirl, who has totally gone way beyond the call of duty.

My editor, Deb Werksman, who loves Jazz and her witch buddies as much as I do.

Mega thanks to Terese Daly Ramin who kept me on track.

To Yasmine Galenorn and Lisa Croll Di Dio for making sure all my witchy stuff was right.

The Witchy Chicks, Yasmine Galenorn, Terese Daly Ramin, Lisa Croll Di Dio, Madelyn Alt, Candace Havens, Kate Austin, Annette Blair, and Maggie Shayne. Your support is much appreciated and I love you all.

About the Author

Linda Wisdom was born and raised in Huntington Beach, California. She majored in journalism in college, then switched to fashion merchandising when she was told there was no future for her in fiction writing. She held a variety of positions ranging from retail sales to executive secretary in advertising and office manager for a personnel agency.

Her career began when she sold her first two novels to Silhouette Romance on her wedding anniversary in 1979. Since then she has sold more than seventy novels and one novella to four different publishers. Her books have appeared on various romance and mass market bestseller lists and have been nominated for a number of Romantic Times awards and has been a finalist for the Romance Writers of America Rita Award.

She lives with her husband, two dogs, two parrots, and a tortoise in Murrieta, California.

When Linda first moved to Murrieta there were three romance writers living in the town. At this time, there is just Linda. So far, the police have not suspected her of any wrongdoing.